PASADAGAVRA

Marta K. Stahlfeld

Book Publishers Network
P.O. Box 2256
Bothell • WA • 98041
PH • 425-483-3040
www.bookpublishersnetwork.com

10 9 8 7 6 5 4 3 2 1

Printed in the United States of America

LCCN 2012908303
ISBN 978-1-937454-37-1

Cover designer: Laura Zugzda
Typographer: Leigh Faulkner

Dedication

To Selah: thank you for all your help and encouragement.
To Lindsey: you can finally read it!

To Given

A book is an ocean; imagination is a ship.

Martin Stahlfeld

11/24/12

Contents

Acknowledgements

Thanks first and foremost to my parents; without their help, I could never have gotten this published. Love you, Mom and Dad!

Thanks also to Barbie Kinney, who has always been supportive and helpful. Love you, Barbie!

Thanks to Selah Elmquist and Colleen Croy for your help in selling *Darkwoods;* without your help, I couldn't have gotten this book ready.

Thanks to everyone who purchased *Darkwoods;* your purchase helped me to get *Pasadagavra* on the shelves.

And finally, thank you to God for allowing me to pursue this road. All praise and glory to You forever, Amen.

Cast of Characters

MICE

Wraith Mice (magical mice that can become invisible)

Crispisin	a Wraith Mouse novice, mentored by Zuryzel
Dejuday	an inept scout, Sibyna's younger brother
Hokadra	king of the Wraith Mice, father of Johajar, Zuryzel, and Mokimshim, mate to Demeda
Johajar	Zuryzel's twin brother
Mokimshim	oldest child of King Hokadra and Queen Demeda; brother to Johajar and Zuryzel
Orgorad	Sibyna's mate
Sibyna	a messenger, friend of Zuryzel, older sister to Dejuday, mate of Orgorad
Zuryzel	(zur-EYE-zel) second child and only daughter of King Hokadra and Queen Demeda, twin of Johajar, sister of Mokimshim

Rangers (mice who patrol the northern half of the earth)

Aspen	Ranger Orlysk, or ordinary soldier
Cinder	Lady Raven's second-in-command, or Hetmuss
Crow	Lady Raven's daughter, future leader, or Herttua, of the Rangers)
Raven	Lady, or leader, of the Rangers, long-time friend and ally of Queen Demeda
Rainbow	Ranger Orlysk
Snowgoose	high-ranking Ranger

Graystone Mice

Opal	one of Feldspar's oldest friends
Chite	one of Feldspar's oldest friends
Feldspar	mouse from the south, looking for adventure in the north

Cliff Mice

Glor'a	Ran'ta's friend; takes refuge in Pasadagavra
Ol'ver	orphan, friend of Feldspar, long-time friend to and in love with Ran'ta
Ran'ta	Ol'ver's sweetheart and long-time friend

Keron Mice

Coll'n	leader of the Keron Mice
Al'ce	Coll'n's deputy

OTTERS

River Otters

Anamay	daughter of Mudriver, younger sister of Danaray, mate to Mollusk
Danaray	eldest child of Mudriver, sister of Anamay
Doomspear	river otter who lost land to sea otters
Moonpath	river otter who lost land to sea otters
Shinar	princess in service of King Hokadra
Shorefish	future chief, vowed revenge against the sea otters
Streamcourse	aunt of Shorefish, occasional helper of the Wraith Mice

Sea Otters

Anemone	member of Mollusk's clan
Crustacean	chief of Mollusk's clan
Current	chief of another sea otter clan
Eagle	Anemone's son
Kiskap	chief of Hoeylahk otters in the far north
Mollusk	poor sea otter, mate of Anamay
Northstar	allegedly a sea otter chief; Kiskap's sister
Saline	Anemone's daughter

FOXES

Blood	deceased Oracle, Fawn's former mentor
Eclipse	Oracle sent to besiege Arashna
Fang	Oracle, recorder of the Oracles
Fawn	Oracle's apprentice to Blood, descendant of old kings
Hemlock	senior Oracle
Ice	corsair posing as an Oracle; spy for Lady Raven
Knife	second most senior Oracle, apprenticed at a higher age than her contemporaries
Sage	runaway Oracle's apprentice, mother of Rosemary
Scythe	deceased senior Oracle, against the war waged by her colleagues

CORSAIRS/ SEA CREATURES

Mercenaries

Ailur	ferret, friend of Queen Demeda
Arasam	slightly untrustworthy fox
Demmons	greedy fox who desires the riches in Pasadagavra
Drexa	low-ranking member of Ailur's crew
Fotirra	ferret posing as a captain
Grayik	member of Ailur's crew, often her messenger
Iddi	low-ranking member of Ailur's crew
Jironi	ferret posing as a captain
Norya	crow friend of Lady Crow who brings messages for the Rangers
Redseg	ferret, captain of the *Deathwind*

Pirates/Adventurers

Epoi	ruthless young fox who used to be Demmons's navigator, now her own captain
Shartalla	pine marten who hunts treasure but still has loyalty
Skorlaid	Shartalla's second-in-command
Tsanna	member of Shartalla's crew

OTHERS

Chipmunks:

Skettle	friend of Lady Raven
Texat	Skettle's brother

Tundra Otters:

Sone	friend of the Rangers
Xar	Sone's brother, friend of Lady Raven's

Prologue: A Dubious Ally

Shartalla sat at a table in the seaside tavern in a city called Diray, slowly drinking a mug of ale. There really weren't very many pine martens on the northeast coast, not even among the pirate ships, which made it a little difficult for her to blend into a crowd.

Her drinking mate, a female ferret called Ailur, looked warily out at the crowd. "It ain't safe," she muttered.

Shartalla put her mug down quietly. "It's as safe as it's gonna be. Spill it. What news? Is someone coming for us?"

Ailur nodded. "Far as I know."

"Good," the pine marten muttered. "I don't want to waste my time stuck here."

Ailur grinned at her. "You can't stand t' be away from the sea."

The pine marten smiled wolfishly. "I'm a sailor—what can I say? What's been happening in the war?"

Ailur twirled her own drink carefully in her paws. "Y' understand that the only word I have on this is a crow, and they ain't the best of messengers?"

"I get it," the pine marten snapped. "Stop delayin'!"

Ailur smiled. "Fergive me, friend. I'm afeared we'll be o'erheard."

The pine marten shook her head impatiently. She had absolutely black eyes, without so much as a twinkle in them. "No one's *in* here except my crew, your crew, and the other crews who're in on this. *Spill it,* Ailur!"

Ailur sighed. "The foxes have finally burst out of Darkwoods in the east. They've pushed the armies there back all the way t' Pasadagavra."

The pine marten nodded. "Good. Almost time, then?"

"Almost," Ailur replied forebodingly. "I've got one o' my crew waiting halfway twixt 'ere an' Pasadagavra. Hopefully, he'll run into the messenger from Queen Demeda. Yer turn. What's happenin' at Arashna?"

The pine marten spread her paws. "More o' the same stuff that's been happenin' fer ages. The foxes keep tryin' t' throw themselves against it, hopin' t' break in, and the defenders keep makin' fish food o' them."

Ailur nodded. "I 'ad 'oped t' have more t' say t' Queen Demeda."

"Her scheme is *working,* ain't it?" the pine marten asked. "'Cause if it ain't, count me out."

Ailur snorted.

The pine marten rose very slowly. "You really don't think that I'll take my crew out of this if the battle's lost?"

"No, I don't," Ailur replied. "Y'er braver than that, Shartalla."

Now Shartalla snorted. "Y'er an idealist, Ailur. No wonder y' gets on so well with Queen Demeda an' Lady Raven."

Ailur inclined her head. "Bein' an idealist don't make me wrong. When I 'ear more from Queen Demeda, I'll let y' know."

"Thank you," Shartalla replied. Then she nodded to Ailur and swept off into the crowd of half-drunk pirates.

Actually, watching the crowd, Ailur could tell Shartalla's crew from the others. Shartalla allowed for drink but forbade drunkenness. She and her crew had far too many enemies to afford carelessness.

"I 'ope I did the right thing in trustin' her," Ailur murmured.

1 The Way to the Sea

Zuryzel breathed a sigh of relief as the Ashlands thinned out and then a second sigh as they stopped altogether. Crossing the Ashlands was the biggest part of her journey.

She followed the river diligently, not stopping, except to get another edible plant or berry or something to stave off her hunger. Limiting herself to sleeping every two days, she had learned to wake herself up whenever she wanted to. Weary after seven days of toiling with very little food or water, she was wishing she had not brought so much weight, but she kept going.

Zuryzel was on her way to the western shores, in search of a wild mercenary ferret named Ailur. Ailur was captain of the frigate *Justice*, and on many occasions in the past, the *Justice* and her crew had aided the Wraith Mice. Several mercenaries like Ailur were employed by the two senior Wraith Mice leaders at Arashna in helping defend against the Darkwoods fox armies besieging the island.

Zuryzel remembered the ferret as clearly as crystal, and she was scared of going to the west.

She closed her eyes and thought of Dejuday, the scout whom she constantly needed to rescue from the Darkwoods prisons, but who had returned the favor by rescuing her from two corsairs. Somehow, she thought she'd be better off in his company now because he had already proven himself a match for the most feared fighters in the land—ah, on the sea. But this was a mission she had to undertake herself. Her mother, Queen Demeda, hadn't actually said that, but Zuryzel got the feeling that her mother intended it.

Suddenly, just in front of her, she spotted something: a fallen oak. Its trunk was only partially burned, leaving the top of it flat. Zuryzel sprinted to it at top speed; at last, a chance to rest! She had made good time, but she still had two days to go following the Dellon. With this improvised watercraft, now she would have only a rough half hour—this could knock two days off her journey! Every minute was precious.

She reached the log and threw her sack and pouch down onto it gratefully. Then she noticed a young oak, still alive and sitting at a tilt, nearly touching the water, half of its roots exposed. Zuryzel could not leave it like this, so she leaned hard on the exposed roots and kicked a lump of ash over them. Then she piled many globs of river mud on top of that.

Yes, she thought, *this tree will survive.*

She patted it softly, and she could have sworn that the tree whispered to her, *Thank you, Zuryzel, princess of the moon.*

Zuryzel found a floating log of usable size and hefted it onto the oak log. Then she hauled herself aboard and used the other log to shove off.

The current bore the huge log off with a speed that Zuryzel had never known. She unsheathed her sword and began hewing away at the last half of the log that she would not need—it was best by far that she travel with all speed. She would need to haul this log to the Eupharra, which was two days away. After she had cut off the back of the log and watched it bumping along for a bit, she used her dagger to slice through the burned parts of the makeshift raft and hewed it down to less than half what it had been. It would not be enough to ride the Eupharra, but she could add rails and attach things later on—it would not be hard. The Daya flowed through an overhanging forest, so she could get the wood as she rode along.

She maneuvered herself carefully around the log as she cut off most of the top. Then she sat down carefully and rested for a little until she saw the sharp turn in the river. Using her other log, she pushed hard against the current, beaching the log in a patch of deep sand.

Zuryzel sat, panting on the bank for a while before lifting up her makeshift boat. It was taller than she was, but she managed to bear it for a while.

"Havin' trouble, are you?"

Zuryzel nearly dropped the boat in her shock.

A young but seasoned ferret warrior sat calmly down practically right in front of her. Zuryzel recognized him instantly.

"Grayik?"

Grayik, the mercenary ferret, smiled disarmingly at her. He was one of Ailur's band, and Zuryzel had grown to like him when she had first met him. He was strong, cunning, and a genius with a blade.

"Not like you to be so far in the middle o' nowhere, but never fear, Princess," the ferret teased, "we'll get you down to the coast in a month or so. Ailur's been anticipating someone coming, but very few could have guessed that you'd be the one a comin'. So, if you need help, I'll get ya down to the Daya for ya."

"Where did you pop up from?" Zuryzel asked, still surprised by his swift appearance.

"Ya're the one who popped up from the river, Zuryzel," Grayik reminded her. "But the point is, ya need t' get to the sea to find Ailur, so I'll take ya t' her. C'mon, look lively. Ya just need t' get t' the river an' ya're practically there."

Zuryzel shook her head, remembering Grayik's unbelievable impudence. "You say Ailur is expecting someone. What does that mean?"

Grayik shrugged. "I dunno. Come with me, I'll get ya t' the sea. Kyka'll be able t' help us."

"Who's Kyka?"

Grayik grinned mysteriously as he tossed the log into the river. "You'll see."

Zuryzel didn't like this at all. "Grayik, I'm sorry, but you just pop out of nowhere and expect me to trust you?"

Grayik clapped a paw to his cheek. "Ah! I almost forgot. This is my token of trust."

From a pocket in his trousers, Grayik drew a long silver chain and held it out for Zuryzel to examine. The chain was made not from links but from little indigo stars. Zuryzel recognized it as her mother's.

"Where did you get this?" she gasped.

"I told ya. Yar mother informed Ailur that somen'd be travelin' t' the oceans and would need `elp. Now, we should get goin' `cause we don't seem to `ave lotsa time."

Zuryzel still didn't like this. But she didn't have a choice.

Darkness was usually a welcome thing to Wraith Mice because it accompanied the night and that meant cover. But all that this darkness accompanied was dirt. These infernal tunnels, leading from Dombre to Pasadagavra, were packed full of creatures making the trek but, unfortunately, not packed full of torches. The tunnel wasn't even solid rock, either—just dirt. Dejuday hated dirt. Not because he was prissy or neat in any way, shape, or form. He hated it because it separated. Because it blocked out the sky. It was worse than a prison, and he would know—he'd been in one a few times. And each time, he'd been rescued by Princess Zuryzel.

Well, at least now he could think about that without feeling that his fur was curling with shame. He had saved her life from two corsairs. The princess, who was rumored to be a better sword-wielder than any princess had a right to be, needed to be rescued by him, the clumsy scout.

"I hope she's all right," he said aloud, thinking of the long miles that lay ahead of her into hostile territory. For him, the hardest part of that journey would be going so near to his home, the island city of Arashna, and seeing it under siege without actually setting paw there. But Zuryzel would have to convince a wild host of corsairs to aid her kingdom and with so little gold.

"Bear King, protect her," Dejuday prayed.

Beside him, his older sister, Sibyna, gave him a scrutinizing look. "You mean Zuryzel?"

He only nodded, a response no one detected in the unlighted passage.

"She's a solid rock of resourcefulness." That was Orgorad, Sibyna's mate. Dejuday couldn't see him, it was so dark. "She can take care of herself. Wherever she is, I'm sure she's safe."

Wherever she is … Those words rang like a guilty bell in Dejuday's ears. However, Orgorad's words encouraged him. Orgorad had a way of being reassuring, if distant, that most creatures found comforting, especially Sibyna. His distance had once almost shattered their relationship, but thankfully, that breach seemed behind him and his mate.

Sibyna looked in the direction of her mate's voice. "I just hope she wasn't captured. The foxes vowed to do all kinds of nasty things to her if they ever got their paws on her."

Even though Sibyna couldn't see his face, Dejuday had to look away. He was the only one, besides Queen Demeda, who knew where Princess Zuryzel was, and it had to stay that way—the only other creature allowed to know was Biddah the squirrel. It made him feel awful, though, to see his sister worrying over her friend and know he had the power to cease her worrying.

But no. He had to keep his word and the Princess's secret.

Corsairs and Cliffs

Knife sorely regretted summoning the corsairs, but she refused to show it. She had Demmons twirled around her paw—he was no trouble as he only wanted a promise of conquest and he had not ever stopped to think. This was the case for all of the fox captains—but the three ferrets were a different matter entirely.

Jironi was a ferret not only of beauty but also of forethought, patience, and wit. Fotirra was not any of these, but she had skill with a blade and with strategy, and she also had an ample amount of common sense and logic, something that, for all Knife's sharp wit and uncommon mind, the fox sadly lacked. She could miss the most obvious things anywhere, but none of the ferrets did. And Redseg, well, he had a fearsome saber, which Knife feared, but he also had lightning speed and a smart-aleck attitude.

When Dombre was left behind and Pasadagavra was in view, as was the original horde of the foxes, Knife overheard Redseg whispering to Jironi, "Huh, is that all they've got? That's about as lacking as ol' Poison's logic—there's not enough room in her tiny head for it! I don' see what she's afeared o'—there's no room for great cats to attack."

Fotirra spoke with a burr in her voice, as she did when she did not want to be overheard and understood.

"Och aye, thou art raht thir, Reedseeg. No' enou' room fer majoor attacks. No' mich lahk the oopen sea, eh? Nae limits thir."

"If you must jabber, then speak in a language we can all understand," snapped Poison from behind.

"I'm surprised you unnerstand me when I speak wi' that Simalan tone," snapped Fotirra impatiently.

"Fotirra," said Jironi in stern warning.

Fotirra fell silent.

Knife had been trying hard to ignore them, but that was hard, especially when she didn't have the faintest clue what Fotirra had said—stuff like that always made her curious.

"You know, she has a point there," said a cool, smooth voice from behind Poison.

Epoi, the only vixen captain Demmons had brought, was smiling slyly at Fotirra.

"You needing to speak in languages we all understand, I mean," she continued. Her voice did not have the twang of the sea as the others did.

"Och, ye great blithermouth, shut ye oop an' speak thee in a tongue *we* all ken, d'ye ken? Nae, ah wager ye dinnae ken e'en the sea's tongue. Hah!"

"You're marching all wrong!" snapped Epoi, annoyed by Fortirra's fearlessness. "It's right left, not left right!"

Fotirra deliberately marched left right, or, as she said it, "lift raht."

Biddah lay, trembling, on the cold stone floor of the tunnel. She had not seen fire for what she guessed was nine days.

Yes, it must be nine days, she decided. They had reached the foot of a huge cliff, rough but fine for climbing. It went up until it was lost in darkness no eyes could penetrate. Syra had said that they would need nine days for climbing, which left nine days for traveling. There was more than enough food, but Biddah was still scared. The great cliff was dominating, and a horrible thought had entered her mind: where would they sleep?

Lady Raven hurried out of the darkness. She kept glancing nervously at the cliff, but she had mastered herself.

"Biddah, Karrum, Marruh, Rainbow, Cinder, Maple, Raspberry, Shinar, Dejuday, Colobi," she called out softly.

Biddah and Karrum stirred.

"Yes, Lady Raven?" Karrum asked her.

Lady Raven shuddered, a rare sight. "We may as well hurry and get up that cliff part of the way. Syra says that there's a large cleft where we could rest for a while, and that's a ways up. Let's hurry, and rest then. Queen Demeda should follow later.

Biddah nodded. Karrum wrapped her blanket about her, and then wrapped his blanket around her, too.

"You go first," he whispered to her. "I'll go behind you to keep you from falling."

Biddah took a deep, uneven breath. She vaguely heard Lady Raven giving quiet orders.

"Rainbow, go find Plum, Hosta, and Dogwood. Maple, find Birch, Aspen, Rowan, and Mayberry. Ouch! Oh, shoot that rock. Raspberry, find Cedar, Apple, Snowgoose, and Foam. Bring them all here, we're going. Marruh, are you ready? Right, don't worry. Cherry! Since you're awake, you may as well come with us. Everyone ready? Shinar, see if there are any others ready to come. Wait here. I'm going to check in with Queen Demeda. Wait for me before you climb."

Lady Raven hurried off into the dark without a backward glance. By the time she had returned, the last of the summoned Rangers had hurried up, their gear buckled on, and Shinar had hastened out of the gloom with Crispisin, Orgorad, and Sibyna in tow.

Sibyna gaped at the tough of the cliff. Orgorad put a paw about her shoulders as Lady Raven came sprinting up out of the gloom.

Considering the speed she had, Lady Raven stopped surprisingly abruptly. "Well," she commented, "this cliff isn't going to get any shorter. Let's go."

Aspen, one of the Rangers, exchanged a nervous glance with Rainbow, his friend. The two Rangers walked over to the wall and gingerly felt it. Lady Raven was just above them, having walked straight to the wall from informing Queen Demeda of their departure. Cinder had found paw holds not too far away, and Snowgoose, one of Lady Raven's captains, was just above him; Orgorad and Sibyna were having little difficulty as they climbed side by side.

Karrum and Biddah glanced at each other. Then, trembling, Biddah walked to the wall and Karrum followed. Tentatively, Biddah hoisted herself onto the cliff, and Karrum followed.

The climbing of the great cliff had begun.

3 Oria

Zuryzel was bone weary, but she kept going. She kept a constant, comfortable pace behind Grayik, following the corsair's eyes. Grayik kept glancing to their left—south, in other words. There always seemed to be something to the south. The forest, thick with trees and blackberries and nettles, made it hard to pass.

"There's Oria," said Grayik, suddenly pointing north.

Zuryzel could see nothing but low, reddening bushes, groves of trees, and all sorts of … not so pleasant things. Then suddenly, through a gap in the groves, Zuryzel saw Oria.

The trees and short green grass and shrubs through which they had been traveling ended abruptly at a far distance, as though a giant paw had drawn a line. Not even a branch hung over Oria. It seemed just to appear out of nowhere. Why hadn't she seen it before? But now Oria—the moor that formed the border to the Ranger's land—stretched as far as she could see.

It was way into the distance—perhaps many days into the distance—but Zuryzel could see it all quite clearly. A stretch of long brownish-green grass dotted with sagebrush and such stretched out northward to some sheer cliffs. It was the biggest moor Zuryzel had ever seen, and it stopped her breath. She found most moors to be peaceful. But Oria was by no means pleasant or peaceful or pretty. Instead, it filled Zuryzel with a warrior's spirit, and made her want to run forever.

Zuryzel suddenly understood what gave the Rangers their unique fighting spirit—they had a broad, sweeping home that they loved.

Darkness and night, Dejuday had learned, were not interchangeable. Night had the light of stars and the moon. This subterranean darkness was punctuated only by a few torches clamped in climbers' teeth. Dejuday, in spite of his loathing of this non-night darkness, refused to take a torch. He didn't want those smoking things anywhere near his eyes.

Hang it all, he was neither squirrel nor worm! Why had King Hokadra done this? Why had he arranged to have his army slip away from their fortresses? Why … hadn't … they … fought … *back?!* He paused in his climbing and mentally rehearsed his story for Biddah once more. He couldn't tell her Zuryzel's end destination, but he could say that she was alive, at least. Maybe he could say a little more—that she was doing something for her father. Then he winced. But, what if Biddah went to King Hokadra for the whole story? King Hokadra knew nothing of his daughter's mission. He'd have to come up with a way of keeping Biddah from doing that.

He could see the squirrel now. She looked worse than he felt.

Biddah was by no means scared of heights or of darkness, but this solidly black cliff was another matter. She did not like it one bit. It seemed to go on and on and on. And above all, there was no guarantee that the next resting ridge would be anywhere within a day's climb, so in spite of their desire to flee from the dark tunnels they'd been enduring for nearly sixteen days, they took advantage of every possible ledge for a rest.

Biddah sometimes heard the cries of those behind them—whenever someone slipped, for instance. Biddah never had slipped, but more than once, the Wraith Mice near had, and so had a few of the Rangers.

To Biddah's surprise, it was Lady Raven who kept them going. Her strong will seemed to have conquered her fear of heights, and she would slide nimbly down the sheer cliff to a ledge she had already left to offer words of encouragement to any she saw there in trouble.

A cry came to Biddah's left. Mayberry, one of the Rangers, screamed as the rock she was using for her pawhold came loose. It had tumbled down the long cliff, for who knew how far?

Mayberry clung onto the pawholds she had found with her forepaws.

Snowgoose, who was just above her, turned nimbly and reached down, grasping one of Mayberry's paws. She pulled hard, and Mayberry found another pawhold and moved her footpaw up to where her forepaw had been.

Snowgoose, an older Ranger, sighed in relief as Mayberry's trembling paw did not give way and she continued climbing.

Biddah suddenly noticed that a shape was looming out of the darkness above her. In a hoarse voice, she called out, "Something's up above us!"

Lady Raven increased her climbing rate. She reached up a paw and touched the dark thing.

"A ledge," she sighed. "Big enough for us to rest on."

Every other creature hurried up after her.

Biddah collapsed gratefully against the solid stone. Karrum dropped in against her, wrapping his tail about her in an effort to warm her.

Biddah hated this dark with every last particle of her. Inwardly, she vowed never to take such a fine gift as the stars, a storm, trees, fire, or food at her paw for granted again.

Before Biddah fell asleep, her paw strayed to her stomach. It was swollen, and she could feel herself getting heavier. The babe she was carrying would be born in Pasadagavra, she realized, and he would be one of the few squirrels outside of the Stone Tribe to know what the inside of Pasadagavra looked like all his or her life.

With that thought, Biddah fell asleep.

Biddah was woken by a gentle shake.

"Wake up," whispered a voice in her ear.

She recognized the voice.

"Syra? What's going on?"

Syra's tail brushed gently against Biddah's face. "Lady Raven wishes to set out soon. Set out with her, friend. You have a long way to go."

You? Earthworms never used the word *you*; they said *ye* and *thou*.

"Syra," Biddah whispered uncertainly.

"Do not fret about my words," the earthworm hissed whilst shaking Orgorad and Sibyna into wakefulness. "I've heard you speaking, and I suppose I picked it up. If it makes ye feel any better, ye need not fear me. Wake up, you lot. Wake *up*!"

Suddenly a thousand echoes shocked the others into wakefulness. Karrum leaped up with surprise. "What was that?"

"Some creature fell *in*," hissed Syra in alarm. "A bit ago, for it will have taken some time for the echoes to reach us. Quickly, quickly, ye have no time to waste! Follow the stairs, they are right there. Hurry! I will make sure everyone knows the position." Syra slid off down the sheer cliff like wind.

Lady Raven held a swift conference with Cinder. He nodded in agreement.

"Rangers, we're heading back down as quickly as we can. Everyone else, keep going! We'll send Syra back up here as soon as we meet her."

With lightning speed, the Rangers vaulted over the edge of the ledge. Biddah saw their paws holding onto the ledge before they vanished as the Rangers continued to climb downward.

"There," pointed Dejuday. "There's something that looks like a set of stairs. Let's try to climb up them—Srozka!" he exclaimed.

Srozka and Layda were slithering down with all speed.

"This way, quickly!" they exclaimed.

The creatures practically ran up the steep stairs until the stairs became too steep to walk up, and they instead climbed from step to step. They were going as fast as they could toward the top of the stairs when, suddenly, the black air was alive with hisses.

Biddah vaguely recognized Creeka, Srozka's grandmother.

"Hold still," they hissed. "We need to get ye up the rest of the way as swiftly as we can. Just stay rigid. Thou wilt be fine."

Like in the tunnel to Dombre from Mirquis, an earthworm gently lifted Biddah on its head and slithered up, pushing her. Only this time, she was not going at an easy pace, but at lightning speed. Biddah tried hard to keep her paws from touching the rock of the stairs. Nearly an hour of pure fear went by while remaining rigid in rushing darkness.

Then the whole passage seemed to break, and they were on flat and solid ground again.

An oaken door stood not far away. "Go there," hissed the earthworms, before they were gone.

Biddah did not hesitate. Her fur was ruffled from the air whooshing past her face when they had traveled, and her body was cut all over and covered with mud, yet she hurried, not looking back for one second nor stopping to think about how she looked. She only rushed forward.

They had not yet reached the main gate when other figures dashed up behind them; the Rangers had turned on the word of the earthworms and now hurried behind them.

"Graeka said to hurry along here as fast as we could," Lady Raven panted.

It was not really a retreat, Biddah decided, but an act of judgment—it was better to leave the horrible place at once instead of stopping to see who had landed in the cave.

The Rangers were breathing hard and looked tired and ragged in the faint light that issued from the crack under the door.

"No time to wait," panted Orgorad. He kept looking nervously over his shoulder.

Dejuday reached the door first. It was stiff as could be, but he wrenched it open and then stood to one side. "Come on, everyone; we haven't got time. Hurry."

"We've got plenty of time," Karrum pointed out. "Whoever fell in, fell in several days march back!"

"How do you know?" Lady Raven shot. "They could have fallen in through one of the air passages. In that case, they could be not far away!"

The thought was frightening. The remaining Wraith Mice, squirrels, and a single river otter hurried without question toward the door.

The tunnel behind it was made of pink alabaster and rather smooth but quite climbable. Lady Raven had long since taken out her bow and had a gull-feathered arrow on its string.

"Cinder, Snowgoose, go quickly," she hissed.

The two Rangers were both nearly ten cycles older than she, and she was not so young. However, she stood with her bow drawn tight whilst jerking her head toward the tunnel.

Somewhat to Biddah's surprise, Cinder and Snowgoose both protested volubly. Lady Raven wasn't just their leader; she was also their comrade. But Lady Raven jerked her head again and snapped something in the Ranger's language. They sulked but obeyed.

Biddah scrambled up after them, blind with fear. Suddenly, behind her, she heard the sounds of many creatures hurrying, heard the faint shouts, and heard Lady Raven's sigh of relief.

"Demeda," Lady Raven breathed.

"You heard the echoes, then?" Demeda panted.

"Of course. Hurry, there's a tunnel over there."

"You come, too."

"Not yet. Go. Rangers, stay here."

"Lady Raven," called a hiss from the darkness, "go. You've no time to waste. Don't worry; we'll handle it if someone fell in. You go and bring the word."

Lady Raven seemed to hesitate for a moment before there was sound of her muttering in bitter assent and ordering her Rangers up the tunnel.

They went. Biddah heard them scrambling up behind her.

Suddenly, bright light of a moon rushed in on the squirrel. Such was the brilliance in comparison to the darkness of the tunnels that she had to shut her eyes. She felt other paws holding hers, helping her out of the tunnel.

When she finally blinked her eyes open, she realized that she was surrounded by white stone—marble, on closer inspection. The sound of a fountain tinkled in her ears. She caught sight of a pink alabaster wall and realized she was in the east side of Pasadagavra.

Karrum had hold of her paw and was gently maneuvering her to the pink wall, where the fountain was. Cinder and Snowgoose were taking a hurried head count.

Biddah waited as Queen Demeda struggled up through the tunnel.

"That's almost everyone," she panted. "Lady Raven and Rainbow stayed behind to make sure everyone else knew where they were going."

"Typical," Snowgoose grunted.

"What day is it?" Demeda asked wearily.

Biddah looked around to see who Queen Demeda was speaking with and realized that she was talking to Jaccah, Tribeprincess of the Stone Tribe squirrels. Biddah had not noticed the Tribeprincess there before.

"Nearly autumn," Jaccah replied.

"Then Zuryzel should be about at the Daya," whispered a familiar voice. Biddah jumped. She had not noticed Dejuday, the clumsy scout, climbing up the tunnel with a few others. And his words made no sense.

"What?" she whispered.

Dejuday glanced around and gently guided her away. "There's something she asked me to tell you ..."

4 Aboard the *Justice*

At the very moment Zuryzel was being discussed by her friends, she was on the Eupharra River, barely a day's sailing east of the sea.

Grayik and she had found Kyka the day before. Kyka had turned out to be a loner river otter who built boats. He had a kindly, friendly smile and twinkling eyes but didn't talk much. He rather reminded Zuryzel of Asherad, her oldest friend; their manner was more or less the same for they were both quiet, friendly, and kind, yet Zuryzel could tell that this river otter had no shortage of courage or skill with weapons, like her old-time friend.

Kyka had declined the offer to come with them. "No, Princess of the Moon," he had said cordially. "I've a good life here. However, on your return, I will go with you. My family was slain by the foxes, those that disease didn't get. I'll be here, finishing a few more boats. Then, we'll have enough room for Ailur and whoever else. So I'll bid you good-bye now and plan on seeing you in forty days or so."

Now Zuryzel leaned on the railing at the front of one of Kyka's boats. It had oar holes and a sail so that there was enough power propelling it beside the current of the river. It was a light little craft but well capable of sailing the seas near the shoreline. It would be quite easy to find the *Justice* in this vessel.

The sea was not far off, Zuryzel knew. She felt it in her fur, in her muscles, in her blood. She smelled it on the air. She heard seagulls crying over the river's noise. And she tasted salt when she licked spray from around her mouth.

The willows that draped over the Eupharra formed a curtain behind which they sailed and made it nearly impossible to see through. Zuryzel was forever putting up her paw to brush away the willow boughs that whipped her face.

Suddenly, the willow curtains broke. There was a boiling sound accompanied by a loud steady pounding. And right in front of Zuryzel, stretching out for miles and days and cycles, was the great sea.

Zuryzel smiled to herself. It had been many long cycles since she had seen the sea and the seagulls soaring overhead.

Grayik tugged on the white, triangular sail, and it billowed beautifully. He secured it to the mast, grinning at the sea breeze.

Zuryzel kept her eyes skinned for signs of a ship—the *Justice* should be around here somewhere—and for corsairs. Some had not answered Demmons' call and were just as evil as he was. The *Justice* might not have been able to get here yet for having to avoid the other corsairs. She needed to make sure that she did not run into trouble with them.

For nearly two hours they did not see a ship. The boat road the waves southward, tacking skillfully now and again.

"Sail t' the north!" shouted Grayik, obviously challenging her to identify it.

Zuryzel hurried to the back of the boat and stared. "Not the *Justice* ... I'd say that we'd best avoid that ship. She looks like the *Redsea* to me. Run by a ferret, name of Immihg. Stay closer to the shore; that ship prefers deeper water." She looked at Grayik's knowing face. "Am I right?"

"Yep." Grayik took the tiller and turned the boat more shoreward. "How'd ya know?"

Zuryzel watched the corsair vessel and realized with relief that she was sailing north and did not seem to have spotted them. "Immihg has always been an enemy of the Wraith Mice. He mounted many attacks against Arashna itself."

After about another hour, just as dark was falling, a city with a huge harbor came in sight on the shore. "Let's make for the 'arbor," Grayik called. "Per'aps the *Justice* will be there."

Once the boat reached the harbor, Grayik called to Zuryzel, "Ya best let me go in there, see if'n Ailur ain't there. Barnacles an' seaweed, there's bound t' be other corsairs in there. I knows how t' 'andle 'em."

He leaped ashore before she could protest and went for a building that Zuryzel took for a seaside tavern.

The wait was not a long one. Before even moonrise, he came hurrying back with another ferret at his heals. Zuryzel recognized Ailur instantly. She wore no tunic but was clad in bright yellow trousers and a dark red shirt, a real seagoer. Brass hoops dangled from her ears. She wore a necklace of golden rings about her neck, a belt of sharkskin adorned with crab pincers (into which were thrust a saber and a curved knife), and a bracelet of lobster pincers and sharks' teeth. Zuryzel tried hard not to look at the sharks' teeth.

"Zuryzel!" Ailur exclaimed, looking surprised. "Great Cerecinthia, I expected someone else. Quite a pleasure to have yeh, I must say. Yeh look like a bit o' shuteye wouldn' go amiss. Don' worry, there's a berth or two aboard *Justice*; yeh can sleep there. No, Zuryzel," she added seeing the Wraith Mouse's face. "I'll talk to yeh tomorrow. You look too wore out to concentrate much on anythin'. Get some sleep. Follow me!"

Ailur led them to the biggest ship Zuryzel had ever seen in her life. It had four masts and a bowsprit with another sail on it. Ailur cupped her paws about her mouth and shouted, "*Justice* ahoy!"

Another ferret appeared over the railing and dropped a rope ladder. Ailur nodded to Zuryzel. "Up yeh go."

Zuryzel found the climb to be not too difficult. Ailur followed her up. The other ferret tipped his sea cap to her in brief salute. "Cap'n!"

"Take the midnight watch, Nuit and Pya."

The ferret nodded. Ailur sucked in breath and bellowed, "Sail watch! Down 'ere on the double. Uku, cummere! Every other ferretjack, keep on watch."

From directly overhead, a ferret dropped right between Zuryzel and Ailur. Zuryzel jumped, but Ailur hardly seemed to notice.

"Zuryzel, stay 'ere fer a moment," Ailur said. "Uku!" she called again.

A figure that had been leaning on the prow railings turned. Zuryzel's instinctive reaction put her on guard. But that instinct lasted for only a moment.

On first sight, Uku was a sea otter. Yet a closer inspection proved that to be wrong: most of the sea otters had sizeable girth, yet Uku was slender as a stick. And, whilst the sea otters wore tunics of fine cotton or extremely refined bark cloth, Uku wore a dress of brown color that looked loose and cool. About her head, she wore a woven hat with small shells tied onto it, and she wore a necklace with a single, beautiful clamshell. Hanging by a blue cord from her shoulder was a huge, beautiful shell.

Uku was clearly young, not much older than thirty cycles, but she seemed to radiate confidence, understanding, and friendliness. Her eyes were dark and wild.

"Zuryzel, this is Uku," Ailur told them. "Friend o' mine. Uku, take 'er to the stern cabins, and fill 'er in a bit."

Uku nodded wordlessly and beckoned to her. Zuryzel followed and tried to engage her in conversation. "So, where are you from?"

"I am from the Hoeylahk tribe on the northern shores."

The breath caught in Zuryzel's throat. She had heard legends about the Hoeylahk otters; but a mercenary ship was the last place she'd expect to see one.

Zuryzel opened her mouth to ask more questions but changed her mind. There was obviously no point in trying to converse with the otter; she was clearly not given to discussion.

They continued scrambling carefully over rope coils and bulky, pointy objects that Zuryzel could not identify. Finally, Uku stopped. A door made out of either oak or pine stood right in front of them. Uku wrenched it open and nodded inside.

It was not quite anything Zuryzel could have expected. Five hammocks lay stretched around the curved walls. One of them was occupied. As the door opened, the head of a young ferret popped up from the nearest one.

"Can't a beast get a wink o' sleep 'round 'ere?!" she yawned.

Uku smiled kindly. "Well, you'll be on watch in a little bit, so you may as well wake up, Iddi. Incidentally, you will be having some company."

"Seas and storms," grumbled the ferret. "Is it nearly midnight?"

"Not for another hour. Iddi, meet Zuryzel."

The ferret stopped rubbing her eyes and blinked at Zuryzel in surprise. Then Iddi nodded courteously. "Pleased indeed t' meet yeh, Zuryzel. Cummin. Those two hammocks are empty." She nodded to the two swaying hammocks in the back of the room.

Uku nodded and wordlessly left as Zuryzel sat down on one of the two. Iddi rolled her eyes in frustration.

"I wish Uku talked more. She's quiet as the bottom o' the sea, quite annoyin'. So, Zuryzel, I guess you've just arrived from Pasadagavra? What news from the war?"

WHAM!

Zuryzel jumped as the door slammed open, but Iddi merely turned her face sadly to the new ferret staggering wearily in.

"Does that mean it's our watch now?" she asked pathetically, her face fallen.

"No," replied the new ferret wearily. "Nuit an' Pya are taking the watch. They're not too happy, but y' know them."

"Oh, *good*!" exclaimed Iddi. "No watch 'til noon tomorrer!"

The new ferret shrugged. She nodded to Zuryzel. "So this is the princess Ailur said arrived tonight. Welcome aboard the *Justice*, finest ship on the 'igh seas. My name is Drexa, an' I'm Iddi's cabinmate."

"So, d' you know where we'll be goin' then?" demanded Iddi.

"' Oo knows. Prob'ly back t' the island."

"But what about getting to Pasadagavra?" Zuryzel protested.

The ferrets exchanged looks. "Zuryzel, that's easier said than done," Drexa explained. "There's a bare fifty aboard, an' that ain't goin' t' make much difference aginst Demmons an' 'is fifty or more cap'ns wi' their crews." She shrugged. "I guess we'll leave at noon—er, sun 'igh—tomorrer. 'Tis the best we c'n do."

"Why so late?" asked Zuryzel.

"'Cause, 'til then it's lowtide, an' the ship ain't able t' sail on lowtide. We needs 'ightide. And we got t' get food an' such. Yeh can't survive fer a week or so at sea without no water. Besides, I suppose Ailur'll want t' get some more crews t' help us, maybe enough t' make a full convoy. That ain't much compared t' the 'orde Demmons 'as got with 'im, but it's somethin'." Iddi smirked. "A few o' the greater corsairs are 'ere, an' they may not be good, but yeh can count on 'em when there's a chance o' gettin' at Demmons."

Zuryzel lowered her head sadly. "This doesn't sound very promising. I don't know what we'll do. You are our last friends."

The two ferrets exchanged glances. "Yeh know," Drexa murmured, "the one thing that Uku keeps tellin' us—it gets on our nerves, it does—is, 'Yeh don't always know where yeh have friends. Yer bound to have friends where yeh don't know. There's always someone willing to help you against yer enemy. Yeh've got friends where yeh don't know, lots o' them.' Yeh'd kind o' think she knows somethin', but either way, I think she wanted us t' tell yeh."

Zuryzel puzzled over what Drexa said. Well, there had been Fawn, she supposed, who had helped Biddah and Karrum escape when they had been captured. No one had expected that. Then, even farther back in time, there had been Lady Raven and the Rangers, arriving matter-of-factly in the middle of the Bow Tribe camp—that was as unexpected as things could get. And then, when Ice had disappeared, whoever had killed or captured her was a friend for sure. And Danaray and Anamay, the pair of river otters who had helped her get Fawn out of the Darkwoods—were they friends?

So many questions, but not so many answers yet, Zuryzel thought. Perhaps Ailur was not their last hope after all.

Zuryzel woke the next morning to feel Drexa shaking her.

"Wake up," advised the ferret. "Ailur wants a word. I'd go wid yer, but I'm on watch. C'mon, wake up!"

Zuryzel struggled up and gazed around. The cabin looked welcoming and safe in the morning light. A heavy swell seemed to have penetrated the harbor, and the ship was swaying cheerfully, though it was rough. The hammocks swung wildly, and Zuryzel's paws were unaccustomed to the swaying. But she picked up the swell easily.

Clambering over the coils of ropes and sharp objects did not get easier the second time. Now that the ship was rocking, Zuryzel had to work on keeping her balance. Several times, she nearly got cut.

"Drexa," queried Zuryzel, "What are these?"

"They're bolts an' such fer our ballista," shrugged Drexa. "It's on deck—I'll point it out t' yeh—an' we use it t' fire at other ships t' disable or t'sink 'em. Though we rarely use ours—we try t' rescue the slaves first—except we do use it t' destroy a mainmast now 'n' again. I've even go'en t' fire one in a battle. It hit the mast, too!" Drexa sounded quite proud of herself.

The two found a stairwell and climbed up until a bright light greeted them.

Uku was leaning on the prow railings again, gazing northward. A ferret was at the stern, gazing the other way, as though on watch. Another two ferrets dropped from the rigging.

Drexa glared at the female one. "Pya, may I asks yeh why yeh volunteered me fer watch? This time o' the morn ain't my watch!"

"I know," grinned the other female, though she still looked groggy with weariness. "On'y, I jus' did yer watch!"

"Yeah, well, it's my watch now, *an'* my watch at noon! That's two watches in a row!"

"Oh, is it? Oh well," shrugged Pya. "Tell yeh what—I'll do that watch for yeh 'cause then it ain't my watch until dawn. That do?"

Drexa still look angry, but she shrugged. "Sure."

"Well, Zuryzel," grinned one of the male ferrets, "I'm Nuit – pleased to meet yer! I'm to take you to Ailur."

Zuryzel followed him, still a little wary. These ferrets were not creatures that she was used to, and she had enough common sense to stay cautious.

Ailur was sitting calmly on the railing not far away, chatting away to another, elderly looking female ferret, who had a considerable girth and a homely face. When the captain caught sight of Zuryzel, she called her over.

"Ah, Zuryzel! Just the one I wanterd t' see. Nuit, go an' git yerself some rest. Now, Princess, tell me everything yeh know."

So Zuryzel told Ailur of all that had happened since the Darkwoods Oracle Scythe's death, down to where she'd left Dombre. Ailur sat and listened with rapt attention, her bright black eyes flickering sometimes, though she held her questions until Zuryzel finished.

"So, Hemlock summoned the warhawks fer 'elp?" she mused. "Hmm … that was foolish. An' then he summoned Demmons … What captains did he summon again?"

"All I know is that he summoned Epoi—I saw her; Jironi, Redseg, and Fotirra—one of the scouts saw them; and Riorat, Snillouf, and obviously, Demmons … What?"

Ailur was chortling with amusement. "Jironi ain't a captain—not fer Demmons, anyway. Drexa and Iddi told yeh part o' my crew was on my father's island, yes? Well, that's what I ordered them to say, but it ain't true. Jironi is my third in command." Ailur grinned at Zuryzel's surprise. "I wish I could take credit, but Lady Raven planned most o' this out. She expected corsairs t' be summoned, and she wanted some'n to be planted right in the foxes' army, some'n who could attack from inside." Ailur paused, grinned to herself again, and then continued. "So, on yer journey on the sea, did yeh spot any vessels?"

"Yes, the *Redsea*, I think."

"Hmm, that makes sense," Ailur mused. "Immihg tends t' be more in the north seas these days." She shrugged. "No consequence, really. But, there's very little I c'n do, wid more 'n three quarters o' my crew absent. We'll need other crews—a few o' the crews up 'ere would 'ate t' miss out anyway. But only yeh c'n convince 'em; yeh've seen it all. Yeh'll 'ave t' come up to the taverns wid me.

Zuryzel gaped at her in disbelief. A ferret tavern?

Ailur laughed.

"Yeah, yeh'll be fine. Just look like yer well armed an' don't back down from any corsair-jack of 'em , an yeh'll be just fine."

Zuryzel gulped at the idea of heading up to the taverns, but at Ailur's word, she hastened back down to the cabin and retrieved her blades.

"Bear King," she murmured, "I hope I can trust Ailur."

She shivered once and scrambled back up to the top deck.

Ailur and Grayik awaited her. "Ready t' go?" grinned Grayik. Zuryzel nodded shakily.

The two corsair ferrets and the one Wraith Mouse descended a ladder and leaped onto the shore. Zuryzel found that it really wasn't difficult to put on a brave face and follow Ailur up to the tavern.

When Ailur pushed the door open, Zuryzel received a minor shock. This tavern was not dingy and filthy and dimly lit as her father had said a tavern was. Four fires filled it with light, and there was no drunken revelry but laughing and occasional singing of gruff voices. A young female ferret played an instrument in a corner, her claws dancing lightly over its strings. Grayik cast a curious glance around and murmured, "Look who's in the corner."

Sitting in the corner opposite the musician was an old fox. He had numerous gray hairs on his face, but his muscles looked hard, and his eyes shone bright. He looked up at the closing of the door, and his eyes drifted onto Ailur.

"Ailur, I was wondering when you'd get up here …," he called. His eyes landed on the Wraith Mouse. "And can this be Princess Zuryzel?"

The breath left Zuryzel's lungs completely. Who was he? How in the name of the Bear King did he know who she was?!

At her name, all activity in the room ceased. Even the musician stopped mid-note and turned her eyes to Zuryzel, curiosity brimming in them.

"May I ask what brings you down here?" queried the old fox, with no real surprise that it was Zuryzel who should bear the message.

"Tell them," hissed Ailur. "The whole story."

"But—a fox? Tell *him* our situation?" Zuryzel asked quietly. The old fox snorted, looking a little offended, and Ailur nodded vigorously. Zuryzel decided to start from the beginning and raised her voice to address the tavern. "Have you heard that Oracle Scythe of the Darkwoods foxes has died?" All the creatures nodded. "Almost immediately after Scythe died, the Darkwoods foxes set out to conquer the world. They've already overrun the squirrel Bow Tribe camp and have captured the Wraith Mice fortresses of Mirquis and Dombre." This last was obviously news to some of the creatures, as Zuryzel heard several gasps. The old fox looked grim. "The squirrel tribes and the Wraith Mice have already lost many soldiers to battle, but the majority of our creatures are making their way to Pasadagavra."

She paused and looked around. "You all know of Pasadagavra, the inland fortress of the squirrel Stone Tribe?" When heads nodded all around, she continued. "It will be attacked next because it blocks the passage through the mountains. The Darkwoods foxes intend to conquer the world, every thing and every place. I come to seek help to stop them before they can control the mountain passage—before they defeat Pasadagavra."

"But the foxes won't be able to defeat Pasadagavra—it's too powerful!"

Zuryzel couldn't see who made the comment, but it came from her right. "Until recently, this was just a conquest by the foxes of Darkwoods.

And if that is all it was, I think you are right—the Ranger Mice have been helping us, too, and I think Pasadagavra could withstand the foxes alone. But about a month ago, many crews of corsairs arrived to aid the foxes, led by Demmons."

Cries erupted from the corsairs, some of comprehension, some of anger and indignation. Zuryzel held up her paw, hoping that it would silence them. Surprisingly enough, it did.

"King Hokadra has sent me with a message to all I could find: We need help defeating the foxes and corsairs. We will offer, to every captain and crew who helps us, a *reasonable*"—she cast a look at Ailur—"amount of loot from either the Wraith Mice fortresses, the Darkwoods fortress, or from Pasadagavra. And of course there would be whatever Demmons and his allies have."

There was silence for a long moment at the end of her speech. Then a ferret spoke up—apparently, he was a captain.

"Ye say that there be other crews aside from Demmons. Which other crews?"

"I do not know all of them," began Zuryzel. "I only know that Epoi, Riorat, Snillouf, and Redseg are there."

"Probably Uddio too," mused the captain. "We ain't seen 'im in cycles."

"Horeb also," piped up the musician. "We ain't seen 'im in ages!"

A ferret leaped up from where he had been sitting. "On me soul, Princess, I'm comin' wid yeh after Horeb! Aye, wid my crew, too!" he declared.

"Same goes fer me 'n' my crew!" added another voice.

As every single captain and crewmember in the tavern yelled his or her agreement, Zuryzel distinctly heard Grayik mutter, "Ach, shovin' back off, an' I only got 'ere yesterday!" But Zuryzel sensed he was smiling.

Two hours later, ten ships, sailing in a tight convoy, left the reefs about the small town and set sail for the mouth of the Eupharra River. Zuryzel stood behind Uku at the bow of the *Justice*.

Uku turned back to look at her.

"Now it begins, Zuryzel. Now it begins!"

5 Halls of Night

The vixen Eclipse had been an Oracle's apprentice her entire life.

Since the day of her birth, twelve winters previously, she had been destined for greatness in the service of the Serpent, or so the elderly Oracle Knife claimed. Eclipse did indeed last longer than most of her mentors. Her first, someone called Slash, had died. Then she'd had three others, whom she had never met, and they'd all been killed. Finally, it had been agreed that her mentor would be Hemlock, another Oracle she didn't remember.

And why had she never met them? Simply because the whole system of apprentices and teachers was only a formality. An apprentice was not required to follow her mentor or even listen to him, but some did both. The other four apprentices—Fawn, Oracle Blood's apprentice; Ice, Oracle Scythe's apprentice; Scorch, Oracle Fang's apprentice; and Poison, Oracle Knife's apprentice—were all with their teachers, helping Darkwoods along the path to victory.

Eclipse had never been on a war band in the East. All of her time had been with the war in the West. At six winters of age, she had been sent to Arashna, technically in command, but in fact answering to another in charge, of the armies on the eternal campaign, which passed south of Graystone and eventually laid siege to Arashna and Dobar. Eclipse grew up in command of the elite armies of Darkwoods.

This arrangement fulfilled the law of Darkwoods—that an Oracle or apprentice had to officially be in command of any army of a certain size—while making sure someone who truly knew how to win a war, such as a seasoned, hardened general, actually took charge. But by the time that competent general who had set out with her to besiege Arashna had died, Eclipse was as much an expert at war as he had been, so, as a mere Oracle's apprentice of Darkwoods, she assumed command.

Her life had been nothing but warfare. And now she hated the very thought of Darkwoods.

She had no idea of the recent happenings in the East, and she would have taken no interest in them had she known. She had been in a never-ending battle that her teachers and her soldiers' comrades could barely imagine. Eclipse was fighting corsairs, and she was feeling the sting of how hard that was. In misery and anger, she stopped sending any messages back to Darkwoods of what was happening at Arashna.

When her generals insisted that they needed to send word of their progress, she laughed mirthlessly and asked, "What progress?"

Her army was still encamped in Kardas, the little farming settlement where the Wraith Mice once ruled. They were still sitting outside Dobar's walls and gazing hungrily at Arashna, sitting imperviously on its island just half a mile out to sea, surrounded by three corsair ships, waiting while a fourth brought in provisions.

Almost inevitably, she began to alienate herself from the Blight, the foul curse of the Serpent that the foxes served. It supposedly gave them extra prowess in battle, and it certainly turned their eyes red. But to keep faithful to it required harshness and extreme devotion, and her life had enough of such adversity already. The land itself in the region was harsh, with precious few glades and grass, lots of nettle and blackberries, and painful rocky outcroppings. But Eclipse had found she was tempted to wander off on an occasional night and find a small clearing, flop down on the grass and pine needles, and gaze up at the stars—and to fall into an easy sleep. When she woke up, she saw the sun tinting the sky many shades of blue, green, and gold. The cedars smelled fresh, the grass was soft, the birds were singing, the taste of salt from the sea was in the air, and the distant mountains were outlined in sharp detail. She felt clean and peaceful when she woke, which changed once she forced herself to return to her army and the bitter life she led.

In short, Eclipse hated the campaign and doubted the Oracles back in Darkwoods even remembered she was alive.

So it was quite a surprise when Oracle Fang arrived one day, demanding to see her in her command house.

Eclipse had moved her army out of Kardas's walls, so she had a tent where she made the plans and did all the technical work. On purpose, she made Fang wait two hours in the damp chilliness of evening. In summer, Arashna and its lands were pleasant enough; in winter, it was always raining, and it usually continued nonstop until summer. The cold, just above freezing, and the dampness got to you. Eclipse wanted to give Fang a taste of what she'd been suffering from for ages—both the weather and the waiting.

When she walked in, she banged her paw impatiently on the table and demanded flatly, "What?"

Fang raised his chin a little at her tone, but he simply said, "Upon the death of Oracle Blood, you have been named Oracle."

"You're lying," Eclipse stated. "I'm the youngest of all the apprentices. I can't be made Oracle."

"You've had the most time as an apprentice," Fang reminded her.

Twelve winters, Eclipse remembered. "Ice has had more than I," she snapped.

"Ah. I take it you don't know what's been going on at Darkwoods?" Fang observed.

"How can I?" Eclipse snarled. "No one bothers to send me messages or reinforcements."

Fang decided to be patient. "Oracle Scythe died at the beginning of last fall," he informed the new Oracle.

"What a shame," Eclipse muttered sarcastically. Inwardly, though, she was disappointed. Scythe had always seemed more moderate than the other Oracles.

"Oracle Ice was chosen to replace her," Fang continued. "Hemlock succeeded her as Eldest Oracle. Not long after that, Oracle Blood also died, possibly from poison."

Eclipse had no problem about that. "Do you mean Oracle's apprentice Poison? Or just plain old poison?" she asked sardonically.

Fang bit his tongue to keep from snapping. "Fawn was chosen to replace him"—naturally, she was the next oldest—"but she was discovered to be losing contact with the Blight. She was betraying the Serpent."

Eclipse said nothing.

"Instead of promoting Scorch or Poison," Fang continued, "who were obviously not capable of dealing with soldiers, we chose to give Claw—you know him, I presume?"

"He used to be part of my army before I sent his division back to Darkwoods to recover from wounds," Eclipse replied apathetically.

"In any case, Claw was chosen to fill in the place for an Oracle until we could find and destroy Fawn."

Eclipse shrugged. "Then where is my opening?" she snarled.

Fang gave her a wearied look. "I'm coming to that."

Eclipse eyed Fang. "You seem to have lost a lot of Oracles recently. A little careless of you, don't you think?" Eclipse commented, baiting him.

Fang looked for a moment as if he would strike her but, instead, simply continued. "Not long after the whole incident with Fawn, we drove the Wraith Mice army from the Bow Squirrel Tribe home where they had been basing operations."

"Well. That would never have happened if Oracle Scythe had been alive. She would not have allowed that," Eclipse said slowly.

Again, Fang looked as if he wanted to claw her, but he resisted. "The defending army was driven from there to Mirquis to Dombre. There they sit, under attack."

"You sure they haven't escaped using those tunnels no one but the Wraith Mouse king knows how to enter?" Eclipse interrupted, beginning to enjoy herself.

"They were in Dombre when I left for here," Fang corrected himself. The last he'd seen of this fox, she was six summers old; something told him she'd become adept at using words to set traps. "Around that time, Oracle Ice disappeared, assumed to be dead."

Eclipse held his gaze levelly for a long time.

Fang grew uncomfortable in her glare. "What?"

"You drove Fawn out, I presume," Eclipse said deliberately.

"She escaped."

"Whatever. It was because she was 'losing connection with the Blight.'" Eclipse took a deep breath to control her anger. "Look at me, Fang. I'm not connected to the Blight at all."

Her blue eyes jumped out of her dark brown fur, and Fang nodded, conceding her point.

"But you are a general. We don't need a spiritual leader at the moment; we need you. And you can always make connection with the Blight again."

Eclipse sat back in a chair, passing a weary paw over her eyes. "How are the numbers at Darkwoods holding up?"

"We just got some reinforcements." Suddenly, Fang felt he shouldn't have said that.

"Oh good," Eclipse muttered. "Then you can send me some—" she broke off, and her blue eyes became wary.

"From where?" she asked coldly.

"What does it matter?" Fang replied airily.

"Fang," Eclipse snarled, "in the past six winters, I've become as good a wordsmith as you. Don't beat around the bush. *Who reinforced you*?"

Fang decided it best just to get it over with. "Knife sent for the help of Demmons and other corsair crews."

Until this point, Eclipse had been holding back her anger. Now, she exploded.

"She *what*?" the vixen practically screamed. "She did *what*? She allied herself with those monsters?" Eclipse jumped from her chair and actually upended the heavy table. "We've been fighting corsairs for six winters! They're dangerous! They'll destroy Darkwoods!"

"You don't know what you're talking about," Fang tried to interrupt her tirade.

"*I* don't? *You* don't!" Eclipse screamed. "I can't believe Knife trusted those barbarians! I've been fighting them for too long not to know how dangerous they are."

Fang stood up abruptly. "I think this interview is concluded, Oracle Eclipse. What has been done has been done. I will rest here tonight and return to Darkwoods tomorrow."

As he left, Eclipse shouted after him, "Fang, I won't ally myself and my army with them! I won't follow Darkwoods as long as those fiends are there!"

When Eclipse's generals found her, she was leaning on the upended table, seething and gnashing her teeth.

"E-Eclipse?" one of them stammered. The idea of addressing her by a title had been forgotten four seasons ago.

Eclipse got hold of herself. "Fang told me that I have succeeded Ice as Oracle," she informed them.

This took her generals aback, but the new Oracle held up her paw. "Relax. We're not going anywhere near Darkwoods. Fang gave me no orders."

Eclipse sat back in annoyance. She did, as an Oracle, have the right to remove her army from this senseless slaughter, and plainly, her generals thought she should. One of them murmured, "Why don't we go back? We can get away from the corsairs."

Eclipse laughed bitterly. "No, we can't. Knife decided that Darkwoods, even with more than twice as many as the opposing armies, needed reinforcements. She summoned corsairs to be her soldiers."

The disgust in her voice added that she had more to say.

One of her generals sat down slowly across from her. His Blight-less eye fixed with hers, and he asked, "And?"

Eclipse felt the honest gaze of all her generals on her. "And if we go back, we could all fall under the conquering ecstasy again. Then we'll only come back here and suffer this all over again."

Eclipse looked out the tent door again. "And yet ..."

"We are the best in Darkwoods," murmured another of her generals. "If we returned, we could easily dominate the others."

Eclipse let out a barking laugh. "As if. I'd wager all the soldiers in this army that Knife and Fang and possibly even our old friend Claw are trying to gain their own power in Darkwoods. We'd return to turmoil and confusion, as well as suspicion."

But still, if they were to get away from this place ...

"We don't have to go back to the castle," one of her generals commented mildly.

Eclipse stared at the maps of Arashna and the surrounding territory on her table. She had to think. She knew that she was not going to sit around here anymore. But where else could they go?

"Leave me," she instructed. "I must think."

6 Never Cross a Mouse with Arrows

Rainbow, the Ranger Orlysk, or ordinary soldier, and her friend Aspen had taken to sneaking out the back way of Pasadagavra through the Last Storehouse onto the mountain. Being stuck indoors—even such a big indoors—without so much as a fresh breeze was not their idea of pleasant, so they explored the mountains. They never actually got lost, though there were incidents.

One of those days, they had made it to the peak of a neighboring mountain and were resting for a time when a black crow glided up and alighted not far from them.

"Hello, Norya Nightwatch," Rainbow greeted the bird. "Looking for Herttua Crow?"

"Is she here?" Norya inquired in a rough caw.

"Nah," Aspen replied. "She and the other archers are tracking a party of foxes going south."

"Ah," Norya dipped her head. "How is Lady Raven?"

"Hasn't changed," Rainbow chuckled.

"Are she and Crow still not getting along?" Norya asked sadly.

Rainbow nodded glumly. "Unfortunately." Her black-and-silver-speckled pelt looked dull against the white of the mountain behind her, but her amber eyes were sharp and clear.

"Craic should be coming soon," Norya continued after a pause. "A raven is always more at home amongst peaks than a crow. Tell Lady Raven that either I or Craic will want to speak with her in about two weeks, once we have had an opportunity to gather information." With that, she took flight.

Aspen and Rainbow exchanged looks and began to make the arduous climb back towards Pasadagavra.

The evergreen forest waved gently to a summery breeze as Warriorqueen Wazzah sat calmly on the precipice where the trebuchet was located. Sibyna had been sent to bring a warm drink to the Warriorqueen. The archer approached cautiously, uncomfortable in the presence of someone who had so recently been an enemy.

Wazzah glanced at Sibyna as the Wraith Mouse approached. "Yes?" she asked in a neutral tone.

"I was asked to bring you this," Sibyna explained, extending the cup of hot tea.

Wazzah took it gratefully. "Thank you, Sibyna," she said politely.

Sibyna's eyes widened in surprise. How did the squirrel know her name?

Before she could back out, two of her fellow Wraith Mice jogged up. One of them was Lurena. "My lady," she panted to Wazzah.

Wazzah looked up sharply. "Yes?" she asked, her tone icy.

"I-I was sent to ask if you had seen anything," Lurena stammered.

"No," Wazzah replied. She gave Lurena a searching look. "You are from Kardas, I gather?"

Lurena blinked in surprise. "Y-yes."

"What is your name?" Wazzah inquired.

Lurena gave the Warriorqueen a mistrustful look.

"Her name is Lurena," replied the dry voice of the third Wraith Mouse.

"And yours?" Wazzah asked.

"Muryda," the other runner replied. "I'm from Dobar."

Wazzah nodded. "I hear you three are extremely competent runners."

"It doesn't require competence to run," Muryda replied calmly. Her black eyes showed no fear of the Warriorqueen, while Sibyna and Lurena had slipped back behind her.

"Which of you is fastest?" Wazzah asked candidly.

"Muryda," Sibyna and Lurena replied simultaneously. She really was. She was the fastest runner in the entire Wraith Mouse army.

"Then, Muryda," Wazzah asked, "could you run and suggest to Queen Demeda from me that another sentry on the wall—or rather, at the wall—would be prudent?"

Muryda nodded. "I will."

Late that night, Anamay was wakened by a terrible scream.

She jerked awake and gasped, surprised and terrified.

Mollusk bolted up beside her. "What was that?"

Anamay lept up, threw her cloak about herself, and hurried to the door. Mollusk followed her example.

They ran quietly through Zurez, searching for the source of the scream. Finally, Mollusk spotted a group of adult sea otters grouped around something, clogging the hall. From a distrance, the little sea otter, Eagle, and his friend, Amethyst, watched. "Eagle," Mollusk hissed, "what's going on?"

"Look's like Current found a prisoner. A mouse," explained Eagle.

Anamay looked closely and gasped. "This mouse is definitely in trouble," she shuddered.

"Do you recognize her?" Mollusk asked.

"Yes," Anamay replied. "There's a tribe of nomadic mice that live along the banks of the Keron River. This mouse is the sister of the deputy of the Keron Mice."

"Think we can help her in any way?" Mollusk wondered.

"She's got a babe with her," Amethyst, Eagle's friend, breathed.

"Driftwood will love that," Mollusk murmured forebodingly.

"Shhh," hissed Eagle, trying to hear Current speaking to the Keron Mouse.

"So, you think you can just stroll into our territory, do you?" he leered.

"It's not your territory," the Keron Mouse snarled back. "I was on the bank of the Keron. That is *our* territory."

"All alone," jeered a voice that Mollusk recognized with a jolt as the warrior named Driftwood. He must have led the patrol. Driftwood was a cruel and extremely dangerous warrior with fiercely aggressive beliefs. He had actually threatened to kill Anamay once because she was a river otter rather than a sea otter.

"On *my* territory," repeated the Keron mouse. "You are trespassers."

"This territory is ours, by right of conquest," Crustacean retorted.

"The river bank is *our* territory. The city of Zurez belongs to the Wraith Mice," snarled the Keron Mouse. "To King Hokadra. You've no right to defile Zureza's grave!"

"This whole place had already been defiled by her grave until we arrived," Current said coolly.

"Now, what punishment for you?" said Crustacean coldly. His usual wisdom and gentleness seemed to have vanished.

"Take her to where we take prisoners, and have her brat killed," replied Current.

His last comment brought the pride off the bound mouse completely. She stared at him in horror before pleading, "Please don't hurt my son. Please, please, he is only three days old. Punish me, but spare him. Please, in the name of the Bear King …"

"How could he even suggest such a thing?" hissed Eagle in horror.

Mollusk suddenly noticed a small, dark shape edging around the knot of sea otters.

"Ana!" he whispered. It was true; Anamay was attempting to dodge around the other adults and the prisoner. Whatever she was doing, she didn't want to be seen by them.

Eagle spotted her too. "Look," he nodded.

Mollusk motioned for them to stay and then followed his mate.

She was out the deserted main gates, across the sandy shore, and into the nearby forest like a shadow. Once in the woods, Mollusk could not keep up. He had a pretty good idea where she was going, but he paused by a huge rock and waited, his grayish fur blending in perfectly.

The commotion came down to the main gates. Mollusk was shocked to see Driftwood roughly dragging the Keron Mouse by her *neck*—and he had thought Anemone's method of capture had been cruel! No way could the female Keron Mouse survive that kind of treatment for long, and it seemed as if most of the watching sea otters were just as appalled as he. The crowd of Crustacean, Current, Driftwood, and a dozen or so shocked other sea otters moved off down the shoreline. Mollusk didn't dare move in case there were sentries by the gate.

After an hour or so, Anamay reappeared, followed by half a dozen dark shapes, clearly mice. They exclaimed in a strange tongue that Mollusk didn't understand, and Anamay replied in the same language—it must have been Miamuran. They were searching the area around the door. Suddenly, one of them gave a cry of surprise.

"Al'ce!" hissed another. But the one who had cried out ignored the reprimand. She lifted up a small bundle. It was the babe Keron mouse.

There was a general murmur of fury. Then the six mice glided back into the night, one of them coming within touching distance of Mollusk.

Anamay stood silently, her eyes following them. Mollusk stood from his rock and walked toward her, stopping next to her, though her face was still on the course the mice had taken, averted from his. "You brought them," he observed.

She turned to face him. Fire glinted in her eyes that he had never seen before. "Yes," she replied. "My father had an agreement with them. As his daughter, it was my duty to honor his promise."

Mollusk blinked. She had never actually acted that way before.

"Besides," Anamay continued, "I was also thinking of the child *we* will have and my duty as its mother."

There was no sight of the mother of the Keron mouse babe. Anamay dreaded finding out what had happened to her.

Gray moorland rolled endlessly until some mountains reared in the south. Two strange creatures flopped down on one of the hills. "Lookolook," the male creature commented. "Thestars theyshine. Beautiful, prettysweet."

"Yesiyes," the other, his sister agreed. "It is prettysweet, Texat, butmountains, theythebest."

"Doyou thinkshe will continue inthis stupidfoolishness, Skettle?" Texat asked his sister.

"Ihopenot," Skettle mused. "Butshe doesn'tstop fornothing. Ibet shewill."

Texat sighed. "Heralliance isshakyshaking. Shemay changersides."

In spite of her speedy speech, Skettle was inclined to think slowly and thoroughly. "Shewillnot. LadyRaven hastoo powefulthreat overher. Shedoesknow wherethe Nyincoey isstanding. Foxesdonot. Shechanges hersides. LadyRaven knowhere tokill Nyincoey. Foxes cannotdothat."

Texat inclined his head. "Truesisser. Truetrue."

7

The Price of Rules

Biddah sighed in relief.

Autumn had come in pleasantly, but it remained warm as summer in Pasadagavra. Her child would be born soon. The foxes had tried many different ways of getting into Pasadagavra, but none of them had worked as of yet.

Perhaps they would simply not conquer Pasadagavra at all. Just perhaps.

Suddenly, she noticed one of the wall guards scurrying past her. His face was grim, and so Biddah decided to follow him.

He hurried through most of the strange streets and over several creeks until he came to the place where Tribeking Fuddum, King Hokadra, Queen Demeda, Warriorqueen Wazzah, and Lady Raven sat, discussing the enemy.

"Yes?" inquired Fuddum, his eyes questioning, as the guard approached.

"The foxes want a parley," the guard explained.

Lady Raven made a funny noise, somewhere between a snort and mirthless laughter.

"They request that you meet them at sundown, out in front of the main gates. They will come unarmed and request that you do so, too."

"They do not come to parley," murmured Raven. An anger shone in the depths of her eyes and they began to darken. Demeda saw, too, and her eyes widened a little with fear.

"Who exactly?" inquired King Hokadra.

"Demmons, Epoi, Claw, Poison, Scorch, Riorat, and Snillouf."

"How many did they say we may bring?" asked Lady Raven.

"Who's *we*?" Hokadra muttered.

"Seven, at the most," answered the guard.

"Clever of them," commented Wazzah bitterly.

"Seven of us, seven of them," mused Fuddum.

"Four of which are corsairs," added Lady Raven. "This sounds bad."

"Well, do we parley, or not?" wondered Hokadra.

"I'd say not," replied Fuddum instantly. "Claw himself is untrustworthy enough, but with corsairs, well, no point in taking unnecessary risks."

"I'm rather inclined to agree with Fuddum," murmured Hokadra. "What do you think, Raven?"

Lady Raven bit her lip calculatingly. Then she voiced her opinion.

"I disagree."

"What, you trust Demmons?" exclaimed Fuddum.

"No," replied Lady Raven slowly. "But I think we should accept."

"Why?"

"Well," Lady Raven murmured, "to find out what they will say. Perhaps the foxes simply wish to go around Pasadagavra. They want our word that we will not attack them from Pasadagavra on their way. In that case, we could use that to our advantage, as long as that is the only promise. There may be many of them, but they'll have to go further north—way further north—if they want to control the earth. Then, a few days marching will bring them to Oria. We can be waiting. We have all the upper paws we could want: knowledge of the land, adaptation to the land, and superior skills of weapons. An ambush would not be difficult to set up. So, I would suggest we could use that."

"Good theory," Hokadra pointed out, "but if they get past you, there's nothing between them and the rest of the earth."

Demeda shuddered; Raven smiled. "That is where you are wrong, Hokadra. There are others—others of a terrifying, barbaric nature—who live on the north seas. They are not really nations; most of them are loners. But if the foxes ran into them, there would, for one thing, be cold that they have never felt—the land up there is made half of ice—and then barbarians of worse nature than corsairs to greet them."

"And supposing, at the parley, they demand we surrender Pasadagavra?"

Lady Raven frowned thoughtfully. "Well, should we pretend to surrender? Have all those who really aren't warriors come out dressed and disguised as warriors?" Her voice became more urgent. "Then, have the real warriors hiding in Pasadagavra … every place where we can, and when the foxes fully arrive, slam the gates shut, and snipe at them … They don't know any back way out of Pasadagavra, do they?"

Demeda gazed at her friend incredulously. "And you say you've never fought wars in a fortress?"

"Just a couple of canyons." Lady Raven shrugged.

"Well, I'm not sure about letting them into Pasadagavra. We've been holding them off very well so far, and that sounds like a huge gamble to me. But as to the parley ...? Right," decided Fuddum. "I say let's do it. Let's see what they have to say."

"Put it like that, and I'm with you," decided Hokadra. "But," he added, "would it be possible to have a hidden guard for the parley? Just in case Demmons decides to play dirty?"

"Leave it to me," promised Lady Raven. "I can position some archers in the woods nearby."

"But I do not think it wise to attack unless you have evidence that they are up to something," Wazzah pointed out warily.

"Makes sense," grinned Lady Raven. Wazzah looked puzzled.

Demeda, however, plainly was not.

"Raven, if you attack them before they attack us, it'll be obvious you're there, and it will be a violation of the rules of parley. We do *not* violate the rules of parley," Demeda warned.

Raven sighed. "Yes, I know. But we already know they're up to something. You know I wouldn't, anyway."

"Well," said Wazzah slowly, "perhaps we should bring only six, then. Make it seem as if we believe them more."

"No, because they'll take it as a sign of weakness," explained Demeda. "It's better to go with seven."

"Well, I suppose we should all go ... With the exception of Lady Raven," Hokadra mused. "That means three more ... Jaccah may as well come ... and Darag, I suppose ... and Sharmmuh?" he suggested.

"Not me, Sharmmuh, or Darag," corrected Fuddum. "We're too old, and we look it."

"Perhaps ..." Wazzah hesitated, looking apprehensive.

"Go on," said Lady Raven.

"Perhaps Deggum?"

Fuddum narrowed his eyes thoughtfully. Then he said, "That's an idea. But why?"

Wazzah's eyes grew cold. "It would shock them."

"Why?"

Wazzah's glinting eyes were dangerous. "Long story."

Fuddum eyed her consideringly, but did not inquire further.

"Perhaps Ornit?" suggested Lady Raven. "They would respect the Tribeking of the Coast Tribe."

"Perhaps Cinder to represent the Ranger Mice?" suggested Hokadra.

Raven threw him a look that was almost scathing. "No," she replied firmly.

"If only Arpaha were here," whispered Biddah to herself.

"Perhaps Mokimshim?" suggested the guard.

"That would make sense. May as well." Demeda sounded fearful of sending her eldest son as well as her husband along with the parley, but she shrugged as if it was of little concern.

"And I suppose Cedar or Rowan would represent the Ranger Mice in the ... mm ... whatever the word is," added Lady Raven.

Biddah decided she had learned all she needed to know. Silently, she slid away to the main part of Pasadagavra.

Before even an hour had passed, it seemed as if every creature in Pasadagavra had heard of the parley, and none felt very good about it.

Biddah saw Cinder, Snowgoose, Cedar, and Rowan—four of the elder Rangers—track Lady Raven down and attack her with questions.

"Raven, you don't seriously think that this isn't some sort of ambush you're getting into?"

"I know, this isn't safe, there's some trick somewhere. But I plan to make sure that there is no real danger."

"How? What are you going to do?"

"I'm going to use the hidden guard tactic."

"But what's that going to do against a warhawk?"

"I don't know, just maybe get whomever out there back in safely."

"No, but what of—"

"I know, but this may be the opportunity we've been waiting for."

"Trickery isn't going to destroy these creatures!"

"Maybe, maybe not, but it may weaken them," commented Raven. "There is very little I can do now, but I plan to make sure it's all safe. Demeda and Hokadra don't know, but I plan to have every single creature there with a hidden guard."

"And you think that will work?"

Raven sighed. "If you can suggest something better, I'm all ears."

Raven waited, but no better suggestion was made.

The five Rangers looked at one another before dispersing.

They were not the only sign of tension Biddah saw. She heard Jaccah arguing with her father about it, warning him what she had heard.

"Sage knows these creatures!" exclaimed Jaccah. "Sage is a fox. She used to be one of their Oracles; she knows how treacherous they can be. I spoke with her just now, and she's against this parley." But King Fuddum soothed her, assuring her they were taking precautions.

And so the discussions went throughout Pasadagavra.

Lady Raven detailed her Rangers to guard the walls. Every one of them wore merely their tunics—except for thirty of them, including Lady Raven.

They had put on their green, stiff cloaks, and each was armed to the teeth: a throwing spear, a shortspear, a bow and quiver filled with arrows feathered with gull feathers allowing for swifter flight, a dagger, a rapier, and two hunting knives apiece. Lady Raven selected twenty of them to guard the whole meeting. She decided on strategic locations for groups of four or five, and they slipped out of one of the many secret tunnels leading from Pasadagavra. The other ten were to surround the meeting at short range, with rapiers drawn. How they planned to stay hidden was a mystery to Biddah, but it seemed that they were the hidden guard.

Various squirrels were also ordered to help guard the walls, including Biddah. She hated it, but she was not about to protest. She decided that she would rather see the parley firsthand than hear it from others.

At that moment, Claw was making a few, final detailed decisions for the foxes' contingent.

"You four, remember, your immediate target is King Hokadra, but if—and only if— the original plan fails, attack both Hokadra and Demeda."

"They'll definitely be coming out then?"

Claw glared at the archer who asked the question. "Of course, dimwit. Whom else would they send out?"

"Tha's no' what 'e meant," sniggered Fotirra.

"Supposing they also bring out Zuryzel?"

"Then kill her with her father or mother!" Claw snarled. "Do you never shut up? Now, you nine, you'll be hidden behind that rise, so don't move until you get the signal. Then rush the others."

"Thou art fergettin' somethin'."

Claw whirled angrily around on Jironi. "What?"

"Thou wilt need a stern guard," the ferret said, ignoring the fox's anger. "Thou dinnae want an attack comin' at thee from the stern, do ye?"

Claw did not realize that Jironi meant "stern" as in the back of a ship, but he understood Jironi was warning against a rear attack. "So what do you suggest?" he demanded.

"I dinnae know. Thou'rt the one who's s'pposedly in command o' shore strategy. Thou hast t' decide."

Claw glared at her for a moment before bellowing orders for archers to cover the back of the army.

"Idiot," muttered Fotirra, coming with Redseg to stand beside Jironi.

"You noticed?" Redseg inquired coolly. "Huh, now the whole earth'll know that archers are to guard the stern, hidden, of course. How subtle."

Fotirra shook her head in despair. "Och, a great, great, fule 'e is, huh. Whaht a ditherbrain. Ah wuhnder if'n 'e'd ken crektion."

"Er ..."

"Correction," translated Fotirra.

Claw pretended not to have heard them. But he definitely understood them.

Biddah felt sick to her stomach. The seven who had been chosen to meet the foxes in the parley were grouped about the postern gate. They were, indeed, unarmed. Or rather, all but Rowan were definitely unarmed. Biddah could not decide if he was hiding a knife or not.

Biddah remembered the fight in the woods where her home had once been. She had been scared stiff as a board, then. Now, fear left her limp as a noodle. Her tail drooped, and her pelt shook. She wished dearly that these terrible foxes were gone forever.

The sun declined from above the hills. The seven foxes began to approach the meeting spot.

"Let's go," breathed Hokadra. He seemed unafraid, but he took a deep, shaky breath and jerked the postern open.

Demeda looked fearless. Her face twisted briefly with hatred as she gazed at Demmons, and she held her head high. The look on Wazzah's face was indecipherable, while Jaccah had a bold face on, though her paws were shaking. Rowan looked impassive and fearless; indeed, Biddah thought he looked as though he was eagerly anticipating the meeting. Why that was, Biddah could not guess. Mokimshim was taking several deep breaths, attempting to calm himself. Biddah did not blame him.

As the small party slipped wordlessly through the postern, the wind picked up. Biddah saw Wazzah's tail being blown sideways, and Jaccah's tunic rippled. Rowan seemed to take the wind most seriously, however. His head shot up, and Biddah guessed that he was scanning the sky for clouds.

If Biddah looked directly down, she could see a small mound of grass that looked like four or five Rangers hidden, watching closely, and Biddah thought she could see the outline of their bows. But she was not sure.

The wind seemed to blow the words away from Pasadagavra, but Biddah listened with all her might. All she heard were a few snippets of their discussion, which was growing heated.

The wind continued to pick up until Biddah wondered if the arrows of the Ranger Mice would be useless.

Then, before Biddah's very eyes, a mass of blackness, dark as night, appeared and was gone. A horrible screech of fury followed and then a terrible thud.

Biddah never quite remembered what happened after that thud. She only remembered what had come before: the warhawk Chiraage had swooped in and attempted to snatch up Queen Demeda, but Lady Raven had seen her coming and, at the last minute, pulled her old friend aside. But one of Chiraage's stiff pinion feathers had caught under the bent Ranger's chest, flinging her backward to land hard against the wall.

Biddah had no recollection of how the parley party and the other Rangers got inside. She knew that Cinder had fired a furious arrow off at Demmons before dashing inside, but it had instead landed in the throat of Snillouf due to the wind. She knew that Lady Raven was unconscious but not with any visible wounds. She saw a few crossbow bolts hitting the earth, but not who fired them.

Biddah desperately sought out Karrum. Not far away, she saw him, struggling toward her. His eyes were huge with disbelief, and his tail bristling and waving.

"I don't believe it," he panted hoarsely. "Did you see that bird? And it was only one of her *feathers* that hurt Raven … Oh, Biddah."

Biddah was speechless with shock as she hugged her mate to her.

"I don't believe this!"

The archers grouped around the back of the army could not see the nearly six hundred bright eyes watching the parley and its disastrous end.

The otter maiden who had witnessed Knife summoning Demmons spoke again.

"Dirty liars! If I were down there, I'd give them such a thrashing with my spear that they'd wish they'd never left the high seas!"

"That was Lady Raven we're talking about, though," pointed out the other female otter hopefully. "She's not a weakling."

"Nor is that bird," pointed out the deep male voice. "And Lady Raven isn't young."

Doomspear turned away from the scene of chaos at Pasadagavra to his companions. "She's older than she was when she was on that slave ship. She can't take beatings and attacks and wounds as well anymore."

Streamcourse, her fur nearly all gray, wrapped her paws around herself. "Do you think Lady Raven didn't survive?"

"It makes precious little difference right now," Streamcourse, the second female, hissed vengefully. "Raven can't be in any shape to command, whether or not she survived."

Moonpath's viciously scarred face was hidden by silken veils. These fluttered as she hissed savagelike. "Demmons may be a corsair, but I still intend to kill him for this."

"You're a powerful warrior, Moonpath," Doomspear murmured. "But you're no match for a corsair. The spear," he said by way of explanation. The spear was the customary weapon for a river otter chief.

He took a deep breath. "Right, we've got to find Crow. I don't know if Lady Raven survived, but chances aren't available to take. You two, go look for her. Keep your eyes open for sea otters, Shorefish, anything. But *go*."

"And leave you here?" demanded Streamcourse in disbelief. "You've only got a hundred … I'll stay. That's a great horde you're facing. Or at least let my warriors stay; I'll be fine by myself."

"*No*. You're facing a concealed danger. Go *fast*. No, don't argue; just do it!"

"But what about you?"

Streamcourse had desperately voiced the question. "Don't forget when I let Sky do this …"

"Well, Nighthawk is dead. The worst threat on this is that Crow Blue Arrows won't be able to get up here in time. Now *go*! Both of you. *Fast*! *Go*!"

Two hundred creatures, all with a last look at their remaining friends turned and ran into the woods in search of Crow Blue Arrows, daughter of Lady of Raven.

Not half an hour later, Zuryzel stood just outside a makeshift camp where the Daya River merged with the Eupharra River. About her sat the crews of over ten large corsair vessels. Uku had come with them, though she was weaponless.

"I'd be useless in a battle. I'm not that great with weapons—Hoeylahk maidens aren't permitted to be warriors," she had said, blustering. "I'm only coming as a healer, and for any news."

"Zuryzel?"

Shartalla, one of the captains Ailur had recruited, trotted up noiselessly and plopped down next to Zuryzel. A pine marten, she was the most unusual corsair Zuryzel had ever encountered. Her pelt was orange as the setting sun, and her eyes as black as the sky that followed, even with a twinkle in them, as if it was starlight. Her voice was a little husky, and her accent peculiar.

"We made good time," Shartalla commented. "Particularly against the current. How much longer, d'yeh say, to Pasadagavra?" she asked, carefully sounding out the last word.

"Oh about ten days more, maybe eleven," Zuryzel replied.

"Tha' sounds right," agreed Shartalla. "What's the course, all river?"

"Not quite," explained Zuryzel. "There are two days of trekking around a mountain."

Shartalla furrowed her brow. "Two days round the mountain and then another river, yeh mean?

"Yes," replied Zuryzel.

Shartalla shrugged. "The boats are light, at least. They can make a shelter an' will be no trouble t' carry. By the way, seems Arasam 'as the report ready."

Zuryzel turned as the captain Arasam marched up from behind her.

"Nothin' to report," he said carelessly, touching his paw to his ear tip.

When Zuryzel had first seen him, she had been terrified of him, though she had, as Ailur had warned, not let it show. He was clad in green, purple, silver, and orange silk trousers and vest. He had a bright blue eye patch wrapped about his head on a braided coral-colored thong. He wore no shoes of any type, though he carried four or five sabers at a time.

"Aye," added one of the scouts he had chosen, a ferret named Skorlaid. "The on'y livin' thing out there is a pair o' black birds, flyin' south. Large 'uns, I tell yeh."

"Large black birds?" repeated Zuryzel blankly. "Cormorants?"

"Nah," replied another of the scouts, a female ferret named Tsanna. "They had too short o' necks. They were prob'ly some sort o' land bird."

"Did they have a tail shaped like a fan?" Zuryzel asked.

"I don' think so," Arasam frowned.

"Yeah it did," supplied Tsanna scornfully.

"Anyway, yeh'd best git somethin' t'eat," finished Arasam. "It'll all be gone, otherwise. Too many fatty-ferrets about." He looked almost directly at Tsanna.

"If that is what 'e rilly thinks," snarled Shartalla to herself, "then 'e 'as lost *both* 'is eyes."

Zuryzel, eying the retreating form of slender Tsanna, could believe it.

8 The Tree of Ice

Warriorqueen Wazzah stepped carefully out the back door of the Last Storehouse, followed by Queen Demeda. The Warriorqueen looked back nervously, her fur fluffed up against the wind. "Are you sure about this?"

"It's what Rainbow and Aspen said," Demeda replied without a worry.

"That's not very recommending," Wazzah protested.

"You sound like Zinnta," Demeda retorted with a twitch of her ears.

"No, I don't!"

"Exactly like." Demeda's amused tone echoed in the mountains. "Craic?" she called. Her words echoed a dozen times.

"I'm right here!" called the raven from atop the dome of Pasadagavra. He took flight and landed next to Queen Demeda. "You're late again."

"Ravens, as you well know," Demeda scolded, "are abominable time keepers."

"Doesn't matter, does it?" Craic asked irritably. His black eyes narrowed nervously. "I heard something from Norya. About a parley or something. Tell me she couldn't see well!"

"She was correct," Demeda replied grimly.

"Is Raven still alive?" Craic asked fearfully.

"Barely," Demeda's tone was sad. "She was flung rather far and hard."

Craic glanced at Wazzah. "I also hoped it was a false rumor that the Sling Tribe was driven from Ezdrid."

"Not so, my friend," Wazzah replied sadly. "But Kappan and Rhonnah and the others are still there, I think."

"I hope they can restore Ezdrid," Craic murmured. "The great cities never once touched by evil are lessening in number. Alkzor fell in the great plague. Kardas was lost in the Dark Ages. Lunep, too, has fallen. Tariakadi on the east coast is near the point of starvation herself. Dombre, too, fell in the Dark Ages and again now. Brikthi in the south was destroyed long ago. The Island City is under siege by corsairs, though the rougher seas have made that harder on the besiegers. Iannia is in no immediate danger but has no warriors to defend it. Miamur faces corruption from within. And now, Ezdrid has fallen. That leaves Denerna, Graystone—which is no longer great—Nyincoey, and Corenthia in the east left still to stand."

"I don't like it either," Demeda agreed, "but it could be said that Zurez still stands."

"Zurez," Craic scoffed. "Held by sea otters."

"Which are not quite what one would describe as evil," Demeda commented mildly. "Crustacean, I detest, and Current, and their cronies. But is the average sea otter truly evil? What of Palm, who is nothing but a pawn? And Foam, his second-in-command? And Northstar?"

"Don't preach to me about Northstar," Craic advised the queen, "when I know who she is, too."

"True," Wazzah agreed. "And while things like the sea otters inhabit Zurez and are no threat to the foxes, there is no immediate danger. It has fallen, certainly, but not necessarily into evil paws."

"Maybe you haven't heard that the sea otters have allied themselves to the foxes?" Craic snapped.

"Current and Crustacean have," Demeda corrected. "An alliance requires more than signatures of the leaders, and a treaty will be honored only for as long as all is agreeable. A time will come when it will be less agreeable to the sea otters to submit to or play along with their leaders." Her voice was full of conviction. "In the meantime, Raven says to tell Zinnta to be careful because Knife almost found out about Nyincoey *again*. And *I* say to tell Northstar to keep an eye out for Crow."

"I thought Torona was doing that," Wazzah objected.

"I know," Demeda replied dryly. "Tell Northstar anyway, in case Torona didn't make it."

Craic nodded and took off, going south. Demeda made an irritated noise. "I didn't tell him to go there *first*!"

"The issue with Zinnta is not so important," Wazzah shrugged.

"Oh, no?" Demeda challenged. "It could reveal the location of one of the still-standing great cities that Craic just mentioned—a city whose only defense is secrecy."

"And numbers," Wazzah soothed.

"That won't be much against corsairs," Demeda murmured worriedly.

"Zinnta will be fine," Wazzah shrugged.

"That's a lot of guesswork," Demeda warned. She sighed helplessly. "We're fighting this war assuming everything that should have been done has been done. I don't know if Ailur was successful, and still I sent my *daughter* out on the assumption that she was. Zinnta may actually *not* be able to hold out. We just have to keep doing what we have to do and leave the tasks of others to others." Demeda sighed. "But as the head of the Wraith Mice intelligence, I don't like not knowing things that important."

They turned to head back into Pasadagavra. Wazzah stopped right at the entrance to glance toward her former home. "Demeda!" she gasped. "Look!"

Demeda turned and gasped. Just across from them was a mountain with an enormous glacier. The wind had whittled away at snow and ice, imprinting the image of a tree growing on the glacier. The sunlight shining on it had made it hard to see, but in the cloudy darkness of the moment, the glare was gone, and the tree's details finely etched out.

"I guess time has to be dark sometimes for us to see something of incredible beauty," Wazzah commented.

The northern moors, home to the Moor Tribe of squirrels, lay just north of the mountains surrounding Pasadagavra. Not many had dared to brave the treacherous mountains; thus, not many knew about the Moor squirrels.

The two chipmunks, not actually part of the Moor Tribe but who sometimes lived in the territory, sat side by side on a small rise in the middle of the moors.

"Whatdo youthink Skettle?" Texat, asked.

His sister shrugged. "Whoknow, Texat? Zinntais dangeroussure, butnotstupid. Shewoulddo nothingto endanger Nyincoey."

"Whyshouldshe stayloyal to LadyRaven?" Texat asked doubtfully. "Shedoesnot needthe aid oftheRangers. Tooskilled isshe. Thatgift—bettershe didnot possessit."

"Butshedoes," Skettle replied firmly. "Strong sheis andwise."

"Just ambitious."

Both chipmunks spun around to see Craic the Raven perched on the rise behind them. "HelloCraic," Skettle chattered politely.

"Lady Raven has been severely wounded," Craic told them without preamble. "Queen Demeda is not sure how long she will survive." Both chipmunks gasped as Craic continued. "I spoke to Jironi, and she advised me that Claw, who is currently in command of the Darkwoods army, seems to have found a way to invade Pasadagavra, perhaps by a tunnel. She asked me to alert both you and Fern the Archer. You may soon be needed."

Skettle nodded. "Howmuch does Demedaknow?"

Craic spread his wings helplessly. "I could not contact her after I spoke to Jironi. Perhaps Norya can warn Demeda, but I do not know." He gave them both a hard look. "Keep Zinnta on a leash," he advised them.

"Weknow," Skettle replied. "Whendoes wemove? Whereis Crow?"

Craic shrugged again. "I don't know. We wait for Queen Demeda or Ailur to tell us what to do next, and as for Crow, she could be anywhere, as far as I know. Demeda may know otherwise, but like I said, I could not reach her."

9 What Do We Do?

Danaray Mudriver gazed impatiently at the parchment map in front of her.

She was trying, with all her might, to decide what to do, though her options were limited. Her otter tribe had been more or less reunited, and she now had definite news of the siege of Pasadagavra. Yet she was faced with several difficult choices. Should she slip around behind the foxes, attack them in the field about Pasadagavra? Should she search for Crow even though she had no idea where the archer was? Should she go to Miamur, plead for help, stress the problem that far outweighed Miamur's? Should she surround the foxes' fortress of Darkwoods, or even take it, whilst the main action was Pasadagavra?

Almost immediately, she dismissed the fourth choice as a viable option. There was absolutely no way she could hold the fortress, it not really being a fortress or capable of withstanding a siege. And as for the first choice—attack the foxes around Pasadagavra— well, if her tribe were skilled at woodland fighting and sniping, at making a small number look like a lot more, that might be possible, but her tribe had next to no woodland skills, so making their small number seem like more would be practically impossible. Besides, her tribe was small and had no archers, fighting mostly with javelins and throwing knives, none of which were easy to replace. That left her other two options: search for Crow, or try to get help from Miamur. Neither seemed very inviting.

The Miamurans were under almost constant threat of attack by the rogue river otters that lived on the plain. They needed to defend their own territory; Danaray had no qualms about *that*. So asking them for help for Pasadagavra didn't seem like a good idea.

Which meant that searching for Crow would be most logical. Yet, even *that* was difficult. Crow could be anywhere south of the foxes' castle, as there were others living that far south beside those at Graystone. If Crow had not caught up with them—which seemed unlikely—those foxes would probably be by Kwang-ha`el, or even into the sea otters' territories.

Danaray gazed through tired eyes at the map. She had been working on the dratted question for four hours now and seemed no nearer to the answer. Admittedly, going for Crow might be the wisest … yet it would be so difficult. Her warriors could make use of the rivers—that would not be hard—but it would still be difficult to find Crow. That included at least another two weeks trekking west to find Graystone, anyway.

Against all logic, she found herself rather inclined to go for Miamur.

Stretching wearily, she knew all that had to be done was to announce it, but she felt strangely reluctant.

But, she reminded herself, *I'll have to sooner or later. May as well get it over with.*

Danaray yawned wearily with fatigue and straightened up. She could imagine the surprise of her warriors—they probably were expecting to go after Crow. But Danaray had no clue whatsoever where she was …

Danaray pushed the tent flap back and called Kermunda, her healer, and two of her elder warriors to her tent. They stood up and obeyed instantly. Danaray still found this rather odd. It had not been that long since she had become the leader following the death of her father.

"Right," she said in a firm voice. "There's not a whole lot we can do about Pasadagavra by ourselves, so the best thing to do is to get some help. We'll head to Miamur, and ask them for help."

"But why not find Crow?"

Kermunda posed the question exactly as Danaray finished.

"Because, unless some news has come in I haven't heard, I have no idea where Crow is. Miamur may be preoccupied, but they're the best chance. Crow could be cycles' march away."

"True," agreed one of her warriors. "And Miamur is only a few days' march away."

There was silence for a moment. Then Danaray ordered them, "Pass the word around, and when the patrol gets back, send them straight here."

The three of them nodded and stood up to leave; yet Kermunda hung back.

"Dana," he whispered softly, once the others had departed, "I don't think Miamur will be much help."

"I know," sighed Danaray, rubbing her eyes wearily.

She felt, rather than heard or saw, Kermunda coming toward her. She felt his warm eyes shine with all the concern he'd ever felt for her. How loyal he had been, always obeying her without question.'

The noise of the patrol returning roused Danaray. She shook herself and commented dryly, "Perhaps they'll have something important for a change."

Dark shapes, over four hundred of them, practically slid through the early autumn undergrowth, dodging branches. In the lead, there were four creatures of different sizes. On the farthest right was a Keron warrior mouse, Coll'n. Beside him was a well-recognized figure: Rain, leader of Kyang-ha'el river otters. Beside Rain was a blood-red vixen with ice-blue eyes, dressed in a green silk tunic, eighteen gold and brass hoops in each ear. The fourth figure, the one on the leftmost side, was inscrutable. Male or female, impossible to tell, or even what type of beast it was, due to a green-and-brown cloak with a voluminous hood that hid its face completely. Yet it carried a huge bow—bigger than any Mollusk had ever seen …

Or was it? Mollusk watched from a distance the figures drawing nearer, crouched in his ambush point. Current had sighted this band coming and had prepared an ambush, and Mollusk got landed with it. All around him, nearly three hundred sea otter fighters of both genders sat hidden and waiting for the signal to attack.

Now as Mollusk gazed hard at the bow, he thought he had seen it before. Well, not exactly that. It was perhaps less aged than the one he had seen in the paws of Lord Jet of the Rangers. But still, it was similar. And the figure was definitely wearing arrows over its shoulder, as Lord Jet had. Though, all these arrows were jay-feathered. Despite the hood hiding the figure's face, dark, sparkling eyes shone through and examined the whole scene in front of it.

Without warning, the hooded figure called, "Halt!" and instantly, all of them obeyed. The figure gazed intently about itself for a while before calling out in a firm voice, "You can quit hiding, sea otters. I can see you. What is your business stopping us? "

Current stood up boldly, and with him, the other sea otters rose as well.

The vixen spoke up rather impudently. "Well, good day t' yeh. Wot's yer trouble? We're in a kinda hurry."

Coll'n the Keron mouse stared at the vixen's boldness and carelessness in disbelief.

Current seemed equally amazed that anyone facing over three hundred could be so carefree, but he glared at her. "You are trespassing on my lands."

"Well ain't that nice t' know? Now we know f'sure where we landed; th' compass was gettin' useless. Could y' step t' the side so's we kin pass 'n' get out o' yer lands?"

Current raised his javelin coldly. "You will take another route!"

The vixen frowned at him, but the cloaked figure spoke up.

"We would, but I am afraid that this is the quickest route to our destination, and it is essential that we reach it soon."

Mollusk watched the other side of the figure carefully. Now he looked closely ... Yes, indeed, there *was* a fifth there, with the same cloak and a bow the same size as the hooded figure. The green cloaks were for disguise! But they were a darker shade of green than the deciduous green of the trees. Wherever these creatures came from, it was not a deciduous forest.

He was so intent on the figure that he missed Current's reply.

"We will be gone before sunhigh," protested Coll'n, looking almost desperate.

Driftwood thrust his way forward. "You will not enter our la—"

A harsh cawing interrupted the fourth figure. "Insolent scum!" it cawed, and everyone looked up, startled, to see a female crow perched on a high branch of an oak. "You dare hinder Marsa—"

"Peace, Norya!" called the first cloaked figure sternly.

It turned back to the two challenging sea otters, its voice suddenly threatening. "You have my solemn word that you will not find me on your lands again," it said, with a hint of a snarl, "And we will be gone ere the sun is midhigh. But we *will* pass, and you will *not* stop us."

"Oh no?" sneered Driftwood. He raised his javelin.

Mollusk did not have time to blink. He did not have time to inhale. Swifter than thought, the figure pulled the bow off its shoulder, notched an arrow to the string, and pointed it straight at Driftwood's eye. At her motion, there was a ripple in the air, and Mollusk now saw roughly forty others, each with drawn bows and notched arrows, all of them garbed exactly as the first hooded figure. Mollusk stared hard at the two figures he could look half in the face, wishing that they would lower their hoods. There was something familiar about both of them, and now that he thought hard about it, there was something vaguely familiar about all of them, as though he had seen them before, long, long ago. Yet the figures foremost … the second one he knew he had seen before, but the first … he had kind of seen. *Kind of seen*? That made no sense. He had seen … its … shadow?

The word struck Mollusk when he had not been thinking, yet it seemed so true.

Driftwood lowered his spear, and the arrow pointed back at the ground. Driftwood glared at it.

"Where are you headed then?" demanded Current.

"That is none of your—" began the river otter Rain, but the shrouded figure cut him off.

"North."

Mollusk sighed with relief. Current hated Rain in particular, and it seemed that Rain hated him equally. Apparently, though, the hooded figure would rather get through this without a fight. *Good luck with that*, thought Mollusk.

Driftwood raised his javelin again at the hooded leader. "You will stop here. Your troop may go onward, but you will not."

TWANG!!!!

Again, swifter than thought, the figure had risen the bow, but this time, it fired. The aim was deadly—it had gone straight through Driftwood's stomach to the paw of one standing behind.

Driftwood croaked and doubled over before lying painfully on the ground, panting and groaning, until his life was extinguished. His body simply lay there, limp and harmless, whilst the sea otter who had been struck with the arrow on his paw began panting, gasping, before collapsing and moaning something about him being on fire.

As Mollusk stared in horror, another arrow seemed to materialize out of that otter's neck, and then his painful cries finished. Mollusk turned his eyes to the archer. It had all happened so fast none of the sea otters had reacted yet.

The figure's hood had fallen back, and Mollusk could see black fur and bright eyes of a dark blue sheen. Mollusk guessed it was a female. He would not apply the word maiden, however, to such a fearsome creature

Something about either the arrow or the figure unnerved Current. His eyes glazed over with fear for a moment before he raised his javelin.

Norya the crow swooped from her branch and lifted the javelin from the sea otter's paw. Wheeling high above the crowd, she snapped it in two.

Current was now weaponless, with his allies creeping cautiously backward, facing what was obviously an experienced and cunning warlady, well armed at that, with arrows that were obviously poisoned.

Current snarled savagely at the warlady archer as Norya alighted on her shoulder. "You will pass today. But if you are ever seen again …"

The whole army of sea otters turned and disappeared.

Except Mollusk. He stayed hidden. He wanted to find out more of this warlady. He wanted to know who she was.

The army passed by him but did not see him. He realized that the army was actually much larger than he had thought. Careful as could be, Mollusk followed, trying with difficulty to keep up with the lead figure.

"Kireeka," whispered the vixen, "doesn't Marsa mean—"

"Quiet, Torona," ordered the warlady. "Storm! Sorry we're late, we had a run-in."

Five more shapes seemed to materialize from the scanty underbrush. One of them held a raven on its shoulder. Another who seemed to be the leader approached the warlady.

"So did we, Crow—Oh, you found Norya."

"Norya found *us*," shrugged Crow, the warlady. "She, er, had some interesting news. Speaking of which …"

Her voice grew deadly again. She turned to the crow perched on her shoulder. "Norya," she snapped, "and Craic, on that log," she ordered, indicating a fallen tree.

Both birds left shoulders and landed where directed. Crow turned to her followers.

"Salal, Owl, Plantain, Storm, you should hear this too. Everyone else, try to set up a camp and get some food, but don't go too far, and don't light any fire."

As the warriors dispersed, Mollusk crouched low in some bracken, not interested in being found. Keenly, he listened to Crow and the crows. *That's kind of funny*, he thought to himself, side-tracked. *She's not a crow; she looks like a mouse, maybe. But she's named Crow, and she's talking to crows, but …* He snapped his attention back to the conversation

"Now," Crow said sternly, rounding on the birds, "I want the solid truth to my questions. *No* fibbing."

Craic cawed "Of course not," and Norya dipped her head.

"All right, first, what are you doing here? Shouldn't you be up north?"

"Quaar brought us here," explained Craic in a croaky voice. "She snuck away."

"Ice-brain!" exclaimed one of the listeners.

Crow motioned her to silence.

"Now," her voice dropped low, almost to a growl. She was holding one of her arrows, and her paw was shaking as she pointed it firmly at the ground. Craic eyed it fearfully, but Norya, though clearly afraid, did not flinch but met Crow squarely in the eye.

"What did you almost say back there, by the sea otters?"

"You know what I almost said," replied the crow, meeting the eyes under the hood.

"What does—"

"Quiet, Storm!" Crow snapped at the figure next to her, in the same motion sweeping her hood off her head. Following her example, the other five swept off their hoods, all of them proving to be mice.

Mollusk drew in his breath.!

"Tell me," she warned, her blue eyes fearful and her paw holding the arrow shaking visibly.

Craic and Norya met her eyes steadily. Craic opened his beak and closed it several times, but no sound came out. Norya finally opened her beak and burst out, "I am so sorry, Crow. But your mother, Lady Raven, is dead!"

Crow let the arrow fall, and her paw fell limply to her side as she stared at Norya. Storm's gaze shifted from Norya to Crow, disbelief and concern mingling in his eyes. One dark brown female opened her mouth but no sound came out. The white male exclaimed "*What?!*" and a light golden, older male asked in disbelief, "*How?*"

"Chiraage," cawed Craic angrily. "Lady Raven saved Queen Demeda from being snatched by Chiraage, but the warhawk's powerful wings threw Lady Raven against a wall, very hard."

The grief and pain in Crow's eyes were joined by hatred. Storm said coldy, "*Indeed,*" before casting a worried glance at Crow. The others stiffened, and the dark brown maiden snarled.

"We need to get to Pasadagavra as quickly as we can," muttered Storm.

"Norya, Craic," snapped Crow suddenly, "go and find Zinnta. She'll want to help. Then go north and bring Xar, Sone, Nrin, Quaw, and Kir down to Pasadagavra. Then, *find Quaar!*"

Both birds nodded. They cawed harshly and flapped into the sky.

Mollusk had heard enough. He cautiously crept away from the group and found a passage where he could creep away unnoticed. He was stunned. Lady Raven was dead! And the warlady who killed Driftwood was her daughter!

As the sun climbed higher, he attempted to melt back into the daily bustle at Zurez, which proved to be extremely easy.

"Oh!" exclaimed Anamay as he opened the door of their room. She appeared to have been reading. She leaped up and threw her paws about Mollusk. "I was so worried!"

"Anamay," murmured Mollusk. "I … guess who the ambush managed to get rid of?"

"Who?" asked Anamay?

"Driftwood," replied Mollusk fervently.

"Wonderful," grinned Anamay, releasing him.

Mollusk closed the door and collapsed on the couch. After a few moments, Anamay said sternly, "What took you so long to get back? The rest of the patrol was back ages ago … I heard them coming in through the corridor …"

"Well, I decided to do a bit of scouting, to tell the truth," shrugged Mollusk. And, starting from where Crow had met Storm, he told the whole story.

When Mollusk got to the part of Crow taking off her hood and he described her face, Anamay put her head in her paws and groaned.

"What?"

"Crow Blue Arrows, the daughter of Lady Raven, Lady of the Rangers! I was supposed to find her and tell her that Streamcourse had gone after the band of foxes, remember?"

Mollusk did remember. Reaching out he touched Anamay's cheek.

"Anyway," he pressed on.

He told her of Craic and Norya, and their news.

Anamay gasped, "Lady Raven *dead? Dead?* Lady Raven … oh no …"

There was a sudden pounding of frantic knocking on the door. Anamay slid back into the shadows while Mollusk stood up and answered.

It was Anemone, but it took Mollusk several moments to recognize her. Her face was tearstained, and blind panic showed in her eyes.

"Anemone?" exclaimed Anamay, rising. "Here, come in …"

Anemone took a few steps into the room, and Anamay led her to the couch.

"Look, I-I-I need … I mean … Look, Northstar and her tribe vanished. Just vanished! And, Current, well you can guess, he thought it was a trick of some sort … Well, there's only one adult left that had ever belonged to Northstar's tribe, and that's me. So he's tagged me as a traitor!"

"What? Why?"

"Because I used to belong to her tribe! And if I can't defend myself …" Her voice trailed off. "But," she added, shaking herself, "until I'm cleared, I … could you look after Eagle and Saline?"

"Of course," replied Anamay instantly.

Anemone's blind panic subsided somewhat, and she thanked them in relief. "They're on the dune. Should I get them?" Anamay nodded, and Anemone continued. "May I suggest that you stay well away from the main crowd? It just isn't safe anymore."

Mollusk nodded. Anemone hurried out the door and did not return.

Not too long later, Mollusk heard a tapping noise. He stood up and, in one motion, swept across the small room and opened the door. Eagle and Saline stood there, Saline looking terrified, but determinedly not weeping. Eagle looked just as frightened.

Without a word, Mollusk beckoned them inside and shut the door.

"Come here," Anamay called.

Saline went straight to her like a sparrow to its nest. Eagle stood stock still for a moment before holding out his paw.

"Mother said to warn you to be careful around the chiefs," he said weakly.

"She told us as much, too. Don't worry; she will be fine," Mollusk promised.

Certainly none of the sea otters would want to see Anemone charged as a traitor—she wasn't!—but Crustacean despised her, and he had all authority to have her exiled, or killed.

That night, Anamay's dreams were troubled. She continually dreamed of her sister, Danaray, and of the mission she had so dismally failed to carry out.

Her dreams spun back and forth from the day she had met Brine and Dana had warned her that she and Mollusk could not have a future together (Dana could not have imagined what had happened) to the day her father had given her the mission and then to day she had met Zuryzel and helped her rescue Fawn.

Fawn! Anamay nearly screamed. Fawn had given them the information necessary to find Crow. And *still* she had failed. Anamay remembered, only too clearly, Fawn's bloodstained tunic, the makeshift bandages, the soft brown eyes, the beaded necklace with its red beads trimmed with gold. She had risked much to give them the news about Crow.

The beads!

Anamay jerked awake with this thought. It had not occurred to her—it had not reached her mind—before this point. But now she understood! Now it made sense!

Her memory flew back to the day when she, Brine, and Mollusk had been out scouting for traces of Anemone's mate. She had unearthed the little bead. It had come off *Fawn's* necklace. So the foxes had captured Anemone's mate after all! He must have been dead for quite a while, now.

Anamay stood and opened the drawer on the little desk in their room. She had kept the bead in here, and now she took it out to examine it. It was, indeed, the exact same as the ones left on Fawn's necklace: red with a gold border. It was, by all means, a beauty.

"So," she murmured, "this is the sea otters' war after all."

10
As Untrustworthy as the Sea

Whoosh!

Zuryzel gasped as all the air was knocked out of her lungs. For a minute she couldn't stir, just gaze at the sky.

"Let me guess," she croaked when she got a little air. "I didn't block both your attacks?"

"Yeh guessed right," Shartalla replied. She did not offer to help the princess stand, which Zuryzel found a little flattering.

The princess and the pine marten had been having practice battles for the last few days. It was actually Shartalla's idea; she wanted to get a grasp of the kind of skirmishing she'd be facing in the upcoming fights. Zuryzel was glad of her idea because she hoped to better her own skills against corsairs.

She was also glad she'd asked to have these duels out of sight of the other corsairs.

As far as fighters on land went, Zuryzel was one of the best. Shartalla had even commented that she could hold her own against most of Demmons's crew. However, Zuryzel had yet to best the pirate captain in any of their mock confrontations. Zuryzel was more bruised than she had ever been in her life—not just her muscles but also her pride. Shartalla had helped her pride by commenting in a throwaway manner that she was a captain because she *fought* like a captain, but Zuryzel sensed that was little more than an opportunity to boast.

After the first few battles in her career as a warrior, Zuryzel tried to remember specific things to look for because she had been taught that tactics in war were an ancient art little changed in the centuries of its existence. There was nothing new under the sun, she had thought, which included battle strategies. Shartalla had blown that away.

"Battle with corsairs ain't a set dance," she'd told Zuryzel after their first three practices. "There ain't no rules to follow, no basic strategies everyone bases their fighting off of. Pirate battle is versatile—it changes every moment, and the one who dies first is the one who can't keep up with the changing. Just learn t' change yer attacks, an' yeh don't *need* t' be good. Be unpredictable. Shake it up."

Zuryzel hadn't expected it to be easy. But to her surprise, keeping up with the change in battle wasn't as hard as she had predicted. Shartalla was just much better at it than she was. Much, *much* better.

"All right," she panted, struggling to her paws. "I'm ready to try that again."

Shartalla did not raise her blade in response. "The last three times yeh started off wi' that flick o' yer wrist," she observed. "Is tha' some kinda trick?"

Zuryzel nodded. "Yes. I was taught not to attack first, but so were half the soldiers in the world. That flick makes them think I'm attacking, forcing them to make the first move."

Shartalla nodded. "Well, that won't be a problem with corsairs. Keep in mind, they ain't great sword artists."

Zuryzel nodded, feeling as if she was in the practice arena all over again, but instead of facing her father, she was confronting a creature who had no qualms with inflicting impressive pain. "I'll remember."

Shartalla nodded. She stepped back a few paces to the middle of the clearing, and Zuryzel slipped behind a tree.

Change things, hmm? All right ...

Behind the tree, Zuryzel ducked down and crept to the right, hidden by the low-growing ferns. When she risked a peek at Shartalla, the pirate captain was still gazing intently at the tree.

She could be faking, Zuryzel thought, *but I can't wait much longer.*

Without rustling the ferns, she slipped back into the clearing and started for Shartalla, standing upright as she went.

If not for Shartalla's excellent peripheral vision, Zuryzel could have flattened her without any battle. She jumped back with a cry of "crackin' crabs!" when she saw Zuryzel only steps away from her and sword ready.

Zuryzel wasted no time. While Shartalla was off-balance, she brought her sword toward the pirate's head. Shartalla dodged and swiped at the princess's shoulder, but Zuryzel caught the pine marten's wrist with her spare paw. She threw Shartalla down in the blink of an eye.

Zuryzel couldn't throw Shartalla as hard as Shartalla could throw her; in a bare breath, Shartalla rolled with the fall and was on her paws again. In a battle between land dwellers, the opposing sides would step back and start looking for an opening again, but Shartalla didn't allow time for that. The scuffle went on for some time before Zuryzel finally hooked her paw behind one of Shartalla's and knocked her down as hard as she could. This time, Shartalla didn't jump back up.

"That was good," she panted. "Sneakin' in like that. Is tha' a Wraith Mouse thing, or do all land creatures pull that off?"

"All the ones you'll be fighting *can* pull it off," Zuryzel replied. "Whether they will or not depends on their commander's orders."

Shartalla nodded and struggled to her paws. "Well, it was good. Y' did a good job of attackin' in more places 'n I could defend."

Zuryzel was panting too. "How do you fight like that for so long?"

Shartalla smiled grimly. "The idea is the fight won't last tha' long. Yeh done?"

"Once more please," Zuryzel requested. Again, she retreated into the woods while Shartalla stood in the center of the clearing.

Shartalla wasn't interested in trying to see or hear the princess; she was just interested in dealing with Zuryzel when she came. Zuryzel had hoped she'd be turning constantly, but instead she just stood absolutely still. Though her eyes did flicker back and forth, she wasn't as jumpy as Zuryzel had been counting on. When Zuryzel attacked, even though it was from a completely different direction and even though she didn't see Zuryzel, she was still caught only a little by surprise. This time, it didn't take long for Shartalla to floor Zuryzel.

"Yer gettin' better," Shartalla observed. "Likely, y' could match up t' anyone from Demmons's or Epoi's crews. I bet yeh could even outlast either one o' them in a fight, an' tha's sayin' some'n."

"How'd you get so good?" Zuryzel asked as she got to her paws. "Who taught you?"

"I just learned," Shartalla replied shortly. "Where's the camp?"

"It's this way," Zuryzel replied, leading off . She hadn't really expected a better answer to her question; Shartalla was incredibly close-mouthed about anything in her past, however trivial.

Dinner was being served when they reached the camp. Shartalla took a plate of stew, no doubt supplied by Ailur, that consisted largely of dried seafood. Zuryzel had identified some edible plants for the ships' cooks, and some of the sailors had tried their paws at fishing, so there was some hint of freshness in the meal. Not much, though; Zuryzel would have been very glad to have the plain fare they served in Dombre, the fortress entrusted to her before the foxes reached it.

The princess sat beside Ailur, who, in a crowd with many other pirates, looked far less wild. The mercenary swallowed her mouthful and said, "Yer bein' careful 'round Shartalla, right?"

"I am," Zuryzel replied. Ailur had been almost taking care of Zuryzel over the journey of the last few weeks. "But she isn't going to hurt me, is she? She doesn't strike me as the backstabbing type."

Ailur looked around casually. "She ain't," she said in an undertone. "Not exactly. She don't backstab very often—but she ain't above it either. She takes care o' herself in ways both honorable and otherwise. I'll give it her that she prefers the honorable, but like I said, she can stoop low if she chooses."

Zuryzel took a bite of stew and tried to ignore the taste. "What's her story?" she asked, for want of something other than the meal to concentrate on.

Ailur let out a bark-like laugh. "I have absolutely no idea. Firs' I ever saw of her was a little before this whole war with Darkwoods started." A grin crept up the mercenary's face. "Now *that* is a story in and of itself."

"Do tell," Zuryzel urged while screwing up the courage to take another bite.

Ailur leaned back against a fallen log and smiled reminiscently. "Unnerstand, most corsairs are mercenaries. Those that ain't are either out for glory or out for adventure. I remember you mentioned Epoi as one o' the captains brought by Demmons? Well, she used t' be Demmons's navigator, but she broke off from Demmons 'n' gathered t'gether 'er own crew 'cause she wanted glory. One o' the fastest ways t' get glory among corsairs is what's largely referred to as a shore challenge. Basically it means that a cap'n goes 'n' stands in the middle of a tavern and brags for a while 'bout 'is or 'er skills 'n' prowess. Then other ones, who think they're better, line up 'n' fight with the braggart one by one. It ain't usually a fight t' the death, but sometimes it is. When Epoi did her shore challenge, it was."

Ailur sighed and her eyes filmed over. "It was a terrible thing t' watch, Zuryzel. Firs' one t' go up against her was some'n I was on good terms with, some'n who had won two shore challenges, an' she just wiped the floor with 'im. She couldn't stop fighting, unnerstand, until there was no one left to fight, and the line of her challengers was up in the twenties. The floor was soon covered wi' the blood o' those she'd slain. An' these pirates were some o' the best! Pirates who'd 'ad more victories unner their belt than any ten could count. She just vanquished 'em. After she killed her eleventh challenger, the line just sorta disappeared.

"I'll never forget how terrible she looked, standing in the middle o' the tavern screamin' 'er challenge t' everyone 'o could 'ear. 'Er knife was drippin' in blood, 'er teeth were bared, 'n' she was laughin'. Jus' cackling. Almost drunk on 'ow no one dared stan' up t' 'er. How powerful she was, 'ow much she was feared Then, when she took a breath, we all 'eard a quiet voice say, 'I'll fight you.'"

Zuryzel remembered now why her mother had taken pleasure in this wild creature's company; her storytelling was first-rate.

"We all turned t' look, an' there in the shadows stood a pine marten. She barely looked old enough t' sail, I tell yeh. She didn't even draw 'er sword as she approached Epoi. They were totally unmatched, we all thought. This new 'un was young 'n' small 'n' didn' 'ave enough scars t' have been in many battles, an' no one 'ad ever seen 'er afore, whereas Epoi had just killed eleven o' the best. I ain't jestin' when I say I thought she *wanted* t' die. The total calm on 'er face 'n' in 'er stance only furthered that. I swear, the pine marten was absolutely calm, stiller 'n the stillest doldrums. Wasn' e'en breathin' hard; didn't even touch 'er sword. Epoi laughed, not so much at 'er but at the thrill of havin' another kill. Then the eleven-times victor charged the challenger."

Ailur smiled faintly, even mirthfully. "Epoi was right on top o' her 'fore Shartalla acted. In just a heartbeat, the pine marten went from calm t' snarlin' an' fierce. She didn' even draw her sword, just dodged Epoi's 'n' threw the fox down hard as she could. Wasn' even a contest. Epoi was flat on her back before she even knew what was happenin'. When she finally figgered out, she looked up all scared, waitin' t' be killed. Shartalla drew back, contempt written all over 'er face. 'Get up,' she snarled, drawin' 'er blade. 'Pick up yer sword 'n' come at me again.' Epoi did, 'n' this time she was more careful. Approached the pine marten all wary 'n' cautious, usin' every trick she knew of. Still no contest. The fight lasted only three seconds afore Epoi was on the floor again. 'Again,' Shartalla snarled 'n' backed off. Bu' again, Shartalla just dominated the fight."

"I think I've seen a bit of that," Zuryzel murmured, rubbing one bruised shoulder.

Ailur shook her head. "Trust me, Zuryzel, this fight weren' nothin' like practice. Shartalla knocked Epoi down three more times; twice more, she allowed Epoi t' get up. The third time, Epoi just lay winded 'n' Shartalla stood o'er her, standin' on her paws so she couldn' rise or fight, sword tip right at 'er throat. Epoi just couldn' believe she'd been beaten. 'Kill me then,' she whispered. Shartalla jus' stood there a while; then she smirked, grunted, and stepped back. She sheathed her sword, then turned 'er back on Epoi and walked away."

Here, Ailur shuddered. "I tell yeh, Zuryzel, the quiet in the tavern was somethin' I never seen or 'eard afore. Every eye was on this young pirate 'o'd just defeated a victor six times, let 'er live, then dared t' turn 'er back. Everyone was silent, everyone watchin' wi' their trap 'angin' open. The crowd parted t' let 'er walk through, an' she jus' went up t' the bar 'n' ordered a drink like nothin' 'ad jus' 'appened. No one said anythin' until another crew arrived fer shore leave. Then she just kinda melted inter the crowd."

"But why didn't she kill Epoi?" Zuryzel asked. "Why let her live? Now all she had was an enemy with a vengeance."

"True," Ailur agreed. "I don' know why, Zuryzel. Like I said, this was somethin' I never really seen afore. Eleven o' the best veterans vanquished, then the victor made sport of."

Zuryzel glanced over to where Shartalla sat, sort of with her crew but really more alone. "I like her," she whispered, grinning a little. "Even more because no one ever heard of her."

Ailur shot her a warning look. "I like her, too," she admitted. "As far as pirates go, she's not false, an' she's fairly pleasant. Bu' I wouldn' place yer good opinion there irrevocably. She 'as more enemies 'n she c'n name fer a reason."

"Maybe because she embarrassed them as she did Epoi," Zuryzel suggested.

"It could be," Ailur replied. "It could be. But yeh never know. Be careful 'round 'er. She also won that challenge fer a reason."

"Yes," Zuryzel replied. "It has been impressed on me how much better a fighter than I she is."

"She is good," Ailur replied. "Obviously. She don' fight much, but I've never seen 'er shy away from a fight. It's just that she's hard t' predict. Hard t' unnerstand. Be careful 'round 'er, Zuryzel."

"I will," the Wraith Mouse promised.

Ailur gave a sly smile. "But jus' 'cause yeh don't trust someone don't mean yeh don't like 'em," she grinned, making Zuryzel chuckle.

Towards midnight, when most of the corsairs were dozing, Zuryzel saw Shartalla sitting by herself on a low tree branch. The princess crept forward, careful not to slip into the night as was a Wraith Mouse's wont, and leaned against a stump beneath the branch Shartalla was perched on.

"I used to think Wraith Mice sleep during the day," the pirate remarked, taking a sip of water from her canteen.

"Wraith Mice sleep when they're tired," Zuryzel replied, smiling. "As, I hear, do corsairs."

Shartalla shrugged. "What's the point o' sleepin' when yeh ain't tired?" But she was grinning faintly.

Zuryzel nodded. She watched the moon, her namesake, for a while, and then said, "I heard one of the captains with Demmons has a grudge against you."

"Just one?" Shartalla grinned. "All of 'em do."

"Epoi was the one I heard," Zuryzel replied. "I heard she killed eleven champions in a challenge, and then you defeated her."

Shartalla snorted. "It weren't eleven—no more 'n five or six."

"Still," Zuryzel pressed, "I heard you didn't even blink when you defeated her— five times."

Shartalla smiled wryly. "I'd watched her through six diff'rent fights. I knew her style, an' I knew what to expect from 'er. It wasn't that 'ard."

"Why didn't you kill her?" Zuryzel continued.

Shartalla turned to look at her for the first time, and her expression was serious. "There are things worse than death. Epoi was fighting hopin' t' become the next chief o' the sea, the next terror that tyrannized the corsairs." The pine marten's serious expression turned into a smirk. "All she needed was t' be taught that that weren't goin' t' happen."

Zuryzel sensed that Shartalla enjoyed talking about her victories. "You issue challenges like that?" she asked.

Shartalla shook her head. "Epoi lost because she was slippin' in the blood o' those she'd killed," the pirate answered shortly. "I don't wanna meet the same fate."

Something about the tone warned Zuryzel not to pursue this conversation. However, Shartalla turned back and asked, "Why'd yeh ask?"

Zuryzel shrugged. "I don't know. It just seemed … really incredible."

Shartalla scoffed. "Princess, how'd yeh get outta Dombre?"

Zuryzel shook her head, not sure she'd heard right. "Excuse me?"

"How did yeh get out of a fortress with a whole army tryin' t' kill yeh?" Shartalla elaborated.

"It wasn't that exciting," Zuryzel admitted. "I just sort of snuck away, and I had someone help me."

"Precisely," Shartalla replied. "But everyone's amazed that yeh got out of a deathtrap with thousands tryin' t' stop you."

"It wasn't that many," Zuryzel protested, confused.

"That's my point," Shartalla snorted. "It ain't nearly as impressive when yer the one that's livin' it. But were I you, I wouldn't disillusion the creatures followin' yeh." She coughed.

Zuryzel nodded. She stood up and made for her bedroll. "I'll remember that," she said. "And I bid you good night."

11 Broken Through

Feldspar sat dangling his paws in the lake. The Graystone mouse had simply wandered off alone, wishing for time to think and attempt to rid himself of his horrible foreboding.

Lady Raven had died three days ago. She had survived for two days, but her body seemed to have broken, and she was not young. She had died at twilight, her breath coming in steady gasps, from what Feldspar heard from the healers. Roughly seven hours ago, Cinder, Mayberry, Cherry, Snow, and some others had left with Lady Raven's body between them on a litter. Word was they were taking her north for burial.

Feldspar had been in Pasadagavra for several months but had seen Lady Raven only once. Yet, that one time had been sufficient enough to command his respect and confidence. Now she was dead, and her daughter was Lady of the Rangers, but who knew how far away she was? Three cycles? Four? Five? Without a leader in place for the Rangers, Feldspar felt nothing but terrible doom waiting on the horizon.

Suddenly, Chite came hurtling through the entrance to the lake. He was panting as Feldspar had never seen.

"What is it?" asked Feldspar, seeing the terror on Chite's face.

Chite gasped only three words. "They've broken through!"

"The foxes?"

"Of course, you ninny! They're already at the Stream Source, heading for the city gates!"

"Oh, no!"

Feldspar did not hesitate. He followed Chite back to where the fortress was divided from the city.

It was nothing short of chaos. The very old, very young, and those who were not warriors struggled desperately away from what sounded like yelling, shrieking war cries, and, to Feldspar's horror, *laughing*.

Arrows were already flying around the two mice, struggling against the rushing crowd, searching for Ol'ver, Ran'ta, and Glor'a. By the time they had reached the back of the crowd, they had not caught sight of their friends, though, as Chite commented, "It's easy to miss them in this crowd."

The only thing keeping the oncoming horde of foxes back in the narrow street were two young Rangers, Rainbow and Aspen. They had their bows out and their arrows pouring into the foe, though their quivers were dwindling. Rainbow did not turn her head as she addressed them as calmly as a child asking for lunch.

"You should get back. We need help. Couldn't you bring the others?"

"Yes, go—wait a minute …," said Aspen.

He had just slain Riorat, one of the captains Demmons had summoned, to reveal a terrifying sight.

The foxes behind had formed something like an advancing wall of prisoners they had grabbed, two deep and five abreast.

"Great," muttered Rainbow. "On second thought, could you stay and help them get away? We'll have to deal with this …"

Behind them, the street was empty toward the city gates. In front of them, the foxes got closer and closer, behind their captives. Regardless, the two Rangers stood fearless, shouldering their bows and drawing their swords.

"You'll get killed!" exclaimed Chite, staring aghast at Rainbow, who had begun to pace forward.

"No, we won't. We'll get away soon as we can. Just stay here and help the others escape," shrugged Aspen.

"Do they often go up against odds like this?" muttered Feldspar to Chite as the two Rangers broke into a run.

"Looks like it," replied Chite, drawing his knife.

Feldspar followed his example, inwardly thinking that Aspen had been lying when he had said they would soon get away.

But he stood beside Chite, watching as the two Rangers thrust their way roughly between two of the captives to get at their captors. Unthinkingly, both the captives darted toward the street. One of them, to Feldspar's relief, was Glor'a, and the other, Ran'ta.

"Feldspar," panted Glor'a, her eyes wide, "wasn't that Rainbow and Aspen?"

"Yes, but get back to the city, *fast*. Is Ol'ver around?"

"No, I think he's back in the city!" Ran'ta shouted over her shoulder as the two maidens ran.

Glor'a paused, glancing back at Feldspar, as Ran'ta rushed on. Feldspar shouted, "Go!" and still she hesitated for a moment before going.

Looking back, Feldspar realized that Rainbow and Aspen had just managed to free another four prisoners, all of them old squirrels who could not move very fast.

"Go quick as you can," Chite called to them. "We'll help you as soon as we can."

"Too much like Aspen," commented Feldspar, fighting to keep his voice from cracking.

"Only I do plan to get to them," agreed Chite, the same panic in his voice as in his eyes.

"True," panted Feldspar, watching in horror as a blade seared across Rainbow's shoulder, narrowly missing her eyes and neck. Chite moaned as she struck back, slaying her attacker with one blow of her sword.

"How she can do that, I'll never understand!" Chite was looking clammy and terrified, as the last captives broke loose.

"Now go!" Aspen's shout rose above the rest of the noise.

Chite and Feldspar, they were later ashamed to say, did not hesitate to help the captives escape, leaving Rainbow and Aspen surrounded by the horde. They were afraid that they themselves would get caught and surrounded by the oncoming army. So they hastened to help the others get back, leaving Rainbow and Aspen surrounded by the enemy.

Yet, many times after getting back to the city, they thanked the Bear King that their cowardly move had not been disastrous.

Epoi the vixen corsair scanned the ground, covered with slain squirrels, Wraith Mice, and a few river otters.

"Huh, not a lot in the way of pickings," she commented, looking around. Movement caught her eye. A squirrel had somehow survived the purge of the Darkwoods foxes. But there was no mercy with corsairs; the law of the pirate was still the law of their conduct.

Claw looked up at the sound of screaming. He saw Epoi lashing her blade against the squirrel, beating him to death.

"Leave him alone!" he shouted to Epoi. "We need the captives."

Epoi stopped her beating. "Huh, too late; it's dead now. Shatterin' sharks, these landlubbers ain't no fun! No gut at all." She strode purposefully off, looking for more victims.

Claw sprinted over to the squirrel Epoi had beaten to death. Its eyes stared at nothing, and its jaws gaped open in an eternal cry of pain. The ripple tattoo on his cheek showed he was a River Tribe squirrel. River Tribe squirrels were tough and strong compared to most creatures on the land, with the obvious exception of the Sling Tribe. How was it that it fell so easily to this corsair captain?

Chite, Feldspar, and the last of the civilians just made it through the city gates as they were closing.

Ol'ver was waiting for them, the usually dark brown face pale, as so much blood had drained from his face. "Oh, thank goodness!" he exclaimed. "I thought you'd been caught by the foxes near the fortress. I was afraid you would be lost like the others!"

"We—what? What do you mean, lost like the others?" Chite asked. Both were gasping from their efforts of getting inside the city.

"Didn't you hear?" asked Ol'ver, his face grim. "I suppose it's not as bad as it could have been. The foxes didn't break through the city gates. They found something like a tunnel outside that led into the Stream Source; that's how they got to the fortress. So, everything but the living quarters, part of the Great Fire, Growing Fields, fountain, Last Store House, and the mountains are cut off since they're on the other side of the city gates. That leaves us with enough to survive, for a little while, anyway, assuming we can keep the foxes penned up in the fortress.

"But we lost a lot of warriors today. The Rangers weren't on guard duty. The Wraith Mice were just making their way down to relieve the squirrel wall sentries, so some of them survived, about fifty, I'd guess. But the squirrel warriors were hit hard. Of course, the Mountain Tribe is fine; they weren't on duty, nor was the Prairie Tribe, from what I hear. But … word is that the Bow Tribe was annihilated, only one warrior survived because he was being treated by Marruh, the healer, at the time the fight began. I guess two babes of the Bow Tribe survived, too—but that's it, I've heard." Feldspar gasped in horror as Ol'ver continued. "The Coast Tribe and the Sling Tribe seemed to have the fewest losses, I think because they're most used to surprises. The River Tribe and Wind Tribe both had a lot of losses, but there's still a lot of them left, too. I think the Stone Tribe is pretty much okay, but both Tribeking Fuddum and Argoss died. So did Onair, poor fellow."

Fedspar looked at him aghast. So many lost! So many dead!

"What else? Who else?" asked Chite urgently.

"That's all I know of right now. I don't know what happened to the Rangers," replied Ol'ver. Suddenly his eyes burned. "But when I get a chance to get at the foxes, you can bet they'll be sorry!"

Ol'ver is definitely a warrior, thought Feldspar. *His attitude is just like Opal's. Grief later and vengeance now. If only I could be like them! Then maybe I wouldn't be afraid of being killed!*

Just then, Feldspar caught sight of something beyond the clear diamond wall of the city. Several foxes were wrestling with two squirming figures, which Feldspar recognized as Aspen and Rainbow.

"Bear King be praised," Chite breathed. "They're alive."

12 Friends from the North

Ol'ver rolled his eyes impatiently at Chite.

"Alive," he agreed, "but for how long? What do the foxes want to do with them?"

It was an ominous thought, though Aspen and Rainbow didn't seem afraid. Rainbow's amber eyes were perhaps a little dull, though that was hardly surprising, as she had a terrible wound along her side, and her usually gray and black fur was paling. Aspen's blue-green eyes were bright, though his white fur was half covered by blood and his tunic was ripped and soaked with blood. Yet in spite of their terrible wounds, both Rangers were struggling, clawing, even biting their captors.

Snowgoose, who was temporarily in charge of the Rangers, hastened to the wall and pushed open an arrow slit.

"What do you want?" she called through to the foxes.

"We have two prisoners here," called a harsh voice. Claw was standing nearby, watching the Rangers' struggles with obvious enjoyment, talking to Snowgoose at the same time.

"*Obviously*," exclaimed Snowgoose, curling her lip contemptuously. "Rainbow, Aspen, are you all right?"

"Oh, yes," called Aspen, disregarding his soaking red tunic.

"We're fine," shrugged Rainbow, though she winced.

"As are several other warriors they have …," added Aspen suddenly.

"From the Bow Tribe and River Tribe …," Rainbow picked up without a pause.

"Maidens, mothers, and babes, too ..."

"Though we don't know wh—" Rainbow's words were cut off as a paw slapped across her face. She bit it.

"What do you mean by parading them in front here?" demanded Snowgoose. Feldspar could see she was playing for time; she had clearly read Claw like a book.

"We were thinking you'd want to get them back," shrugged Claw, still with his eyes on the Rangers.

"Indeed. Well, it would seem rather obvious that is impossible."

No, it's not, thought Feldspar desperately.

"Nothing is impossible. You can get them back."

"How?"

"You, and any other of your warriors, come out with your blades above your heads," sneered Claw, his red eyes turning to look into Snowgoose's black ones.

Snowgoose said nothing. Her eyes focused hard on Claw's until he looked away.

"I will consider," answered Snowgoose finally. "Give me ten days."

"Three," snapped Claw.

"Ten, or I swear by the Bear King that you will regret it."

Claw plainly had no fear of the Bear King, but the ferocity in Snowgoose's voice was threatening anyway. Claw's nerve failed him.

"Ten days, but at dawn on the eleventh day, either come out, or watch these two die."

"Then," called Snowgoose swiftly, "bring them here for me to see every sunhigh that I may see they are alive."

At the same time Snowgoose avoided Claw's trap, she set a trap of her own, Feldspar guessed.

Claw went straight into the trap, whatever it was. "Very well."

That night, Feldspar and Glor'a kept their eyes on Snowgoose. She seemed to be keeping watch for something—what, it was impossible to guess. Yet her black eyes kept combing the dark mountainside. Once or twice, she jumped; though, what she thought she saw seemed to be nothing but a mound of snow.

For four nights, this continued, and after each night, there came a sunrise and then a sunhigh where Aspen and Rainbow were paraded in front of the city. They quite clearly were not "all right," but they were well enough to walk and struggle against their captors. Rainbow's fur was getting paler and Aspen's tunic was solid red, but none of this seemed to bother them.

On the fifth night, something happened. Snowgoose, at her usual post facing the mountain, suddenly stiffened before she stood up and swept toward an arrow slit.

"Cinder?" she called softly.

"Snowgoose?" called Cinder's deep voice. "Good, we were afraid we'd be too late."

"The foxes made it into the fortress of Pasadagavra," called Snowgoose, still barely loud enough for Cinder to hear. "Wait a minute, I'll show you a way into the city!"

Silent as a shadow, Snowgoose hurried away from her post and out of sight. Feldspar and Glor'a rushed to where she had stood.

Down below them were roughly ten dark figures. About eight of them were milling about, nervously looking this way and that, but two of them stood stock-still and immobile, looking calm and reassuring. Feldspar thought he saw something moving on the rocks, but a moment later, he was not sure.

Then Snowgoose's shape flitted into his view. One of the milling figures started, but neither of the still figures reacted. Feldspar would have guessed that they were made of stone … until they began to follow Snowgoose back toward where she had come from.

Feldspar guessed, by Snowgoose's timing, where they would enter.

Holding Glor'a's paw, he hurried around and up to the fountain. Sure enough, when he got there, the door that led to the mountain was opening, and the Rangers entered the fountain room.

As it was well past moonrise, the fountain was off and the lights extinguished. Glor'a's light-golden fur was not so visible, and Feldspar could not see his own fur, so the two mice hid by the clear diamond walls and were not seen.

Jaccah's voice sounded out of the gloom. "Cinder, may I ask who's with you?"

Hoods left heads as Cinder explained. "You know most of us, Jaccah, but this is Fern." He gestured toward a smallish mouse with dark brown and black speckled fur. "And somewhere around here, wherever they got to—Great Cerecinthia!"

Two small, dark shapes dropped down right in front of him. From what Feldspar could see, the two creatures would have reached his shoulder, had short, brown fur with a white stripe down their backs, rounded ears, long, sharp claws on their forepaws, bushy tails, and handsome, dark, serious eyes that did not quite match their cheerful voices.

"Ah, suresure, noneed "troducing us, Cinder. Menames Texat."

"Suresure, an' I his sisser, Skettle, at yourservice."

Cinder rolled his eyes. "Texat and Skettle, pair of nuisances, but insisted on coming. And these are," he nodded to the two still immobile creatures, still hooded and cloaked, "Xar and Sone."

Xar and Sone finally swept off their hoods. Feldspar sucked in his breath. The first word he would have used to describe Xar and Sone would have been fuzzy. But on second glance, "ragged" was a better word. Their long, coarse fur was white, which would explain the black cloaks, and had been cut away at the face. They leaned on long spears, longer than any Feldspar had seen, and which seemed not to be made of wood. Feldspar guessed they were otters of some sort.

He missed what else passed between Cinder and Jaccah; neither Feldspar nor Glor'a caught it. Both of them snuck away and gazed at each other. Then, after a bit, Glor'a said, "I think we're in for another weird twist."

Two dawns later, Zuryzel crouched fearfully in some scanty undergrowth just south of Pasadagavra. The whole band of mercenaries and corsairs was hidden in a field roughly three hours' swift running away. The only companions with her were Shartalla, Tsanna, Grayik, Skorlaid, and Arasam.

Tsanna frowned. "Mmm. Seems 's though the foxes broke through," she observed. "I c'n see 'em millin' about up there."

Cold fear covered Zuryzel at Tsanna's words. Had the foxes, indeed, broken through? Her family, and her friends—were they, all dead?

"But look 'igher, inter that great clear dome," Grayik pointed out, his claw extended marginally. "See, there's beasts up there that ain't foxes or ferrets! Huh, doesn't look as though those ferrets, what's their names, Jironi, Redseg, and, uh, Fotirra, were helpin' much, do it? They're the ones all laid out lazy-like."

"Searin' storms!" exclaimed Arasam suddenly. "That's never … no, it ain't … is it?"

"What?" demanded Zuryzel, fear building in her throat again.

"A tundra otter?"

"A *what*?"

"Tundra otters," explained Skorlaid quietly. "They are otters that live in the far north, on the isle of Tundra. The vast majority of it's tundra climate—yeh know, ground, but frozen, barren in winter, large fields in the summer, lots o' the dumb animals there too, like fish on the land, and stuff like that. But the northern third o' their isle's covered in snow. There's one place up there, called Seal Inlet, that 'arbors seals. Tundra otters are otters born pure white of fur an' practic'ly designed t' hunt the seals, evil things too, seals are."

"Which means, if one o' them is in Pasadagavra and there are Rangers in Pasadagavra, the 'ole city 'asn't fallen yet, *and* there is a way in," added Shartalla. "But this puts us in a bad position. What d' we do?"

"What has happened?" Zuryzel whispered. "That city is the strongest city in the world. Those gates have never even been imprinted on. So, how did the foxes get in? What has happened?"

No one could answer her wondering. Then …

"Zuryzel you said there were tunnels leading to Pasadagavra. P'r'aps through a tunnel *into* Pasadagavra?" suggested Tsanna.

"Maybe. Seems logical," agreed Zuryzel. "Perhaps we could find their tunnel and surprise them?"

"Nah," rasped Shartalla. "Demmons ain't no fool. 'E'll 'ave though' o' tha'."

"Maybe he isn't, but Claw is," Zuryzel pointed out. "And Claw will be in charge if Knife isn't here, and Knife plainly isn't here."

"Still, let's lie low fer a bit," suggested Arasam. "We needs t' make a proper plan."

"True," agreed Zuryzel.

The small scouting patrol slid out of the bracken almost noiselessly (Grayik stepped on a pinecone and yelped aloud), and in no time, they were scurrying toward the field.

Anamay glanced back at Zurez.

The sea otters were returning inland for the winter, even though the fall had barely begun yet. Anamay suspected it was because of what had happened to Driftwood. Foam's clan would be in the worst danger since the Keron flowed through their territory. Brine had warned that she had seen many more Keron Mice than Current reported, but Foam seemed unafraid. Anemone was now officially forbidden to see anyone but Crustacean, Current, or Foam, including her own children. Anamay was run ragged with watching Eagle and Saline, and felt sincere admiration for Anemone for keeping her two children in line. Anamay could not imagine how she had done it. Crustacean seemed to be remorseful about Anemone, though Anamay knew by now that his old, wise pretense was nothing but a fake.

If she were watching Eagle and Saline, he might come over and say how he regretted that Anemone could not look after them herself and more such nonsense. Anamay privately thought it was about as true as old rags were fine. And to cap matters, Anamay was expecting a child.

She had been delighted when she first realized she was expecting, but now she was nervous. The child would be born in late winter or, she hoped, early spring. Anamay knew perfectly well that winter was the worst time for childbirth. She herself had been born in late winter, and her mother had died. Anamay had almost died, too. But the winters were much worse on the prairie than in the forest, and her homeland was a long ways north. Yet still, she had heard tell of someone who had not only lost a child but also her life in the winter. Anamay was nervous. Early fall though it was, already the air was getting colder and the nights longer. Winter was going to be a bad time.

Anamay stepped on something hard. She longed to pick it up but was afraid that Crustacean would suspect something. So, she bent down and scooped up Saline and swiftly swept her paw back to where the thing was and pocketed it without a second thought.

The prairie grass rolled endlessly from the gleaming white towers of the Miamuran palace. The Miamuran banner—a blue field with two wide, white wings—drifted from the towers. Around the walls were clustered the many houses belonging to the city that surrounded the palace. To the east, the rich farmland spread out for miles and miles. To the west, the little copper mine was bustling with workers.

Danaray Mudriver turned away from the well-known sight and north towards the one she was unused to. Spread out across the golden prairie, out of sight of the castle, was an army. It wasn't a large army or a heavily armored one but rather about four hundred warriors, if that many, who looked as though they were drilling.

It was not unusual for Miamur to have an army. What *was* unusual was that they should be doing anything other than fighting the eastern savages that harassed them. The Miamuran Queen Regent was not the sort of monarch who paid much attention to armies. All she was doing (thankfully) was holding the throne of Miamur for her eldest son, Galledor, until he became twenty-one seasons old, the age at which Miamuran princes were considered eligible to be king. In any case, this army was too far west to be a defense against the wild marauders, and it likely wasn't commissioned by the Queen Regent.

Danaray puzzled over the strangeness for a while, nibbling at a grass blade. "They're up to something," she decided out loud. She stood and stretched before readjusting the ceremonial knife in her belt. All river otter chieftains had these knives; they were symbols of position and a constant reminder of the responsibilities of a chief. Danaray's was made of iron with a garnet-studded hilt and a huge garnet set as the pommel stone. The cross-piece was short but very hard. This knife had once been her father's, and his father's, and so on and so forth. *My kind worry too much about tradition!* she thought as her hand left its grasp on the jeweled top.

Now she had to decide what to do about the Miamurans on the plains perhaps two miles away. It was always a good thing to check before allowing an armed force to parade on your lands. Danaray debated between sneaking and boldly striding. She hadn't done much sneaking since her sister Anamay had defected to the sea otters—yet again she cursed them for seducing her sister away from her while praying that Anamay was well with Mollusk—and she had done a lot of bold striding since her father had died. She let her paw touch the blood-red pommel stone at her waist and made up her mind: she was going to stride. She could sneak some other time, but when it came to finding out the reason for an inexplicable anomaly, it was better to act the chief.

For a moment, she wondered if she should get a patrol to come with her, but she really didn't like the idea. An armed patrol could look like a threat. So sporting her chieftain's knife and her long, thin javelin, she began a comfortable jog toward the Miamuran army.

When she reached the edge of their encampment, she expected to be challenged, but to her surprise, the drilling soldiers allowed her to walk straight down the row of tents, barely according her a second glance. Those not drilling sat at the entrances of spacy, square, white-gold tents sharpening weapons or polishing armor. Most of them were mice, but Danaray saw the odd river otter. She even recognized a few former members of her band that had traded their rural ways for city life; they saluted her as she strode by them.

At the end of the avenue of white-gold tents, she saw a particularly fine open-air pavilion with a table, chairs, and a chest that probably contained cold refreshments. There were six or seven mice gathered in the tent, bent over a map on the table. Most of them were strangers to Danaray, but three of them she recognized.

The gray mouse closest to her was Asherad, one of the Miamuran princes. He wore a suit of strange armor made from something that resembled leather. His own crest was on the front—the Miamuran white wings around a pool of blue water.

Princess Kiarna stood next to her brother, and she wore a dress made of the same material as her brother's armor. Unlike Asherad, however, she wore a princess's diadem and had outlined the white fur around her eyes with black paint. On her wrists jingled bracelets made from exquisite stone and metalwork. Her crest—Miamuran white wings above a blue rose—was also painted on the front of her dress.

But the one who drew Danaray's attention the most, though he was dressed the plainest, was the tallest in the pavilion. A brown mouse with his siblings' deep blue eyes, Galledor carried an air of silent dignity about him, from the simple copper band on his brow to the massive sword at his waist. He wore armor similar to his brother's, and his insignia was a sword in the center of a tongue of fire, flanked by the characteristic white wings. His voice was deep and purposeful.

"They have surrounded Pasadagavra on all sides," one of the strange mice was saying, tapping the map. "Some of them tried bringing a battering ram against the gates but didn't even make a dent."

"Timing is crucial," murmured Princess Kiarna. "And winter halfway through."

"Asherad," Galledor ordered, "take the generals with you and make sure the drills are being executed with all precision, especially the ones concerning the turtle."

"Right away," Asherad replied. He and the other strange mice exited towards the huge parade field, leaving Kiarna and Galledor.

"If this endeavor goes wrong," Galledor said to his sister, "then likely four armies will be scattered in the middle of winter. If it goes right, several dangerous threats will be eliminated."

"Indeed," Kiarna agreed. "And you will have established yourself as Crown Prince."

Galledor waved his paw. "That doesn't matter. No one can challenge me anyway. What does matter is that the situation is precarious. It all depends on one princess's timing."

He looked up from the map and smiled in Danaray's direction, as if he wasn't at all surprised to see her there. "Welcome, chieftainess."

Kiarna jumped and hastily pushed aside one of the maps. "Danaray!" she exclaimed.

"Your Highnesses," Danaray replied, not sure whether that was a real form of address or not.

"I was sorry to hear of your father. Please accept our deepest condolences," Galledor added, his eyes making obvious his sincerity.

Danaray blinked quickly and replied, "Prince Galledor, may I ask what an army is doing preparing for war?"

Kiarna chuckled, and Galledor replied, "We mean to aid in the war our neighbors are engaged in."

"Forgive me, but the last I had heard, Miamur intended to stay neutral," Danaray replied swiftly.

"This army is not Miamur," Kiarna replied calmly. "This is an army independent of the Queen Regent."

"But not of you, I see."

Galledor shook his head. "No, indeed."

"And were the warriors involved informed of this?" Danaray inquired. "I saw former members from my tribe, and I would not like to think they were being manipulated."

"Oh, they are," Kiarna replied unabashedly. "This army has been told they are gathered for self-defense in case the Darkwoods foxes *do* head east."

"What is your true purpose, then?" Danaray challenged.

Kiarna began to respond defensively, but Galledor waved his paw. "She is right to be cautious. Her tribe is used to having these grasslands to themselves." He turned to face Danaray.

"I know it looked as if the superpowers of this world sat back idly and watched while Darkwoods grew in power," he began, "but that isn't true. Certain monarchs have been in secret contact for several seasons, and plans have been made."

"How secret are these communications?" Danaray pressed.

"Not even Asherad knows of them," Galledor explained. "He is under the same illusion as the soldiers."

"But you mean to march?" Danaray persisted.

Kiarna smirked. "As soon as we're given the word."

Danaray gave them a bewildered look. "By whom, if not your mother?"

Galledor smiled rather smugly. "Queen Demeda, of course. She is the center of our plans."

"I still don't understand," Danaray protested.

The brother and sister shared a cautious look, as if trying to decide if she was trustworthy enough to include in secret plans. Galledor nodded and softly reminded his sister, "Her father was a part of this."

Danaray hid her surprise.

The princess laid the map she'd snatched back on the table and rolled it out flat. There were markings on it in several different colors. A black star was to the west by the Cliff Mouse cities, a green one to the south among the sea otter lands, and a white one right over Miamur. Lines extended from these stars in the same color and snaked through mountain passes and over rivers, but all three of these met at Pasadagavra.

Danaray touched the star over the sea otters and whispered, "Are these stars where armies are?" Crow would be by that green star. And the black one … the Wraith Mouse army from Arashna, perhaps? No, Arashna was to the south of the star. But the white star was obviously the Miamuran army.

"That's right," Galledor replied quietly.

"What is to the west?" Danaray inquired.

Kiarna smiled sadly. "If all goes well, a very young, good friend of ours."

"That is unimportant right now," Galledor cut in.

"Are you asking for my tribe's aid?" Danaray inquired, suddenly seeing their purpose for telling her.

Galledor smiled. "We like all the help we can get."

13 The Secret Corsair

Knife returned to the castle the next day, drenched by a heavy rain, and was greeted by a worried look on both Fang's face and that of Cutthroat, the healer.

"What?" she snapped, her temper shorter than usual.

"It's Ice," explained Cutthroat. "Something's happened, and I don't like it."

"What?"

"Follow me."

She scurried past the open red gates, up through many passages and stairways, into the room that had once been Ice's.

It was unlike any room Knife had ever seen, and she had seen quite a lot. Strange, wood paneling covered much of the stone walls with things painted on it here and there in a strange writing neither she, Cutthroat, nor Fang could interpret. Above some of the writings were paintings that were extremely crude. One of them depicted something that was solid black with monstrous curving claws and evil, amber eyes that set Knife trembling. Beneath it was the writing:

Tηε Ρυσηακκ

Another picture showed what looked like two serpents emerging from great, foam-topped waves, of revolting green-blue color with milky white fangs and hideous, but deathly beautiful, heads with eyes black as midnight without any twinkle of star shine. Beneath this picture was the inscription, carved, not painted:

Σιδον ανδ Σψρα

The bed, a mere hammock but of canvas cloth not at all familiar, had minor tears in places, but nothing too bad, and faced the paintings of the terrible monsters that so baffled Knife.

Cutthroat moved silently to a dark corner and lifted something up. It was a heavy chest with carvings of waves, mussel shells, sharks, and dolphins, though neither Knife, Fang, nor Cutthroat could identify the shapes for what they were.

Cutthroat bent down and opened the strange chest. It was completely empty.

"When Ice was ill once, I knocked this over by accident. She didn't know I saw what was in here, but I did. In here was once strange things—a knife, curved strangely, I think in the shape of a sickle. And there was something I think called a compass, and things that looked like bird eggshells, but they were strong—unbelievably strong."

"Things that come from the sea," Knife surmised. "Where did she get them?"

Cutthroat frowned. "Oracle, you may be well advanced in cycles, but I'm much, much older than you. Now, if I recall rightly, one autumn, I think the autumn before you were apprenticed to Scythe, a corsair by the name of Torona was found wandering about in the woodlands. She was brought here and more or less learned our ways. I guess Ice wrestled all these things from her somehow. But who has taken them now?"

Fang and Knife exchanged looks. Knife had warned Fang what she had found out at the shallow pool. Finally, Fang said, "Thank you, Cutthroat. Go and attend Hemlock. We will handle this."

Cutthroat nodded obediently and left.

"Do you have the writings of Scythe still, Fang?" inquired Knife coolly.

"Yes. I haven't studied them much, though, so I really don't remember what Cutthroat was talking about."

"Nor do I, but I'll find out."

The two foxes entered Fang's study, which was only a few rooms down the hall. Fang opened a cabinet door, which was filled with stacks of paper. He selected perhaps the last quarter of the stacked heavy sheets and laid them on the table.

"Here they are, the autumn before you became her apprentice and beyond. Now let me see ..."

He thumbed through them for a minute, careful to not rip the pages with his claws, before exclaiming, "Here it is!"

He held out about ten sheets and began to read, as Knife was a slow reader.

Just two hours ago, a young vixen was discovered wandering on the moor just outside the woods, looking very beat up but alive. She was brought straight to me, as I am the oldest Oracle. I questioned her. She asked where she was, who I was, and a lot of other questions, but answered very little. I did not blame her much. She was in a terrible state. The only things answered were her name and age her name is Torona, and she is barely ten cycles old. And she said that at one point in time she was a corsair, though she gave it up over four cycles ago. She did not say why, though she seems frightened. We gave her a room by my study, and she strung up a hammock she had been carrying with a spare set of ragged clothing. She had absolutely no decent weapons save for a rusty sickle knife. I have never seen a sickle knife, and I never will. But, this corsair, Torona, she described it all to me. I hope that one day, she will be my eyes. I have had none since my accident with the warrior mouse.

Here, Fang stopped reading and gaped at Knife. "Did I read that right?"

"I think you must have," replied Knife in disbelief, flabbergasted at this news.

"Did you know Scythe was blind?" demanded Fang.

"No. Read on," ordered Knife.

Fang scanned the page. "Huh, for four days all she wrote about was Hemlock … though, that was when he was made an official oracle. Oh, here we go—Torona."

I saw Torona again today. I confess I have become fond of her. We did not sit in my dusty study. We took a walk in the woods. Torona is young and strong, but I could feel her terrible stress. My young friend has led a hard life, short though it still is. She has told me about why she deserted her ship, but nothing else, save that her father was a land-dweller (she used the phrase "landlubber") and her mother a corsair on a vessel known as the Sea Monster.

"Wow!" exclaimed Fang. "She even got the ship-script right. And she was blind!"

"Keep reading!" snapped Knife.

"Her mother was not a kind one. She sometimes beat Torona when she was either too loud or if Torona asked questions. Torona told me that her mother was slain by a poisoned arrow when Torona was two cycles old. Torona had no bitterness to the creature that had done it. She said merely an hour later, the *Sea Monster* was taken over by strange creatures. The word "Ranger" has crossed my path now and again. I sometimes wonder if the black mouse that blinded me was a Ranger. Torona told me that the Ranger leader, Lord Condor, took over this ship because his daughter, Raven, had been captured. He had taken over another ship, called the *Wave Hawk*, and renamed it *Deathwind*.

Torona told me that Demmons, one of the corsair crew-foxes, avoided death by hiding up on the rigging. He had snatched her and held her up there. She had been gagged, so she could say nothing. When three of the Rangers shinnied up the mast to loose the sails and sail away, Demmons slew one of them, knocked another into the sea where Torona lost sight of him, and then flung himself with her into the sea. After several hours, both of them were picked up by another vessel. Demmons secretly slew the vessel captain and claimed captaincy. He named the ship *Waveslayer*. Torona, from two cycles old, was forced to serve the vile captain. Then, when she was roughly seven cycles old, she found her chance, and she took it. She deserted her ship. She'd heard her father left his home by the sea and had moved this direction, so she made for here. That was where we discovered her.

I, in turn, told her my story—how I was blinded. I would have told her something else, but she had already noticed my blindness. I was used to it, but I did not expect others to realize it. Yet Torona seems to notice everything. She was my eyes today. I told her how the black warrior mouse had ruined my eyesight with his arrow. Torona seemed amazed by this tale.

"That was the Lord of the Rangers!" she exclaimed. "His arrows are poisoned! He must not have been using his poisoned arrows."

Now, remembering what a single arrow did to Torona's mother, I am grateful instead of resentful.

I know no more of Torona, save that she has both sharp eyes and a sharp mind. I will keep my eye on her.

"Why did you stop?" Knife asked.

"Because it stops talking about Torona. Except for this bit though—oh, ha, ha, get this:

> Today, I was given an apprentice. Her name is Knife. I must admit, she seems clever, but I rather wish that Torona would be my apprentice. She has shown an interest in being an oracle, and she is much cleverer.

Hahahahahaha!"

"Oh, very funny," snapped Knife, her temper rising. "Read on."

"There is nothing else about Torona," shrugged Fang, riffling through the parchment. "Oh wait, yes, there is! Here …"

> My cycles are running. I am weary, weary beyond all belief. My friend, Torona, is growing. She is no longer the scared, sad, weary child who came to us so long ago. She is grown and strong. I do not fear for her for, when I am gone, she will survive here. She has been given a new name and has told me many secrets that I will not record here. Save I will say this: Torona has adorned her room. There is wood paneling where once was cold stone. She had painted scenes of a corsair on the wood, with old corsair sayings as well, and ballads and any number of things from the sea. She has described them all to me, so I will describe two of them. One of them is a picture of a black, ancient ferret with amber eyes. It is female and, therefore, more ferocious. Her name is Rushakk and has faced Lord Condor's daughter, Raven, who will be Lady Raven, now. Rushakk's name in the script Torona used is thus:
>
> Τηε Ρυσηακκ
>
> Another is of the two sea serpents, Sidon and Syra, brother and sister, who range the seas now and will guard the sea that separates the Serpent's land from Cerecinthia, land of the Bear King. They are ancient, more ancient than Rushakk. They are all that is left since the Morning of Time and yet are the first warning of the Night of Time. The inscription beneath them is thus:
>
> Σιδον ανδ Σψρα
>
> Alas! My cycles have finally run. I am tired, yet I feel as one who is going to rest.

Why did I write of what Torona did? Because, when these are read, none will be alive who truly remember the corsair Torona, only the Blight-stricken fox she seems to be now. Yet she is not. There is still much of the sea in her heart, and I sincerely hope that she will return to the sea and leave this terrible place. When I am dead, none will be alive who truly remember her. My friend is safe.

I, Scythe the Oracle and Recorder of Darkwoods, have written all these records with my own paw. I can write no more.

Knife repeated one of the lines. "None will be alive who truly remember … But she was wrong. Cutthroat lives. I wonder who Torona is now?"

"Well, there is …," began Fang cautiously. "I mean … these inscriptions are the same as on the wall in …"

Both foxes looked at each other, and then shrugged.

"Impossible."

Knife suddenly whipped around at Fang. "You ordered Cutthroat to go attend Hemlock," she said. "What was that about?"

"Oh, simple," grinned Fang suddenly. "Our plan is working. Hemlock has gone insane."

Night fell on the great Miamuran plains. Galledor watched as the messenger ran up to his tent, panting heavily. Kiarna and Danaray were bent over the starry map, Kiarna explaining the finer details of the plan.

The messenger was a river otter who limped in her left paw. Around her neck was a chain with a star pendant. She was employed in the service of King Hokadra.

"Hello, Arpaha," Galledor greeted her.

"Prince Galledor," she panted. "I came as soon as your message arrived. What's wrong?"

"What all do you know of Queen Demeda's schemes?"

Arpaha blinked in surprise. "Schemes? What do you mean?"

"I mean, where have you been since you left the Wraith Mice army?"

Arpaha winced. "I didn't have much choice," she muttered nervously. "River otters aren't meant to be cooped up. We fight with the water and the forest. We—"

"That's not the point," Galledor interrupted. "I mean, what have you *seen*?"

Arpaha shook her head, bewildered. "Nothing. I don't know what you mean."

Galledor nodded, convinced. "Here is what I need you to do. Go towards Pasadagavra with your tribe. Doomspear will meet you on your way."

"Doomspear?" Arpaha protested. "He and I were never on good—"

"He will explain to you what you need to do," Galledor went on. "It's crucial that you listen to him. And this time, you cannot run off. It's vital that you stay there."

"And get my tribe killed?" Arpaha inquired. "You know that this war hardly affects my tribe. We live wild in the woods, and it doesn't bother us who sits on some distant throne. Why should we get killed in a war not ours—for nothing?"

Galledor could have met any price she named, but he merely shook his head coolly. "Shame on you, Arpaha. You sound just like the sea otters."

Arpaha blinked and recoiled. "I'm sorry, but you expect me suddenly to befriend someone I've been an enemy with and risk my entire tribe without telling me *anything*? Really, prince of Miamur?"

Danaray stepped forward and said very calmly, "If that isn't war, then what is?"

Arpaha eyed Danaray curiously. "I heard your father had died. I'm sorry. But you should learn caution, young chief. That was your father's gift."

"Actually, my father was a part of all this as well," Danaray replied, resting her paw on the map. She tilted her head back proudly. "He was a large part of it."

Arpaha sighed. "I respect his courage. But honestly, my tribe has thirty fit warriors. What good am I supposed to do?"

Galledor reached into his pocket. "Doomspear will tell you that ..." Out of his pocket, he drew a distinct seal shaped like a sword. "When you meet him at Pasadagavra ..."

At the sight of the sword-seal, Arpaha's eyes grew wide. "You could have said so before," she muttered sullenly, "instead of making me look like a sea otter. I'll be there."

After she left, Danaray sighed and tapped her knife. "I can't believe Arpaha was so reluctant," she admitted.

"She just wanted proof that the orders came from King Hokadra. She owes her loyalty to him, not me. Hence this." Galledor turned the sword-seal over in his paw.

"What is that?"

Kiarna answered. "It's King Hokadra's seal."

14 The Rescue

Biddah found herself shaking in the cold. She had been captured by the foxes, though, thankfully, not slain. Not yet, anyway. She hoped Karrum was okay—*oh, Bear King, please let him be alive and all right!*

She sat shivering in the cold—the Great Fire on this side of the gates had gone out—with a baby mouse called Nathan'el asleep on her lap. Both his parents had been slain, though he had miraculously survived. Biddah had taken it upon herself to care for him. He was barely two cycles old. He lay, curled on her lap, his dark brown eyes staring into hers as he tried to sleep. Biddah sang softly to him, cradling him in her lap. He was hungry, but Biddah could do nothing to help him. Seven days after their capture, and the foxes had merely brought soup and water—just enough for about two days. Biddah had taken only enough water for herself to survive, with the odd gulp for the unborn babe she carried. Nathan'el had once drunk his fill thirstily, but now, he seemed to have gone into a helpless melancholy. He cried for his parents, and Biddah had not yet had the heart to tell him that they were dead.

The two of them were kept in an isolated room. Biddah longed for contact with some other creature, but she kept the lights out when she could have lit them as there were more than enough fire-makings in the room. She hoped the foxes might think this room deserted.

Suddenly, before Biddah had time to hide, the door swung open. A stern-faced ferret stood outlined in the door.

"Come yeh wi' me," the ferret ordered.

Biddah stood up, trembling.

"Och, hurry oop, Ah'm no' goin' tae 'urt yeh oehr the babe."

Biddah followed the ferret from the room.

"Lassie, yeh're in nae dangehr; just stay wi' me."

Biddah rushed in the wake of the strong-boned, swift-pawed ferret. The ferret seemed to be taking her to another room, a room along a deserted corridor. She stopped rather abruptly outside a rather plain door. "In 'ere," the ferret ordered. She pulled the door open.

Biddah stumbled in. To her surprise, this room had a bed, a comfortable couch, a table, five lit lanterns, and a door at its other side.

"Go on in; I'll be back soon with food fer yeh," the ferret promised. She turned and left, locking the door behind.

There was something about the lit lamps, the polished mirror on the wall, which intrigued Biddah. This room had been previously made up.

"You all right, maiden?"

Biddah jumped. She hadn't expected another occupant. But now she looked, there was a dark figure, standing by the extra door. It had spoken in a deep, guttery, rasp of a voice. It wore a cloak as dusty pink as the stone behind it, so Biddah found herself squinting to see it.

"Sit down," said the cloaked figure, indicating the couch. "Don't worry, I won't hurt you."

Biddah sat, with Nathan'el still on her lap.

The figure swept off its hood. Bright blue eyes that smiled kindly at her rested first on Biddah, then on Nayn. Biddah guessed that this strange creature was some sort of otter, though she had never seen an otter quite like this one before.

"My name is Xar," added the strange figure. "I, as well as my sister, Sone, am friend to the Rangers. We live in the far north, on an island. I came south with Cinder when he returned from the burial of Lady Raven. Now, realizing the position, a plan is in action to rescue you and bring you away from the foxes."

"So we're heading toward the city?" Biddah asked, clutching a sleeping Nayn hopefully.

"That is essentially it." Xar tipped his head to one side. "The guards are bringing Aspen and Rainbow. Swiftly, get under the bed. Don't make a noise."

Biddah ducked under with her sleeping bundle just as the door was flung open. There came a sound of stumbling footsteps, of swishing whips, and a single agonized groan.

"Stay in theres, till yer mates git ye out!" shouted the harsh voice of Demmons.

The door slammed shut. Biddah peeped out from under the bed. There were no foxes, only four more footpaws of Aspen and Rainbow. She slid awkwardly out from under the bed, heart hammering.

Aspen and Rainbow were unrecognizable. Most of the fur had been ripped off Aspen's face, and his face was bloody, as was his tunic. Rainbow's face was pale gray with mere flecks of black standing out, like charcoal among ashes. Her amber eyes stood out jarringly, and already she was looking thin. Two or three of her wounds were still bleeding badly, and she winced with every movement. Yet she managed a smile for Biddah.

"Well, Fotirra managed it, I see. You'll be getting away soon, friend. Xar, did you manage the others?" she grimaced.

The snowy-white otter materialized from the stone wall. "Yes, I did. Now it's only you lot that have to get away." His voice still had a rasp to it.

Rainbow eased herself gently down on the sofa, wincing all the same. "Well, you'd better get away fast. The guards are still out there."

"Right," rasped Xar. "I'll come back for you in a bit."

Aspen and Rainbow exchanged looks. Aspen sat down beside Rainbow. "Um, well … we've been talking it over, and, well, there's no point in rescuing us. The minute *we* disappear, the foxes will go searching for the rest of their captives. Then you'll never be able to get them away."

"You mean, just leave you here?"

Rainbow shrugged. "Don't see much choice. We're too badly hurt to make the climb anyway."

"She's right," Aspen murmured. "We could never make it without reopening our wounds and bleeding to death."

"But they'll kill you."

Xar's ominous statement set Biddah trembling. She wanted more than anything to say, "You must come!" but she could not muster the words. The thought that anyone would suggest simply forgetting them, letting them die, was horrific to Biddah. True, she had seen courage when defending her land against the foxes before their major conquest, but she had never seen half as much courage as in Rainbow and Aspen. That they were willing to die, helpless, even with their friends abandoning them to it, was extraordinary to Biddah.

Xar held their gazes and finally sighed wearily. "Very well. Friend squirrel, we must hurry."

Biddah followed him to the other door, but not before casting a last, incredulous glance at Rainbow and Aspen. Rainbow nodded and Aspen smiled, and Biddah turned her head and did not once look back. Her heart hammered.

The second room was slightly smaller, but Biddah did not take in her surroundings. She clutched Nayn to her, wondering, to take her mind off the two brave Rangers, who would adopt Nayn. *She* hardly could—she was a squirrel, and Nathan'el was a mouse.

There was a single window in the room. Xar slipped through it and perched on the sill; Biddah climbed up rather clumsily. She was amazed to find herself just above a dip in the walls that was padded with earth. Gingerly, she slid down and landed on the earth that many winds had blown there over the cycles. Yet, it was not the sod that Biddah was used to; it was more like sand, and it scattered as she landed on it, though it was soft and warm, even with the early autumn air beginning to turn nippy.

Xar slid down behind her, as there was a crash from within. "Great snow mounds," he panted. "The guards came back in already. Good thing I closed the door!"

There were loud shouts coming from within. As Biddah listened, she gazed over the walls at the field. What she saw there nearly made her heart stop.

"Look, what are they doing?" she breathed to Xar.

Xar stared in puzzlement. In the field below, there were foxes scurrying back and forth, bringing rocks, wood, and oil. The rocks were being piled into something like a flat pedestal, and the wood lay beside it. Oil was dousing both the wood and the rocks. As Biddah watched , there was a *whump* beside her, and she jumped.

A strange figure had landed between herself and Xar. Biddah had, admittedly, not seen very many strange things, with the exception of Ice. But this was ridiculous. The figure had long, shaggy, white, coarse fur and wore what looked like a dress of something slick and strong and was decorated with what Biddah forced herself to think was wood carved into shapes of claws and teeth.

Without turning, it addressed Xar in a strange tongue. Xar did not react to its news, though he turned to Biddah. "This is my sister, Sone," he explained, tipping his head to Sone. "She brings news. The guards promised Snowgoose ten days to decide whether or not to surrender all the Rangers. At the end of the ten days, Rainbow and Aspen would be killed. Now, after seven days, they have taken Rainbow and Aspen, and said that if Snowgoose did not come out immediately, they would be killed. I think they found their prisoners were escaping. Naturally, Snowgoose refused. So, it seems that they will kill Rainbow and Aspen now."

Biddah gasped. “It would not be safe for you to go up yet, friend,” Sone added, with even more of a rasp than her brother. “Not until dark.”

Xar shrugged. “No—it’s more dangerous for her to stay here—someone could see her up here.” He turned to Biddah. “You must climb up. Sone, did you get the others up?”

“*Nahnim*. There are too many guards milling about—we’d be seen.”

“Friend,” murmured Xar to Biddah, “you’d best climb up as swiftly as you can. There are others above a few levels—climb to them with all speed. Tell them—the others we have not managed to help get to the city—that we’ll get them to safety come moonhigh. Go!”

Without question or comment, Biddah tied Nayn to her shoulder, turned around, and began to climb the wall of Pasadagavra.

At first, it was not hard to climb as there were plenty of pawholds. Then there came a stretch where the pawholds got narrow and shallow, and Biddah chanced to look down.

She should not have done that. The drop behind her was huge and dizzying. She could see no foxes—they must be inside the city. She remembered the cliff in the cave, remembered groping for the pawholds in the dark for nine days. This was worse. Much, much worse. She hadn’t eaten much in the last seven days, which affected her strength. And there were no earthworms to help here. Just a dizzying drop and others waiting for her up somewhere above where she could not see them.

After about an hour, at a place that she thought was only stone, a dark brown, comical face appeared. Biddah was so startled she almost let go. A shot of fear went through her.

“Asuresuresure, youhaven trouble? Letme helpyou.”

Biddah stared in disbelief at the face that was grinning at her from above. “Who are you?”

“Menamed Texat,” shrugged the figure. “Letme helpyou,” Texat repeated.

Could she trust this strange creature? She wasn’t sure, but she was very tired and Nathan’el was getting heavier by the minute—she could use some help. Deciding she would risk it, Biddah gingerly lifted one of her paws and held it up. Texat, to her amazement, scrambled down the sheer wall without bothering with the pawholds, and snatched her paw. Half dragging her up, he clambered back up a couple of paces.

“Great Sesitha, Texat, begentle!”

A second face, almost exactly like Texat’s, popped from in between the stone. The owner of this face proved to be another of whatever species it was, the same as Texat. Somehow, Biddah deduced that this one was a female.

Lightly, she crawled down the wall until she reached Biddah. Her touch was gentle, and her gaze reproachful as she looked at Texat.

"Comecome, maiden. Texat, gofind outwhatis happening!"

Without a word, Texat bounded away on the wall.

"Myname Skettle, Iare Texat's sisser. Comecomeyou. Fourothers waitforyou."

"Four others?"

Skettle's paw was gentle, and she guided Biddah slowly up the wall to the dip in the outer shell. "Guardsare moving, nottime for'scape. Wewait till nightshades."

"Nightshades?"

"Youcall midnight," shrugged Skettle. "Newmoon tonight."

Skettle was infinitely careful, especially for Nayn, but she kept a cheery smile on her face and a careless stance on her body.

"Soso, youlastone? DidXar sayso? WhereisSone?"

It took Biddah a moment to translate the questions.

"Yes, I am the last one. Xar said so. And Sone is watching … What is going on?"

By this point, they had reached the top of the level, and another dip lay in front of Biddah. It, too, was filled with sand, and four creatures sat in the crevice—two squirrels, the Wraith Mouse runner Muryda, and Jaccah's daughter, Shaynnah. She was curled up by herself, trembling with either cold or fear, and her eyes were wide. Biddah pitied her, but did not go over to her because, at that moment, Texat bounded down.

"Badnews, badnews!" he chattered. "RainbowAspen, foxeschange-mind, burnthem, nownow!"

Biddah barely understood, Texat was talking so fast, but she guessed enough by the urgency in his voice, and she suddenly comprehended the piling up of wood and stone.

"Looklook!" cried Skettle.

A mass of foxes and ferrets (entirely corsairs, Biddah noted) were exiting the main gate, dragging Aspen and Rainbow along with them. There were cries from below, as though Rainbow and Aspen were putting up a very good fight, though there was little they could do to free themselves.

Four ferrets dragged a white shape between them. Pulling and fighting, they dragged Aspen to the wood. A fifth ferret dropped a torch on the wood, and it flared up so fast that Biddah was dazzled. A white shape fell on the blaze.

But the scream that reached Biddah's ears was not that of a mouse but … a ferret!

"Good shot, Tsanna!"

Zuryzel crouched in the undergrowth, watching as Grayik, Tsanna, and Skorlaid rapidly picked off the unsuspecting ferrets attempting to thrust Aspen and Rainbow into the fire.

Grayik turned to Tsanna. "Ah, that was a good shot, but keep yar peepers on this 'un!"

He took skillful aim and shot the ferret that was presently trying to shove Aspen into the fire. He, too, collapsed, and his body went up in flames.

"Nice shot," grinned Tsanna, blinking flirtatiously at Grayik, who gazed away and smiled. Tsanna rolled her eyes in amusement.

"Yah, that's all very well," retorted Skorlaid mockingly. "But watch this one!"

He, too, took careful aim and slew a third ferret. Aspen managed to break free and desperately darted toward the three foxes holding Rainbow down. Tsanna snatched up another crossbow bolt and fired at one of them, and Aspen wrenched Rainbow away from the other two and half tugged, half supported her along the uneven ground as Skorlaid finished off the two foxes in quick succession.

Tsanna turned her playful flirting on Skorlaid, though she seemed to keep half an eye on the approaching Rangers. "That was fast firing, Skorlaid. You sure have a quick paw with a crossbow."

Skorlaid gazed down at the ground as Rainbow and Aspen hit the scant foliage about the pine trees. The foxes were trying to find where the attack was coming from, but it was utter chaos around the fire, and so far, they had not been able to attack in return.

Aspen panted heavily as they reached the snipers, grinning lopsidedly at Zuryzel. "Might've known it would be you, Zuryzel. Good timing!"

"Good timing nothing, we've been watching this place for two days, trying to figure out how the foxes made it into Pasadagavra. But let's get back to camp first; then we can talk! Grayik, stay here, and keep them from burning anyone else."

Several days ago, Tsanna had spent hours making a barely visible pathway of soft, almost rotten pine needles. Paws made no imprint on the pathway, and by now, the corsairs were learned enough in woodland ways not to leave marks, even though most of them kept up a bitter stream of complaints about being so far from the sea.

The two Rangers stumbled along on terribly wounded paws and legs, and Aspen's tunic was stiff with dried blood, while Rainbow's fur was almost pure white, she had lost so much blood. Yet they kept on running, their eyes bright as stars, their lips bit, their paws stumbling. Zuryzel felt wretched pity for them and sheer admiration for their courage. She stubbornly grabbed Rainbow's paw and wrapped it around her shoulders to support the injured Ranger. Skorlaid did the same with Aspen.

Zuryzel had long since moved the camp to a sheltered clearing in the woods. This was much more convenient for the frequent scouting missions she constantly went on and much more sheltered than the grassy knoll just east of Pasadagavra—not to mention well out of sight of the Ashlands. Not that they were a danger; they were just disturbing.

As the small group neared the camp, Rainbow and Aspen panting hard, they heard an outbreak of painful squealing. In the blink of an eye, Zuryzel had drawn her sword.

"Who's there?" she called out threateningly.

"Zuryzel?"

Out from behind a tree emerged a shockingly familiar figure.

"Arpaha?"

Arpaha, the river otter, stepped out in plain view. Her tribe had once been part of King Hokadra's army and was technically still in his service. She was holding a ferret by the ear.

"Leggoo'me, yowyow!"

As Arpaha drew nearer, Zuryzel recognized the ferret as one in her company.

"You can let her go," she advised the river otter swiftly.

Arpaha removed her swimming claws from the ferret's ear without hesitation. "We saw Ailur and the others. I recognized several of them, but I wasn't sure this one was a friend," she explained.

"Who's 'we'?" Zuryzel asked, tipping her head to one side.

"Doomspear and me and our crews." Arpaha blinked. She had caught sight of Rainbow and Aspen. "Great Cerecinthia, what happened to you two?"

Aspen shrugged. "Long story."

"We'd best make ourselves scarce," suggested Tsanna. She had been listening hard. "Someone's coming after us."

Without further words, they continued on the pathway toward the camp.

15 The Stump

Sibyna sat hunched in a corner of a large chamber in the city of Pasadagavra. She had survived the battle with only one shallow slash across the shoulder. Many of the Wraith Mice were not so lucky. Karena nearly lost her eyes and had ugly-looking wounds on her face. Dikiner's back had been slashed by a saber, and now he seemed to not be sitting easily. Sibyna's brother, Dejuday, had lost an ear. Johajar had taken an arrow through his side, though fortunately, it did not seem to have hit any vital organ.

The door to the chamber opened, and in hurried three warriors. The first was Shinar, the river otter, her muddy brown eyes dull, limping painfully. The second was Muryda—Texat and Skettle had plainly managed to pull of the escape for the last remaining prisoners—and the third, Dejuday.

Shinar collapsed beside Dikiner, massaging her left footpaw, and Muryda sought out some of her friends. Sibyna gazed hopefully into her brother's face as he sat down beside her.

"I'm sorry, Sibyna. I didn't find him."

Sibyna could not prevent a tear from gliding down her cheek. Orgorad, her mate, had been one of the many who remained missing.

For days, the Wraith Mice had been trying to find all their friends, whether alive or dead, but many remained unaccounted for. Eventually, Hokadra had ordered all of them to this chamber, hoping then to account for everyone. But the method was not working. Over a hundred had remained undiscovered—thankfully, though, Muryda was no longer missing.

Sibyna could not see how Orgorad could still be alive. If he had been, she would have seen him or heard about him before this—nearly eight sunsets after the battle.

Her brain was numb with grief. She could not think. She hardly registered her brother, massaging her shoulder gently, looking as though trying to say words of comfort but coming up with nothing to say.

Sibyna suddenly became aware of another pair of eyes watching her. Blinking away her tears, she recognized Dikiner, his gaze traveling between her and Karena. She sighed, sparing a moment to be grateful that she had a caring brother and a loyal friend. Even through his anxiety about Karena (she'd been missing for several days), Dikiner had always had time to ask Sibyna if she had found Orgorad or give her suggestions where to look. And Dejuday had always helped Sibyna look for Orgorad.

The chamber door opened again, and Queen Demeda hastened in, her black eyes searching frantically, until they found her two sons, Mokimshim and Johajar.

Sibyna missed their sister, Zuryzel, very much.

"I wish she were here," she said aloud.

"Who?" Dejuday asked.

"Zuryzel," Sibyna shrugged. "I miss her. But I suppose there was nowhere else she would have wanted to ...," she trailed off.

Dejuday felt an attack of guilt, the same way he did every time his sister mentioned her missing friend. "There's no proof Zuryzel's dead," he pointed out awkwardly, trying hard to block out his last memory of the princess.

Sibyna gave him a long, thoughtful look. "Are you trying to convince me or yourself?" she challenged softly.

Now Dejuday inwardly cursed her sharpness. "There is no proof she's dead. She could very easily have been isolated from the tunnels and be in the forest right now, watching for an opportunity to get inside."

Sibyna lay her head on her brother's shoulder. "If you want to believe that, then believe that. I want to, too, but I'm too tired to convince myself of it."

"Dear sister," Dejuday smiled. "It'll be all right."

"I miss them," Sibyna repeated, in that sentence lamenting her mate and all her friends who had died in the war.

Dejuday watched as his sister finally fell asleep. It had been so hard for him to come up with the story of Zuryzel waiting in the woods when playing in his mind's eye was his memory of Zuryzel beginning a journey west across a completely gray land. He prayed desperately to the Bear King that his princess—and several-times savior—was safe.

Zuryzel sipped at a beaker of warmed spiced wine and sat down opposite Doomspear.

"You said you had some interesting news. I'd like to hear it."

Doomspear gazed at her through light brown eyes in a heavily scarred face. In one calloused paw, he held a cup of wine; in his other rested his spear. He was muscularly built, and nearly a head taller than Zuryzel. He reported to her in a deep, strong voice:

"Streamcourse and I were watching the sea otters in Crustacean's clan for some time, I forget how long. Anyway, at the beginning of last spring, Kite, one of the older warriors, captured a river otter maiden, name of Anamay, sister of Danaray. You know her?"

Zuryzel nodded and Doomspear continued. "Well, after a week or so, Nighthawk attacked the camp. Anamay's ankles were wrenched, so she was just sitting in front of one of the tents, her knife held ready. She saw Nighthawk and slew him. I don't blame her to be honest, but don't tell Streamcourse I said that."

Zuryzel nodded with understanding. Nighthawk was, after all, Streamcourse's brother.

"Anyway, Crustacean took her into his clan, as a way of thanks, if you will. Do you know, she's got a mate in that clan now?"

Zuryzel shrugged. If a river otter princess chose to take a mate from the sea otters, that was that; she was free to make her own choices. The river otters would consider it as the offense of all time, however, so she tried not to show her indifference to Doomspear as she inquired, "Anything else?"

"Yes," replied Doomspear. He lowered his voice. "Streamcourse and I ran into Moonpath a few hours after Nighthawk's attack. She veered off to the east to keep her eye on the castle. Once she heard about the corsairs, she shot off west again, but Streamcourse and I were already headed north. She kept her eyes on the sea otters again, and she discovered …" His voice trailed off. When he spoke again, his voice was so low Zuryzel could barely hear it.

"Some of the sea otters, including Crustacean, Current, and that jerk Driftwood, have allied themselves to the foxes."

This news was no news to Zuryzel. Time had shown her the scene in which Current had offered to send all his prisoners to the foxes.

She sat there for a moment, mulling it over, thinking. Then a new idea hit her.

"Why didn't you attack them?"

Doomspear shrugged. "Because those sea otters may be soft and overblown idiots for the most part, but there are a few who aren't so bad. And besides that, there were a lot of them. It wasn't worth the risk."

That makes sense. She gazed thoughtfully into her cup of wine.

One of the two healers in the crew of *Justice* hastened up to the tiny fire where Zuryzel sat. "Princess, yeh wanted t' know when Aspen or Rainbow'd be ready t' talk t' yeh. Aspen is in good 'nough shape, but yeh'd have t' make yer questions limited."

"Right. Thank you," Zuryzel answered her, dipping her head politely.

She gave Doomspear a respectful nod and rose, following the healer.

Aspen sat at one of the few large fires. He wore a clean tunic (it fit him a little oddly, as it had been made for an otter) and was wrapped in a blanket sipping a foul-smelling concoction that the healer had made up of seaweed, saltwater, and some sort of dried and powered shellfish.

Bear King save him from corsair remedies, Zuryzel thought with an inward grimace.

He looked up as Zuryzel approached.

"You want to know how the foxes got into Pasadagavra." His voice carried no question.

"I would like to know," she replied calmly, "how they broke into Pasadagavra."

Aspen gazed up at her. "They did not break in. You know of the many tunnels that leave the place? Somehow, they found one of them and used it to invade. They came up between the fortress and the city gates.

"How many died?"

"Not as many as you'd think, but it was bad enough. Tribeking Fuddum died, as did Argoss, Jaccah's mate. She is now Tribequeen. Tribequeen Sharmmuh also fell. None of the Wind Tribe survived. Most of the Wraith Mice did, though," he added, seeing her face. "King Hokadra, Queen Demeda, Mokimshim, Johajar. I saw that Sibyna, Muryda, Harclayang, Dikiner, and Dejuday survived. I do not know who else died or lived."

"How many were wounded?" Zuryzel pressed on, trying to ignore that Aspen had no information about Karena, Shinar, Karrum, or Biddah.

"Just about all of the ones who survived. None escaped wounds—not even those not yet grown."

Zuryzel was stunned, but she tried not to show it.

"Did the foxes find Sage?" she added, suddenly alarmed at what that would mean. Sage was a runaway Oracle's apprentice. She had abandoned the foxes and would be given a traitor's punishment if she were captured by them.

Aspen, to Zuryzel's relief, shook his head. "They did not. If they had, it would have gone much worse."

Zuryzel did not doubt that. But what did alarm her was that the foxes and their corsair friends could batter down the door into the city of Pasadagavra. With the inhabitants so wounded and decimated, it would be easier to conquer the city. Somehow, Zuryzel had to get aid to them fast.

"Aspen, would it be possible to climb the mountain and join them from there?" she queried.

Aspen shook his head. "When Cinder and his helpers returned, there was little wind. Two days ago, there was plenty of wind around the mountain, and there was an avalanche. I don't think it would possible to climb it now."

The only other ways Zuryzel knew of were the gates and the tunnels. The gates were obviously not options, and the entrance to the tunnels were days away in Darkwoods-held Dombre. There was no other available way in, unless ...

"Could we try to take on the foxes?"

"I doubt it. They're sheltering in Pasadagavra's fortress—it is autumn, and before too terribly long, it'll be winter—and besides, they don't want to be susceptible to attack."

That made too much sense for Zuryzel's liking. She gazed questioningly at Aspen.

"Rainbow heard them talking about it," he explained.

"You said they got in through a tunnel. Would it be possible to find that tunnel and break in that way?"

"Probably not. It's the same tunnel that led from Dombre, you know. The tunnel entrance is very wide—I saw it myself—but Demmons will have about two score corsairs guarding it. I heard him bellowing the orders."

Zuryzel sat there, gazing down, thinking. But she could think of only one option.

"Then we've got to get them to our own battlefield."

A rumor spread around the Wraith Mice, brought to them by the river otter Shinar. Aspen and Rainbow had escaped, aided by arrows coming from the woods.

"I saw it!" Shinar insisted. "The corsairs trying to kill them all fell down dead! It must have been arrows. Perhaps it's Arpaha! She must still be honoring her bond with King Hokadra."

Any and all Wraith Mice demanded to know exactly what she had seen, some even shaking her for news. She only repeated that she thought it was Arpaha, which drove her comrades crazy.

Dejuday turned away from the ring of excited faces, pressing for more potential news of their former comrade. He didn't recall any archers in Arpaha's band of otters. They might have picked up bows at one point, but the bonfire had been so far away from the trees! Most bows couldn't shoot that far, much less hit targets from that distance.

But crossbows could.

It might be Zuryzel. It just might be. Pirates, mercenaries maybe, would have come with her, and they would have crossbows. He prayed once more for her safety, and prayed also that they hadn't come too late.

Then he added one more request to the Bear King.

16 The Plea

Claw sat calmly beside a fine oak tree, munching away at a clump of strawberries. For the first time since Knife had left him in charge, he felt as if he truly was in charge. Demmons had come up with the idea of the surprise parley, but he hadn't seemed to mind Claw being in charge, and he had been strangely cooperative. Yet the corsairs had been unimportant altogether in the whole thing. They had done absolutely nothing to help conquer Pasadagavra, but he had managed to order their crews to do guard, and Fotirra had even submitted to doing guard duty herself. Jironi had kept well out of his way, and even Redseg had not given him any snide remarks.

The three ferrets had always rankled him, as though they were sticking his pelt with pine needles. The whole Pasadagavra situation hadn't changed that.

Poison trotted up beside the oak tree and dipped her head to him. Claw felt enormous satisfaction as he queried, "You want something?"

Poison stood in front of him, though she threw him one of her coyest smiles. "Claw," she said politely, "Pasadagavra was well captured. But there is more territory to the north, and surely some of the enemy live there. I would, with your permission take four hundred of our own, no corsairs, to root out whoever lives up there." She blinked flirtatiously at him.

Poison's beautiful face began to have its usual influence on him. Claw fought desperately against the helplessness Poison engendered in him, but he felt himself giving in. "Very well. Take six hundred, just for extra measure," he head himself say.

Poison nodded. Claw knew what was happening, but he couldn't stop it. Poison smirked and left.

In that moment, Claw realized that Ice was really gone and she was not coming back. If she were, she would have been back by now, and Poison would have been the first to know, and Claw the next. Ice would have stepped in to report to Poison, to tell her coldly that she would not be going anywhere.

On the other hand, she would have been in charge of the army.

Claw sighed. If only he could have stood up to Poison's plea.

The day was waning for the third time after Rainbow and Aspen had escaped. Zuryzel was out scouting by herself. She had scarcely slept for the past three days and spent all night out scouting. The Wraith Mouse magic of becoming invisible in the dark made them particularly useful for night scouting—Zuryzel knew that, but she still didn't like night scout assignments.

Doomspear and Arpaha with their tribes had been welcome additions to those Zuryzel had gathered. It meant that the corsairs, those so skilled and at ease on rolling ships and sandy shores but so clumsy in the forest, no longer went on scouting trips. Doomspear had sent five otters after Moonpath. Streamcourse would have to continue looking for Crow, as her tribe was most accustomed to tracking. Zuryzel had hardly a moment off her paws, from watching the mountain behind Pasadagavra at night to spending hours on end debating about the next action they would take. She had long since discovered that most corsairs had a fondness, reaching a passion, for arguing, or, as Doomspear scornfully described it, "the stating of opinions."

The night scouting hadn't been fun. Zuryzel hated crouching in scanty bracken, keeping her eye on the entrance to the city on the peak of the mountain, and glancing at the main gates from time to time. It was cold work, even though the nights were getting shorter and noticeably warmer. And, to cap it off, mist constantly swirled around the peak, making visibility almost nil. In the late hours of the night, Zuryzel often thought she saw creatures on the mountain, struggling around the sheer cliffs and rocky crags. Once or twice, she thought she saw a gigantic mound of white fur not too far away from her, but when she blinked it was gone, and when she went to check the place, there was no print or sign that the snow had been disturbed. Just a couple of snow mounds all around her. On one occasion,

Zuryzel half thought that she saw the shape of a black bird. But she blinked again, and the illusion was gone again.

The wind was blowing strongly tonight, and it cut through her fur. She shivered like a baby out in the snow. For a moment, she melded her body into her wraith-like condition, and it let the wind pass through her, but it only made her colder.

Suddenly, Zuryzel saw a pale shape flitting through the trees. She tensed. The fur was pale, like a squirrel's, but a squirrel would be in the trees. Was it a ferret?

Without thinking more, she drew her knife and set off after the pale figure. When she was right behind it, she knelt down. She was utterly silent and had no touch in her body. She was a living wraith. In a heartbeat, she thrust her body out of her wraith-like state and wrapped her paws around the intruder's ankles.

The fox yelped as she twisted in the air and landed on her back. She pointed her shortspear up, but Zuryzel had backed out of range and had sheathed her knife.

"Fawn!" she gasped, holding out her paw. Fawn, like Sage, was a deserted Oracle's apprentice. But she had had a more … eventful time of getting away. She and Zuryzel had barely escaped capture by the foxes right in their vile castle. After they had crossed the moor to the Bow Tribe camp, King Hokadra, Zuryzel's father, had sent Fawn to parley with foxes in the south for help.

Fawn relaxed her tense body. "Princess Zuryzel. I've been tripped up before, but I must say, you're the most methodical."

"Sorry," Zuryzel apologized, helping Fawn up. "What are you doing here? I thought you were sent down south to—"

"They wouldn't come," said Fawn flatly.

"The sourthron foxes?"

"The very ones. They wouldn't come."

Zuryzel let out her breath. "Oh. That's … disappointing."

"Has Pasadagavra been captured?" Fawn demanded.

"Half of it," Zuryzel explained. She gave Fawn a quick rundown on everything that had happened since the vixen had gone south. Fawn didn't say a word through it all. Her eyes were no longer red, but brown, proof that she didn't have the Blight anymore.

"So," Fawn surmised at the end of the telling, "you have at least around three hundred corsairs with you?"

"Mm, yes."

"And they were all … just … at this tavern?" Fawn added skeptically.

Zuryzel nodded, but Fawn's words opened up a whole range of possibilities she hadn't considered before. Why *had* the corsairs all been there? The jetty had been bursting at the seams with all the ships, and the tavern was too packed for such a small, rundown town. There had been the right number. And the right ones. Just what Zuryzel had been hoping for. Was it pure chance that brought them all there at the right time? Or had someone … arranged it?

"Come on. I'll take you to the camp," Zuryzel told Fawn.

Fawn gave her a faint smile. "Thank you."

As they walked, Zuryzel let her mind wander. Who *had* arranged for all the corsairs to be there? Had it just been chance? No, it couldn't be, she realized, because there was one more important factor. There wasn't a single corsair there who would've been *against* Zuryzel.

She remembered other odd happenings. Grayik had been waiting for her on the course that was the most obvious one to take from Dombre to the sea, but how would he—or Ailur, for that matter—have known someone was coming to the sea for help? Kyka the river otter should have been at Pasadagavra ages ago if he lived alone, so why wasn't he? Ailur had been in that small town, but what was she doing in such a small town when she could have been in a place where her skills were needed? And that old fox in the tavern at Diray had known right away who she was, but *how*? Zuryzel wondered if her father had some paw in it, but Demeda had said Hokadra knew nothing of her sending Zuryzel to the coast. Was it her mother? But how could she have managed it without Hokadra knowing? Had the decision to send Zuryzel to the sea not been hers? Had someone persuaded her to make it?

Lady Raven?

Zuryzel remembered Lady Raven had referred to an old River Tribe squirrel as one of her friends. *One* of her friends. She must have had more—perhaps not in Oria. She had been traveling around, Zuryzel knew, in her youth. Had Lady Raven arranged all this?

Three nights later, Zuryzel crouched in the same spot she had been when she had found Fawn. A dark cloud hung over her mind. She couldn't get the thought of Lady Raven out of her head. Had it indeed been the Ranger who had arranged for all of her allies?

The faint moon climbed the sky as Zuryzel crouched in the undergrowth, shivering, quietly cursing the bitter wind that pierced through her fur. Usually she did not curse things, but all the same, it was freezing. The last rays of the sun lingered, perhaps reflecting on the sea, past the deciduous woods that covered the earth from Mirquis to Zurez, from Dombre to Graystone. The wind picked up, swirling strongly between the pines, whispering as if it were alive. It only made her colder.

Suddenly, the wind brought to her a strange voice, but one vaguely familiar, calling quietly out to many others. Strong, rippling quietly on the wind, calling out warnings to companions.

Silently, Zuryzel stood up, using all the magic guile of the Wraith Mice to blend in with the night, desperate not to be seen. She followed the voice, going against the powerful wind, yet letting the wind pass through her body, as though she truly were a wraith. Her paws made no impression, and her breath made no noise, yet she could hear the pounding of her own heart.

The closer she got, the louder the voice became, but the wind got quieter, until she could hear many voices when there was no wind at all.

Ah! She recognized them.

"You say there are *ferrets* inside Pasadagavra, Storm?"

"Yes, there are plenty of them." Zuryzel called quietly.

Lady Crow Blue Arrows, almost invisible in the night, whirled around to face Zuryzel with an arrow on her bowstring, but when she caught sight of the princess, she lowered her weapon and gazed disbelievingly at her. "Zuryzel!"

Zuryzel approached Crow, a small smile on her face. "Good timing. We were about to send out messengers looking for you!"

Crow shook her head, a smile on her face. "Owl," she called over her shoulder, "get the others and bring them back here *fast*." A dark brown she-warrior nodded once and slid off into the pine forest. Crow shook her head again. "Why are you outside the fortress, Zuryzel? And what happened?"

Zuryzel shrugged. "Long story. What about you, did you find that band of foxes?"

Crow nodded. "You found Danaray and Anamay, then?"

Zuryzel nodded in return. "What happened? Did the foxes not go very far south?"

Crow shook her head. "Nah, they just followed the Keron River. We caught up with some river otters—Wave and Rain. Do you know about them?"

"A little," acknowledged Zuryzel.

"We were about three miles north of Zurez when we literally ran into a band of sea otters. A little way further north, we ran into Moonpath and her crew—but we didn't stay long with them." Crow shuddered. Moonpath was known for being insanely vengeful. "By the way, Zuryzel," Crow added, "do you, by any chance, know of the Hoeylahk otters?"

Zuryzel's heart began to pound. "A little."

Crow shook her head. "I knew them, too, but for Cerecinthia's sake, would you have guessed that some of them, with families and everything, were posing as spies against the sea otters?"

"I beg your pardon?"

Crow nodded. "Seriously! Kila, the sister of the present Kiskap, was posing as some chieftain or other. I don't know why. They were keeping tabs on the sea otters, I guess. But it's scary—they shouldn't be there at all!"

Zuryzel could not reply. She had not guessed it, but she should have. *You don't always know where you have friends. You're bound to have friends where you don't know.* The Hoeylahk otter Uku had said that herself. She had been talking about part of her tribe.

This was yet another strange happening. And Lady Raven almost certainly had arranged this, as well. How long had she foreseen this war?

Storm rolled his eyes expressively, not noticing Zuryzel's silence. "Imagine the surprise! Anyway, a little later, we ran slap bang into a small patrol of sea otters, around three hundred."

"That's hardly small," protested Zuryzel.

Crow shrugged, opened her mouth to say something, then closed it again as a chickadee's song drifted through the trees. She imitated it perfectly. Without warning, at least two dozen other dark shapes emerged from the gloom, practically gliding.

"Zuryzel!" hissed a familiar Ranger's voice. Another muttered in quiet surprise, while still others gazed unblinkingly at her.

The many eyes unnerved Zuryzel, but she had long since learned not to show it. She merely half leaned against a tree, watching back.

Crow broke the illusion.

"What exactly happened in Pasadagavra?"

Zuryzel raised her voice, loud enough to be heard by all, telling how she had first left Dombre in search of help and then had returned to find the fortress of Pasadagavra in the hands of the foxes. She then explained everything that Aspen and Rainbow had told her of what had happened in Pasadagavra. There were many whistles of disbelief at what she said about the attack on Pasadagavra.

Crow made no motion at all during the telling. She only watched Zuryzel through dark, narrowed eyes, thoughtful as could be. Finally, she said, "So, Knife summoned the corsairs, and Demmons showed up with Redseg, Fotirra, Jironi, Epoi, and others?"

Zuryzel nodded.

Crow frowned deeply.

"And when you went to the coast, the nearest city you found on the coast was where Ailur had harbored, yes?" added another Ranger.

Zuryzel nodded, aware that, in the Rangers' minds, something wasn't making sense.

There followed a silence, when the wind swirled slowly around the trees, and then another Ranger added, "And *Shartalla* was at this city?"

Zuryzel nodded. "That is correct."

Suspicious silence again lingered.

Then Crow queried, "Where is this camp?"

"Follow me." Zuryzel turned and headed off.

At first, Zuryzel was unsure of the way, but it took her only a little time to find her bearings, and then her paws took her almost automatically toward the swiftest, safest way back to her camp.

"Crow," she whispered, just loud enough for only the Ranger leader to hear her.

"Yes?" Crow hissed back.

"You looked worried when I mentioned Redseg and Fotirra and all that. Why?"

"I'll explain later."

The journey passed rapidly. Whomever Crow had with her did not exactly follow Zuryzel but instead bobbed and weaved, keeping Zuryzel within their sights, always making sure that they never lost sight of her.

Once the small opening in the woods wove into view, a fire-colored head popped up out of a hollow log.

"Good timing, yer 'ighness!" Shartalla grinned. "Arasam was just …" her voice trailed off as she caught sight of Crow. She swallowed hard. "*Marsa Kireeka*," she spluttered. Hastily she struggled out of the log and nodded respectfully. Her eyes widened when she spotted other shapes drifting behind Crow. "Seas o' blue 'n' green!"

"Hello old friend," Crow grinned, obviously amused.

From overhead, there came a scrabbling noise. Zuryzel looked up to see Tsanna and Grayik scrambling down a huge pine with many branches.

It was all Zuryzel could do to keep from laughing out loud as Tsanna's eyes widened at the number of other creatures Crow had brought—forty archers, Zuryzel could tell, now that they were standing still. "Golly," Tsanna commented in an undertone.

Crow called something over her shoulder in her own tongue, and instantly the creatures began to disperse. Tsanna leapt the last few feet to the earth, and Grayik swiftly followed her. Crow turned to Zuryzel.

"You wanted to know what worried me about the three ferrets with the foxes— Redseg, Ailur, and Fortira?"

Zuryzel nodded.

Crow looked uncomfortable. "I really do not know the whole story, but I will tell you what I know."

She sat wearily down on the log. Zuryzel sat next to her, carefully balancing her weight. Crow met Zuryzel's eyes squarely.

"Do you know of the *Deathwind*?"

Zuryzel nodded.

Crow continued almost sadly. "Redseg is the captain of the *Deathwind*. Ailur is his sister. My grandsire, Lord Condor, trusted Redseg to be the captain of the *Deathwind*. That ship in the wrong claws is dangerous. I trusted Redseg; everyone has for a long time. Now you tell me Redseg followed Demmons and is with the foxes that have taken the fortress of Pasadagavra? I would have said that Redseg would have had nothing to do with Demmons. I am stunned.

"Also, the city you arrived at on the coast was Diray. Ailur would never be there except for a very, *very* good reason. It's a nasty little town with no one but cutthroats and pickpockets. And as for Fotirra … she isn't a corsair, or for that matter, even so much as a fighter. She's a servant to an old king on one of the northern islands. And Jironi—"

"I know who Jironi is."

Crow shook her head despairingly. "I would bet every inch of my territory that it was Lady Raven who gave them a good reason. Somehow, she found out about the foxes, and she suspected the sea otters too—Kila the Hoeylahk otter proved that."

"Who?"

Crow blinked. "Kila, Northstar, sister of the present Kiskap, their leader, you know?"

Zuryzel shrugged.

Crow continued almost wearily.

"Kila was an old friend of my mother's. Mother placed spies around the earth, and somehow or other, she managed to keep them passing her information. Do you know of Torona?"

"Who?"

Crow's weariness faded and turned into wry amusement. "Torona. She's a fox whose mother was the slavedriver of the captain of *Sea Monster*, the ship that captured Mother and a few others. Somehow Torona and my mother became great friends—my mother would have trusted Tonona with her life." Crow looked sideways at Zuryzel. "Torona managed to make it to Darkwoods and is currently known there as Oracle Ice."

Ice?! Zuryzel could not prevent her eyes from widening. "You're serious?"

Crow nodded, grinning. "She's not with me; she's somewhere on the coast now, keeping her eyes on Zurez. But it's just like with the corsairs and the Hoeylahk otters. She shouldn't have been in Darkwoods. It's too obvious. And for everyone to be here now is … unbelievable."

"Do you know who was passing this information to your mother?"

Crow's face became serious again. "I can't guess. Perhaps Craic—"

Crow broke off, her eyes widening. "What's that?"

Zuryzel had heard it, too, as apparently Shartalla had, because she came hurrying up. Never before had they encountered such a loud, long sound.

The gate of Pasadagavra was opening, not just the postern, but the whole main gate.

17 Scout

Zuryzel watched as Poison's army marched out smartly. Beside her, Crow's pelt was bristling, but Shartalla merely looked with calculating eyes.

"Nothin' fer it," she warned quietly. "They'll have t' be followed."

"Who, just you?" Crow muttered.

"I could go," offered Zuryzel.

"By yerself?" Shartalla muttered. "Not wi'out me, yeh won't!"

Crow glanced at them. "If anyone should go, I should. I can find my way back."

Shartalla rolled her eyes. "Come on, Crow. Yer the *Marsa Y' Ianne*, Lady of the Rangers. Yeh can't jest go off followin' anything. Besides, you got the longbow and poison arrows; yeh'll be needed 'ere. But Zuryzel an' I won' be, anymore. We'd be better qualified. Come on."

Before Crow could say another word, Zuryzel and Shartalla were scrambling after the army of foxes.

Zuryzel glanced back. Crow shook her head, but apparently, she thought Shartalla was right.

Zuryzel took the lead, using every clump of grass as cover. Shartalla's fiery pelt would give them away if any fox looked their way, but both knew the meaning of speed, and Shartalla was the least of Zuryzel's worries. If the need arose, Shartalla could fight her way out of any mess. After watching Shartalla at sword practice, Zuryzel doubted that her own sword skills were very good.

To the relief of the princess and the captain, the army turned north, skirting the large mountain backing Pasadagavra. As the day progressed, the army of foxes marched in a valley between two other mountains with almost unnatural speed. There wasn't a trace of the scanty green scrub brush that had hidden them earlier, and Shartalla's pelt stood out vividly in this world of gray rock. They would have been spotted instantly if any of the foxes looked backward, but fortunately, they were intently focused forward.

As night closed in, through which the foxes apparently planned to march, a cold wind started blowing, and Zuryzel began to shiver violently. Shartalla already had a thick, long-sleeved tunic on, so she passed her black cloak to Zuryzel.

"I don' need it; I'm used to cold." The pine marten's wild black eyes were unusually dull, but she did not complain. Zuryzel wrapped the cloak around herself gratefully.

Once the sun came up, Zuryzel took off the cloak, and they continued following the foxes. Shartalla had not said a word throughout the entire march, but that was not unusual. She had become quite good at walking silently, and her eyes picked up things more easily.

Around sunhigh, the first incident happened. A harsh cry from above pierced the air, followed by a long panicked shout from the foxes. A bird that would have frightened a warhawk wheeled above them on the wild jet stream. It let out another cry and plummeted, dropping like a stone toward the huge army.

Instantly, the six hundred foxes scattered, but not fast enough. The eagle snatched up two of them, one in each claw. Then another eagle swooped down and snatched up another two. More eagles kept appearing as the foxes searched desperately for any place in the rock to hide, but they numbered too many and the terrain held too little protection.

The birds did not let up their attacks until nearly sundown. Zuryzel and Shartalla were either very lucky, specially protected by the Bear King, or recognized by the eagles as ones who did not taste good, for no eagle came within spitting distance of them. Once the eagles vanished to their nests in the rocky crags, Poison regrouped her army and took a headcount. Shartalla's keen ears picked out her count—the eagles had snatched up nearly a hundred. Before continuing with their march, the army lifted up their shields in a defensive formation, covering their heads and flanks.

"Smart. But they won't be able to march very long in that formation," Zuryzel pointed out.

Shartalla shrugged. "I'm jus' here t' keep yeh from gettin' yersel' killed. I ain't used t' things like shields; to me, 'tis only a waste o' time an' effort."

Zuryzel shrugged back and crept after the continuing army, Shartalla silently in her wake.

In spite of the cold, more attacks from eagles, and the danger of being seen by the great army, Zuryzel felt almost at home on the interminable journey. As one of the best—and most frequently used—scouts of the Wraith Mouse army, she had gone on numerous scouting trips for her father. This was better—it was as though her paws already knew the way. She had been the one to see Oracle Scythe die. She had been the one constantly to find Dejuday in the cells, as he had no scouting talent. She had been the one to weave her way past guards, patrols, even Oracle Ice, to help Jaccah escape. She had been the one to find Fawn, plunge a whole courtyard into darkness, drag the vixen literally from the claws of Knife. She realized now that, for all her complaints, she had enjoyed it. And she enjoyed scouting now, using all her guile and magic to follow this army, who knew where? When she had been in command at Dombre, it had not been so free, so satisfying. She liked being a scout; perhaps, after all, she didn't want to be a queen.

For five days, the journey in the mountains continued. Yet, when the mountains opened up, they led onto moorland.

Zuryzel drew in her breath. She had never seen such a wide, sweeping, hilly place. The hue of the ground was somewhere between green and gray. Zuryzel could tell that the vast army was relieved with the exit from the mountains, but Zuryzel was worried. The moorland had no hiding places, and the wind here was strong and never ending. The scene in front of her was more foreboding than the mountains.

At first, Zuryzel wondered if they had crossed into Oria, but then she realized that the moor of Oria was many more days north. As Zuryzel adjusted her eyesight, could see that a forest was a week north of her now; perhaps it was a cedar forest. Zuryzel guessed that Oria was somewhere around there.

The foxes continued marching north for three more days. The nights were getting colder, and the wind stronger, and one night, it rained. Zuryzel and Shartalla had managed to find a small cave that was dry, but there were no such accommodations for the huge army. The cave impressed Zuryzel; there was no pattering on the roof, for the grass above muffled it all. The earth within—somewhat sandy but also unbelievably soft—reminded Zuryzel of loam. In this terrain, moss was nonexistent, as were ferns, but the heather that did grow was equally soft. Outside, the grass muffled the wind as well as the rain, and there was no way of being seen, even with Shartalla's pelt.

The next day, around sunhigh, the first sign of inhabitants of the moors revealed itself to Zuryzel—or rather, to the army.

Zuryzel was crouching in a scanty gorse bush by Shartalla when the whole army stopped. Zuryzel exchanged but a single glance with Shartalla, and they simultaneously began working their way up to where Poison stood at the head of the army.

A thin *something* of gray stood in the way of the army.

Feldspar was in the middle of a beautiful dream. He was back in his home, Graystone, the peaceful, unbelievably beautiful woodland settlement. It was late summer. Bees droned, a gentle breeze stirred warm air, and clover and dandelions waved their greetings. About him, the inhabitants took their ease, relaxing in the shade of the gray stone walls of the little village. *Heavenly.*

He was wakened from his dream by a prod from something sharp and icy cold. He blinked one eye open. He was back in Pasadagavra, and the cold, sharp thing was a saber point.

Feldspar shut his eye swiftly. By now, he knew to think before he acted. He listened carefully.

Many paws in strange shoes milled about the small chamber where Feldspar had laid his head to rest. He was petrified with fear. Something was not right. The voices that reached his ears were hushed and twangy, not like he was used to.

"I ain't certain we really are in 'ere. Yeh sure we ain't dreamin'? No one made it in 'ere before."

"You ain't dreamin'. We really are in 'ere."

Corsairs! The city had been invaded.

Feldspar lay as still as he could, desperate for the corsairs not to know he was awake.

"Listen, mouse," murmured the corsair standing over Feldspar. "I won' 'urt yeh. When the action starts, get to the walls fast. 'Tis yer only chance t' escape."

Feldspar dared to open one eye a slit. Redseg stood over him, his saber pressed lightly against Feldspar's neck. Feldspar forced himself to relax so that his pelt would not bristle. He listened carefully. What action had Redseg meant?

There was a sudden uproar. Feldspar listened carefully. From what he could understand, it sounded as though one of the captains had been laid low by an arrow. Feldspar lay still, but he blinked once to see an almost black something, flitting around by the walls. Fern the archer, it had to be!

She fired off another large arrow with deadly accuracy. This time, she struck a female ferret in her ear. The ferret wrenched the arrow out, but only a few seconds later, she was screaming with agony. Fern zinged off another arrow, this time not far from Demmons. Feldspar saw terror cover the corsair's face as he watched another fall to poison.

Feldspar leapt up like a spring and shot toward the nearest wall. On the way, he spotted Glor'a, trembling under the sword of a Darkwoods fox. He shoved the fox away from Glor'a and yanked her up, dashing for the wall.

Glor'a sighed with relief. "I thought they would have killed you."

Feldspar hugged her briefly. "I'm all right. I got very lucky."

Glor'a managed a smile. "Ran'ta already escaped, but I don't know about Chite or Ol'ver."

Ol'ver was the least of Feldspar's worries, but Chite was not really skilled in self-defense. Feldspar's eyes searched frantically amidst the hubbub, but all he saw was the door. It led up to the fountain room and the passage out of Pasadagavra.

"Glor'a," he hissed, "we need to make it to the door. Stay behind me."

Inch by inch, staying well hidden from the scene of chaos, the two mice crept toward the door. Fern flitted in and out of their vision, and as others broke free of their captors, they snatched any weapon that came to paw, slaying the befuddled enemies.

All of a sudden, Epoi, the vixen captain, appeared out of nowhere. She stood, barring the mice's way, her teeth bared in a terrifying leer.

"Going somewhere?" she mocked.

Suddenly, she jerked and fell in an awkward heap. Feldspar looked up. Lodged in the cracks and supports were what looked like whatever was left of the Sling Tribe warriors, among them, Wazzah, who had slung the stone that took Epoi's life.

Relief surged through Feldspar. He led Glor'a to the door.

Glor'a sighed as she stepped on the steps. "Come on, we need to get away."

A thought had been growing in Feldspar's mind. Wazzah's stone had settled his resolution.

"I'm staying to fight."

Glor'a looked appalled. "But … surely … Feldspar, please come!"

Feldspar hugged her again. "I love you Glor'a," he whispered.

A tear glided down Glor'a's cheek, but she did not beg him to stay. She merely murmured, "Please try to be careful."

Feldspar smiled. He drew his knife and hurtled off into the fight.

It was worse than he expected. He could scarcely keep up with the speed of the fight. Fern had not yet been caught, but she had lain plenty low. From time to time, Feldspar glimpsed other warriors he thought he recognized; he was certain he saw Ol'ver now and again and Bow Tribe warriors from when he had been rescued by Sibyna. In fact, he could see the Wraith Mouse fighting now, back to back with her brother. Feldspar realized with a jolt that he hardly recognized Dejuday. The usually amiable Wraith Mouse now was filled with wrath. Feldspar shuddered when he saw Mokimshim, the Wraith Mouse prince; he fought hard, but his skill was limited.

An unearthly screech filled the chamber, covering even the noise of the battle. A warhawk had swooped through the open gate and now circled above the fight, glancing from side to side, screeching every few seconds. Stones and arrows were loosed at it, but none of them did any damage.

And Fern had used all of her poisoned arrows.

Momentarily distracted from the fight on the ground, Wazzah hurled a stone at the warhawk. In the blink of an eye, Scorch, the Oracle apprentice, threw his spear at the Warriorqueen.

The fight literally stopped for a moment as the spear struck Wazzah. The squirrel's eyes widened, popping with shock. She clung onto the stone spur she perched on for a few heartbeats. Then, as if in slow motion, she fell.

She landed with a sickening thud that reminded Feldspar forcefully of Lady Raven. Wazzah's eyes were dull; her paws gripping her sling in a death grip; her chest ominously still.

Wazzah, Warriorqueen of the Sling Tribe, oldest enemy of the Stone Tribe, was dead. And she had died defending the Stone Tribe's home.

18 Defeat

Fang had called Hemlock insane. Knife disagreed with him. The eldest Oracle had summoned the other two to his chamber. Knife could easily believe that this was the same one who had seemed so impressive as he led the army to war.

Hemlock looked up as Knife entered. "Ah, Knife, my old friend! The war goes well, I take it?"

Knife nodded. "Yes, but … Sire, I bring bad news. Ice has vanished. I do not know what happened to her."

Hemlock shrugged. "Ice was always an idiot. We do not need her. We will manage just fine. You have done well, Knife. Return to your duties."

Knife left bewildered. Hemlock did not sound so insane.

Feldspar slashed desperately with his blade. He could not believe Wazzah was dead. She was so indestructible, so powerful.

What happened next was something he would remember forever.

Fraeggah, Wazzah's younger sister, stared in horror as her sister's body hit the stone floor. She let out a shriek of fury and launched herself at Scorch from her high position. Feldspar's heart thudded. No one could fall that distance and hope to survive. But Fraeggah did not hit the floor. The warhawk snatched her out of the air before she fell even half way.

Deggum, her brother, gasped. He tried desperately to slay the warhawk with a pebble to its eye. The warhawk did not even seem to notice. And what was worse, Deggum lost his grip on the rafter he clung to.

He was very lucky—he landed on the body of a fox and was not killed. But maybe not so lucky—Feldspar could guess how little time he had to live.

Then a thought pushed its way into Feldspar's mind. The foe did not seem to be fighting to kill; they were fighting to capture. Feldspar knew there was only one thing for it—to fight to kill. All he had been doing so far was trying to wound, to put out of action. But now, he had to kill.

In his next strike, he ran a ferret through with his blade.

Shock paralyzed him, but he steeled himself. He had to continue fighting. He could be shocked later.

Suddenly, all went black as a spear butt thudded against his skull.

When Feldspar's eyes blinked open, all he could see was the inside of a blindfold. The past battle came back to him, and he felt bitter tears reaching his eyes when he thought of Glor'a. Was she all right? Where was she? On the mountain? Yes, probably on the mountain. Many would use whatever shelter it offered, but most likely, it would provide very little.

A horrible thought entered his mind, one that paralyzed him with terror. *What about Sage? What if they find Sage?* Feldspar didn't want to think what would happen if they found her. But he was certain without thinking that it would go badly for all—especially the renegade vixen.

"Bear King, don't let them find Sage!" he murmured.

"Over here. He's awake!"

Feldspar felt the blindfold being torn from his face.

Claw's savage face leered back at him. "Not so proud now, are you mouse?"

Feldspar spat at Claw. "You're very brave facing me now. Try facing me when I'm free!"

Feldspar meant every word.

"Ah," said Claw. "Free. I thought you would say this. But you *aren't* free."

Feldspar did not reply.

"You could be free, though. All you have to do is help me get at those who are hiding in that special room. Tell me about it. Is there a way in?"

Feldspar spat at him again.

Claw shook his head pityingly. "You are indeed a brave mouse. Or maybe just stupid. You may delay us awhile, but we will get in. And when we do, for every creature that defies us, we will slay four creatures. Not all of the mice are as brave as you."

Feldspar knew he was right. What if they slew Glor'a?

He went limp with the thought. Finally, he muttered, "What do you want?"

Claw reached out and grabbed Feldspar by the throat. "You get us in there."

Feldspar spluttered and choked until Claw released him. One of the guards cut his bonds and then grabbed his and bound them again.

"You'll be doing no attacking," sneered the fox.

Feldspar glared at him.

"Come on," he snarled, dragging Feldspar roughly by his paws.

Claw jerked the mouse prisoner along the stone corridors of Pasadagavra, past the city gates, about halfway up the stairs that led to the fountain room.

A voice hailed them, gruff, low, and unfamiliar. "Who goes there? If you be friend, do not hesitate to come. If you are foe, clear out fast or taste my lance!"

"I am a friend of Pasadagavra," Feldspar called.

"Then come quickly," called the Pasadagavra warrior.

"But there are enemies with me! Beware!" Feldspar shot out and immediately threw himself to the stone floor. He hoped fervently that the warrior was ready for Claw.

His hopes were not dashed.

Something whistled over his head, and there was a sharp *whack!* The fox guard holding Feldspar collapsed.

Claw darted away, and Feldspar used all his strength to leap up off the ground and dart past the warrior.

"Sage!" Claw cried.

Feldspar made it past the threshold of the room and looked around.

Claw stood where he had stopped. His burnt orange pelt rippled with shock. He looked scared, shocked, and delighted at the same time.

"Sage," he said again, this time softly.

Feldspar did not want anything more to do with Claw, so he scampered, back toward the mountain. He would go back to help Sage after he had seen Glor'a alive and well.

Suddenly a strange thought struck Feldspar. Why hadn't Sage attacked Claw first? That answer was obvious; with a lance, it would have been easier to attack the one holding Feldspar first, as he was closer. By the sound of it, Sage had only knocked him out. So Feldspar could guess that she had used the butt of the lance and then had whirled it around to stab with the point. But why hadn't she?

Then, he remembered what Sage was. As a fox, perhaps she hadn't stabbed Claw because she was wary of killing him. But she should be more wary of letting him live. If her former comrades found her, she was doomed to who-knew-what horrors. But worse, if Rosemary was found … Feldspar didn't like to think about that. Perhaps Sage had thrown the lance after all. Feldspar listened hard but heard no sound—no patter of paws, no heavy breathing.

He shook himself and carried on toward the mountain.

Biddah groggily blinked her eyes open. All she could remember was a beautiful dream. But she couldn't remember what the dream was about. Then she felt a throbbing pain in her skull. She blinked.

"Yer right, she ain't dead!"

A rough paw shook her. Suddenly, she realized that she was upright, next to a tree—a pine, by the smell. But there were no pines in Pasadagavra! She opened her eyes properly, and in a flash, she became aware of three things: her paws were tied, there was a blade at her neck, and a glittering pair of brown eyes was watching her.

She blinked again. A sickening thought raced into her mind—her son! Only a few days ago, Biddah had given birth to a babe, whom she had named Garrow. But where was he? She blinked again—and her blood ran cold.

Fotirra the ferret was staring back at her.

Biddah let out a cry of panic. What had happened? She tried to scramble up the tree, but she was tied. She tried to cry for help.

"Nae any'un kin 'ear thee t' help." Fotirra's voice was soft and sad, like a helpless child caught out in the rain. It soothed Biddah's terror but filled her with despair.

"My son," was all she could gasp out.

"Dinnae worry, lassie, thy bairn's there." She nodded to the base of the tree. Glancing down, Biddah saw Garrow, trembling with cold but at least out of obvious sight. She began to cry.

"Hush, lassie," advised another ferret, sitting hunch-shouldered beside Fotirra. "Dinnae draw attention t' thyself oor the bairn. 'Twill be fine—thou'll see."

Biddah did not see how it could be fine.

A terrible screech filled the squirrel's ears, and she glanced about her. She was unsurprised to see Chiraage the warhawk, proud as a blackbird, watching the field about Pasadagavra with a fierce eye. Her gaze landed on Fotirra. Fotirra stared boldly back. After only a few moments, Chiraage looked away. Biddah was too distressed to admire the ferret's willpower, but she did note the warhawk's gaze traveling around the pines.

Biddah realized the tree she was tied to was on the edge of the field, and there were many around her. She spotted Dejuday, wrestling viciously with a few foxes as they attempted to tie him to a tree. Sibyna, her head down, was slumped against her bonds, looking as if she had no strength to continue living. And, to her dread, she saw Rosemary the fox child.

Claw came tripping and stumbling, looking unpleasantly shocked about something. His gaze flitted backward and forward, almost clandestine. They passed over Biddah, over many others, through trees and shrubs, until they rested for a few seconds on a single point.

On Rosemary.

But it appeared that Sage had not been found, and Claw did not dwell on Rosemary. Instead, he transferred his red gaze to the postern door of Pasadagavra.

More foxes were bringing out other captives. Biddah's heart lurched when she saw King Hokadra amongst them. The proud king's paws were savagely tied behind his back, and his head was forced down, but he was fighting every inch of the way. Behind him, Johajar, too, struggled even though he was covered from nose to paw with deep wounds. He fought on, his eyes smoldering with rage. Biddah was not shocked to see that Jaccah had been spared but captured; so had her two children, Rhonndan and Shaynnah. Biddah caught sight of Verrah, the Coast Tribe squirrel, who at least was not hauled out roughly; the corsair holding her paws merely led her to a tree to which he tied one of her footpaws.

As Biddah glanced about, she saw many corsairs—mostly ferrets—lounging around on piles of pine needles or ferns, looking bored, but not moving toward any of the captives. Biddah wondered at this. She had, for herself, seen what corsairs did to their captives—normally they took sport in tormenting the helpless victims. So what were they doing now, for the most part, ignoring them?

19 The Stoneflower Will Rise and Be Victorious

Shartalla rolled her black eyes at the gray squirrel barring the army's way. "Seas o' silver, what dominatin' springull that 'n is!"

Zuryzel gazed curiously at Shartalla. "Springull?"

Shartalla shrugged. "Means a young warrior."

Zuryzel risked a peek over the top of the gorse bush. Shartalla was right, in her sarcasm at least. The squirrel was very small, perhaps a head shorter than Zuryzel, but as for its age, it looked as if it was about, well, ancient. Zuryzel had never seen such a gray-furred squirrel *anywhere.*

"Let's see what's taking place," Zuryzel suggested. Simultaneously, the pine marten and the Wraith Mouse slunk up to where they were almost level with Poison.

"You will not go further north." The squirrel had a peculiar accent, carried a long, thin spear, and wore … something weird. If it was a tunic, it looked nothing like the tunics Zuryzel knew.

Poison sneered in the squirrel's face. "And who are you to bar our way, old one?"

"The ruler of this territory," replied the squirrel unafraid.

"Oh, are you now?" Poison's voice was like honey mixed with salt—smooth but irritating—to the ears.

"Indeed. Kindly take your rabble back where you came from."

The more Zuryzel watched, the more she realized that this was no ordinary squirrel. The squirrels she knew of were—with the exception of Wazzah the Warriorqueen, the Sling Tribe, and the vast majority of the

River Tribe—peace loving, generally well fed, softened by good living, and normally well dressed. Not so with this squirrel. The scars on her face plainly told of her experience as a warrior, her lean and muscular body hinted at a tough life, as did her tattered garment, and she had a hard aura about her, though her face was completely impassive. And, although her fur was completely gray, her face radiated youth and vigor.

Poison seemed to be getting uneasy, too, but she did not back down. "You are hardly in a position to make demands, squirrel. We are hundreds to your one! Go on then. Throw that spear—or are you too cowardly to do so?"

It was the wrong move. A thin smile crossed the squirrel's gray face. "Call me a coward," she warned quietly, "after you have stood up to *my* lot."

Zuryzel saw the squirrel wave her tail once, and then it remained perfectly still. Meanwhile, Zuryzel realized that her own tail was being blown by the constant wind.

Shartalla yelped aloud as her paw was pricked on a gorse thorn.

But neither the flick of the tail nor the yelp was noticed by the foxes for the moorland behind the squirrel seemed to rise up and was suddenly full of squirrels, all dressed, armed, and shaped exactly like the first.

The blood left Poison's face completely. Not only did the squirrels look swifter and stronger than the foxes, but also they *outnumbered* them. Zuryzel had never seen the Darkwoods foxes outnumbered before. And it looked as though Poison hadn't either.

The squirrels attacked, and in the blink of an eye, it was chaos as Zuryzel could hardly believe. Spears lashed and stabbed through armor, shield, and throat. Cries of the wounded were swiftly cut off. Zuryzel glimpsed Poison and a few others racing south, glancing over their shoulders in terror, while those in the battle screamed for mercy. But the moorland squirrels were merciless, and in only a few moments, every last one of the foxes who had not fled south was slain.

When everything seemed to have calmed down, Zuryzel and Shartalla stood up cautiously. Immediately they were surrounded. A viselike grip on her neck had Zuryzel paralyzed, and it seemed the same for Shartalla. Neither of them moved.

The female squirrel that had challenged Poison thrust her way to Zuryzel and Shartalla. She glanced at them once, and commented, "Well, you were not with the redpelts. Though for the life of me, I cannot see why you were not. You have a red pelt yourself, sea-fox."

Shartalla grinned back fearlessly. "Yeh know what they say. Fire-pelts on ferrets means fire courage."

You're not a ferret, thought Zuryzel in amusement.

A twinkle lit up the squirrel's eyes. "I take it, then, that you are friends."

Zuryzel dipped her head. "I am Zuryzel, and this is Shartalla."

Eyes blinked as Zuryzel said her name. "I see," commented the squirrel. She waved her paw. Instantly, the squirrels let go of Zuryzel and Shartalla.

"I am Warriorqueen Zinnta," the squirrel explained. "This, as you may have guessed, is my tribe. But you look hungry; food would do you no harm. Come with us."

Without waiting for a response, the whole horde of squirrels broke their surrounding ring and jogged off.

Zuryzel and Shartalla followed them nervously. Shartalla's quick eyes darted to and fro, and after a while, she commented, "Soaring seagulls! Yeh know, I've seen plenty o' great numbers in my time. The cities on the south coast, the taverns are always full. The whole crews o' 'bout sixty ships're always up, and there're lots. But I ain't ne'er seen anythin' like this. There must be ten thousand!"

"Save your breath," Zuryzel advised. The pace was quickening.

Both non-squirrels were breathing heavily by the time the squirrels stopped.

"Mazhog, go tell Loaki to get something in the way of a meal ready," Zinnta called. A female squirrel waved her spear in acknowledgment.

Shartalla frowned. "I thought all squirrel maiden names end in 'ah' or 'uh,'" she said under her breath to Zuryzel.

"Nanyet, Piyma, find Ressif and have her see to the wounded. Iro, Kleop, see to the weapons."

"Apparently not," Zuryzel murmured back

Sweet aromas permeated the air. When Zuryzel and Shartalla caught up to Zinnta, they were looking down on a hollow filled with moorland grass and heather. What met their eyes below was a town bustling with activity. There seemed to be little shelter, as far as houses were concerned, but it looked like a good place to live. Older squirrels lounged by a fire, smiling as they bounced younger ones on their knees. Juvenile squirrels tended to the fire, brought the elders food, and almost always paused to listen to the elders talking. A small, barely visible wisp of steam curled up from an overhang of loamy soil where many adult squirrels busily tended pots simmering over fires.

Zinnta waved her paw airily. "My village, Nyincoey. Anyway, what are a night-mouse and a fire-pelt doing this far north?"

"We were only following that horde."

"You come from Pasadagavra."

Zuryzel nodded. "That's right."

"Yet Pasadagavra was captured."

"Most of it was."

"And one of the Oracles summoned one of the sea-foxes?"

Zuryzel frowned; Zinnta seemed to know already all of the details and was merely confirming them. "You know rather a lot."

Something akin to a smile hovered on Zinnta's features. "It is a long story that surely can wait. You must be hungry and tired. Come with me."

Her paws ran lightly down a path toward a pile of soft earth covered with heather; she ducked around it, Shartalla and Zuryzel following. Zinnta flitted toward the overhang where the fires simmered.

She bent over a pile of pottery bowls, picked up two, and after shouldering her way through to one of the cauldrons, filled the pair with whatever smelled so good. Nimbly she picked her way back toward where Zuryzel and Shartalla waited. She tipped her head to one way and set off at a swift pace, balancing the bowls expertly. It seemed as if she was trying to keep Zuryzel and Shartalla from asking questions.

Zinnta took a route that was obviously the long way around, but she eventually led her guests to the edge of the hollow. She pulled aside a curtain of gorse and disappeared behind. Zuryzel and Shartalla glanced nervously at each other.

"Yeh know, they may not be friendly," Shartalla warned.

"They've just killed a whole ton of foxes for us," Zuryzel pointed out.

"Just 'cos they're a foe t' our foe don' make 'em friendly; they could be our enemy too."

"Got any other suggestions?"

Shartalla looked around, and shook her head.

"Let's go."

Zuryzel pulled the gorse aside.

Inside was a cave, not too unlike the one she and Shartalla had spent the previous night in. There were piles of soft heather flowers mounted up around a mound of some form of table on which Zinnta had carelessly placed the bowls. She indicated the piles of heather. "Help yourselves."

Zuryzel and Shartalla sat, though Zinnta did not. The Wraith Mouse was willing to bet that Zinnta never tired of moving about. Zuryzel sipped at the broth in the bowl hungrily, as she had eaten little for many days. Zinnta said nothing, but her eyes appraised the pair of them. Some secret lay buried in the squirrel; that much was obvious, but Zuryzel did not feel uncovering it called so urgently that she should stop eating.

Zinnta nodded as they finished.

"You may as well sleep," she advised. "Come with me."

She led them out of the cave, around the edge of the hollow, and into another one. This had a bare floor strewn with rue, heather, and a comfortable layer of dried grass. Squirrels lay all over, curled up, and Zuryzel guessed this was the sleeping quarters. Zinnta led them to a secluded corner.

"You would do well to sleep," she said, in a voice quiet enough not to wake the others dozing. She then turned and stalked off.

Shartalla shrugged and plopped herself down. "She's right. If'n they'd wanterd t' kill us, they'd've poisoned the stew or the bowls or attacked us afore now. Let's sleep."

Zuryzel sat slowly, looking around. Shartalla was right; they might want to kill prisoners or do something else with them, but they probably would have done so before now. Silently, Zuryzel let her head sink down and her mind drift into sleep.

Immediately, she opened her eyes to whirling darkness and gentle warmth. She blinked.

"Zuryzel."

Time! Oh no. It had been a long time since her first vision from Time. Had Time another to show her?

"Watch, Zuryzel. I have two visions to show you tonight. All are in the past as you call it, and all are connected."

Zuryzel felt the whirring sensation begin, and quite suddenly, she stood in a stone chamber at Dombre.

"You can get help from the coast."

For a moment, Zuryzel's heart leapt, and she forgot this was only a vision. Lady Raven! She was here! Then Zuryzel remembered. In the here and now, Lady Raven was dead.

But in this vision, she was not only alive but also not alone.

"What help? Raven, Hemlock has pushed just as far at the coast as out here. What good is there?" King Hokadra waved his paws in exasperation.

"I was not speaking of the Cliff Mice. They could not much help you even if they were not already hard pressed. I was speaking of other corsairs."

Hokadra looked at her as if she were mad. "Other *corsairs?*"

There was a rustling noise, and Queen Demeda stood up. "*Raven, you're not telling anyone everything.*"

Lady Raven pulled a wry face. "*Have you ever known me to have perfect confidence in anyone? You said so yourself—I never share secrets.*"

"*So what are you suggesting?*"

Lady Raven barely let her finish. "*Sailing has proven not as prosperous as staying on the coast for many corsairs. Offer them a small reward, and they'll be most interested in getting their blades into Demmons's throat. That is the way it is with corsairs—you should know, Demeda. Send someone to Diray, by river, if possible. Many ships are docked there, and all can be trusted enough to help.*"

Demeda frowned. She opened her mouth, but Hokadra interrupted her. "*And how do you know all this, may I ask?*"

Raven shrugged. "*Long story that would take quite some time to explain. Look,*" she added, her eyes suddenly darkening, "*just trust me. It is better that only one know all secrets—otherwise, death would be spelled out for just about everyone. Trust me—you've got to! There is a worse danger here than the Darkwoods foxes.*"

"*One we have not seen*?" Hokadra challenged.

Lady Raven did not meet his eyes. "*One that you would refuse to see.*" Bitter pain welled up in her eyes, mixed with self-contempt and fury. But she swiftly blinked it away.

Then Zuryzel's blood ran cold. Lady Raven had turned her eyes away from Demeda and Hokadra and was staring right at Zuryzel, as though she saw the princess. "*One you would refuse to see.*" She repeated.

Zuryzel's stomach jolted. What was going on?

Demeda was right. Lady Raven knew something she wasn't telling.

Hokadra lowered his head and sighed. "*I'll think about it. Raven, could you check on the squirrels and see if they're ready to go?*"

So this was right before the journey through the tunnel?

Raven swept out. Hokadra looked at his mate. "*What do you think, Demeda?*"

Demeda shrugged. "*I think Raven is right when she says we need help, but I'm not so sure that corsairs are the answer.*"

"*What would you do?*" Hokadra asked. Zuryzel frowned. Hokadra was uncertain—that seemed strange to her. She had never seen him waver in any matter.

"*I would take the chance,*" Demeda admitted. "*We are short on time; all we need to do is hold out at Pasadagavra until winter. The foxes, ill equipped, will suffer in winter, and we can sweep them. But winter is not as close as I like. Miamur will not help us, the river otters are scattered—though,*" she added, seeing Hokadra's face, "*they would have been of little help, anyway.*"

The decision to let Arpaha and her crew go roaming off as guerrillas, Zuryzel realized, had been Hokadra's choice, and Demeda plainly didn't like it.

"The Sling Tribe is all but destroyed, and the Stone Tribe has great skill but pathetic leadership—an old Tribeking and an arrogant Tribeprincess. The River Tribe and the Wind Tribe are good fighters but have never fought corsairs. The Coast Tribe, the Prairie Tribe, the Mountain Tribe, and especially the Bow Tribe simply have no fighting experience of any kind. We need help badly with virtually no time to seek any."

Hokadra sighed heavily. "*You're right, as always.*" He gave his mate a fond look. "*What would I do without you?*"

"*There are a dozen other fellow leaders you could confide in,*" Demeda shrugged, but the smile on her face spoke volumes.

"*But I can't tell them what I'm about to tell you,*" Hokadra grunted. "*The decision is yours.*"

Zuryzel hadn't expected that, and neither, it seemed, had Demeda.

"*Beg your pardon?*"

"*It's up to you if you send someone for help,*" Hokadra explained. "*I don't care who you send or to whom, but I definitely don't want to know about it.*"

Demeda blinked. "*Like the plan involving that message?*"

"*Precisely.*" Hokadra answered. "*Do you know what Raven meant?*"

Demeda sighed. "*I have a fairly good idea.*"

To Zuryzel's disappointment, the whirring began again, and the vision of her parents faded. When the blackness lightened, she suddenly found herself in the tavern the ferret Ailur had taken her to. It was dark, but she could make out distinct shapes. She heard the musician and saw the very old fox in a corner.

"*What's in iht fer mhe?*"

Zuryzel couldn't quite recognize the voice but saw the pine marten, leaning coolly against the wall, speaking to a cloaked creature.

Zuryzel did not know the voice that answered.

"*A chance at Demmons's head, and a bounty from our territory.*"

A Wraith Mouse? No Cliff Mouse could make that kind of offer. Zuryzel guessed this was before even the main war with Darkwoods had begun, though perhaps not too much before.

Shartalla, the fire-colored pine marten, shook her head. "*Yeh know tha' ain't wha' ah wahn'. Try agaihn, Lady.*"

Eyes gleamed craftily from beneath the hood. "*Adventure for your crew, the knowledge of other captains, if they agree, and respect from every corsair.*"

"*Now, yeh're talkin',*" Shartalla nodded. "*Duhn.*"

Shartalla had sounded only a little like this when Zuryzel had found her. Zuryzel assumed this scene must have happened not too long after the pine marten had injured her throat—a long time ago.

"Remember, you must speak to no one of this."

"Why?"

"I cannot risk word getting back to Darkwoods."

"Yeh dinnoh' truhs' meh?"

"I do not trust corsairs when they have had grog or wine, friend. I trust you."

"Whell, Ih'll tell mah crew. They desherve t'knhow. An' none of mahn get drunk—Ih see to thah'."

"All I ask is discretion," the stranger replied. *"But you know your crew better than I."*

"An' whah' ohther cap'ns'll be cohmon'?"

"I do not yet know, but you will be the first to find out."

"Sphose thah' means Ah'll haff t' anchor mah ship elsewhere an' trehck bahck," Shartalla commented ruefully. *"Ah, well ..."*

The confrontation dissolved into the mists of Time again.

"That is what I had to show you, Princess," Time said softly.

Zuryzel blew a sigh of frustration. "What was Lady Raven not telling Mother and Father?"

Time sighed. "Oh, Zuryzel, there are many things that no one wants to see. But you must only know that there is a danger that your mother and father will not—cannot—deal with. You are the one who will have to face it."

"What danger would my mother and father refuse to see?"

"You will find that out."

"Did Lady Raven know I was there?"

"She guessed I would show you that."

"Does this danger have to do with Mokimshim not being able to lead?"

"Zuryzel, you would not believe how close and far from the truth you are at the same time. You have been right for many cycles—your brother is not as bad as he, at times, appears. But there will come a day when you wish him dead."

"*Dead?! I* will wish him dead? Then the trouble is with me!" she realized. "With my desire to lead! It's my fault!"

Again, Time's breath felt warm on her cheek, almost as if he were gently smiling. "You did it again. The trouble involves you, yes, but not your desire to lead. It has everything to do with Mokimshim and everything to do with you. But it has nothing to do with Mokimshim's leading abilities and nothing to do with your will. At the same time, it will have everything to do with both of those."

Now Zuryzel was really confused; asking questions had not cleared up her mind, only fogged it up more. "That doesn't make any sense! Why will you not tell me clearly?" she wailed.

"Because that is what will make you strong enough to carry the burdens you must carry: your finding out with your own abilities what will happen. It will make you ready for when it does come. Now morning calls; time to waken."

Zuryzel woke with a start and looked around. She was in the sleeping cave, and she heard the snores and mumblings of others. A little diffused light came into the room; glancing at the entrance, she guessed it was dawn. She had slept for a while.

"Shartalla," she hissed.

"Yer awake?"

Zuryzel blinked in surprise. Shartalla sat upright, looking neither tired nor wary, simply observing. "You haven't slept?" she mumbled.

"Oh, I did sleep a little. Yeh sure were tired, though, by how yeh look."

"Shartalla," Zuryzel whispered, "you were staying at Diray. Who was it that bribed you to wait for a call for help?"

Shartalla looked curiously at Zuryzel. "What're yeh talkin' abou'?"

By now, Zuryzel knew that trick too well. "Don't play stupid. Someone bribed you with a chance at Demmons's head, plus adventure, to wait at Diray and to come when she called you for help. Did you know who she was?"

Shartalla frowned warily. "An' 'ow did yeh know?"

Zuryzel decided not to keep secrets from the corsair. "Would you believe me if I told you I dreamed of Time himself?"

"Prove it," Shartalla hissed back, though there was no aggression in her voice.

Zuryzel had strung the small bead Time had given her on a thin chain, which she wore under her tunic, along with the strange raven image Crow had given her. Making certain Shartalla did not see the raven, she drew the bead from beneath her tunic and held it out in her palm: the pale silver crescent moon.

Shartalla reached beneath her sea-garment and took off a piece of twine she wore about her neck. Making certain none could see but Zuryzel, she held out the tip of the crude necklace.

On it was not a moon but a flame, made out of some reddish orange stone, etched with gold. Zuryzel's eyes widened; nowhere could there be such a skilled craftsman anymore, not to mention such a fine type of gold that seemed to glow.

Shartalla hastily stowed her own Time-bead beneath her garment again. "All right," she said, as though trying to get things straight. "Time showed yeh the scene when I agreed t' wai'. Yeah, I knew who she was, but as fer tellin' yeh—"

"Don't bother," Zuryzel snapped. "I know what comes next. You have a very good reason for not telling me, but you can't tell me what the reason is."

Shartalla chuckled. "Time talked mystic'ly with yeh as well, I see. Zuryzel, I canno' tell yeh because I believe someone else will tell yeh soon. Tha's all I have to say on the subject."

"What was wrong with your throat, though?" Zuryzel asked curiously. "You were speaking all huskily."

Shartalla shrugged. "Don' remember any more—tha' was several cycles ago, see."

"How old are you?" Zuryzel asked, curious.

Shartalla grinned dryly. "Na' much older 'n' you," she replied. "I don' know jus' how much exactly, 'cause where I grew up in the eas' we've a different style o' calendars. Anyway, wha' else did Time show yeh?"

Zuryzel went into detail about her other dreams from Time, starting with the one in which she had seen Current.

To her astonishment, Shartalla could make more sense out of her dreams than Zuryzel could. "Lady Raven rules—ruled—over all kinds o' creatures," she explained. "There's a lo' o' creatures in their lands, and—"

"Wait a minute," Zuryzel interrupted. "There're only about two hundred Rangers."

Shartalla chuckled. "Zuryzel, what do you know about Oria?"

"Uh—not much, I guess."

Shartalla shook her head. "The Rangers are the *army* o' the region. Their tribe's the Ianne, but there are mice in tha' tribe who don' want t' be Rangers. They live in a city called Iannia. Then there're the chipmunks and a few islands in the north sea, plus some other cities in Oria. They all have their local gov'ments, but Lady Raven ruled them all. An' she had a network of informants pretty much all over the world 'cept the Wraith Mice cities, so she woulda heard the whispers of trouble stirrin'. And she woulda done something about i'. I would bet my ship tha' the little conversation she and yer mother had with yer father was planned out b'tween the two of 'em."

"But what has that got to do with anything?" Zuryzel protested.

"I'm comin' t' tha'. As yeh know, the Darkwoods foxes ain' the only trouble on earth. This trouble tha' yer parents would refuse t' see is somethin' tha' Lady Raven was preparin' for."

"But what would my parents refuse to see?"

Shartalla opened her mouth to say something but stopped as one of the squirrels approached them.

"Warriorqueen Zinnta would like to see you."

20 Marsa Kireeka

Biddah glanced around her. As far as she knew, every single creature that had taken refuge in Pasadagavra had now been taken captive, save those who had hidden in the fountain room. Biddah sensed four feelings around her: defiance, calm acceptance, triumph, and despair. It was mostly the Rangers who were defiant, and the Darkwoods foxes who were triumphant.

Biddah could barely see Sibyna, slumped, neither awake nor asleep, in a kind of stupor. On the other side of the field, Dejuday, her brother, was not much better off. She did glimpse Fern the archer, her green eyes blazing with savage courage, facing up to Demmons, who sneered in her face. Cinder snarled and fought, his gray pelt stained with blood. Biddah spotted Shaynnah, Jaccah's daughter, tied to a low-hanging bow.

A scuffling sound broke out behind Biddah.

"Hold hard, git her tied!"

"Cummon, it can't be too 'ard!"

"Ouch!"

Someone was being tied to the tree with her. By moving her head, she saw it was Queen Demeda. Biddah had never seen the Wraith Mouse Queen so ferocious. She struggled viciously against the stern paws of her captors, and she even bit one that latched around her throat.

Go on, Queen Demeda! Biddah thought.

But she was small strength against six or seven corsairs, and before too terribly long, they her tied her to the pine.

"Biddah," Demeda hissed, as the ferrets sauntered off. "Are you all right?"

"Yes," Biddah whispered back. "What happened?"

As Demeda opened her mouth, there was a loud *CLANG!*

Demeda looked up, startled, before a slow smile crept along her white face.

"Oh my, they're trying to capture Xar!" she commented.

"Is that good or bad?" Biddah whispered apprehensively.

"Depends which side you're on," Demeda smiled. "If you're against him, then …"

There was no need to explain further for Biddah saw the mound of white fur surrounded by red foxes. He was certainly making a fight of it. There were nearly thirty foxes with ropes wrapped round his paws, body, and tail, but whenever they tried to get a rope round his neck, he gripped it in his teeth and snapped it.

"Oh, watch this," hissed Demeda. "Or if you have a weak stomach, don't watch."

Biddah ignored the last bit of advice, but she sincerely wished she hadn't.

A corsair got too close to Xar, with a blade in paw. Immediately, Xar was on him, claws slashing and teeth biting. Blood spurted from the corsair's throat, covering the tundra otter's face. Biddah shut her eyes tight, not wishing to see what became of the corsair.

She didn't know how, but somehow or other, in nearly an hour, the corsairs managed to drag Xar over to the same tree where Biddah and Demeda were tied.

"That," commented Demeda when the foxes left, "was disgusting."

Biddah kept her eyes shut, but she heard Xar spit. "I didn't have much choice, Demeda," he retorted.

"I saw."

There was a sudden commotion not too far away. Biddah opened her eyes a teensy bit to see the Coast Tribe Verrah being hauled toward the center of the field where a pile of oiled-down wood was stacked. Biddah felt sick.

"Wait!"

"You can't kill 'er!"

Scorch rolled his eyes at the corsair captains who had objected. "And why not?"

"She's o' the Coast Tribe. It's bad luck to slay 'em!"

"If you do, the seas'll drown the 'ole earth!"

Scorch rolled his eyes again scornfully. "I have never heard such rubbish before in my life."

"Don't slay her." The calm command came from Claw, who hurried to the commotion. "Just tie her back up."

Biddah silently promised herself never to complain about superstition again.

"Right," Claw continued. "First things first. Secure the fortress, but don't worry about the top room. Keep silent once you're within hearing distance."

A couple of foxes hastened over toward the postern. They were cut down in their tracks.

Claw looked up, furious. "I thought you had the place secured! Who shot those arrows?" he thundered. "You, you, and you, get your divisions, and have them use their shields to get inside," he added, calling to a trio of older captains.

Nearly thirty assembled, shields up to the fortress, eyes determined. A volley of crossbow bolts cut them down from behind.

Claw was beside himself. He knelt down, ripped a bolt out of one of the bodies, and turned to the corsairs under his command. "Who fired this?" he hollered.

No one moved; Fotirra looked genuinely surprised. Biddah began to think she was as good a liar as Lady Raven.

By this point, clouds were massing, and the sun was no longer visible.

Claw shouted orders to some archers. "Start firing at any enemy you see," he snapped to them.

Almost as soon as he turned his back, a shaft was loosed, and a red fox fell from the mountain straddling Pasadagavra. It was one of the foxes who had left with Poison on her march to the Moors.

Claw was really furious now. "*IDIOTS!* Look before you shoot! Make sure it's an *enemy* first!" Claw was practically jumping up and down in frustration.

"Poison, are you there? Whoever's up there, get down here fast, or you'll be under fire!"

Poison and five others slid down the snowy slopes, panting and shivering, so tired they were barely able to stand. Poison staggered to stand before Claw, threw a tired salute. Claw forestalled her speaking with a raised paw.

"Is this all that remains of the army that went with you, Poison?" Claw asked with deadly calm.

Poison nodded.

Claw looked at them.

"How many attacked you, vixen? Two hundred? How many? Or did all the six hundred I sent with you fall off a precipice?"

"N-n-nine hundred at least. They jumped us on moorland, ten days steady march north of—"

Claw slapped her face, leaving four streaks of blood across Poison's fine features. "Arm yourself and do something useful, you idiot!" he snarled.

Poison attempted a pretty smile. "But perhaps—" She ducked as Claw attacked her again.

Then Claw dropped flat, as a volley of arrows came from the slits in Pasadagavra's mighty wall. Keeping his head low, Claw signaled to the five remaining corsair captains, Demmons, Jironi, Fotirra, Horeb, and Redseg.

"You're supposed to be expert fighters! Get your crew into Pasadagavra and root out whoever is in there!"

They left with alacrity, though he did not see that Redseg, Jironi, and Fotirra, instead, snuck off to their former positions on the edge of the field.

As the other corsairs began to sneak toward the fortress, they fell flat as one, dipping down and slithering along the earth, bobbing and weaving. They were un-attacked until the first ones reached the doorway. A volley of arrows so thick that Biddah could hardly see past them cut the many corsairs down in their slithering tracks, and the survivors, including Demmons, slid back to the mass army. At that moment, a hail of arrows flew into the back of the foxes.

Claw regained some of his composure and rapped out orders. "Shield bearers, make a perimeter with your shields. Archers, spears, javelins, in the center. Swords, pikes, lances, in between the shields. On the double!"

Biddah took stock of what was inside the barrier of foxes. The pile of oiled wood had been lit; Biddah tried not to think about that. Then she saw something that made her blood run cold.

Nayn, the mouse baby she had cared for for a short time, was in the cruel claws of an old vixen and being thrust over the fire.

Biddah tried to scream, but before she could do so and before Nayn was over the fire, an arrow hit the old vixen with such force that she was knocked backward fully five steps and yet totally missed Nayn. What shooting! It could only be a Ranger! The vixen crumpled, Nayn held safe in her dead paws. Fox archers fired toward where the arrow had come from. But there was no longer anything there.

"This one!"

Biddah realized in fear that the foxes were now intent on *her*.

One of them cut her bonds with a single blow. Another grabbed her front, nearly stepping on Garrow. Biddah flailed desperately, fear of the fire lending her strength. But she was no great match. Within a short time, she was literally over the top of the fire, her fur beginning to burn.

When the arrow struck her holder, Biddah fell right onto the blaze. Agony as she had never known engulfed her, but she managed to roll off the fire, screaming as she threw herself on the ground. The pain was so intense she forgot everything else. She rolled desperately, and the flames that had taken hold of her were soon smothered. But the pain continued, and she could not stop her agonized screams. At this moment, even death would have been welcome.

As if in reply, the clouds burst open like a watering jug, and the rain finally came. In seconds, the field was covered with standing water. Biddah gratefully pressed herself into a puddle, welcoming the coolness.

From her prone position, she ignored her pain, listening and watching hard what was going on.

"We could try climbing the mountain," suggested a scout.

Claw glared daggers at him. "Go check it out and tell us if it's safe. Go!" Immediately, the scout made himself scarce.

"Perhaps we could use the prisoners for shields," suggested Poison.

Claw rolled his eyes. "At last, a good idea from you, vixen." He raised his voice. "All shield bearers get a prisoner and use them as a shield. Try to get out of here!"

Two adventurous soldiers grabbed the nearest to them—a light brown mouse and a dark-furred Stone Tribe squirrel.

"Ol'ver!" A maiden's voice rent the air, filled with distress and terror. The mouse fought desperately, but there was little he could do as he was severely wounded.

Their two guards forced them forward. It seemed to be working—no one shot at the foxes. Immediately, others snatched up the nearest prisoners, dragging them upright.

Biddah wasn't sure she believed what she saw next. Although the mouse seemed to cover almost all of the fox holding holding him, an arrow suddenly appeared from the neck of the fox, and the mouse was dropped. The same happened to the fox holding the squirrel. The squirrel quickly fled, but the mouse tried to fight his way back until his feet were yanked from under him, and he was dragged into the forest by unseen paws.

Chiraage the warhawk watched Claw's frustrated face. "Perhaps if we flew over to the castle? Two of my younger warriors will attempt to do so." She shrieked out orders in her own language. The two birds rose into the air. Astonishment continued to wash over Biddah as she watched events unfold. Now, a black bird, a raven, hurled itself at the warhawks, wings kept well away from their talons. After attacking the eyes of one warhawk, he winged high and called down.

"Kyaaaayaaaaah! I am Craic of the mountains, slayer of eagles! Come to me, and I will be your death!"

Though Biddah fervently hoped the raven was right to be so bold, she was afraid that in the end there was little chance of a single raven defeating so many warhawks. But what happened next was burned into her memory forever.

Following the soldier through the Moor Tribe encampment, Zuryzel and Shartalla had no idea about the fierce fighting taking place that very moment at Pasadagavra. But they knew that time was short, and they were getting anxious about further delays. They also knew they needed to bring help to Pasadagavra. So they eagerly approached the Warriorqueen, hoping they could persuade her to send the desperately needed help.

As they sat down, Zinnta poured both Shartalla and Zuryzel a goblet of wine.

"Now," she began, "those foxes we sent on their way came from Pasadagavra—I recognized some of their plunder. That means at least part of Pasadagavra was conquered. I do not want explanations—there is no time for them. Listen to me: there is a creek not far away—I'll take you to it. Follow it for a little while, and the creek will broaden. Where it broadens, there is a boat. Shartalla, you will have to be good at steering—the creek leads to the Keron River. Keep to the west side of the river, and you will be fine. My tribe will follow through the mountains. We do not like boats and are swift enough of paw."

In surprise that they would not need to do any persuading to obtain help, Zuryzel hastily downed her wine. She wished she hadn't—though sweet, it was also very strong, and she began to choke a little.

"Good wine," commented Shartalla, covering up Zuryzel's spluttering.

"Talk about cool in the face of danger," grinned Zinnta. "Come on."

The Warriorqueen was not one to hesitate once a decision had been made. It was good thing Zuryzel had gotten some sleep and a meal because she was going to need her strength to get back to Pasadagavra. *Actually,* she thought, *I need it just to keep up with Zinnta*! She followed the Warriorqueen at full speed, desperate to get to her family and friends as soon as possible.

Zinnta first passed the cooking fires, taking two full packs.

"You will need these," she said, handing them to Zuryzel and Shartalla.

She then led them on a path out of the hollow, glancing back once at her town.

"Move quietly," she warned. "There are some not so pleasant things on the moorlands."

"Then why do you live here?" murmured Shartalla, her blade held ready.

"Because even so, the moor is a good place. Here, my tribe has a life to live," Zinnta replied. Her voice was so quiet Zuryzel could barely hear her.

Zuryzel could understand why having a gray pelt was an advantage on the moorland. Zinnta was practically invisible. She flitted from bush to bush, cresting hills and sliding into dips with barely detectable motions. Zuryzel's pelt was unobtrusive enough, also, but Shartalla would attract attention the same way flowers draw bees.

After quite a while, Zuryzel heard the sound of a creek. Zinnta stood up, shading her eyes. When Zuryzel and Shartalla caught up to her, she waved her tail in the direction of the sound.

"We meet again at Pasadagavra." She dipped her head once and vanished into the moor.

"Nothin' fer i', Zuryzel," shrugged Shartalla. They found the boat and began their journey back to Pasadagavra. Zuryzel hoped they would not be too late.

Biddah tried to look dead, sighing softly as the rain soothed the pains from her burns. Nevertheless, she kept one eye cracked open, watching the airborne battle between the raven and two warhawks.

The raven had risen high above the pair and hovered on the wind for a while. Both warhawks shot up toward him.

Immediately, the raven dropped, shooting in between the outstretched claws of the monster birds. The warhawks were so close that the claws meant for the raven ripped at each other instead. Blood fell with the rain, spattering the ground, dark red and revolting. The rain sped up, and thunder rumbled behind the clouds. Biddah distinctly heard one of the corsairs say, "It's like a seastorm!"

Despite the fury of the rain, the clouds were not dark; a pale light shown behind them, illuminating the fighting birds. The raven, whoever it was, was unbelievably nimble and even more cunning, cawing out, "For Marsa Nidra!" at frequent intervals. Did he mean Lady Raven? He flew straight at one warhawk, dropping at the very instant its beak slashed at him, making the the bird pull out one of his fellow's pinion feathers. This time, the raven hurled himself at the injured warhawk, attacking his eye.

As the other approached, the raven rolled from the eye, and the warhawk's claws blinded the terrible red eye of his companion.

Now the raven flew up again. "Can you not catch the raven Craic?" he screeched.

Maybe they could have, but they did not—the Bear King was with Craic.

This time, instead of flying down, the raven flew up. The higher he went, the thinner the air got, but it did not seem to bother him. Ravens lived in the mountains; thin air was natural to them. Not so for the warhawks. After quite a while, they dropped, semi-conscious, toward the ground, hitting it with a booming thud, and lay still. By the time they hit, Craic had disappeared.

Claw was in a quandary. Nothing was working. Nothing was getting them out of the field, much less into Pasadagavra. His only option was the mountain; Biddah knew it.

She heard Claw quietly ordering several surviving corsairs toward the mountain.

The Bear King was truly in control of time and sequence. At that very moment, a scream issued from the mountain, followed by the sound of a body dropping heavily.

Despite the urgency of his situation, Claw did not hurry. He paced slowly over to body of the fox lying on the ground, furious disbelief written all over his face. Bending down, he examined the bite wound around the fox's throat.

"What happened to the white otter?" he growled, his voice soft and filled with rage.

Biddah glanced around surreptitiously. Xar and Demeda had, indeed, escaped their bonds. As had most of the Rangers. And, not far away, Biddah spotted Fern the archer, creeping toward the still, weeping little bundle that was Nayn. Expertly, she scooped him up and, half-crouching, sped for the nearest opening.

Fern made it to the trees before she was noticed, and by then, only a crossbow bolt could be loosed at her. Biddah did not see if she dodged it or not, but she heard laughing from the trees. Biddah's fear slowly left her to be replaced by amusement. She almost chuckled out loud.

Claw looked blank with anger, but not Scorch.

"Well," said the vile fox under his breath, "the queen escaped. I know how to get her back."

"Oh," snarled Claw. "How?"

“Watch.” Scorch began to creep toward four of the prisoners with a fine, golden dagger drawn. Claw did not guess what he was up to until too late.

“You touch Hokadra with that blade, and you will regret it. I’ll make certain your death takes the better part of a lifetime!”

If Scorch heard, he gave no sign. In a flash, the blade plunged toward King Hokadra’s exposed throat.

It was all Biddah could do to keep from screaming as blood poured from the proud king’s throat. Scorch, to her horror, withdrew the blade from Hokadra and pierced him again in his lungs. The king began to sputter and cough, blood rising from his lungs to his lips. Scorch withdrew the blade a second time and plunged it a third time into Hokadra’s heart.

Hokadra gasped with pain. He glared at Scorch. He tried to say something but choked on blood. Finally, he managed one word that echoed around the clearing:

“Pasadagavra …!”

Then his head fell forward, and his body went limp against the bonds binding him to the tree, an unspoken word left on his lips: Demeda.

From inside Pasadagavra, Feldspar watched as the king died. He had thought that Wazzah’s was the most horrible death, but she had died fighting, died whirling her sling in a death grip and a snarl on her face. Hokadra was murdered, tied to a tree, stabbed thrice, and not been given the honor Wazzah now had, lying on a bed of soft grass covered in a golden silk mantle. To the Warriorqueen, no matter how honorable, death was still death, but not to Hokadra and not to Feldspar.

Feldspar watched Demeda as well. From her position at an arrow slit, she had done everything she could to save her mate, but in the end, there had been nothing she could do. She had tried to give herself up, but Ailur the mercenary had clamped a paw about her muzzle and held her fast.

Ailur had gotten into Pasadagavra by the now unguarded tunnel and had thrust her way up the stairwell shouting, “Sage, I am Ailur the mercenary, a friend to Pasadagavra!” Sage had not clubbed her. With Sage help, some of the corsairs managed to open up another tunnel. Up until Scorch had approached Hokadra with the knife, a sinuous fighting motion had been in action—each corsair or mercenary used an arrow slit once before moving to the next one, like a great snake, through the tunnels. This had continued outside, with the help of Ranger archers. It had stopped as soon as Scorch approached Hokadra: Hokadra was too far away for the archers to reach, and they hoped if they stopped firing Scorch might spare the king.

But if Scorch had even noticed that the attack stopped, it made no difference. He had killed Hokadra anyway. The arrows had not yet started firing again.

Demeda broke free of her friend's paws, her eyes wide with horror and her face twisted in pain. "Hokadra! No …," she whispered, grief stricken. Her panic faded, replaced by stunned shock.

"You," Ailur snapped at Feldspar. "Run t' the sickbay quick-like an' tell 'em t' get a bed ready. An' I'm only tellin' yeh 'cause yer the closest. Go!"

Feldspar ran along now-familiar paths toward what had once been the Flower Gardens and the Spider Streams. A sanatorium had been set up there, and plenty of beds full of the wounded lined the walls. As he raced past, Feldspar saw Deggum in one, barely alive, tossing and turning with fever.

"Feldspar?" called one of the healers. It was not the first time he'd had an errand.

"Demeda," he panted. "She's in shock."

"Demeda? How? Why?"

Feldspar paused and then quietly told the healer the awful news. "Hokadra was killed. Slaughtered. By Scorch, while still tied to a tree."

The healer's eyes flew wide with shock. "I see. Get back to the wall; tell them we'll be there directly."

Feldspar sprinted back off.

Ailur was waiting anxiously, having guided Demeda away from the slit. Feldspar hastened to give the corsair the healer's message, before scurrying over to take up a bow and quiver of arrows. Maybe he didn't have experience fighting, but he would fight just to prevent anyone else from losing someone they loved.

"What do yeh think yer doin', Feldspar?" called Ailur.

Feldspar glared at her defiantly. "I'm going to fight!"

Ailur gently removed the bow and arrows from his paws. "Yer a brave creature, Feldspar, but lackin' in experience. Yeh'd be in the way o' those who *do* know how t' fight up 'ere. I'm not callin' yeh coward or fiddlepawed, but yer not cut out fer fightin' up 'ere. I'm sorry." She held out her paws.

Feldspar saw the truth in her words. He relinquished his weapons.

Ailur came up with an idea. "What yeh could do, though, if'n yeh want t' help with the figthin', is keep a bow an' quiver wi' yeh, an' dole out arrers t' the archers. Yeh'll help them shoot faster 'n' yeh'll get a shot in now 'n' again."

Feldspar was only too eager to do what Ailur suggested. Immediately, he picked up a smaller bow and the quiver that went with it. Then he grabbed spare quivers full of arrows and rushed along the line of archers, offering arrows and bolts whenever needed. With the constant onslaught,

Feldspar was kept too busy to fire any arrows himself. The defenders had returned to the fight with a relentless salvo. Spears, javelins, stones, and knives, as well as arrows, flew out the arrow slits and from the woods. There was no discretion between foxes or ferrets anymore, save with the crew of the three ferrets; now it was continuous bombardment. Rangers' arrows hit paws and went through to prick others; they no longer aimed for hearts or throats. Screams of pain ripped from the throats of those who were so much as touched by the tips. Feldspar glanced questioningly at the archer Storm.

"Poison," Storm explained. "Crushed vlizhak seeds are made into a liquid, which is dipped onto arrowheads. Once the seed liquid mixes with blood—or any form of warm liquid—it begins to grow and multiply quickly, causing so much pain the victim dies." He grimaced at Feldspar's look, whilst gliding to the next arrow slit and firing another arrow. "It isn't pleasant, and we only use it when things are desperate, but it's a way of surviving. Hurry back," Storm called as Feldspar hurried on. "The corsairs will need more bolts soon."

Claw was so furious he kicked Scorch's paws out from under him. He drew his blade and slapped it across the hapless apprentice's face, but Biddah felt no sympathy for Scorch.

Claw then did something that astonished Biddah more than anything that day.

Claw threw his sword at Scorch and then seemed to get control of his temper. Taking Hokadra's sword from the sheath at his side, Claw slashed at Hokadra's bonds without touching the king's body. The ropes severed, and Hokadra's body fell forward. Then in a most remarkable move, he knelt down and laid the sword under Hokadra's paw.

As the battle raged in Pasadagavra, Zuryzel and Shartalla continued their voyage down the Keron Ricer. Zinnta had not been joking about the speed of the Keron. What had taken Zuryzel and Shartalla more than a day to cover by land took only a few hours by boat. Zinnta's watercraft was light as a feather, and in no time, Shartalla recognized the mountains around Pasadagavra. Using a huge pole she had found in the bottom of the boat, she shoved the boat ashore at the base of the mountain. Zuryzel became aware of a sullen roar.

"Not too soon," Zuryzel commented. "That's a waterfall you're hearing."

Shartalla shuddered. "No waterfalls at sea."

It took them another hour to see Pasadagavra and yet another to reach it. The snows that had once covered the back entrance had melted somewhat and then frozen, making the going icy and difficult but possible.

Shartalla suddenly fell and tumbled backwards a good distance into a snow mound. "'Tis worse than bein' in a fog bank a' noon!"

"It gets worse," came from the snow mound.

Shartalla nearly fell backward again with astonishment. "Who are yeh?"

The snow mound rose slowly and turned into a creature. "I am Quaar, priestess of the Tundra otters."

"You're a tundra otter?" Zuryzel whispered, sliding down to meet her.

Shartalla's shock reduced to rueful recognition. "Quaar, I shoulda known."

Quaar turned to face Zuryzel. The otter looked exactly like Xar and Sone, with a long, shaggy white coat and pale, misty blue eyes. "Princess Zuryzel." Her voice rasped worse than Shartalla's had, but she had no difficulty pronouncing words and no painful coughing.

Zuryzel's black fur was not exactly invisible, and Shartalla's pelt stood out like a beacon, but it was hard to locate Quaar in the snow. Only her blue eyes gave her away.

"You came when I expected you to," she continued. "But you are needed inside. Come!"

As Quaar began to slither up the mountain, her clothing—a white dress decorated with teeth and claws for beads—made an odd hissing noise, like wind over snow, undisturbed by trees. As Zuryzel and Shartalla toiled uphill desperately, their paws numb, their teeth chattering uncontrollably, a black beak emerged from the doorway.

"Princess Zuryzel," called Craic the raven. "You are not a minute too soon. Come quickly."

21 Warhawk

In the field outside Pasadagavra, Sibyna had given up all hope. She had lost Orgorad. She was certain that Zuryzel had died at the battle of Dombre. Dikiner, her old friend, was nowhere to be seen. Her brother looked barely alive, though he held on … for now. Sibyna had nothing left to live for. She had been begging the Bear King to take her life ever since the storm had broken. Her spirit was in agony; even death by the fire was welcome compared to this.

All the prisoners in the clearing had seen Hokadra die. Everyone despaired at the loss. But the others still had loved ones to live for. Not Sibyna. Sibyna wished she could fade away and never exist anywhere again. She had lost *everyone.*

Claw lost his temper again at Scorch, but before he could unleash his fury, Chiraage flew between.

"Let's save fighting each other until after we get out of this mess." Chiraage sounded disgusted with the foxes. "Here's an idea: supposing my warhawks flew you to the castle, but do't worry about little things like that raven. No creature alive can slay a warhawk; the raven did not! Those two were merely unprepared. I will start by taking a prisoner; we can afford to lose one or two of them."

She did not wait for their consent. Chiraage rose into the air and landed alongside the prone Biddah.

"You are alive, squirrel," sneered the warhawk. Without further ado, she lifted Biddah up in her talons and flew into the sky. Biddah screamed with fright and pain.

Sibyna watched as Chiraage glided over the trees. Her dark shape mingled with the clouds. Her cries were filled with victory. *There's no hope for Biddah*, Sibyna realized. *She will die in the claws of a warhawk*. Sibyna bitterly wished the warhawk had taken her instead.

Sibyna glanced at Claw and realized that his expression was less than happy. But if he felt anything other than triumph, the end had come for him also.

Suddenly, there was a *TWANG*, barely loud enough to be heard over the rain. Something streaked across the sky, brilliant and glorious, and in its wake was a trail of calm, where the raging storm ceased and rain fell softly.

Chiraage gave a shriek, but not of fear nor of anger.

Of *pain*.

The arrow had hit the warhawk in her chest. Chiraage flew high, trying to get out of range of other arrows. Then her flight began to falter. She began to sink, and a cry of pain escaped her beak.

"Can't … fly …," she gasped. Then, as if in slow motion, she flipped over and plummeted like a stone. The only sound leaving her came from Biddah's screams from where she was lodged in the talons. Sibyna saw the warhawk slam hard into the ground but could not see what happened to Biddah. She was no longer screaming … she probably did not survive the impact.

Chiraage's death ended the battle for Pasadagavra then and there. Warhawks took flight in terror, winging far off north, where they disappeared and were never seen again. The Darkwoods foxes broke all discipline and fled. Whatever was left of the corsairs scattered, save for Redseg's command, all of whom stood warily, looking from side to side.

"Let them go!" the command rang through the trees. "We have things to tend to first."

Shadowy shapes emerged from the pines; corsairs, river otters, the few Wraith Mice that had escaped, Lady Crow, and her archers.

Sibyna stared in disbelief as the gates of Pasadagavra opened. What had happened?

One white face stood out among the hundreds now filling the field. Ailur, the ferret mercenary who had always been a friend to the Wraith Mice.

Sibyna looked up and felt a spark of hope kindle deep insider her. Her friend Dikiner loped up to her, marks on his neck still showing where bonds had dug into him. So he, too, had been tied up.

Without a word, he drew a dagger and slashed at her ropes. She fell forward, every particle of her body numb with shock and pain. Dikiner hovered for a moment, looking torn, before he knelt beside her and took her right forepaw, rubbing the life back into it.

Sibyna blinked gratefully at him. "Thank you."

He smiled. "You're so cold," he whispered.

Sibyna shrugged as best she could. "I'm just worn out. There are creatures with worse injuries."

Dikiner began rubbing her left forepaw. "Not many that aren't being attended to." Dikiner suddenly looked up into her eyes. "Sibyna—did you see? Zuryzel is alive! It looks as if she found Ailur and some others, too. I've seen Shartalla, Arasam—all the ones who can be won over with a good offer." He smiled faintly. "I think Queen Demeda has some explaining to do."

Sibyna knew he was trying to be helpful and optimistic, but there was a trace of concern in his voice. Sibyna twitched her paw and touched his to reassure him. Suddenly, life did not look so bad to her. Dikiner was alive, as was Zuryzel. Glancing past Dikiner, she saw Dejuday. He was all right, too! She had not lost everyone after all.

"You'd best get inside," he added, helping her to her paws. "You'll need to warm up, or you'll catch a cold."

A cold was the least of her worries. Sibyna stumbled after him, her numbness returning. They might have won a victory in the end, but at a terrible price. Over five thousand had died only one sunrise ago, and most of the survivors were so injured they were unable to fight. That wasn't a battle—that was a massacre. She clung onto Dikiner's paw, filled with the unreasonable fear that he would be taken from her again. He led her to the postern and through it. Sibyna tried not to seem too weak, but she could not support her own weight and leaned heavily on Dikiner.

As they entered the infirmary, Sibyna's wounds stinging her but her paws a little less numb, a healer rushed up.

"Your wounds may not be life threatening, but I bet they hurt," she commented critically. "Come on." She took Sibyna's weight and helped the Wraith Mouse over to a mound of soft feathers and moss. Sibyna sat up, wincing as the healer tended to her wounds.

Then she saw Zuryzel.

Her friend was hunched beside her mother's bed, her black eyes wide with grief and her whole pelt bristling like a cactus. Blood flowed from a recent wound on her shoulder, but she didn't seem to feel it. She was shocked, stunned.

Sibyna stood carefully.

"Be careful how far you walk," cautioned the healer.

Sibyna nodded. Putting her weight down gingerly, she hobbled toward Zuryzel.

The Wraith Mouse princess started as Sibyna approached, tearstains on her face, but she relaxed after a few moments. "I don't believe it. My father … my father is dead."

Demeda lay, eyes closed, but she opened them as Sibyna approached. For a moment, she was confused. Then she recognized the archer. "What is it?" she managed.

Sibyna shook her head. Her heart twisted with pity for Zuryzel. Hokadra had been everything to her. He had taught her how to fight, to speak in many languages, to be a leader—and now he was gone. Just like that.

There was a pattering. Sibyna did not recognize the approaching creature, and her fur pricked defiantly, but Zuryzel stood up.

"Sibyna, this is Shartalla," Zuryzel said quietly. "She's a friend. Shartalla, Sibyna."

Each nodded curtly.

"Queen Demeda," Shartalla stammered, looking wretched, "there's a council o' war, but if …"

Demeda began to rise, but Zuryzel pushed her down. "I'll go, Mother," she insisted. "You rest here. Don't worry."

"I should go …" Demeda groaned.

By that point, both Zuryzel and Shartalla had left, but Zuryzel returned, poked her head around the door to the room, and panted, "Look after her, Sibyna." Then she was gone again.

"I'm sorry 'bou' yer father, Zuryzel," sighed Shartalla.

"Don't," Zuryzel begged. "Not yet. I can't fall apart yet."

Shartalla nodded. "Yeh could be a corsair cap'n, pardon the expression."

Zuryzel bowed her head in acknowledgment of the compliment. "Was your father anything like mine?"

Shartalla nearly tripped. Her voice was evasive as she answered. "Zuryzel, I never knew your father."

"You heard about him from me."

"Well, I don't remember my father much," Shartalla stammered. Her black eyes were narrowed, and she seemed stiffer than she had been.

Zuryzel did not press her.

Shartalla led her to the armory. Inside the dark room, a few torches burned, and a table lay in the center. Arpaha, Ailur, Doomspear, Crow, Arasam, Jaccah, Craic the raven, and the seven other corsair captains were all gathered in the room, milling about, looking disturbed.

Zuryzel tried to appear confident and faced them, hiding her grief and shock.

Crow straightened her shoulders.

"Zuryzel, Shartalla," she said in way of greeting. "We need to decide what to do next. Do we stay here and give ourselves a chance to rest and regroup, or do we follow the foxes while they are on the run?"

"There ain't anythin' t' decide," interjected Arasam. "We gotta attack now while we got the advantage. Give 'em time, an' those dirty dogs'll regroup an' be able t' defend better!"

"The problem with that plan of action, Arasam," Jaccah replied coolly, "is we leave our weak and wounded alone without any means of defending them." The Tribeprincess of the Stone Squirrels looked grim at the thought.

"Arasam didn't say all of us should go," Zuryzel pointed out. "If we blitz them now, we have the advantage."

"Zuryzel's righ'," added Shartalla. "All we 'ave t' do is send enough t' destroy them!"

"Who is left who can do that, though?" Arpaha asked skeptically.

Zuryzel got her first taste that day of why corsairs said, "A fire-pelt means a fire-courage."

Shartalla leaped onto the table, her black eyes blazing with combined delight and vengeance.

"If yeh think that, yeh don' know corsairs. Any corsair an' partic'larly my bunch'll swim the land fer a chance o' adventure. A minor scrap like they engaged in yesterday won' weary 'em none. Now's the time t' set our sails!" For effect, she drew her sword and tossed it into the air.

"Right!" Doomspear exclaimed. The river otter leaped up and brandished his sword as well. "Arm up all fit fighters; we've got some conquering to do!"

That did the trick. Crow backed against the wall as the corsairs rushed out. Doomspear and Arpaha exchanged irritated looks. "Do they always have to be first?" Doomspear muttered to Arpaha and Jaccah, who shrugged, following more slowly. Shartalla, however, did not move from the table. Crow caught the Wraith Mouse princess by the shoulder.

"Zuryzel, there's one thing with this whole plan," Crow warned.

Shartalla looked at Crow as if she expected some sort of double cross.

"What?" Zuryzel said, her voice a deadly low.

"If it is to work, you-you'll have to stay here."

Before Zuryzel could explode, Shartalla did it for her. "Tha' ain' fair!" she cried. "It was 'er father tha' was killed! She deserves t' get 'er blade inter Scorch's scrawny neck!"

"Zuryzel, please," begged Crow, ignoring the fiery pine marten. "You are an excellent leader, and you'll be needed here if the foxes somehow defeat us and return to attack Pasadagavra. Jaccah is hardly in any position to do anything. You must stay here!"

Zuryzel was not convinced. "I want to punish Scorch."

Crow nodded emphatically. "I understand. You aren't the only one who has lost loved ones in this war, you know," Crow added softly. The she gathered herself. "But that's not the point! You're needed *here*!"

Zuryzel looked hard at Crow. The Ranger Lady's eyes were desperate, and Zuryzel knew perfectly well she wouldn't ask something like this of Zuryzel idly. She did understand Zuryzel's need to seek justice for her father's death.

"Fine," she muttered.

"Swear to me you will stay!" Crow insisted.

Zuryzel was shocked. "Crow, a Wraith Mouse shouldn't—"

"I *know*. But this time, you must!"

For a Wraith Mouse, a sworn oath was absolutely binding. If she gave such an oath, Zuryzel would be forced by her own nature to abide by it until it was fulfilled, or until she died. Wraith Mice never gave a sworn oath lightly—and often did not give one for years at a time. Zuryzel stared at the frantic-looking Ranger. She sighed softly. "I swear I will do my absolute best to lead Pasadagavra until our forces come back from attacking the foxes!"

Crow released her. "I'm sorry," she murmured.

Zuryzel shook her head. "Not now!"

Crow nodded and bounded after the other leaders.

Shartalla leapt nimbly down from the table. "I ain' no Wraith Mouse, but I swear on our frien'ship I'll stay 'ere with yeh, Zuryzel. I'm a cap'ain, an' me word is stronger 'n' my sword!"

Within an hour, most of whatever was left of the Pasadagavra fighting forces was gone, including, though Zuryzel did not know it, the mouse Feldspar. She had not seen Feldspar since she had left him in the Darkwoods castle before the war had begun.

22 Invasion

Six days trekking through barren ashen wilderness had left Feldspar weary, hungry, and determined to get his arrows hard at the foxes. He would fight with all his strength; for Glor'a, for Pasadagavra, for Ol'ver, Chite, Ran'ta, Opal and the friends he'd left in Graystone, and many others. He vowed that he would slay at least five foxes. His former, shocked self had vanished into a hard warrior. Feldspar liked the transformation.

The hornbeam forest he had seen so many cycles ago lay in front of him. He remembered having been captured by the Oracle, and … was it *Fawn* who had been with the Oracle? It was all knit together, the entire war with many other battles.

In the middle of that forest lay the Darkwoods Fortress, where Feldspar had been held captive. He grew a little cold just thinking about it.

Crow tipped her head to one side. "All right," she said finally. "Here's the situation: we need a plan of action. Whoever has been in this fortress before, take two others, a window, and try to capture and hold out at a room. The rest of us need to deal with the problem of the door."

Feldspar swallowed hard. He knew perfectly well Crow's orders included *him*.

Knife sat with Fang in his study. He was frantically searching the old records for some mention of the poisoned arrow that had slain Chiraage.

"Poison didn't have a vision showing the future clearly. Her dream depicted the Rangers as mountain cats," Knife realized.

It was the poison that lost the foxes the battle at Pasadagavra and created such terror among the troops. Every last one of the foxes was wounded in some way, and stories were spreading.

Fang glanced out his window. "If only I knew the na—" He suddenly gasped and then toppled over onto Knife, dead.

Knife's eyes found the mouse, perched on the windowsill. Perhaps he should have shot Knife first, but he had slain Fang for his sweetheart—a mouse maiden handed over to Fang because her kin were too cowardly to defend her.

Knife barely dodged the second arrow, which nicked her ear. With a cry of panic, she dashed from the study. On her way through the corridors, she saw Hemlock, running with all his might and Scorch, looking bewildered. Knife just ran until she was out of the castle, forest, and on the moorland. She was shocked at her panic, but the vengeful look in the mouse's eyes as he shot Fang … Knife's shaking began to subside, and she began to feel cheated. She had planned on killing Fang herself. Then, she would truly rule the Darkwoods foxes … if there were anything left to rule.

Chaos reigned inside the fortress. Dead bodies of foxes lay everywhere, but those still alive and who had found weapons fought hard as the Pasadagavra forces pressed the attack. It was taking hours to clear, one bit at a time.

Feldspar, Ol'ver, and Chite surveyed the room that Knife had fled. "Crow should be up here soon," Feldspar commented. "All we have to do is hold the door."

"That isn't going to be easy," Ol'ver pointed out.

"We'll manage," Chite replied dismissively.

Much to Feldspar's surprise, it was easier than it looked. The foxes blundering toward them had no weapons ready and were easy to surprise. Only one or two managed to put up a fight. Before long, they had slain ten among them.

"Call me a southern-lily now," Chite dared Ol'ver.

Ol'ver said nothing as another fox darted around the corner.

Feldspar put paid to it with his arrow. "We're doin' good," he commented.

It was dark when Ol'ver waved both mice off to the back of the room. "Get some sleep," he advised. "We'll take this in turns."

At sunrise, Chite shook Feldspar awake. "Your watch, mate. Little activity going on. Have some water," he added, holding out a canteen.

As Feldspar gulped and new strength flowed into him, he noticed the canteen was the one Opal had given him. Perhaps this was where she got her strength.

Feldspar saw no more foxes until sunhigh, when two shot around the corner.

"Run!" one of them screamed.

Feldspar dealt with both. "Ol'ver," he shouted. "Your turn!"

The cliff mouse jerked awake and leapt up to take Feldspar's place. Feldspar yawned and moved to the back of the room.

As Feldspar nodded off, he heard a shrill chickadee's call. "Crow," he commented, relieved. It had taken two days, but the fortress was captured.

Crow Blue Arrows hastened down the hall, calling to them as she passed.

"Well done. Come on, just one more floor."

Zuryzel had not slept for twelve days. Neither had Dikiner, Dejuday, Johajar, nor hundreds of others. There was simply no time. Pasadagavra was in ruins, almost literally. The Great Fire had gone out and needed to be rekindled, but for days, until it was going well, the whole city was cold. Then there was the gardening, feeding, lodging, tidying, arranging, and more to be done. Plus, she had to arrange for patrols in near areas, guard watches, weapons checks, etc. just to make sure they would see an attack coming and be prepared. On top of that, a message had to be sent to Zinnta, though, thankfully, Redswift had taken care of that. It was difficult work.

Dikiner never complained, and Dejuday hardly said anything anymore. Shartalla treated the whole dilemma with indifference; she was used to days on end without sleep or common comforts such as warmth and adequate meals. Shinar complained a lot, but did her share of the work unflinchingly, and Johajar worked with a fierce passion—mostly, trying to get Mokimshim to move.

Mokimshim was a major obstacle to making headway. He was Hokadra's heir and was needed to lead in this crisis, but it was nearly impossible to budge him in any way, and he had totally collapsed. There was not much for it but to leave him alone, but Johajar ignored this bit of sense and continued haranguing his brother, normally with a few solid kicks. Mokimshim ignored all.

It was a relief to Zuryzel when the Miamuran army showed up at the gates with Kiarna and Asherad catching her black eye immediately. Zuryzel surveyed the army quickly.

“That can’t be Galledor!” she murmured, taking into account the brown mouse in the lead, standing head and neck above the crowd. Slung across his back, he had a fearsome sword nearly as tall as he was. Zuryzel was willing to bet that the Miamuran army would still be in Miamur if not for him.

When Jaccah called, “Open the gate!” the army marched in.

“We thought you’d need help,” explained Galledor, indicating the army. “I see we were wrong.”

“Rraaak!” squawked Norya the crow, riding on Kiarna’s shoulder. “You weren’t wrong!”

“I could do with the help, but for now, take your ease,” Zuryzel offered.

Kiarna and Asherad glanced at her once and slid off to position the troops out of the way; Galledor stayed where he was. “Why isn’t your brother here?” he inquired, his head tipped knowingly to one side.

“Johajar’s right here,” Zuryzel nodded at him. Galledor didn’t say anything, just cocked on eyebrow at her. “As for Mokimshim … ask Johajar,” Zuryzel advised.

“I will in that case.” He made as if to stride off. Then he turned. “Zuryzel,” he said, “I’m sorry about your father.”

Zuryzel threw him an admonishing look. “Please. Later! I can’t lose myself now! If I do, nothing will get done.”

Galledor’s blue eyes glowed sympathetically. “I know—my father died during a war, too, remember?” With that, he strode off to find Johajar.

He wasn’t referring to his true father, the dead king of Miamur. He meant King Hokadra, who had been more of a father to him, Kiarna, and Asherad when they were young.

“Zuryzel.” It was Sibyna.

“Mmm hmm?”

“You got some pretty nasty wounds in that last little scrabble, and the healers insist you need sleep and treatment.”

Zuryzel shook her head stubbornly. “Tell them I’ll be treated and rested when everyone else has been.”

“Everyone else is being dealt with,” Sibyna reassured her. “But you’ll be no good to us if your wounds get infected. Come on.”

She firmly grasped Zuryzel’s arm and guided her toward the infirmary. Zuryzel blindly followed. She was too tired to do otherwise.

But she wasn’t too tired to think about everything that had happened and needed to be done … She wasn’t going to rest with those thoughts going through her head! Zuryzel desperately sought for some distraction to calm her.

"Sibyna," she asked, in a soft voice, "when you said someone really liked me … not Harclayang … did you mean Asherad?"

Sibyna's eyes twinkled like stars. "No, though I bet the description would fit him too."

"Then who did you mean?" Zuryzel persisted, confused.

"My brother."

"*Dejuday*?" in her surprise, Zuryzel's voice rose a little. She glanced around nervously, but there was no one besides Sibyna to hear. She lowered her voice again. "You're joking!"

Sibyna shook her head. "Haven't you ever noticed how he looks at you? Or how he always glares at Asherad when he is around?"

No, she hadn't. "You're imagining things," she said stoutly. But she remembered the day Asherad had asked her for a walk. And she remembered seeing Dejuday glaring at him with fury. She hadn't understood it … Could Sibyna be right?

Sibyna glanced at her. "Just you wait and see."

The next turn led them to the infirmary.

The healer inspected her carefully. "Your back wound is infected, and you need a lot of rest." The healer spread some medicine on her back while she talked. "Go over to those beds. You see them? Go to sleep, and we'll look at that back wound again when you wake up," the healer ordered.

Zuryzel shook her head. "Too much …"

The healer stopped her with a hand on her arm. "Zuryzel, you've done well," the healer whispered. "Crow will be back soon. A few hours of sleep will not disrupt the safely of this place. If necessary, we will awaken you."

After a moment, Zuryzel nodded. She wasn't breaking her oath to Crow, after all.

She stumbled toward the beds and collapsed on the nearest one. Immediately, all the tears she'd been holding back spilled, and silently she wept herself to sleep.

Her dreams were confused—ships ranging the seas, birds soaring in the sky, streams trickling, and wind blowing, mixed with wars, death, despair, and loss. An image of what happened to her father blossomed in her mind, and she screamed. She could not help herself. Suddenly, the whole world was burning hot, a choking confusion of fire, smoke, ash, and—

"Zuryzel, wake up!"

Shartalla was crouched over her, and a cool feeling pressed against her forehead and Shartalla's Time-bead against her shoulder. Shartalla realized this and yanked the bead back into her tunic.

"Perishin' pilchards, yer so ho' I could cook a fish on yer face! Or burn a fish, anyway. Lie still, yeh got a severe fever."

"How long have I ..."

"Been here?" Shartalla finished the question. "Two days. Not a big deal. Crow is back with her bunch. They said some o' the Darkwoods foxes escaped, 'cludin' all the Oracles and apprentices save for Fang. No, don' geh up; jus' lie there. Sounded like you were havin' a bad dream!"

"Horrid ... but just a dream."

Shartalla understood.

To the surprise of many, including Biddah the squirrel, Shartalla stayed with Zuryzel for the rest of the day until the Wraith Mouse's fever broke. Setting sun poured through the many windows and set the pine marten's pelt on fire. Shartalla spoke softly to the ill princess, ignoring the wondering stares from the healers. "Tha's what happ'ns," she scolded the princess, "when yeh have only a few scratches and yeh don' geh 'em tended t'. They geh infected, and yeh geh sick!"

Zuryzel managed a fevered smile, thinking of Marruh, the healer for the Bow Tribe that fussed so over tiny wounds. Shartalla carried on talking.

Healers who were pretending to check their medicine or bandages were really watching Shartalla with disbelieving eyes. Her crew and the crew of many other ships kept pretending they had some task that brought them through the gardens just to see a corsair tending to a sick princess. Tsanna the ferret murmured to Grayik, "I'd never've believed it of 'er. She's so strict and stern, sometimes."

Tsanna was not the only one surprised. Biddah and some of the Wraith Mice who had said they were Zuryzel's friends looked on almost guiltily—a corsair apparently showing greater compassion than a Wraith Mouse? But none of them approached the princess. Most of the surviving Coast Tribe looked on wonderingly—to them it was a miracle worthy only of the Bear King.

But Shartalla ignored all their stares and bewilderment, merely concentrating until Zuryzel's fever broke.

In only a few days, Zuryzel was well again. She took to walking around Pasadagavra alone and unassisted, keeping herself under tight restraint, helping where needed. At night, she got little sleep because her dreams were disturbed and terrified. One starry night, she stood in a lone balcony, gazing out to the heavens, wondering what the stars really were, when she heard footsteps behind her.

Turning, she saw Dejuday, his missing ear swathed in bandages, his black eyes cautious.

"You all right?" he asked softly.

Zuryzel nodded. Normally she would be irritated with Dejuday, but not tonight. She was too tired. She was always tired these days.

Dejuday, to her surprise, glanced out the window himself. He, too, watched the stars, eyeing them as though counting them.

"What do you think the stars are?" Zuryzel asked him.

Dejuday shrugged. "Who knows? Perhaps nymphs or those dead or just specks of light."

Zuryzel kept her eyes on one of the brightest stars in the sky. Suddenly, she turned. "Dejuday?"

"Mmm?"

"I-I'm sorry I left you in the Darkwoods prison that last time. I was fed up with always getting you out of there."

Dejuday shrugged. "No big deal, at least not now. I deserved it." He smiled slightly. "I'm sorry I always got caught. My mind was just … elsewhere."

Zuryzel blinked sympathetically. "Have you slept at all recently?"

Dejuday shrugged. "Not really. No one has."

Zuryzel glanced back out at the sky. "What do you really think the stars are?" she asked.

Dejuday shrugged. "Sibyna says they're … well …" He watched a comet streak the sky. "She says they are the tips of the Bear King's whiskers."

Zuryzel felt the corners of her mouth twitching at the thought of that. She looked back at Dejuday to see he was grinning. Grinning! His was the only real smile she'd seen in days, except for Shartalla's. She turned and leaned against the diamond window. "My mother always joked that there was one star in the sky for every complaint that was ever uttered on the earth."

"I like that one better," Dejuday agreed. "That sounds like something a mother would say."

"Didn't your mother ever say stuff like that?"

Dejuday looked away awkwardly. "She, um, she left my father after I was born. Maybe she had a good reason. Someone told me my father attacked her sometimes."

Zuryzel's eyes widened. "I'm sorry!"

Dejuday only shrugged. "I don't know whether I believe that, though. I remember my father. He was kind to everyone—it's hard to believe he'd attack his own mate. But he died from disease when I was young, so I can't ask him. His sister raised Sibyna and me."

The princess tried to sympathize. "I have a friend back home whose parents died. She said she thinks her father and mother fell ill also."

Dejuday nodded. "There was a plague back when we were young. I don't remember it very well."

Zuryzel shook her head. "I don't remember it at all."

Dejuday smiled again. "But I bet it terrorized our parents in their day—the same way this war has terrorized us."

A spark of hope lit up Zuryzel's eyes. "And you think that we won't remember this either?"

"Time can heal almost anything," Dejuday replied.

Zuryzel's hope was so strong she almost laughed for it. "Dejuday, in spite of the fact that you're a clumsy scout, you are a very wise mouse."

Dejuday looked embarrassed. "Well not … I mean, others have said—" He broke off at Zuryzel's patient smile. "Thank you," he said finally, smiling at his own clumsiness.

23 Sage's Story, and Rumors

Fawn wandered the banks of the lake, searching for some food. It was almost time for dinner.

But then she saw a shape that made her forget dinner.

"*Sage!*"

The vixen looked up and looked around; her brilliant green eyes lit up with delight at the sight of Fawn, but she did not shout.

Fawn was thrilled. Leaping lightly over bushes, she shot toward her old friend from her Darkwoods days. Sage merely watched as Fawn approached, reveling in the sight of her old friend.

"Fawn," smiled Sage. "You shed the Blight, too! Wonderful! Oh, Fawn, I'm so glad to see you!"

"And I, you! I've missed you so! Why did you leave Darkwoods?"

The smile drained off Sage's face like water. "You couldn't have asked a better question? Or at least at a better time? All right, sit down and I'll tell you."

"Look, you don't need to …"

"No, I should." Guilt was all over the vixen's face. "Sit down. It's a long story …" After a moment, Sage began a tale that sent Fawn's head spinning.

"Did you know Claw was my mate?"

Fawn's jaw dropped like a stone. "But you were an Oracle's apprentice!" she blurted out.

Sage shrugged. "Not for my whole life, I wasn't, and Claw wasn't always Claw then, either. When we were mates, his name was Reed. He was wonderful then, and I miss that part of him." Sage sighed heavily and then went on. "I discovered I was to have a child—Claw's child—a little after I became an apprentice to an Oracle. Maybe it was due to carrying the child, maybe it had already started and would have happened anyway … I don't know. But anyway, the Blight began to lose its hold on me." Sage stared off into the distant memories.

"As I began to look around, I realized just how evil the Blight was. And the Oracles. I couldn't stand the thought of becoming one of them and, even worse, having my child raised in such a place. But you don't just walk up to the Oracles and say, 'I've changed my mind, think I'll leave.' They would have killed me before letting me go." She suddenly focused sharply on Fang. "And my child. So … I fled. Claw helped me out of the territory and told me to head north to Zinnta's territory—Zinnta, of the Moor Tribe."

"I know," replied Fawn. She had recently spoken to Zuryzel.

Sage continued. "I was out in the wilderness when I gave birth. I was so weak I could not continue going north. I was found by some squirrels from the Stone Tribe and brought here. I haven't seen Rosemary—my daughter—since. But I hear reports about her—it seems she is very happy."

Fawn thought for a moment, but was still confused. "Why didn't you tell Oracle Blood? He didn't have the Blight, you know. He would |have helped you."

Sage spat. "Maybe he would have helped, maybe not. The Blight isn't the only problem, you know. The Blight wasn't always the law at Darkwoods. It's pretty new, Fawn. The Oracles were evil before the Blight was given to them. Losing the Blight didn't necessarily mean Oracle Blood would be any less evil." Sage looked directly at Fawn. "Even before the Blight, Oracle Blood made your parents' life a misery."

"Sage?"

"Mm-hmmm?"

"Did you really know my mother and father?"

Sage's green eyes brimmed with memory, and she almost smiled. "I certainly did. Your mother looked almost exactly like you. Her name was Dust. She was gentle and kind and just as skilled with the shortspear as you are. Your father, on the other paw, was fiery orange and looked a lot like Scorch—I think they were some sort of cousins. He was called Bonfire. He lived up to his name, too. I think you inherited your personality from him."

Fawn's mind was spinning with things to think about. "I'm sorry, Sage. You could come with me. I'm going to Miamur."

Sage shook her head soundly. "No. I'd never be welcome, and I don't want much to do with them, anyway—the queen, the current monarch, is such a blown-up idiot. I've seen her. But—if she agrees … obviously—will you raise Rosemary for me at Miamur? I've heard of it. It sounds like a good life, and I trust you with my daughter." She gave a harsh laugh. "I'm not sure I trust myself is all."

"I will," Fawn vowed.

Feldspar had noticed strange things going on.

Ever since he had come back, cold eyes were turned on Lady Crow. Not from her own tribe, but from others. He didn't understand. Why? Then he saw the other archers getting the same treatment. Now he really was confused. What in the name of the Bear King was going on?

One night it all became clear. Feldspar and Ol'ver both caught sight of a Wraith Mouse hastening down one of the hallways toward the lake. Ol'ver blinked in surprise. "I think that is the Princess Zuryzel."

Lurena, one of the Wraith Mouse runners, glanced up from polishing her spear. "Princess, hah! She is a coward. Vanishing in the middle of the night and showing up after the battle!"

"Queen Demeda explained all that," snapped a Wraith Mouse sitting further away down the hallway.

Feldspar was stunned by this accusation.

Ol'ver looked more … well … angry. "Running off, did you say?" he challenged. "Have you never been to the coast, runner? Corsairs are dangerous. She wouldn't run off toward corsairs, bringing back a few crews, on her own unless ordered to!"

"Or if she had nothing to fear," Lurena retorted. "If, say, they knew her, she would have nothing to fear! Or perhaps she is the spy Fawn spoke of! She belted down and spied for Hemlock! Coward!"

There were murmurs of agreement; a few of them, to Feldspar's horror, came from Rangers. Suddenly, Feldspar understood the treatment the others were giving to Crow: she and her crew of Rangers had left just before the major battles. Just like Zuryzel.

A swift glance had shown Feldspar that Fawn was not around. Then he retorted heatedly, "You would trust an Oracle's apprentice over your own kind?"

"And you call her a coward?" a deep voice added. "I could call you worse things."

Feldspar jumped and looked around. Deggum, the only survivor of the Sling Tribe, leapt lightly down from a nearby oak. He glared at Lurena murderously; Lurena shifted backwards.

When Deggum spoke again, his voice was a quiet growl the whole room heard.

"You say your princess is a coward. She is braver than you! You do not dare speak of such to her face. And moreover, even when convoys from my tribe to your fortress of Kardas constantly called for help, telling you we were under attack from warhawks and the Darkwoods foxes, you and your king ignored them. Or perhaps, he simply didn't ever hear them, for none came back, as I recall. While you were sitting safe inside Kardas—don't look so surprised; I can tell you're from there by the way you speak—our tribe, once the most numerous of all tribes, was being picked off one by one. My mate and three children were carried off by a warhawk, even before Chiraage promised her allegiance to Hemlock. You call your princess a coward, say she might have been the spy, but perhaps it was *you,* Lurena."

"Yes, perhaps," snapped another voice.

It was Muryda, the fastest runner the Wraith Mice had. She limped a little, but she had entered upon hearing Deggum's voice. "That would explain why you weren't around when Zuryzel wanted a message taken to Pasadagavra from Dombre and why Sibyna and I had to take the message instead!" she added.

Lurena muttered, "I told you a thousand times I was on patrol!"

"Sure," retorted Dikiner, who slid in behind Muryda. "*I* never sent you on patrol. I never sent *any* runner on patrol."

Ol'ver shook his head. "There's no point to all these accusations now. We may as well forget the whole thing. The foxes are *gone*, and that's the last of it. I saw for myself them fleeing toward the southeast!"

At the mention of the southeast, Muryda looked up sharply. Dikiner's eyes flashed, and Lurena shuddered.

"What did you say?" Feldspar murmured.

Ol'ver looked startled. "I don't know—what did I say?"

Muryda sat down suddenly and began to scrub her blade with mud to get off the littlest bits of grime.

Feldspar crept over to sit by her. "Muryda?"

He had made the runner's acquaintance on the trek over the Ashlands. She turned to look at him with her normally friendly black eyes, though she still breathed heavily with anger. "Yes, Feldspar?"

"What's in the southeast?"

Muryda shrugged. "This little place, called Teggap, down in the prairie. It's like Denerna, one of the cliff mouse cities. A beautiful place, but weak when it comes to defenses." Muryda's eyes narrowed. "Its just … I saw it marked on Knife's map once when I was spying on the fortress. I'm guessing the foxes will try to regroup there, attack Teggap." She shrugged. "The mice living down there aren't idiots, though. They can at least get themselves away and get help from the roving mercenaries. I'd say you're right—we're over and done with those foxes."

24 An Empty, Dying Land

Zuryzel didn't want to sleep, so in the evening she deliberately curled up into an uncomfortable position, trying to keep herself awake. When midnight came, all stirring in the city ceased.

Zuryzel stood up slowly and looked around. Everything was quiet, so she set off to wander through the ancient, monolithic city. Nighttime or daytime, Pasadagavra felt the same—no bustle, no signs of life, no crowds. How could it be otherwise? So many had died in the battle. Only eighteen squirrels had survived from the Stone Tribe, three from the River Tribe, and two—Biddah and Garrow—from the Bow Tribe.

At the thought of Biddah, Zuryzel shook her head in confusion. Biddah had been just as cold to her as Lurena. Zuryzel didn't understand that; Biddah had always been her good friend.

Zuryzel continued to tally the terrible losses. Only twenty-one survived from the Mountain Tribe. All of the Wind Tribe had been lost—not one had survived! Twenty-eight from the Coast Tribe survived, seven from the Prairie Tribe, and of the once mighty and indefatigable Sling Tribe, the only survivor was Deggum, brother of Warriorqueen Wazzah.

The Wraith Mice had also taken heavy losses, though not as much as the squirrel tribes. About seventy Wraith Mice survived, but over three hundred had died. Among them were Orgorad, mate of Sibyna, Crispisin, the novice Zuryzel had been mentoring who had been almost old enough to become a fully fledged warrior, and Zuryzel's beloved father, King Hokadra.

The few river otters involved in the action had escaped notice and, therefore, had escaped with their lives. But Sone, the female tundra otter, was killed when she was forced off the mountain, and Snowgoose, elder of the Rangers, had been slain when a warhawk attacked her.

So many lost! So many dead! Zuryzel wandered around in a trance, wishing not to feel, wanting anything else but this.

"Zuryzel?"

The deep, gentle voice shook her out of her thoughts. "Dejuday?"

The soldier approached, his black eyes hard to read. Zuryzel felt her pelt prickle, remembering the last encounter with him. He approached her almost warily.

Her heart thudding like a drum, she commented quietly, "You're up late."

Dejuday blinked. He was taller than she, but not by much, and she had to keep her eyes up to meet his. "No later than you are," he whispered.

Zuryzel blinked, suddenly nervous and unsure of herself. "I- I … true."

Dejuday tipped his head sideways. "Something occupies your thoughts?"

Zuryzel attempted to shrug. "Not … really." She smiled knowingly. "That's rich from you."

Dejuday shifted guiltily, but his good humor and optimism had returned. "I concede the point."

"Dejuday?" she whispered.

"Mmm?"

"Thank you," she said quietly. "For helping the past few days."

Dejuday's cheerfulness faded a little. "Of course."

Zuryzel decided to try something. "Did you know the Miamuran army is leaving tomorrow?" She knew Dejuday didn't know that yet, and it was almost amusing to see his eyes spark with hope.

"No," he shrugged. "I didn't."

Zuryzel had to smile. "What?" she teased. "You know they've been helpful."

"Sure," Dejuday muttered, still smiling a little. "They've been helpful. At guarding the field."

Zuryzel laughed out loud. Everyone knew guarding was the easiest, if not the most exciting, task any warrior could ever be given. And a field was the easiest to guard.

"I'm planning to go with Shartalla's crew to Ezdrid," she added.

Dejuday's eyes glinted. "This is the second time you've gone off on some important mission and informed me about it. I don't suppose that *this* time you might be persuaded to let me come?"

Not an icicle's chance in a forest fire, was Zuryzel's first thought. But she smiled and shook her head gently. "No. You'll be needed here."

Dejuday inclined his head in acceptance. "Then I will bid you good-night and good travels," he said formally. He turned and disappeared into the darkness. Zuryzel turned and went her own way. There was no stirring in her heart, no eager breath, no nervousness in her.

Still, Dejuday's words left her thinking, even when she realized there was no reason to.

Early—but not *too* early—the next morning, Zuryzel sought out Galledor, the eldest prince of Miamur. She was used to having him in charge.

"Deggum is going to Ezdrid to bury Wazzah today," Zuryzel explained. "Shartalla and her crew are going also, and I was going with her, in case there are any foxes."

Galledor nodded. "I'll tell your mother. Don't worry about your family; they'll be safe."

Zuryzel nodded.

Galledor continued. "Have you ever been to Ezdrid?"

Zuryzel shook her head. "I don't think the Sling Tribe would welcome strangers often."

Galledor tipped his head in agreement. "I've seen the tallest tower. Believe me, without a bunch of magic in her territory, the Sling Tribe's land would be in a spot that you could see from the ocean."

Zuryzel didn't know what he meant, but she uttered a quick farewell and hurried to join Shartalla.

The pine marten looked a little uneasy. "Deggum is in such a state. I don' know if 'e's sane. Livin' alone in some ruins tha' once were great ain' gonna help his sanity. 'E should be in Pasadagavra, not Ezdrid."

"Jaccah would do the same for Pasadagavra," Zuryzel pointed out.

"An' I would say the same thing about 'er," Shartalla argued stubbornly.

"We'll see," Zuryzel agreed.

Deggum was waiting for them just outside the city. Shartalla had two of her crew carrying Wazzah's enclosed body between them. Deggum had taken a lot of persuading before he agreed not to go alone. He met Shartalla's eyes and Zuryzel's eyes and then murmured, "This way."

He turned off, trekking southeast. Shartalla jerked her head, and her crew followed her and Zuryzel.

"How far to Ezdrid?" Zuryzel asked Deggum, trying to strike a conversation.

"Ezdrid is two days southeast of Darkwoods. On the route we're taking, it is about six days."

"Could the foxes have fled there from Darkwoods?"

"Probably. It is where they would go. Ezdrid is large enough to hold them, and a few of my tribe were still holed up in small places in the city. They might try to root them out."

"Wazzah left spies in the city?"

"Not spies. Defenders, called *Tarlks*, or Immortals. Their sole purpose is to stay in those small places and high towers if the city were ever conquered and try to win it back. They are guerillas, and not easily caught."

Zuryzel nodded.

"But they are not exactly squirrels." Deggum's eyes lightened a very little. "You will like them."

"Are they like the chipmunks, Texat and Skettle?" Zuryzel asked.

"A little bit. But they are much more understandable and down-to-earth, figuratively. I find it kind of ironic, actually."

"'Ow come?" Shartalla asked nervously.

"You'll see."

Shartalla didn't look reassured, but she said nothing.

They passed the Onyx Watchtower at sundown, and entered the Sling Tribe territory just as night had fallen. Deggum led them to the grove of trees where Danaray had once spied on the suspicious and jumpy squirrels that the Sling Tribe had become. But if the rest of their territory was conquered, it was no wonder they were jumpy. The corsairs took to the trees for sleeping for the most part, but Shartalla wandered out a little on the prairie and collapsed out where she could still see the stars. Zuryzel joined her.

The corsair looked reminiscent and weary, but her eyes were fixed on the western sky, and she was murmuring names as though remembering constellations. Zuryzel listened to her whispering, trying to make sense of it, but she hadn't heard the names of any of those stars.

"What are you talking about?" she asked Shartalla.

"The names of the Guides," Shartalla murmured. "O'er the western sea, there are thirty stars in the sky tha're used fer navigation. One of 'em ne'er moves. They say's a city tha' was los' in the sea long ago and some'ow made it through the earth t' the sky. The city's name's Cyama, so the star's called Cyama Lio, which means the City Star in the sea's tongue."

"The City Star," Zuryzel murmured. "Are there many legends like that on the sea?"

Shartalla chuckled softly. "More'n I c'n count. There're tales o' nymphs and battles and heroes. The sea ain' entirely savage, Zuryzel. When the

Dark Ages were on the mainland, the sea kep' some o' the old legends an' histories, though it is now so long ago that it's 'ard to tell fact from legend." She turned her midnight black eyes on Zuryzel. "I love the stories tha're half real and half myth."

"Half myth," Zuryzel repeated. "No one in Arashna—or any other Wraith Mice city—knows the real story of Zureza, the first queen. They think that because her mate died, she was made queen and ruler. There was a great battle against evil, and she saved Arashna. That is what they think."

"Tha's all?" Shartalla asked, sounding disappointed. "Tha' ain' e'en a complete story."

But Zuryzel had fallen asleep.

Dejuday was trying to sleep beside one of the stream-like fountains in Pasadagavra, but he was finding this difficult. He used to sleep on his left side, but now, with his left ear missing, it felt stranger than strange. The clumsy scout tossed about for some minutes, trying to get comfortable with little success.

There was a rustling nearby, and he sat up to see Karena, one of the messengers and Dikiner's younger sister. She looked disturbed.

"'Sup?" he mumbled.

She turned to look at him with bleak black eyes. "They're not gone," she said curtly. "The Darkwoods foxes."

Dejuday closed his eyes. "That's not news, Karena. Everyone in our army knows they're out there somewhere. We just don't know if they mean to attack us again."

"So why is Prince Mokimshim acting as though they aren't?" Karena demanded.

Dejuday opened his eyes again. "What's that supposed to mean?"

Karena bit at her lip between speaking. "He's been dismantling the guards and telling the armorers to take the day off."

Dejuday frowned. "He doesn't have that authority."

"Whether he has it or not, he is using it," Karena replied.

Now Dejuday was fully awake. "Has someone informed Queen Demeda?"

Karena shrugged. "I assume so."

Dejuday leaned back on one paw, thinking. Then he stood up. "Karena, how close are you to the Queen?"

She blinked. "What's *that* supposed to mean?"

"You know what I mean," Dejuday told her bluntly. "The Queen asks you to do special tasks for her. She has for a while."

"She hasn't asked me anything she couldn't have asked of you," Karena shot back.

Dejuday didn't have time to argue with her. "I'm going to inform the Queen," he sighed. "Maybe Prince Mokimshim is following her orders."

Karena snorted softly. "Maybe. Maybe stones fly."

Dejuday tried hard to ignore that Karena had a very good point. Queen Demeda wouldn't do something to jeopardize her defenses before she was absolutely sure it was safe. As he made his way through the gardens of Pasadagavra, he tried hard to ignore the whispers of foreboding in his head.

The morning dawned cold and misty. Zuryzel and Shartalla were wakened by the chill and hastened back into the grove of trees. Deggum had lit a fire in a pit with stones lining the edge. Beside him was a skeleton of a squirrel. He kept stealing sad looks at it.

When Zuryzel looked at it questioningly, Deggum explained. "She was my mate's niece. The tribe had come here a little while before we went to Pasadagavra. Two otters were passing by and trying to keep themselves hidden. One of them slew my niece when she saw them." His voice broke, and he took several calming breaths before he continued. "Less than an hour later, the foxes arrived. Wazzah didn't know it, but I snuck back when we had made camp just around the Onyx Watchtower—huh, it took Wazzah days to decide to throw her whole tribe onto the mercy of Stone Tribeking Fuddum and Tribeprincess Jaccah. I had a job keeping hidden. I found my niece's body. She had rich ornaments because she was related to me, the Warriorqueen's brother. The foxes were plundering her gems. There were too many of them. I could not sneak in to bury her or even keep them away from her." He blinked away a stream of tears. "She was the last relative of my mate."

"What 'appened t' yer mate?" Shartalla asked gently.

"She, my two sons, and my daughter were taken by a warhawk. They have plagued us since the end of the Dark Ages."

"So you ne'er 'ad a rest from war, did yeh?" Shartalla asked quietly.

As Deggum shook his head, Zuryzel realized that it was the closest she had ever heard to a corsair complaining about war. She only ever heard one other corsair complaining about conflict in her life.

And she never saw a battle that Shartalla, or any other pirate, would avoid.

Shartalla kindly changed the subject. "Where's the crew?"

Deggum gestured. "Still asleep."

Shartalla rolled her eyes in annoyance. "Six days, jus' six tha' I was gone on the moors, an' they star' sleepin' t' the late morn. Land's made 'em soft, I tell y'!" Without further ado, she launched herself into the nearest tree with a jump. Zuryzel heard her berating her crew, waking them.

Deggum chuckled. "She's something."

"She is," Zuryzel agreed. There was a *whump* as Skorlaid slid from the tree bough where he had slept. Tsanna scrambled down from a different tree, her eyes bleary.

"Brr," Skorlaid shivered. "It's cold!"

"No colder 'n a misty mornin' at sea," Shartalla retorted, dropping neatly from the tree.

"Maybe t' you, but yer the one with a pelt thicker than an ice floe," Tsanna muttered icily.

"Wha' was that, Tsanna?" Shartalla called.

"I said the day is still new, but the mist is thick, an' it'd be nice t' get going."

The rest of Shartalla's crew was awake by now, rubbing their eyes and murmuring gratefully for the fire. Deggum had slipped off into the cellar of the camp and found some dried fish that was still good. They ate quickly as Shartalla sat next to Zuryzel.

"What *did* Tsanna say?" she asked.

"She said 'Maybe to you, but you're the one with a pelt thicker than an ice floe.'"

Shartalla nodded. "Thought so. Ah well, she's too good at watch; I can't get rid o' her."

They trekked across the misty prairie, which quickly turned into a hilly, barren region. The grass reminded Zuryzel of the grass in Zinnta's Moor Tribe territory, and the sod of the prairie had become loam, though it was warmer this side of the mountains. Eventually, even the moorland gave way to rocky outcrops and grassless dry dirt. Deggum came to a rock hill covered with straggling vines and sighed.

"This area," he indicated the rock and two others, "was called the Garden of Vines. There was a stream that flowed here—you can almost see its trail—that watered the ground just around here. We grew grapes and berries here. Down there in the rocks is a small cave where we made wine and medicines." He sighed again.

They walked for about another hour. The ground became harsher, and many of the corsairs were without shoes. Shartalla murmured, "Mm, Deggum, maybe we should stop."

"In a few minutes." He pointed to a grove of pines just a little ways ahead of them. "There is better lodging in there."

Shartalla did not complain.

They made the trees just as night had fallen. Deggum explained the significance to Zuryzel and Shartalla. "This is called *Nuremene*, or Child's Paradise. Just a little ways in there is a village where the very young children, or those who were expecting children, would go in the summer. Attacks on Ezdrid from rogues—or nomad kingdoms wandering the Unsettled Lands—were more common in the summer, and it made it harder for the children to survive the danger. We took them here, where they could spend the summer in a safer place. Sometimes the elders came here too, but only the very oldest, and they would be carried in a cart." His eyes softened. "I remember when I took my sons here. They made sport of trying to swim."

"Where's there t' swim?" Shartalla asked.

"Just past the first few trees. Listen."

Zuryzel did, and the sound of rushing water reached her ears. Deggum began walking again, this time into the trees. Zuryzel followed him, and a few steps brought her to the waterfall.

It came out of the ground. Zuryzel blinked, but the illusion didn't change. There was a cliff just in front of her where the water spewed out. It flowed as a river for several hundred yards and then disappeared into another, smaller rise, where Zuryzel stood. Zuryzel could hear the river thundering underground. Deggum explained it.

"The river was a highway in days of old. It was a way to travel swiftly and out of the weather. It has several estuaries. Over the top of these estuaries, the oldest cities of the world were built. A few still stand, but most of them are ruined. Alkzor, on our northernmost border with the Stone Tribe, was once a city of ours that specialized in growing food and shipping it to all the places of the world. But it fell into ruin when a great sickness swept here from the south. Bugs and locusts came carrying the disease, and when the bugs bit the squirrels, they fell ill. The locusts ate the crops, and so those who did not fall ill starved because there was no food. Alkzor was smaller than Ezdrid, and the disease, though it left at least a fortieth of Ezdrid's population, destroyed Alkzor. It was abandoned. Wazzah wanted to rebuild it, but then the foxes struck Ezdrid." He grew silent.

"When did that happen?" Zuryzel asked.

"Less than six cycles before we went to Pasadagavra."

Shartalla had been sniffing the air. "Deggum," she said, "I smell vegetables."

"There is a garden here that is tended," Deggum explained.

"By whom?" Zuryzel asked.

"A Tarlk."

"An immortal?" Shartalla remembered.

Deggum set off along the riverbank. "This way."

He turned from the river and set off into the woods. The ground was carpeted with soft moss, and little, star-shaped flowers. It was soft underfoot and cool, though not cold. They passed the garden, which was big, but it wasn't hot, sunny, or dusty. It was shaded and cool looking. There was no sunlight that penetrated the forest, but it was light, and light streamed down, giving the place an awesome, enchanting aura. It was beautiful.

A rather large cluster of houses sat nestled on a rise. They all had tattered tarps strung between them, making spaces that would be dry in rain. Their walls, neither wood nor plaster but green stones piled on top of each other, had patterns of precious gems on all sides. It must have cost a fortune to build each one.

Deggum explained, "They are decorated because of a favor paid us a long time ago. The fox king of Lunep, a castle, wanted to give his two daughters, Silver and Cobalt, practice in making beauty. They practiced here, making these houses. Silver was childless, but Cobalt had many children, one of whom became the next king of Lunep. He also had children, and Cobalt's line has not yet died out. But Lunep was overthrown by wandering foxes, and King of Lunep was exiled along with most of his kin. After the overthrow, we found the king's brother not too far from Lunep. He was very ill, but he survived, and he lives now in a different place. Since the king of Lunep was exiled, Lunep took a different name—now we call it Darkwoods."

Zuryzel gasped. She had not seen *that* coming!

Shartalla's crew had, by this point, entered the tiny houses, and it sounded as if they were settling down on beds. Shartalla turned to Deggum. "What's the name o' this king of Lunep?" she asked casually.

Deggum turned and looked at Shartalla, smiling slyly. "Burnish," Deggum replied. "The king's brother's name is Bonfire."

Shartalla gasped. "But Burnish is—"

"In the corsair tavern at Diray. I know."

"So that's who that old fox was in the corner!" Zuryzel realized. "I wondered how he knew my name, and he sure didn't look like a corsair."

"He was your father's friend," Deggum added, looking kindly at the princess.

"Huh. Who would've thought it—old Burnish, a king!" Shartalla shook her head in amazement. Then a new thought occurred to her. "I've 'eard Burnsh refer to a son sometimes—like 'e was dead . . . ?" Shartalla asked, her eyes narrowing.

"Yes," Deggum replied darkly. His voice filled with anger. "Burnish had . . . has . . . a son. He's not dead. His name is Scorch." Deggum looked around. "Scorch betrayed his father and betrayed his home, turning the beautiful Lunep into Darkwoods. And then betrayed all his father's friends, helping the Darkwoods foxes to attack all of us."

Zuryzel felt her blood boil. Deggum looked at her again, and his eyes were flaming too. "Zuryzel, your father hated and despised Scorch also; to betray one's father is a crime not easily forgiven." The fire in his eyes died, and his shoulders drooped. "But come. We must get enough rest to travel tomorrow." Without further ado, he paced toward one of the houses.

Zuryzel and Shartalla exchanged a look, but they did not enter the house. Instead, they flopped down in one of the spaces covered by a tarp. They did not speak of what they had just learned—it required some time to consider before talking over. Instead, they lay quietly, listening to the night.

The sweet smells of the woodland overwhelmed Zuryzel, and she flitted into sleep. She was, again, in the midst of whirring. It would seem that Time was about to show her something new. But this time, he didn't greet her. The whirring blackness melted into shapes, and she was suddenly seeing . . .

On the grayish moor. Zinnta, Tribequeen of the Moor Squirrel Tribe, was sitting on a rise, and perched on her knee was the raven Craic. His eyes were wide with worry, but Zinnta seemed only calm.

"*What message does Lady Raven—*Crow*—have for me*?" asked Zinnta.

"*Lady* Raven *said before she died to tell you that her spy—the Oracle Ice—said that Fawn is Bonfire's daughter and, more important, has forsaken the Blight.*"

Zinnta nodded. "*Zuryzel did not tell me that.*"

"*But just as important . . . Knife still speaks to the wind,*" Craic continued, "*and she almost found out about you.* Again."

Zinnta stiffened, but she said, "*I do not know what you mean.*"

"*Don't be so foolish in the future,*" Craic snapped. "Y*ou spoke to the wind, and Knife heard about you. You do realize that half her prophecies were what the wind told her about you, don't you?*" Craic shook his head. "'The Stoneflower will rise and be victorious. The one who thought she was senseless will find the answer.'"

"*The rest wasn't about me.*"

"*Yes it was,*" Craic snapped. "'Feared by the ones who know no fear. Find out who she is.' *That was* you, *Zinnta.*"

Zinnta sighed, but Craic kept talking. "*You found out who you were when Wazzah's father found you wandering alone out in the wild after having been abandoned. You believed you were an idiot when you were younger because everyone told you so, and yet look at you now. That's all good, as long as Nyincoey stays hidden. It has survived evil because it is hidden. It is your city that is in the highest point—in the sense that it is held in highest esteem by invaders and hardest to conquer. But if it gets discovered because you were foolish enough to keep talking to the wind …*"

"*Then what hope is there for squirrels?*" Zinnta finished. "*I know. I forgot who I was when my mother took me into the wild to protect me from the rogues who found Nyincoey. But they all died, my mother also. It is true I was found wandering and Wazzah's father, Krartarn, identified me. It all fits, and yet, I do not think the wind spoke of me.*"

Craic shrugged. "*There is no one else that it can speak of.*"

"*No?*" Zinnta challenged. "*My story cannot be unique.*"

"*Your name is mentioned,*" Craic pointed out.

"*Maybe so,*" Zinnta conceded.

"*It is just as well that Zuryzel did not need you at Pasadagavra,*" Craic continued. "*You'd have to tell her the whole story, or Knife might see you and recognize you.* 'She will be identified by the speaker of these words.'"

"*Knife is not the speaker of those words,*" Zinnta retorted. "*The wind is. It has already identified me.*"

Even in her vision, Zuryzel was startled: this was happening *right now!* The whirring began again, but Zuryzel woke before she could confront Time.

So *that* was whom the stupid prophecy was about! Zinnta! *She could speak to the wind!* That actually explained a lot. *That* was how she knew all those things about the war in Pasadagavra.

Zuryzel looked around, but Shartalla wasn't there. Zuryzel stood up and began to call for the corsair quietly.

"I'm 'ere," Shartalla's voice sounded out of the woods. It was still dark, but Shartalla's flaming pelt stood out like a beacon—as usual—in the night.

"Where've you been?" Zuryzel asked.

"Looking for the Tarlk Deggum spoke of," Shartalla grunted. "'E said I prob'ly wouldn' find 'im, but I 'ad t' look."

"*Did* you find him?" Zuryzel asked.

"I think so." Shartalla sounded rather shaken. "'E was flyin'."

"You mean it was a bird?"

"No, I mean it was a flyin' squirrel."

Zuryzel blinked in confusion. At Arashna, a favorite sport was taking a parachute, jumping off the westernmost tower, and seeing how far out to sea you landed. Demeda had flat-out refused to let her children try it, though her father had convinced her to let them do it once. Zuryzel, with her luck, had been sick on that day, and Hokadra never swayed Demeda again. "Do you mean it had a parachute?"

"No, it 'ad wings," Shartalla replied. "Gray with the same markin's as on the body. Wings. Flyin' squirrel."

Zuryzel shook her head. "That doesn't make sense."

"That's what I saw." Shartalla was obdurate.

The sun was visible through the trees when Shartalla roused her crew. It was all Zuryzel could do to keep from cracking up when she heard Shartalla's crude curses.

"Glorified geese, get yer tails out there! Wake up! Burnished barnacles, 'ow c'n y' think I'm gonna let y' sleep till noon? Cummon, wake up, y' bunch o' wallowin' whales!"

"Glorified geese," Zuryzel giggled. "That's a new one."

Deggum appeared out of the trees. "This is quite an interesting journey. Those pirates can't keep their curiosity at bay. Twenty-three of them, counting Shartalla, went out trying to find the Tarlk. None but Shartalla caught sight of her."

"What exactly is a Tarlk?" Zuryzel asked.

"A Tarlk is a squirrel that can fly," Deggum chuckled. "Sort of. They have skin between their arms and their sides, and if they jump off a high area, they glide down, like a bird. But they can't fly up. Still, closest a squirrel will ever come to flying! There are many legends about their origins, but they have always lived in Ezdrid."

"So Shartalla *did* see a flying squirrel," Zuryzel realized.

"She certainly did."

This dawn was clear and warm, clothing the air in gold. Zuryzel was somewhat sorry to take leave of Nuremene. It was beautiful, and there was something to be said for the houses made of gems. But she was all too ready to see the rest of the Sling Tribe territory.

Once they left Nuremene, the land became flat, harsh, and brown, but this time there were visible signs of past beauty. Zuryzel could see houses here and there, straggling remains of gardens, and even a few stagnant streams that held just a little moss in them. Zuryzel knew that in good days, there would have been gardens everywhere and streams filled with soft moss and crayfish, a Sling Tribe delicacy. Some of the streams had fallen trees lining their banks. Zuryzel knew that they were once shady arbors. Surely not even corsairs could cause this kind of damage? When they neared a piling of broken stones, Deggum sighed and explained.

"This was once called the Plain of the Ten Thousand Gardens. This plain, they say, was where the Bear King stopped to speak with many creatures, including six other kings. But it was the Sling Tribe who offered him first Ezdrid but then the land when the Bear King said that an open plain would be better. He blessed this plain, saying that as long as there was a king—or queen—of Ezdrid to rule this land that had claimed his right, there would be flowers and gardens. When a new king was crowned, he need only touch this statue. When a king died, the gardens would wither until the new ruler made claim." Without further ado, he stepped forward and touched the statue.

There was a subtle rustling sound, like wind through tall grass. A green shade spread out from the base of the statue across the plain until the harsh, rocky surface was covered with short green grass. Streams began to flow with clear water. Moss sprouted from inside them. Flowers grew up in delicate patterns, looking like blue stars or silver moons. There was even a type of flower that looked like a ship's sail—when Shartalla saw it, her eyes grew wide.

It blossomed into a garden of the kind Zuryzel had never known. Flowers of every kind unfurled their petals. Arbors gave welcome shade here and there. And fountains just came out of the ground. Some of the flowers were magical, Zuryzel could tell; they had water coming out of them like fountains or glowed like little lights or even moved on their own, swaying in a swirling pattern as if they were dancing. It made the gardens of Pasadagavra seem like wilderness.

Deggum smiled gently when he looked at the garden, stretching on for as far as the eyes could see. Zuryzel sensed him perk up a little, as though he felt less devastated by the destruction of his Tribe.

Shartalla bent to sniff one of the flowers and jumped back with a start. "Wooh! That thing just squirted dust at me!"

"Not dust," Deggum laughed. "Pollen. When it's ripe, you can suck honey from it."

Shartalla brushed the golden powder off her nose. The rest of her crew began to meander around, examining the flowers. Tsanna touched a purple-and-red flower and got a jet of wine in her face. Skorlaid cautiously touched a blue flower, and a song emanated from the petals.

Enchanted by the garden, Shartalla was wandering around with her crew, touching flowers gently. Deggum merely watched.

Zuryzel was listening to the song that came from the blue flower, trying to decide if she'd heard it before.

Deciding the tune was unfamiliar, she stood and then noticed another wonder. "Deggum, what is *that?*"

She pointed to something that looked like a rainbow.

Deggum smiled slyly. "That, Princess, is the Astyre."

"Astyre!" said Shartalla sharply. "Don't that mean somethin' like 'bird's 'ome'?"

Deggum looked surprised. "I did not know you were at all instructed in the old languages."

"*Ashire* is the word for 'sky' in the sea's tongue," Shartalla explained, "but it means 'bird's 'ome' literally."

Deggum shook his head in wonder. "Astyre means 'sky's eye.' It was the tallest tower in the world before the Dark Ages. Still is."

Shartalla nodded. Deggum gave her a curious look. "They still use the old tongues at sea?"

"Jus' one," Shartalla shrugged. "All of 'em are known by most captains in speech, though not many's the number that c'n read in any o' the tongues."

"Well can I comprehend that," Deggum commented dryly.

Shartalla turned to her still-bewitched crew. "Come on! We'll be comin' back this way. We gotta go *now*. We need t' get t' Ezdrid fast in case there're any foxes there."

That shook her crew awake. With a last, wistful look around, they plodded on through the garden.

25 Ezdrid

Between Ezdrid and the statue Deggum had touched, the gardens stretched on for three days. The sixth day of the whole journey was rising when they topped a rise and the gardens stopped, falling away behind them.

"Why don't creatures live there?" Zuryzel asked. It had been more pleasant than Nuremene. A sweet scent perfumed the air, and flowers sang soft lullabies. Zuryzel had even heard, much to her amusement, Shartalla humming reminiscently along to some of the tunes.

"Some did, before the Dark Ages," Deggum grunted. "But the Serpent is angry because of the existence of the plain. Though he cannot harm the flowers, which the Bear King blessed, or the creatures that live there, he causes raging storms high above. It is a scary sight. He did not do it to us—perhaps because we were only passing through—but if creatures live there, terrible storms are always there. Most prefer to live in Nuremene because the sight of storms does not leave a Sling Tribe's heart unbothered. Most of my tribe prefers—preferred—the sight of the blue sky."

Ahead of them, the ground fell away into dark brown earth, rolling and undulating, covered in wildflowers. A road of stone, with walls on the sides and benches along it, stretched out from their paws. "This road leads right to Ezdrid's *Morthomolohk*, the Arching Gate. Those gates almost always stayed open in the good days, long ago. Around here," he indicated the rolling moor with the wildflowers, "was farmland. There is farming land inside Ezdrid, also, but not as much as in Pasadagavra because the city was made to be less visible."

As he said this, Zuryzel looked up the height of the Astyre as it reached into the clouds—the day was overcast—and disappeared. Shartalla muttered, "It would prob'bly be perfectly unvisible if not fer the Astyre."

Deggum smiled slyly. "You cannot see the Astyre unless you passed through the Plain of the Ten Thousand Gardens or you are born in the city. It is a magic tower."

"Is there anyplace in the Sling Tribe's land tha' *ain'* magic?" Shartalla muttered.

"A few places."

Shartalla shook her head irritably. "Swipin' swordfish."

Deggum led them along the pathway. They grew silent as they neared the city. There were no foxes around the gate, and there were no sounds from inside the city. The walls, Zuryzel noted, were about her height and made of golden stone—hardly a good defense. The walls were hard to see, but the gate itself was overlaid with silver and bronze and studded liberally with curiously carved gems of every shade of blue, green, and purple. The intricate gems and shining metals made Pasadagavra's diamond-backed gates seem crude.

Poking just above the walls were some shapes, that might well have been sculptures made of bronze and steel. The bronze caught the sunlight and glowed an intense golden color, and the steel shone like white fire. The features of the half-revealed city surprised Zuryzel, but Deggum smiled at her knowingly. "This is just the beginning."

Shartalla held up her paw. "Listen!"

Shouting—some definitely in the sea's accent—sounded from within, as if it had just started. Shartalla nodded. "This is where the foxes came," she confirmed.

Deggum nodded. "It's not too hard to get in, but I want to wait until Kappan gets here."

He had barely finished speaking when a grayish shadow began gliding down from the top of one of the sun-touched sculptures. It had the shape of a squirrel minus the bushy tail, and it did have wings. *Ah*, thought Zuryzel, *this must be a Tarlk!*

The Tarlk landed neatly in front of Deggum. "Sire," he bowed. His voice had a soft, subdued, almost dusty tone to it. His fur was mostly gray with black markings—similar to Rainbow's—and his eyes were blue-gray. He wore a kind of smock that accommodated his wings.

"Hello, Kappan," Deggum replied.

"They are in the southeastern section of the city," Kappan reported, still with that quiet tone. "They have not fortified it."

Another gray Tarlk launched itself from one of the spires and landed beside Kappan. "What happened to Warriorqueen Wazzah?" she asked. "And Princess Fraeggah?"

"Dead," Deggum murmured sadly. "Everyone else in the Sling Tribe is dead. I'm all that's left."

The new Tarlk lowered her eyes and sighed. Her voice had the same soft tune as Kappan's. Deggum patted her shoulder consolingly. "She died with honor, Rhonnah," he murmured.

"But death is still death," Rhonnah sighed, "and our tribe has followed her."

"We must now cleanse Ezdrid from the defilement of the Darkwoods foxes," Kappan advised grimly. "And grieve later."

Rhonnah nodded. "We are ready to take the customary action," she added.

"Do so," Deggum ordered in a voice that was clear but quiet.

Both Tarlks took flight again.

"What did they mean?" Zuryzel asked. "What customary action?"

"It isn't all that customary, actually," Deggum told them, smiling slightly. "Only the Tarlks can do it. Remember the flowers that played the lullabies? If you dry them out and grind them up, they make a sleeping powder. The Tarlks will fly above the foxes and drop the powder to put them to sleep."

"Then we move in," Shartalla grinned. "I like Sling Tribe strategies an' tactics. Do y' s'ppose I could purchase a vat o' that sleeping powder fer my ship?"

"No."

"Oh."

Deggum patted the gate, and it slowly creaked open—another example of Sling Tribe magic—and he led them through.

Zuryzel caught her breath when she saw Ezdrid. It was huge—almost bigger than Pasadagavra. It was in a deep canyon, at least a thousand feet below her, spread out over several thousands acres. The sides of the canyon were perfectly straight and made of limestone with little jewels set in with no particular pattern. The streets of the city curved instead of going straight, so Zuryzel saw little chevrons and figure eights all over. Every street was made of a different type of gem, so each street had a different color. Counting the colors, Zuryzel saw that there were only eight very long streets.

At various intersections of these streets, an enormous building stretched to the top of the canyon walls with some fancy rune on top—these were the sculptures that Zuryzel had seen—that seemed to designate markets or places of trade. The houses were color-coded too; in one section of the city, there were red houses, and in another, green. Some houses were built into the wall and were colored indigo. Going away from Zuryzel, the city was just about three miles wide, but at least a hundred in the direction of the Astyre. The Astyre stood in what Zuryzel guessed was the center of Ezdrid, towering above all, made of every single color in the city. Zuryzel craned her neck, trying to see to the top of it, but she couldn't.

"Let's go down," Deggum suggested, his eyes alight with mirth at his companions' awe.

A blue set of stairs just in front of them led down from the gate. Deggum trotted confidently down this road, Zuryzel and the others still looking in awe at the city.

"Deggum," Shartalla asked nervously, "is this street made o' sapphire?"

"Mm, hmm." Deggum nodded.

"Where'd it come from?"

"Lunep."

"Those houses on the wall," Tsanna pointed out, "they've got lotsa fancy stuff. Are they more importan'?"

"Those houses belonged to the richer families in Ezdrid," Deggum explained. "They all had something extra special—like a waterfall—that was usually the boundary between their property and their neighbors'. One family with many children had a zigzagging slide that they would play on. Another family had a limestone track with a cart they could ride around in, with gardens and statues on the side of the track. My mate's family had a silk pavilion with a maze in it. Everyone had lots of fun trying to solve it." His eyes twinkled. "Only her family knew the answer. I spent a whole month trying to worm it out of her." He snorted with self-directed derisiveness. "I think she was enjoying watching me struggle to find it out."

"What is the secret?" Shartalla asked.

Deggum grinned. "Tell you later."

As they progressed, Zuryzel's awe at the beauty around her began to turn into sadness in the sense of decay. The city was beautiful, but there was no life here anymore. Where once there had been families and markets and who knows what all, now only silence filled the streets.

They had almost reached the yellow street when Rhonnah glided down in front of them. She spoke quickly in the language of the Sling Tribe before taking flight again. Whatever news she had was good because Deggum started chuckling.

"What?" Zuryzel, Shartalla, and Skorlaid all asked at once.

"I don't believe it," Deggum grinned, "but the corsairs are hiding in the maze!"

Zuryzel frowned. "That's not good," she murmured. "How are we going to fight them?"

"You wanted to know the secret?" Deggum asked. "There is no answer. There is only one door into the maze."

Night was falling when Deggum led them around on the blue street. They kept to the edge of the walls, their ears pricked for any sounds of the foxes or corsairs.

Deggum finally halted and pointed to one of the houses on the wall. Beside its colorful walls, there was a silken pavilion with sides rolled down. The silk, in faded grays, gave subtle evidence of once-grand greens and purples. There was a tiny door in the closed-sided pavilion, behind which shown no light.

"This is the doorway to the maze. The Darkwoods corsairs are in here," Deggum explained. "The Darkwoods foxes are in another section of the city. The Tarlks will take care of them. Now, we need one to stay here and guard the entrance to make sure none get out. Shartalla, your pelt stands out so much, I'm afraid that may be you."

Shartalla's eyes betrayed her disappointment, but Zuryzel objected first. "But she's one of the best fighters here, and she knows the corsairs best."

"She won't have the advantage of surprise," said Deggum doubtfully. "That will be most important."

"I can take care of that," Zuryzel promised.

Deggum still looked dubious. "Are you sure?"

"My father taught me how," Zuryzel assured him.

"I'll stay out here and guard," Tsanna offered. "My eyes ain't that good in the dark like others."

Shartalla nodded—maybe a little too eagerly—and Deggum continued. "If you're sure. The maze goes back into the hillside, so it's much bigger than it looks. There aren't any dead ends until you reach the edge. When you reach the ends, keep going to your left along the wall until you get back to the door and go back into the maze. There are stairs and ramps and some slides here and there, so watch your footing. Keep your voices down, because the maze is known for echoing. There's a pool of water in the center, and there might be a lot of Darkwoods corsairs around there, so don't go into the open there without lots of help. Be careful. Bear King be with you." He murmured something in his language and raised his paws, like a blessing, and then turned and entered the maze.

"If it starts getting colder all of a sudden, then back away fast," Zuryzel added, loud enough for Deggum to hear. "It's a Wraith Mouse that's invisible—could be one of our spies."

Tsanna nodded and took her position by the door. Skorlaid took a deep breath and plunged into the maze. Shartalla's crew slowly followed him.

Zuryzel led Shartalla into the maze until the light was dusky. Then she turned to face Shartalla.

The pine marten looked nervous, and she gave her friend a suspicious look. "What're you goin' t' do?" she asked carefully.

"I'm going to make you invisible," Zuryzel explained.

Shartalla blinked. "You can do that?"

"The more powerful Wraith Mice can," Zuryzel answered. "My family's always been able to."

"Why couldn't you do that to Fawn when you were rescuin' 'er?" Shartalla pestered.

"I was exhausted then, and it takes energy to do that. Quiet."

"You're gonna exhaust yerself now," Shartalla warned, "and yeh'll need all yer strength fer fightin'."

"I'll be all right. I'm not tired now."

A few moments went by. Shartalla glanced at her paw. "I ain't invisible," she observed.

"You won't be able to tell the difference," Zuryzel answered, concentrating.

"Can't you jus' trial-and-error it?" Shartalla persisted.

"I don't have *that* kind of energy, Shartalla. Quiet. I have to get this right."

"It feels cold!"

"It is cold. Quiet."

Zuryzel let herself sink into the darkness, immediately getting the smooth feeling again. This time, she kept her eyes on Shartalla's fiery pelt. She could feel Shartalla sinking with her. The strain felt as if she was carrying an extra sword on her back. But she could take it, at least for awhile. When she was done, Shartalla's pelt looked gray to her.

"Slick," Tsanna called. "I can't see 'er!"

"Let's go," Zuryzel shrugged. The strain wasn't bothering her that much.

"Do I 'ave t' stay with you?" Shartalla asked curiously.

"No, but it would be easier on me."

"Hey, I c'n see!" Shartalla crowed in a whisper.

"Concentrate on listening."

Shartalla shook her head. "Corsairs don't listen; they watch."

"Fair enough. I'll listen. Quiet."

Silently, the two friends glided into the maze. It was a strange experience for Zuryzel. The walls of the maze stretched almost as high as the halls at Arashna, giving Zuryzel a very small feeling. After just a few feet, the silken sides became stone, and the ceiling was lost in the darkness. Shartalla was shivering, but her black eyes were quick and alert.

The first corsair they saw was a fox, slinking back toward the entrance—or was he? Shartalla hissed in rage. "Demmons!" she growled. "Let's take 'im!"

Zuryzel slipped her magic from Shartalla, feeling the relief immediately. The pine marten's pelt shone in the gloom like real fire. "Demmons!" she said sharply.

Demmons had been looking over his shoulder and didn't see the younger corsair in his path. He was far enough away, however, that his momentary surprise didn't last long enough for Shartalla to take advantage. Shartalla sprinted forward like the wind, slashing her sword at her enemy's face.

It was swordplay as Zuryzel had never seen. Corsairs are masters of swords, and these two captains excelled at the deadly game. Demmons had much more experience with thousands of battles and tricks under his fur. And he had the advantage of seeing Shartalla easily because of her vibrant fur while she had more trouble making out his much darker fur.

But Shartalla had youth and strength in her favor. Pine martens were known to be quicker and nimbler than foxes, and Demmons had a kind of stiffness that came from being in the cold for days. And, although both of them already had wounds, Demmons's injuries, though lighter, affected him much more because of his age. To Zuryzel, it was a well-matched battle.

Their blades seemed to dance, flickering like snake's tongues, delivering blows both effective and delicate. For Demmons's part, they were light parrying, mostly deflecting Shartalla's strokes away from his face. But Shartalla, instead of being thrown off balance by every powerful counterstrike, merely slid her blade off and aimed another blow. Zuryzel's strategy was to have a blow with all the weight behind it so strong that her enemy could not effectively parry it. Shartalla, however, had light, swift strokes that used little energy and seemed mostly deceptive. All she had to do was dodge Demmons's powerful parries and turn that into an attack. To Zuryzel, she seemed to turn every lunge into offensive, mostly driving Demmons back.

She aimed her attacks mostly at her adversary's face and torso, whilst Demmons simply parried her strikes. Zuryzel saw a problem with Shartalla's strategy: it was much too repetitive. She had made variations of the same sword move again and again. It would only be a matter of moments before Demmons realized this.

But Zuryzel had grossly underestimated her friend's cunning. Demmons finally took the offensive and slashed a dangerous blow at Shartalla's head with the flat of his sword. Shartalla let out a cry of pain and doubled over, backing away from Demmons. Demmons laughed triumphantly. "Got y' at last!" he cackled, taking two steps to get closer to Shartalla.

His mistake was so simple it dazzled Zuryzel. Actually, it wasn't really a mistake. Demmons raised his blade to bring it crashing down on Shartalla's bent spine. At the same time, he lifted one of his foot paws. Zuryzel guessed the point of this move was to bring more weight behind the blow when he brought his foot down at the same time as his blade. Zuryzel had never seen that trick before, but Shartalla had realized what he would do and come up with a counteraction before Demmons could lower his blade. Because the sword was high over her head, Shartalla didn't have to worry about it when she swiped neatly at Demmons's footpaw. That was an old trick, and Demmons reacted immediately with a swift hop back. But because he had been on one paw, his landing was unbalanced. Shartalla, in the same motion of swiping at his paw, threw her whole weight against Demmons, knocking him back.

Zuryzel had crept around behind him, and when Demmons came hurtling at her, she automatically raised her sword. Demmons gasped as he found himself impaled on Zuryzel's blade. The whole move took less than a second.

"Well, nice of you to show up and finally help," Shartalla said with a smile as she lowered her sword.

Zuryzel nodded and then slid Demmons's body off her sword, looking up at Shartalla. "Your technique's a little repetitive," she observed conversationally.

"No it ain't," Shartalla corrected. "It's a trap. Some o' the more creative corsairs could see through it, but older ones are always using old tricks 'n' moves that have long outlived their day 'cause they ain't creative enough t' think o' their own technique. I normally don't fight wi' the same move over 'n' over, but I 'ad t' lull Demmons into some kind o' confidence. I'm surprised he didn' figure it out, though."

Zuryzel nodded. "Got it." She recast her magic.

Zuryzel wasn't bothered by the cold, but Shartalla was shivering like, as Zuryzel once heard her say, "a salmon on an iceberg" (as if Zuryzel knew what that meant).

"Can't we jus' sneak aroun' 'n' you cast that spell whene'er some'n' gets around us?" she complained after their third engagement with corsairs. She had almost been heard because her teeth were chattering.

"Takes too long," Zuryzel replied. "And I'm starting to tire, which means it takes even longer."

"But this is—"

"Shartalla," said Zuryzel sternly, "I don't like it either."

Shartalla paused. "Maybe if you could un-unvisible yerself?"

"Then I wouldn't be able to see any Wraith Mice—or you, for that matter."

"Y' don't honestly think the spies went 'ere with the foxes?" Shartalla asked.

"Who knows? There were nearly ten unaccounted-for Wraith Mice after the battle. Bear King protect us, they could all be spies for all I know."

Shartalla shook her head and murmured a reply. "Wouldn' Hemlock 'ave simply killed 'is spy t' prevent us from doin' exactly what we 'ope t' do?"

"And lose his chances of getting more information? He doesn't care what happens to the spy," Zuryzel reminded Shartalla.

"That's true, I got that," Shartalla insisted. "But think about what the spy could've seen when 'e—or she—was makin' the way t' report ter Hemlock?"

Zuryzel drew in a sharp breath. "You mean the names of the other spies?"

"Other spies, secret weapons, discoveries tha' the Wraith Mice c'd benefit from? Yeah, stuff like that."

"Do you think that would occur to Hemlock?" Zuryzel barely moved her lips. "He's not a corsair, and he *is* old. Do you think he might not have realized that?"

"I don' think 'e would've realized 'e coul' find out more by riskin' 'is spies."

"He still has to find Fawn," Zuryzel reminded her. "He may push all other potentials aside in trying to find her. It's their law since she's a renegade Oracle."

Shartalla inclined her head to accept that Zuryzel had a point.

At that moment, Skorlaid burst around the corner, panting heavily. He stopped dead, inhaled sharply, and gasped, "Who's there?"

"It's us, Skorlaid," Shartalla assured him. Zuryzel cast off her magic.

Skorlaid regained his composure immediately. "Cap'n," he panted, "there's another Wraith Mouse 'round 'ere. I was walking along and think I 'eard the sound o' talkin' an' then felt the cold. It was real sharp!" He shuddered.

Zuryzel nodded. "Wraith Mouse almost certainly." *Orgorad, perhaps,* she thought. They had never found him.

"Show us where," Shartalla ordered, glancing expectantly at Zuryzel.

Zuryzel shook her head. "Just stay behind us, Shartalla," she instructed. "He'll feel us before he can see us, but we can disguise ourselves this way."

Shartalla nodded silently and they set off in the way Skorlaid directed them. Zuryzel kept her ears pricked for any noise while Shartalla searched relentlessly. Skorlaid merely stayed in front, padding along in quiet confidence. He was with his captain and the best blade-wielder on land; what did he have to fear? He wasn't even alone, and that was what had spooked him.

Skorlaid rounded a corner and stopped. "'Twas here," he declared. "Just around here."

There were three other pathways leading away from that corner. Zuryzel stepped momentarily in each, judging which was coldest. She pointed to the one going to the left. "This one," she indicated.

She was in front now, with Skorlaid next to her and Shartalla and her fiery pelt behind them. They kept going along the coldest passageway, taking each turn carefully, until they turned into a brightly lit chamber.

Zuryzel didn't have time to think before she acted. She threw her magic over herself, Shartalla, and Skorlaid in a single heartbeat. Skorlaid threw a paw into his mouth to stifle his gasp as the chill of Zuryzel's nightly magic washed over him.

They had walked right into the chamber holding the lake at the center of the maze. And there *were* a lot of corsairs gathered here. They didn't seem to be watching for intruders, and Zuryzel could tell they hadn't been seen. But the chamber was smaller than Zuryzel had imagined, and it was less than a moment before one of the corsairs felt her magic.

"Hey!" shouted one of the foxes closest. "What's that?"

Zuryzel thrust her paws backwards toward her companions, but she needn't have bothered. Shartalla and Skorlaid grabbed her paws, and the three of them turned and ran back into the dark tunnel leading away. Alarm gave Zuryzel a shot of adrenaline, and the cold, musty passage with its earthen top seemed to fly by. She was running faster than she had ever run before, very nearly panicking. There had been at least a hundred corsairs there—how could Shartalla's small crew destroy that?—and she had very nearly been seen.

One Spy, Two Spy

When they finally stopped, as far away from the enormous gathering as they could go, Skorlaid shuddered. "Did yeh see them? There 'ad t' be a hunnert! 'Ow're we go'n' t' deal with them?"

But Shartalla's attention was not about the horde waiting by the lake. "Zuryzel?" she asked with concerned.

Zuryzel had stumbled a few steps away, tripped, fallen to her knees, and not gotten up. She was breathing heavily as though wounded. And when Shartalla put her paw on the princess's shoulder, she trembled and didn't respond.

"Is she all right?" Skorlaid asked worriedly.

"She's just exhausted," Shartalla guessed. "That was a fair distance t' run 'n' she 'ad t' keep her magic on us."

Skorlaid walked around the kneeling princess to face her and gave a gasp of alarm. "Oh no!"

Shartalla quickly dropped down beside her friend, touching the black fletch of puffin feathers. "Crossbow bolt," she murmured. "Zuryzel, c'n y' 'ear me?"

Zuryzel nodded dimly. To her, a great black curtain was closing over her eyes, so solid that the darkness before seemed light as dusk. Her strength was fading, but not disappearing. She knew she wasn't dying; she could feel her strength in her somewhere, but not in her muscles. The bolt had shocked her more than it had hurt her.

Shartalla had made the same conclusions. "Find Deggum," she ordered Skorlaid. The ferret raced off in the twinkling of an eye. Shartalla touched the bolt again, measured it against her paw, and then said, "This will hurt."

It really didn't; Shartalla was so quick that the only pain Zuryzel felt was a deep throb after the ordeal was over.

"It didn't go very deep," she announced. "Actually, it hardly went deep at all. Jus' buried the arrow tip an' that's it. It's most likely bothering yeh 'cause we just moved our tails so fast an' yeh had the strain o' yer magic. Yeh'll be all righ'."

Zuryzel nodded numbly; she could feel her strength returning a little. Shartalla lifted a wooden canteen from her shoulder, pulled the fancy stopper out, and put the neck to Zuryzel's mouth. Zuryzel drank the water greedily; there was a kind of sweet taste to it, reminding her of wind and sky.

"It's from the sail-shaped flower," Shartalla explained. "Water dripped off it like rainwater from a sail after a typhoon. Tastes nice, don't it?"

"Yes," Zuryzel gasped out. Already she was getting stronger.

"Don't tell Deggum."

"I won't."

Shartalla then dabbed a bit of the water onto the hem of her tunic and washed that into Zuryzel's wound. The bleeding seemed to slow, and when the pine marten held the hem over the wound, it stopped. Zuryzel flexed her shoulder, and it didn't bother her.

"That does it," Shartalla murmured, almost irritated. "I'm getting another o' these canteens o' that water."

"I doubt Deggum will let you."

"'E won' know."

"That's stealing, Shartalla."

Shartalla opened her mouth, preparing to object, but then closed it. "Yeah," she murmured. "I guess so." It really wasn't, the corsair thought, because Deggum didn't actually own flowers any more than she owned the water in the ocean. Perhaps Zuryzel didn't need to know, either.

There was a pattering noise, and Deggum approached. "What's wrong?"

"Nothing anymore," Zuryzel replied, "but we found the cave with the corsairs. There are over a hundred!"

"I know," Deggum nodded.

"How are we going to deal with so many?" Zuryzel asked.

"Block and hide the entrance," Deggum shrugged. "No problem."

Shartalla narrowed her eyes. "Why, pray tell," she growled, "didn't we do that first?"

"We had to get rid of the ones that were strong enough to move," Deggum explained. "They could move the obstruction. Then we'd have to fight them in the city, which would be considerably harder. Besides," he added, "I wanted to know if there is a spy around here."

"There is," Zuryzel assured him. "We've got to get him first. I intend to bring him back to Ki—Queen Demeda."

Shartalla gave Zuryzel's shoulder a gentle pat. "Sounds just enough t' me. I'll go with you."

Deggum nodded. "I'll start rounding up your crew, Shartalla," he offered. "Skorlaid, come with me."

Skorlaid glanced at Shartalla, who nodded, and followed Deggum. Zuryzel staggered to her paws and took a deep breath. "Let's go find our spy." She had almost said *Orgorad*.

Shartalla came up with a pretty good plan: Zuryzel was tired, so she put her magic over only Shartalla. The spy wouldn't suspect anything if he or she saw Zuryzel without magic. Shartalla could creep around behind and knock him or her senseless. Zuryzel didn't like it much, but it was sound.

They worked their way carefully through the maze. Zuryzel couldn't see her friend, but she could definitely tell that Shartalla was there. She also discovered that she could see almost as well as when she used her magic.

The only warning she had before the attack was a soft whispering noise; it was just enough to whirl around and dodge the blade aimed at her throat. She jumped back until she was against the wall.

The Wraith Mouse spy slipped out of the magic shadows. It wasn't Orgorad.

"You!" Zuryzel gasped, stunned.

"Don't look so shocked, *Princess,*" Lurena sneered. "Who better to be a spy than a messenger?"

"How did you get away?" Zuryzel snapped, her temper rising.

"It wasn't hard at all," Lurena retorted contemptuously. "Your mother is a hopelessly inept leader. She doesn't even know how to set up an effective guard."

"You slunk off with the Miamurans?" Zuryzel guessed.

"Maybe you're as good as Orgorad thought," Lurena retorted acidly.

"He was a spy, then?" Zuryzel guessed.

"Another one of Hemlock's," Lurena confirmed. "He *loathed* it, but Hemlock cowed him into it. He was absolutely hopeless, too." Her voice crowed. "And just so you know, Princess," she added in a contemptuous sneer, "so was your little pet novice."

"*Crispisin*?" Zuryzel gasped, shocked even more than when she'd been shot.

"Of course," Lurena smirked. "He didn't like the high and mighty princess teaching him tricks for children. He gladly accepted the opportunity to destroy you and your pride when Hemlock offered it."

Zuryzel remembered Crispisin's thanks after she had been teaching him a little. He had seemed so sincere, so honest, so dependable. Zuryzel had dedicated hours and hours to training him to be one of the best. How could he think she did so out of arrogance? How could she have been so stupid as to act that way?

"I'll be a hero when Hemlock returns," Lurena continued arrogantly. "And make no mistake about it, he will return. He will destroy you all the next time!"

"If you think Hemlock would have the guts to do that, you're a complete idiot," Zuryzel scoffed dismissively. "Knife is the real ruler."

"But she will be deposed when I give my information to Hemlock," Lurena sneered.

"What information?" Zuryzel was trying to keep Lurena talking, to learn as much as she could about what Lurena knew.

"Lady Raven's death, of course," Lurena snapped. "They're all terrified of her—and they should have been—but she's dead, and Crow isn't nearly as good as she. Oh, grow up," she snapped at Zuryzel's look of fury. "She's too easily lost to prejudice—you know how much she hated her mother—and she won't be able to take example from her mother because of her unreasonable narrow-mindedness. She hasn't got nearly as much intelligence, anyway." Lurena's black eyes sparked. "Demeda won't be able to function without Hokadra, Wazzah is dead and so is her tribe, and there hasn't been a worthy leader of the Stone Tribe since before the Dark Ages." She laughed. "Darkwoods will win because there is no strong leadership against them."

"What about Ailur?" Zuryzel reminded her.

"Nobody's going to follow a corsair," Lurena sneered.

"Just what makes you so certain the Oracles will believe you?" Zuryzel challenged.

"I've given them good information in the past," Lurena crowed. She had clearly been dying to get to this point. "Hemlock knew Hokadra knew about the spy and the information about the secrets of Mirquis and Dombre. But it was I who turned the advantage—"

"What advantage?" Zuryzel snapped.

"What other one?" Lurena snarled. "The advantage of using a tunnel that the worms dug. *I* told Hemlock about the tunnels. And much more.

Lady Raven trusted me completely—the fool. She sent a dispatch to you through me, giving the full details of the escape plan. Even that wasn't the real treasure. The treasure was Lady Raven's footnote—a list of creatures to trust, agents of her intelligence network, which she operated without your mother's knowledge. They were all the creatures who had been trying to find me and the other spies. But *I* found *them* first!" Her voice rose in a triumphant crescendo. "I gave Hemlock the gold! He will reward me! You never got the message about whom to trust or ask for secret messages—Hemlock got it instead. I gave it to him!"

"You were meant to!"

The words left Zuryzel's mouth before she could stop herself. She hadn't meant to say it, and she didn't mean to keep talking, but her mouth wouldn't stop. She hardly knew what she was saying, but the words came, and Lurena's triumph diminished as Zuryzel talked. "*You* are the fool, Lurena! It was one of Lady Raven's schemes. She gave you false names. I don't know what the names were, but they weren't the names of her agents. Chances are she gave the names of Hemlock's other spies or Knife's spy or Fang's. Your victory is but a greater victory for the Wraith Mice."

Lurena's expression congealed until it was quite different from her previous triumph, but that wasn't what Zuryzel was focusing on. There was a buzzing at her neck where the Time-bead was hanging. She kept talking; she couldn't seem to stop. "Lady Raven has been through ordeals that you can't even imagine, and almost all of them had to do with treachery. She knew exactly how to deal with spies. She probably knew you were a spy since before Fawn told Karrum and Biddah there even *was* a spy." As she spoke, her paw moved, seemingly unconsciously across her throat and up to her shoulder. It brushed against the Time-bead. The whirring started, and Zuryzel knew she was about to see another episode—but how she could was a mystery when she was awake. She had to keep Lurena talking.

"I don't believe you!" Lurena breathed. "You're bluffing."

She *was*, but that didn't stop the princess from continuing. "What makes you think that? I am a princess, and as such I was sometimes confided in—just as Mokimshim and Johajar were."

Her view of Lurena in the dark gloom didn't waver, but in the back of her mind was a vision she seemed to remember … but something she had never seen. The vision was in Darkwoods, at a spot near the castle. Oracle Scythe, silver-furred and wrapped in a very thick cloak, sat on a fallen log. "*I don't know, my Lady*," she rasped in the vision.

"They would never have trusted such a scheme to a princess!" Lurena wailed.

A flicker danced behind Lurena at the same time a flicker occurred in Zuryzel's mind. In the present, Shartalla was inching around behind Lurena, wary of making a move that would alert the Wraith Mouse. In the past-vision in Zuryzel's mind, a dark-furred mouse stood up and was pacing.

"Of course they would have," Zuryzel retorted to Lurena.

"*If those carrion keep this up*," the vision-mouse muttered, "*they'll win by simple subterfuge*."

"Why?" Lurena challenged. "There would have been more than enough involved already."

"*I agree*," vision-Scythe commented. "*But what worries me is the fact that once Hemlock realizes how far he's gone, he may decide to go further and try assassination through one of his spies*."

"I was the receiving end," Zuryzel reminded Lurena.

Shartalla sprang forward and slashed, and Zuryzel let her magic go at the last moment. Shartalla's blade thudded against Lurena's skull.

Shartalla opened her mouth to make a victory cry, but then she stopped. Lurena was writhing as though she had been poisoned. Blood poured from her mouth, staining her white face. Then she choked and was still.

"What the …?" Shartalla gasped.

"I don't know." Zuryzel held up her paws. "Can you see the scene from Time?"

Shartalla shook her head but fell silent as Zuryzel watched the rest of her vision.

"*You have been more of a help than can be repaid*," the cloaked vision-mouse murmured gratefully.

"*Don't thank me, Your Majesty. I am doing what I must to return Lunep to my king*." Scythe paused. "*But destroying these foxes may not be so difficult. The princess Fawn lives, and her anchor in the Blight is in sand. The winds of the Bear King are shaking her. If the Bear King will bring her to him, all the rest of those descended from the original inhabitants of Lunep will rise behind her. All you have to do then is aid her, and you will have every advantage you need*."

Fawn was a princess? The thought flitted through Zuryzel's mind as she continued to experience the vision.

"*Fawn is only the niece of King Burnish. That may not be enough*." The mouse stopped pacing.

"*Either way, I won't be alive to do any good*," Scythe hissed irritably.

"*Several schemes have been imagined*," the vision-mouse said. She hesitated, as though trying to decide whether to continue. "*We know who one of the spies is—Lurena the runner. We've been feeding her false information.*

In point of fact, Ailur has massed about fifty adventurers and mercenaries waiting at Diray; Northstar is waiting by the sea otters to keep any rogues down south from coming north and hitting our flank; Prince Galledor of Miamur has several hundred warriors patrolling the Unsettled Lands; and Zinnta insists that her warriors can protect what the leftover Rangers cannot in the north. You know the rest."

"Zinnta is more dangerous than ..." Scythe's voice trailed away.

"Zuryzel!" Shartalla gasped, abruptly cutting off Zuryzel's vision. "Look a' this!"

She had kicked Lurena over to see that her back was covered in claw marks! Zuryzel dropped to her knees, examining the wounds. "Great Cerecinthia—no creature on the earth has claws this big!"

One mark was bigger than Shartalla's entire tail, and Lurena's back was covered in them!

"I swear, she didn't 'ave these wounds when I slipped up on 'er from behind! I would 'ave seen 'em!" Shartalla's voice was intense and scared. She kept looking around as if she expected something to attack. "'Ow did they ge' there?"

Zuryzel shook her head. "I'm guessing the Oracles do have some magical power, after all. There must have been some kind of enchantment on her so that she would die if she ever fell into our paws."

"Zuryzel," Shartalla said deliberately, "the Blight is o' the Serpent. Serpents and snakes and earthworms and all those crawly crittery thingees don't got claws, so why would we see claw wounds if the Oracles did it?"

Zuryzel hesitated. "The Bear King himself, you think?"

Shartalla nodded. "Yeah, the Bear King."

"Shartalla," breathed Zuryzel, "the Bear King would never get involved in something like this."

Shartalla frowned. "Why not?"

Zuryzel was left nonplussed. "W—he's the *Bear King*. Why should he?"

Shartalla looked just as bewildered at Zuryzel's question as Zuryzel was at her peculiar belief. "'Cause ... we're 'is creatures! 'Is children! 'E protects us!"

Zuryzel shook her head. To her, the Bear King had always been someone who created the world and then only watched its development. Shartalla, it seemed, didn't think that way.

"Wha's the point o' protectin' us long ago," Shartalla continued, "if not t' protect us now?"

"Who knows?" Zuryzel shrugged. Then she artfully changed the subject. "Where do you think Deggum is?"

"Somewhere," Shartalla gestured vaguely. She unhooked a compass from where it hung on her belt. "Let's keep goin' west, and we should find the edge. Then all we 'ave t' do is keep going left."

Zuryzel took a last look at Lurena's body and turned to follow Shartalla

They were the last ones out of the maze, and Deggum was waiting for them. In hushed tones, they recounted Lurena's boasting tale of her spying and then described the marks on Lurena's back. Deggum nodded sadly. "She must have gone into the Astyre. The Bear King himself kills any who enter with the intent of conquering Sling Tribe land. He must have waited to kill her until after you got the information out of her." He straightened. "Come," he said. "It is time to deal with our original adversaries."

At the edge of the stone part of the maze, he slammed shut an enormous door and laid a bar across it. "They will not leave," he declared.

He turned and led them down the blue road again. At the third intersection with the yellow road, he turned onto the yellow road. "This is made of topaz," he told them.

"Wow, Deggum," Zuryzel breathed. "This place has more stone than Pasadagavra!"

Deggum shook his head. "Oh no, Princess. Pasadagavra has *much*, much more wealth. Theirs is simply not as prominent."

The place in which the Darkwoods foxes were hiding was a circular basin in between two enormous sculptures, one a flower, the other a tree. Kappan and several other flying squirrels were perched on the tree; Rhonnah and two others were resting in a dip on the flower.

Deggum clambered nimbly up the steel flower and held a hasty whispered conference with Rhonnah before scrambling back down. She nodded briefly and then began to play a flute.

Like Jaccah's magic flute, this too had powers. Zuryzel couldn't see what the song played of as she had with Jaccah's flute; she saw only indistinct shapes. This music was making everything swirl and seem unsteady. It wasn't creating unreality; it was blurring reality. The foxes, already weary, must have felt it hard. Rhonnah increased the volume, and it began to echo.

As the volume increased, Kappan and his friends spread their wings and glided across. A second later, Rhonnah's companion began to sing a lullaby. The flying squirrels opened the small, lightly bound bags they carried, and a blue dust began to fall onto the foxes. The sleeping powder worked its magic, and t

The foxes dropped one by one.

Zuryzel hissed. "There are only a hundred. There should be *three* hundred!"

"They probably wen' off in diff'rent directions," Shartalla realized gloomily. "Some of 'em went t' Darkwoods an' then ran elsewhere; some ran 'ere."

The sleeping foxes all lay sprawled out. Zuryzel stood to go finish the job, but Deggum halted her. "Never mind," he sighed wearily. "Let them drop poison on our enemies. We must rest, and it is a long way there." He gave the princess a soft look. "You are exhausted—that lullaby almost put *you* to sleep. We all are tired." He sighed. "But, Ezdrid is free. A good day's labor."

Deggum led them to one of the indigo houses. Inside it showed obvious signs of having been spoiled, but two female Tarlks approached at the door. Deggum explained sadly, "This was my mother's house before she became Tribequeen."

The Tarlks had cleaned it out a little bit, and there were soft, clean beds to go around. Zuryzel longed to nod off, but Shartalla's tossing was getting disturbing.

"It's too hot," she hissed. "All these plains is too hot 'n' dry."

Zuryzel shook her head. "Then go ask Deggum for some of that sleeping powder. Or," she added with a bitter inspiration, "go plunge yourself in some icy water. I'm sure the Tarlks have some somewhere."

Shartalla sat up straight. "Good idea!" She bounded off.

Zuryzel finally managed to fall asleep.

Zuryzel woke again when the sun was rising steadily. Shartalla was still asleep, so Zuryzel stood up and glided out of the room, looking for Deggum.

He was in what appeared to be a common room. Unlike the outside, the inside was made of common brick, although several pastel colored windows gave the room a cool feeling. The Warriorking was reading a book with tattered covers; Zuryzel recognized the script of the ancient languages making the title. He looked up at the sound of Zuryzel's steps on the carpeted floor.

"I think we must return soon to Pasadagavra," she explained awkwardly.

Deggum inclined his head. "Of course." He closed the old tome softly. "There is a pathway marked through the garden and also through Nuremene." He stood. "I wish you the best of fortune in the rest of your life, Princess Zuryzel." His eyes twinkled. "We may yet meet again. Not here, I think, but somewhere more sacred to you. Farewell, Your Highness."

Zuryzel nodded. "Farewell, Your Majesty," she murmured respectfully and left the room. She had gone about five paces from the door when she stopped.

Another Time-dream vision filled her head—two, in fact, one right after the other. The first was Demeda deciding to send her daughter to the coast and the tavern at Diray.

Maybe it was the absence of the cloak that had done it or maybe a more familiar surrounding than the tavern she had visited only once, but this time, Zuryzel recognized the voice of the vision-mouse.

Zuryzel brushed her Time-bead.

"*Yes?*" Time's misty voice asked.

"I recognized the mouse that recruited Shartalla," she announced abruptly.

"*It is of no consequence now. It was important you not know who she was when you challenged Lurena. That need is now no more.*" With that, Time's voice left.

27 Revealed

Zuryzel and Shartalla took only four days returning to Pasadagavra, as they could move more swiftly than the wounded Deggum had been able to travel. It still took several threats from Shartalla's colorful repertoire to get her crew through the Plain of Ten Thousand Gardens, however. The night was misty as they approached Pasadagavra.

Shartalla barely took time to tell her crew to rest before she drew Zuryzel aside. "Yer gonna have t' report t' yer mother," she warned softly.

Zuryzel nodded. Lurena's prediction about Demeda rang in her ears, and she was afraid of what she might find, but she set her paws at a deliberate pace, hastening up to the room where Demeda was lodged.

Zuryzel was terrified her mother would be in some comatose condition, but in fact, Demeda was bent over a report, and her eyes were bright and clear as mountain air when she looked up. They brightened even more when she saw her daughter. "Welcome home, Zuryzel," she smiled. "I'm glad you're safe."

She pressed her daughter about Deggum's condition and how the foxes and corsairs were defeated and a lot of other things. Zuryzel didn't mind; she actually intended to do a bit of pressing of her own.

"Mother," she said finally, "I have a few questions for you."

"Oh?" Demeda replied. Her black eyes were strangely guarded.

"Did Lady Raven play some kind of ruse with Lurena? I mean, did she give Lurena false names?"

Demeda blinked. "Yes," she replied slowly.

"She had spies of her own inside Darkwoods, didn't she?" Zuryzel pressed. "Like Scythe?"

For a moment, Zuryzel almost thought she saw disappointment in her mother's eyes. "Scythe was the daughter of one of the kings of Lunep—I trust Deggum explained the castle's origins to you? Of course," Demeda added wryly, "she was a princess a long time ago. I think she was ancient in the time of my father's infancy. But she did indeed feed us information, and she really did go to pains to keep the war from commencing before she had a chance to poison Knife." Demeda smiled wryly at Zuryzel's gasp. "Really, Zuryzel. Politics, especially with enemy governments, truly do involve quite a bit of poisoning. Anyway, Raven knew Scythe pretty much from the time of Lord Condor's death to the day Scythe herself died."

That was the opening Zuryzel had been looking for. She did not meet her mother's eyes as she commented quite calmly, "But Scythe was *your* spy, not Lady Raven's."

Zuryzel raised her eyes to meet her mother's. Demeda, to her surprise, was smiling proudly. "Why, yes," Demeda smiled. "She was indeed."

Your Majesty was the sort of greeting a high-ranking official might use to greet a queen from a different nation.

"You also recruited Shartalla, didn't you?" Zuryzel pressed her mother, feeling more confident.

"Very good, Zuryzel," Demeda complimented her daughter. "Actually, it was Ailur's idea. I didn't like the possibility of recruiting corsairs, but there is no denying Shartalla's prowess with a sword. Especially not after her bouts with Epoi."

"Did you see those?" Zuryzel asked.

Demeda nodded. "I did. Not at all something I'd care to relive, although it was quite something to see Epoi go from the height of respect to the depth of humiliation."

"You found a good recruit in Shartalla," Zuryzel informed her mother.

Demeda stood up and began to pace. "I also found Arasam and the others as well, and I had Grayik wait for you at the bend in the Dellon River. I also had Redseg slip into the horde of corsairs." She gave her daughter a mysterious smile.

"I thought Lady Raven and Ailur did that," Zuryzel protested.

Demeda shrugged. "We split it three ways. Ailur sent the vast majority of her crew with Jironi. Lady Raven found the slave Fotirra and sent her, along with many other mercenaries, to Denerna, where Demmons was gathering the Darkwoods corsairs. And I sent Redseg." She smiled mischievously. "As a matter of fact, it was I—disguised of course—who caused the pirates and scum Demmons brought with him to stay at the coast instead of filling the real ocean. I whispered tidbits of gossip about the riches of Pasadagavra to their captains. Then I fired Demmons with stories of plunder and easy victory. By the way, if Kiskap of the Hoeylahk otters is successful, all their ships have been sunk at the wharves."

"You actually helped them to get to Pasadagavra?" Zuryzel gasped at her mother. "Why?"

"You forget, Zuryzel. Kiskap was in the harbors—as a matter of fact, unless Craic has reached him by now, he is marching toward Pasadagavra with his warriors. His sister, Northstar, is mingled with the sea otters. She, the Keron Mice, and Crow—who was chasing nothing but a band of rogue foxes, by the way—were to come up from the south. Prince Galledor had massed several hundred warriors in the east. The whole theory was that they would sweep in and flank the corsairs and Darkwoods foxes at the same time as Redseg and his friends attacked from the inside."

"I would have been coming from the coast also with the corsairs who were our allies," Zuryzel realized.

"If the foxes hadn't found that tunnel going into Pasadagavra, they would have been outflanked," Demeda agreed. "Kiskap was just a little behind schedule, or you would have met him too."

"But what was the point of this?" Zuryzel asked, bewildered. "All the trickery?"

"Think, Zuryzel," Demeda urged. When Zuryzel still looked confused, her mother sighed, betraying a little disappointment. "The Darkwoods foxes had made many conquests, Zuryzel, but religious leaders have never made good emperors. Conquest is one thing; ruling day to day is something else entirely. That is why the Dark Kingdom in the time of the Dark Ages was so powerful—all of its opponents were being led, officially or in actuality, by a powerful religious figure. In the minds of most pagan religious leaders, policy changed every week. The Darkwoods foxes would have crumbled before Hemlock died. After all, they are only rogues with leaders touched by false spiritual ecstasy and installed in a castle. All they had to make themselves a threat were great numbers and one leader with a fairly high level of intelligence."

Zuryzel blinked. When Demeda had spoken of them before, her tone indicated fear. Now the Queen's voice was laden with scorn.

"The corsairs are another matter," Demeda continued. "They don't bother consulting with false gods; they do whatever is best for them. They don't bother being cautious; they throw their entire strength, wit, and energy into one thing. Usually, that particular goal is victory. Not the lands that come with it, not the prizes, sometimes not even the respect, but just the pure victory. They could very well have been dangerous. You know that there is no navy that could really match them in strength. But still, they needed to be eliminated. The lack of a fleet ruled out overwhelming them at sea; therefore, they had to be attacked on land. We rather effectively destroyed the most dangerous of corsairs and warded off many others."

"So now there is little in the way of threat coming from the sea," Zuryzel realized. "Arashna is safe."

"There is always danger from corsairs, and there always will be," Demeda shrugged. "Immihg is still at large, and I don't trust Arasam at all. But Demmons is gone, thanks to you and Shartalla. Epoi is gone, and so are many others."

Zuryzel actually managed a smile. "So there can be peace for at least a while?" she guessed.

Demeda's face, formerly bright with triumph, darkened. "I don't know, child," she murmured, not meeting her daughter's eyes. "When I was your age, I thought wars were a thing of the past and only once in a while did one erupt. I have since learned differently. War is natural. More natural than peace, I think." She gave Zuryzel a long, penetrating look. "I do not think peace will last particularly long."

"But the corsairs suffered heavily in this war," Zuryzel objected, "and the Darkwoods foxes are no more, except for some bands here and there."

"I know," Demeda murmured, "but the fact remains: there are power-hungry creatures left in all good tribes and countries and, unfortunately, not much in the way of worthy command. Lurena was right when she said there has been no talented leader of the Stone Tribe since before the Dark Ages, and yet they are now the most powerful tribe remaining south of the mountains. Miamur suffered virtually no losses in this war, but their leader—the Queen Regent, I think she's called—is a selfish, spoiled hag, though thankfully only ruling for a little longer. Nighthawk and Shorefish's raids on the sea otters did not deplete their numbers much, but now that Northstar is no longer with them, we wouldn't know if they have ambitions that go beyond Zurez. Eeried did not help us at all, but the mercenaries there are fierce warriors. Zinnta's tribe lost only a score or so of fighters, but her alliances were never very firmly fixed. I shudder to think what she could do if it entered her mind." Demeda's face was grim. "With all of this instability, it would be a miracle if peace persisted for more than twenty cycles. Let even one of these powerful forces got the wrong ideas—well, the old superpowers of Lunep and Ezdrid are no longer there to keep them in check."

"There are the Wraith Mice," Zuryzel pointed out. "And the Rangers."

"I know," Demeda acknowledged. "But I do not know much about what Crow would do if war broke out. It is a rare leader of the Rangers that would leave such a wild place to aid in a war that would not affect them. They have battles of their own, you understand. Lady Raven I knew. I do knot know Lady Crow well at all. And as for the Wraith Mice, I do not think their power will last that long." She closed her eyes for a moment.

"You are a much better queen than Jaccaha or Zinnta," Zuryzel insisted.

Demeda smiled briefly. "Thank you, Zuryzel, but I am not young." Her black eyes betrayed something approaching fear. "And I worry over what your brother could become."

With Johajar and Dikiner and everyone else, Zuryzel had dismissed those worries and insisted that Mokimshim would be a great king. However, coming from her mother, the dark possibilities finally penetrated the stubborn princess. "You think he cannot rule?" she asked nervously.

Demeda, who had always defended her children fiercely, now looked almost lost. "He isn't that bad," she conceded, "but I seriously doubt that his level is up to what it should be."

"He can't be that inept," Zuryzel protested. But unlike before when her defence of her brother had been fierce and convicted, the impact of Demeda's mistrust and uncertainty had shaken all the strength from her own statement.

Demeda's eyes, however, flashed some violent emotion. "I don't know that he is, Zuryzel. I don't know how good he is. At this point in time, I really don't care. All that I am concerned with at the moment is that he isn't fulfilling a potential I know he can—that he knows he can."

Zuryzel had no idea where her mother's vehemence had come from. She was about to ask what was bothering her when the Queen turned calm eyes to her daughter. "So you found out that Scythe was my spy," she said, returning to the first subject. "Who else?"

Zuryzel shrugged. "How many foxes can one creature have that are disloyal?"

"There were only two—three, actually, but one of them was apprehended and killed six cycles ago or so. Scythe was another; Ice was a third."

"I knew about Ice—Crow told me," Zuryzel explained.

Demeda inclined her head. "However, didn't it make sense that I had agents trying to find Hemlock's creatures?"

"Spies in your own army?" Zuryzel gasped.

"Of course. Ice told Raven that there were about eight spies that had infiltrated us. In actuality, there were six. Four of them, unknown to

Scythe, Raven, and Tribequeen Sharmmuh, were my agents, passing along false information."

Zuryzel blinked in surprise and relief. "Then Crispisin—"

"Was one of mine," Demeda confirmed. "He was Fang's only spy, actually, and Fang paid him a fortune for tidbits of false information." Her black eyes grew sad. "He tried to slip some poison into Fang's cup once but didn't succeed. He got out all right, but didn't manage to survive the battle in Pasadagavra."

"And Knife's spy?" Zuryzel pressed.

"We never did find out who Knife's spy was," Demeda explained regretfully. "He or she was a little bit smarter than we anticipated."

"Who were the others?" Zuryzel pressed.

"Can't you guess?" Demeda challenged mischievously.

Zuryzel thought about it for a long while. "Mmm …" Then a name popped into her head. "Shinar?"

Demeda nodded. "Indeed. As a river otter and veritable mercenary, she was easy to slip in."

"I thought all spies were Wraith Mice!" Zuryzel pointed out.

"Ice was just guessing. She reasoned that only Wraith Mice could sneak away and avoid the sentries so often. Anyway, Shinar uncovered the alliance between Hemlock and Shorefish, as well as the alliance between Hemlock and the sea otters." Her eyes sparkled. "I'm sure you can decipher the significance of *that* intelligence."

"Shorefish probably wanted help getting rid of the sea otters," Zuryzel guessed, grinning, "so you told Shorefish?"

"I did indeed," Demeda smirked. "Shorefish was *furious*."

Zuryzel thought some more. "Dikiner?"

Demeda shook her head. "Close, but someone near to him was already spying for me."

"*Karena*!" said Zuryzel triumphantly—and a little incredulously.

"Precisely," Demeda nodded. "She pretended to be cowed by Hemlock. As a scout, it was easy for her to slip away. She was the one who discovered that Lurena was a spy."

"So you could feed Lurena false information," Zuryzel agreed. "And the fourth …" She paused, running over names in her head. Strangely, though she couldn't think of any that made sense. Carefully, she tried to remember the names of the others. Lurena was accounted for, and so was Knife's spy, though they didn't know the name. Karena, Shinar, Crispisin, …

That left only one possibility.

"Orgorad?" she asked in a small voice.

Demeda nodded. "Correct. He devoted most of his efforts into finding the other spies. Gavenya, that young noble maiden from Arashna, was approached by one of Hemlock's captains. Orgorad found out about it and prevented her from joining them."

"That's why he was so friendly with all those others," Zuryzel realized. "He was trying to find out if they were spies. All this time, I thought he was spying on us … but he was loyal after all."

"Yes, he was loyal. He really wasn't being friendly with the others, not as you mean," Demeda corrected her. "You've spent most of your time with your brothers, so you haven't seen how much effect an innocent little comment from anyone can have on a young maiden who spends her first cycles in the army. A little encouragement, just some friendly remarks, and Orgorad could glean all the information he needed. Besides that, young ladies gossip like you have no idea; they could have picked up anything." Demeda paused. "You can tell Sibyna that, by the way."

Zuryzel nodded. "I will. But that doesn't seem like a very … well, *sound* tactic to use."

"I didn't have a choice," Demeda scowled irritably. "Originally, I had an old veteran friend of mine who was the gentle encouragement—the guiding voice. She must not have been very good because, somehow or other, Orgorad found out about my actions. Then I had no option but to have him assume that role." She gave her daughter a tired look. "Tell Sibyna *that,* too."

"Of *course,*" Zuryzel reassured her mother.

Demeda rested her head in her paws for a few minutes. Then she raised it. "I'd still give a good part of my treasury to find the name of Knife's agent."

"Shartalla thinks that one of them may have spied for both," Zuryzel told her mother.

Demeda shook her head. "I don't think so. I told you, I know who most of those spies are, and I can guarantee none of them spied for Knife." She shook her head. "You must be exhausted," she said at last, "and so am I. I think night has long fallen."

"It was dark when I got here," Zuryzel replied.

"Then I have one more question for you," Demeda decided. She sat down and faced her daughter seriously. "When did you start guessing about these spies?"

Zuryzel ran over in her mind the past few cycles. "Mmm," she thought. "I … I guess it was about the same time I asked you about the Hoeylahk otters."

Demeda nodded. "I had rather hoped that you would start working it out earlier. I got desperate when you didn't stop and think about whether or not anyone could be whispering your modifications of Dombre to Hemlock and Knife. I had Shinar drop a few hints about any topic that I thought would get you thinking. In point of fact, I spent the last few cycles trying to get you to see the allies we had and the schemes of Lady Raven on your own."

"Why couldn't you have just told me?" Zuryzel protested.

"I didn't want to be eavesdropped on," Demeda explained. "And I was also hoping you could learn to spot irregular patterns."

"I only noticed it was irregular when I found Fawn that one night," Zuryzel murmured shamefully. "And even then I had to have her point out that the presence of the corsairs was odd."

Demeda smiled gently. "No matter. Now you know what to look for, and when you're older, you'll be better." She stood and stretched. "Let's go sleep."

Demeda and Zuryzel were on their way to the chambers set up for sleeping when a Wraith Mouse scurried by carrying a large number of arrows. "Where are you going?" Demeda's words stopped him imperially.
The mouse inclined his head. "His Highness Mokimshim is dismantling the defenses of the outer walls, Your Majesty."

Demeda actually cursed. "Get these arrows back to the wall *now*. There will be no dismantling of the defenses." She turned to meet her daughter's eyes. "I fear my rest must wait." Her black eyes were strangely weary. "I will see you in a bit." She turned and hurried away toward the walls.

Zuryzel thought now she understood her mother's former vehemence. It seemed as though Mokimshim had been overstepping his authority. What startled Zuryzel was the Wraith Mouse's reference to Mokimshim as "Highness." No one referred to the three royal children like that. It was always "Prince Mokimshim" and so on.

There was the sound of soft steps behind her, and she turned to see Dejuday walking unhurriedly towards her. "Princess," he said respectfully. "You should know that Prince Mokimshim ordered a dismantling of the outer defenses."

"I know," Zuryzel replied, trying to mimic her mother's manner. "Queen Demeda has already gone to handle it."

Dejuday nodded. "I rather thought she might have. She and your brother have been at odds since you left. Johajar has been trying to needle Mokimshim as much as he can, and Mokimshim has done a thousand things that seem to have no more purpose than to rankle the Queen. She won't let herself get rankled, but she won't give Mokimshim a free paw either. It's been a pretty tense situation."

Zuryzel could hardly believe her ears. When she had left, Mokimshim had been in a dazed state of shock. How had he recovered so fast?

"I think I had better see this," she murmured, forgetting to appear majestic. "Where are they?"

Dejuday made a gesture with his paw. "This way." Zuryzel noted that he could have told her where they were without leading her, but he seemed to want an excuse to guide her.

He went, of course, to the Main Gate on the lower level. Zuryzel was startled by the scene that awaited her. Creatures were clustered more or less in a rough circle around Mokimshim and his mother. The two of them stood perhaps ten feet apart. Mokimshim's tone hovered on the verge of disrespect. "The defenders are exhausted," he pointed out. His black eyes were defiant; Zuryzel shied away from the term "malicious." He stood as he did before a battle, with his head erect and his shoulders squared. "There has been no sign of Darkwoods," he continued. "What is the point of holding a weary defense?"

Demeda held his eyes. The look in those charcoal depths said quite plainly that she was the queen and that she didn't need to justify herself. Her next remark was addressed to the soldiers clustered around her. "Tell me, soldiers of Arashna," she declared in a ringing voice, "would you rather be weary or dead? Two hundred Darkwoods foxes are unaccounted for. They know where the passageway into the city is. If we are not on guard and they mount a counterattack, there will be a massacre as bad as the one we just survived." She turned her black gaze to her son. "There will be no dismantling of the defenses yet, Prince Mokimshim. I am the Queen, and this is my decision. Return the defenders to the walls *now*." Her voice carried the threat of hidden daggers.

Mokimshim's eyes blazed, but he dipped his head. "As you wish, Your Majesty."

As if he has any choice, Zuryzel found herself thinking.

Johajar appeared beside his sister. "Hello, Zuryzel," he said quietly. "Welcome home."

"How often has that sort of thing been happening?" Zuryzel gasped.

"Very," Johajar replied sourly.

"Prince Mokimshim seems to be doing nothing but causing bedlam," Dejuday picked up.

"You know, when he was at Mirquis, I thought he actually tried to avoid anarchy," Johajar hissed. "I'm not so sure anymore."

"I am of the same mind as your brother," Dejuday agreed.

Zuryzel looked between the faces of her brother and her fellow scout. "Are you sure you aren't exaggerating?"

Both shook their heads. "Zuryzel, ask anyone in Pasadagavra. He's been a pain in the tail." Johajar looked at the piles of weaponry being replaced. "I'd better go help," he decided. He flashed his sister a look of mingled exasperation and amusement.

"Perhaps I should help too," Dejuday murmured respectfully.

"Not just yet, Dejuday." Just like in Ezdrid, Zuryzel hadn't intended to let the words slip out, but she had done so anyway. "Tell me everything that has happened here," she said quickly to justify her slip.

Dejuday shrugged. "Not much," he admitted. "We did see some of the Darkwoods foxes not too long ago." His black eyes grew wry. "Just yesterday, in fact."

Zuryzel nodded and then was at a loss for what to say. Dejuday's black eyes flickered. "Did you see any foxes in Ezdrid?" he asked artfully.

Zuryzel seized the opening. "We saw around a hundred. I didn't recognize any Oracles, however."

"What about Scorch?" Dejuday asked.

"I did not see him," she replied regretfully.

Dejuday looked away. "I suppose I should help," he said, meaning with the defenses. "And you must be exhausted." He turned and went over to help a squirrel lift a heavy barrel of arrows. Zuryzel watched him for a few minutes. Strangely enough, he seemed to be working the hardest. She slipped back and stood against a rose-colored wall where Dejuday could not see her and simply observed for a few moments. He really did work hard, and most of the creatures he helped were likely total strangers.

After a few moments, she turned and made for the sleeping chambers. But, exhausted though she was, the thought of Dejuday kept her awake for hours. The diligent side of him she had never had the time to see confused her. But as the sky turned gray, sleep had pity on the bewildered princess, and she finally drifted off.

28 Mists of the World

Water from clam holes squirted Zuryzel's paws as she splashed in the sand forming the tidal flats just outside Arashna. The black castle dominated the seaward landscape, and the sun glinted on the sea, where waves bigger than the princess pounded against the rocks that outlined the Island of Arashna. Landward, the fortress of Dobar, built on a steep hill nearly two hundred feet tall, protected Arashna from land. The trees started about fifty feet away from the shoreline.

This, *this* was what life should be like! The soothing sound of waves, just enough sun to warm her fur, calm skies above—it was all beautiful. Zuryzel flopped down in the sand, feeling it conform to her. Content, she closed her eyes against the sun.

When they opened again, she was flat on her back in dusky gray light. *Did I fall asleep*? she wondered.

Then she saw that she was on soft grass instead of damp sand and groaned. She was still in Pasadagavra. Zuryzel sighed in exasperation and closed her eyes again. That had been such a perfect dream.

Then she felt someone shake her urgently. Blinking, she saw that Karena was kneeling over her.

"Yes?" she asked hurriedly.

"The remnant of the Darkwoods army has been spotted near the corsairs' old camp, Your Highness," the scout whispered. "Queen Demeda wants an attack party to deal with them."

"I'm coming," Zuryzel hissed, jumping up.

Zuryzel pelted down to the postern and slipped out to find Demeda's war party was massing. Demeda's eyes were slightly alarmed. "They do not seem weary," she whispered to her daughter. "It appears that they have found some sort of advantage. We must hurry and destroy them."

Zuryzel nodded. Beside her, a splash of color announced her corsair friend.

"They won' be able t' stand up t' my crew," Shartalla declared in a low voice, even though there was no way the remnants could hear them.

"Zuryzel," Demeda added urgently, "I want you to go and get a head count of roughly how many are out there. Quickly!"

"I'll go with you," Shartalla offered. "Skorlaid, you command the crew!"

The captain and the princess ran through the postern post haste. They kept low and close to Pasadagavra until they hit the trees, still running. Zuryzel crouched down, but Shartalla sprang into the trees. Slowly but surely, they moved toward the camp they had set up when they had come from Diray.

They heard the voices long before they reached the camp and saw the foxes massed there.

"No corsairs mixed in," Shartalla whispered from her tree.

Zuryzel pulled herself up alongside her friend and counted the foxes as best she could. "I recognize some of the livery from the foxes we didn't catch," she whispered back, "but I also see a lot I don't recognize."

She examined the latter for a while. They bore signs of a long, arduous march, but there was more than that. Their armor was unpolished and their fur shaggy, as if they'd been living wild for many, many seasons. There was a sense of misery and resentment around all of them, and most of them bore mighty wounds but looked indifferent to their pain. A lot of their gear showed signs of water damage, but that didn't make sense. It had been relatively dry. Unless they'd tried to swim, or …

Or been living in a place famous for rain.

Then it hit her and she gasped. "Shartalla, look for a dark vixen a little younger than I am!"

"There!" Shartalla pointed an instant later. "Sulking."

"I knew it! It's the Oracle's apprentice Eclipse!" Zuryzel felt a surge of joy so powerful she nearly screamed. "These are the foxes that were once besieging Arashna!"

Shartalla's eyes lit up. "That means that Arashna ain't under siege no more!"

"We've got to report this!" Zuryzel breathed. But for a few moments, she watched Eclipse. "Eclipse looks happy, doesn't she?" she added sarcastically.

It was then that Zuryzel noticed something else; Eclipse was wearing the many shawls and scarves of a vixen Oracle, but her eyes were a piercing blue, not red with the Blight. She sat on a log, sulking, glaring at her colleagues whilst the other soldiers that must have been under her command at Arashna had similar expressions on their faces. Zuryzel also saw Claw, and he didn't look very happy about the proceedings either. Knife was nowhere to be seen, but Zuryzel did see Hemlock. Without Knife, of course, Hemlock and Eclipse and presumably Claw were the only Oracles present. But it looked as though Hemlock couldn't hold onto Eclipse and Claw's loyalty.

Zuryzel remembered her mother's comment about a conquering army led by a religious leader and how Demeda had predicted that Darkwoods would fall apart before Hemlock's death. Just twelve hours later, here was Darkwoods, falling apart, half of her remaining soldiers glowering mutinously at their old and half-frayed leader but turning trusting eyes on two equally resentful insubordinates.

"Are you ninnies!" Hemlock screamed. "Rouse yourselves! We will take Pasadagavra this time!"

"Ain't 'e in denial," Shartalla chuckled. "'E ain't got enough fighters t' retake 'is own castle!"

"Oracle Hemlock," Oracle Eclipse retorted, "my soldiers have been harassed and beset at Arashna for over six seasons. Half of them were killed and another quarter injured—your finest soldiers! And for what? Nothing! Arashna still stands! *None* of us is ready for another drawn-out campaign. Most of us would rather die."

"But it will not be drawn out, Eclipse!" Hemlock protested. "We now know there is an entrance through the back!"

"Up the mountain?" Claw interpreted. "Forget it!"

"This is insubordination!" Hemlock screamed. He snatched a spear from a nearby soldier; Claw already had his own sword out. Hemlock was so feeble he could barely lift the heavy spear, but Claw was very conditioned. He raised his own sword menacingly.

"It is the will of the Serpent that you obey the Eldest Oracle!" Hemlock charged him.

Claw's next remark reminded Zuryzel of one of Demeda's tactics: he turned and addressed the soldiers, both those who were glowering at Hemlock and those who were glaring at him. "The Serpent! Brethren, fellows of Darkwoods, my kin—we have been slaughtered on behalf of the Serpent and his overpowering Blight!"

He turned a little so Zuryzel could see his eyes; they, too, were Blightless, now a forest green color. Zuryzel suddenly felt sure that Claw could see them, hidden in the trees, but he made no sign as he continued his speech.

"You have seen your mates and sons and daughters slain all for the supposed glory of the Serpent. But to what end? What good did this bring us? Have we risen in triumph to rule the world? No! Have we gained riches worthy of true conquerors of old? No! We have been left stranded in these woods, fighting for food, fighting to keep alive. Are you all so devoted to something that will destroy you?"

It might have been Zuryzel's imagination, but Claw seemed to lift his sword just a little in her direction, like a sign of recognition.

Dejuday had heard enough about how his sister, Sibyna, would not be part of a war party ever again as long as she lived. He saw her with one of their friends, Dikiner, waiting just outside Pasadagavra, but he could tell they were beginning to hate the thought of battle.

He looked away, annoyed. Battle was sometimes necessary to protect the innocent—had his sister forgotten that part? The way she was talking made them all sound evil. Well, his sister would be herself; she was Dikiner's to worry about.

Dejuday turned his thoughts to his favorite—and least favorite—subject: Zuryzel.

It was no surprise Demeda had sent Zuryzel out to spy on the enemy. She was the best scout. And he was still on pins and needles, waiting anxiously for her to return.

When she does ... he toyed with that idea for a while. When she did return, would she maybe listen to him, talk with him? He doubted it. He and Sibyna were of low class, and after all, he had made a fool of himself many times in the Darkwoods prison. His vivid imagination had thoroughly explored both possibilities, and the rational part of him knew that no princess would be interested in someone as low-born as him.

But then, no princess would stoop so low as to pull someone like him out of prison so many times, either. That thought gave him a small glimmer of hope. True, Zuryzel had been ordered, and Wraith Mice couldn't disobey a direct order, but he was sure that if Zuryzel had pleaded with her father enough she wouldn't have been ordered. So she did have a *choice.* And she really had ...

Ah, but he was being an idiot.

Or was he?

There was no way any princess would glance his way.

But had she already? It wasn't as if she didn't know he existed.

Still, another prince had his eye on her, and Dejuday couldn't compete with that.

But what if he didn't have to? What if …

He shook himself sharply. That kind of back-and-forth inner arguing had become a habit over the past winter, and that part of his love for the princess was driving him insane. Sometimes he found himself talking aloud, though (thankfully) unintelligibly, and his fellow soldiers nudged him in annoyance. Dejuday didn't blame them; it annoyed him more than anyone else.

In none of the romance stories Sibyna insisted he read was annoyance a significant factor. Of course, Dejuday had always associated annoyance with romance because he was so annoyed with his ridiculously romantic sister and her fluffy stories.

His eyes wandered around the other soldiers, all bunched up against the wall, ready to rush back inside if the enemy attacked. King Hokadra's strategy had been largely defensive, and most of the soldiers were conditioned to react defensively. But Dejuday didn't lean against the wall; he stood a little apart and let the wild grass brush his paws. He had heard whispers that Queen Demeda and King Hokadra complemented each other so well because they were opposites.. If those rumors were true, then Dejuday would happily bet all the money he owned that Demeda proved to be more offensive.

He glanced toward Pasadagavra and thought of those two mice—Ol'ver and Feldspar? He barely remembered them. But he definitely remembered talking with them about King Hokadra. He had spoken admirably of the king, and with reason, but he had never revealed the true reason he was awed by the king. It wasn't because of battle strategy, that was for sure. Any king could fight a battle, or he wouldn't be king very long. What impressed Dejuday was that the king had also made time to raise his family.

And there it was. His thoughts always circled back to one creature.

The sound of rushing pawsteps alerted him to the arrival of Zuryzel and Shartalla. They passed him without saying anything, but once past him, Zuryzel turned. Now she was running sideways, still keeping up with Shartalla's brisk pace, but she met his eyes and solemnly raised her paw. He inclined his head respectfully; when he looked up, she was smiling. Her black eyes sparkled, and her smile spread wide and carefree, and it won a return grin from Dejuday. With a jerk of her head, she invited him to listen.

Dejuday couldn't have kept away even if he had tried, and as he slowly followed the princess, he hoped his grin wasn't foolish.

Shartalla noticed nothing as she and Zuryzel hastened up to Queen Demeda. They both radiated success as they reported to the Queen.

"Perhaps six hundred!" Zuryzel panted eagerly. "All in the glade where our camp was."

"Where on earth did the other four hundred come from?" Demeda gasped.

"From Arashna!" Zuryzel cried. "Eclipse was telling Hemlock that they were defeated so badly there they'd rather die than go into another campaign!"

At that moment, Dejuday strode up. Though he stayed in the background and said nothing, Zuryzel had to fight to take her eyes from him.

"An' most o' thuh foxes from 'ere seemed t' think so, too!" Shartalla added, also breathing heavily. "Both Eclipse and Claw 'ave normal eyes."

"They've forsaken the Blight!" Johajar, who sat beside his mother, said gleefully.

"They're arguing amongst themselves like no one's business!" Zuryzel finished. "We could sweep them like dust!"

Demeda frowned. "Argue all they want, we still have less than a third of their number."

"So what?" Zuryzel argued eagerly, still breathing heavily. "They mounted no guard; they aren't listening to their leaders; they could even fight amongst themselves!"

"We can't take that chance," Demeda countered. She knelt down by the map drawn in the sand. "We have to take into account that they have three times our number."

"My crew alone could take them on," Shartalla declared stoutly.

"On a ship, maybe," Demeda murmured. "But those four hundred that Eclipse brought with her are the best from Darkwoods, and they'll be even better after fighting the armies at Arashna." She lifted her black eyes to meet Shartalla's. "And what's more, they've been on the coast for the past several seasons. *They* know how to fight corsairs, and they've probably come up with some technique that would cause a lot of danger to your crew."

Shartalla grew quiet. Zuryzel suddenly understood the enormity of the problem. "And those four hundred are also probably united under Eclipse," Demeda continued.

"But they're puttin' all their energy int' resistin' 'Emlock," Shartalla argued sharply. "They set up no watch, no defenses; they ain't even 'oldin' their weapons."

"Claw mentioned that they were fighting over food, too," Zuryzel added.

"Probably meaning that they haven't had time to forage for food for Eclipse's group," Johajar reasoned. "That means that those soldiers just arrived; *that* means that they're likely exhausted."

"They looked weary," Zuryzel murmured thoughtfully. "But that weariness looked more like they had just woken up from sleep and found that they have no hope."

Demeda frowned. "If they think they're already defeated, maybe they'll listen to terms."

"It looked t' me as if Eclipse tried t' talk terms at Arashna," Shartalla replied. "Apparently, the mercenaries at Arashna gave 'er the choice t' get out or die."

"How do you know?" Demeda asked curiously.

"On the back of 'er neck there was a sort o' x-like scar," Shartalla explained. "Tha's what one o' the seagoing mercenaries I know does when someone tries t' surrender. Sort o' like sayin', "'X marks the spot—next time I'll 'it there!'"

"That means Eclipse won't talk much anymore," Demeda murmured.

"Why destroy someone trying to surrender?" Zuryzel protested.

Demeda waved her paw dismissively. "He probably thought Eclipse hadn't taken enough hits to seriously want to surrender and must have suspected some kind of trick." She stared at the map and cursed. "We don't even have enough soldiers to surround them anymore," she muttered.

Afraid of conflicts breaking out amongst the various armies and previous enemies, Demeda had paid most of the corsairs their fee and let them return to the sea; only the best, Arasam and Shartalla and Ailur remained at Pasadagavra. Shartalla had a relatively small crew of about seventy, but they were tired after the long journey and not a few of them had wounds that had gotten worse over the trek. Arasam's crew was a little bigger, but his fighters were also wounded; and of Ailur's fifty, nearly thirty had been put out of action. They, Zuryzel deduced, were not the best of corsair fighters. Among them, the three corsairs could muster about a hundred ten fighters. The rest of the small army were mostly Arpaha's soldiers, the few Wraith Mice who survived unhurt, and twenty of the best Rangers. More fighters had survived the mass slaughter, but some of them were still occupying Darkwoods, and even more had returned to their homes. Zuryzel wondered why Demeda had let so many fighters go, but then she realized that almost a month had passed since the massacre.

"The camp wouldn't be surrounded anyway," Shartalla shrugged. "There's a big rock formation right against one edge with a narrow pass through it; on the other side, about twenty feet away, there's a mash of a marsh."

Another soldier who had drawn close to listen murmured to Dejuday, "Why did Queen Demeda send all the fighters away so soon?"

"Little catfights were breaking out all over," Dejuday scowled. "The Stone Tribe didn't want all the other squirrel tribes they recently warred with in their home, most of the corsairs are used to being enemies, the Rangers *have* to get back to their home to take up the defense there, no land dweller likes the corsairs much anyway, and Doomspear and his river otters weren't really considered to be safe creatures – most thought them too wild. What's left of the Wraith Mice contingent from Mirquis and Dombre are mad at the Wraith Mice company from Dobar and Kardas, even though the latter lost their homes first, and all of them are angry with Arpaha for leaving the army to join the other river otters in their guerrilla war. Amazing how quickly everyone forgot that, if we hadn't banded together, we'd have been picked off a piece at a time by the Darkwoods foxes. A whole other battle could have broken out right here."

Demeda ignored their whispering and stared hard at the map.

A soldier looked around helplessly. "Do you think it's possible that Queen Demeda will just let the foxes vegetate until she can recall Doomspear?"

"I doubt it," another guessed. "The more she waits the more chances of Darkwoods reunifying."

"She sent Shinar off somewhere earlier," a young one whispered conspiratorially. "Do you think she was already looking for someone?"

"Like Doomspear?"

"Maybe, but I thought Doomspear said that Moonpath was in the area," whispered a voice Zuryzel recognized as Sibyna's. "I thought maybe Shinar was supposed to look for her."

"I don't think Queen Demeda is so desperate that she's willing to work with that barbarian princess," Dejuday scoffed. "Trusting her is more dangerous than attacking the Darkwoods elite with only a third of their number. No, more likely she's looking for Doomspear."

Shartalla looked long and hard at the map in the sand. "The instan' we attack 'em, they'll run away from us as quickly as they c'n. Maybe it's enough just t' scatter 'em—kill some an' separate the rest."

Demeda frowned at the idea. "I thought corsairs taught that the best enemy was a dead enemy?"

"They're already beginning to break up," Zuryzel pointed out. "Knife is missing, and so are Poison and Scorch. There must have been more—families and such—that ran from Darkwoods a while ago."

"All the more reason to destroy what's left of the army," Demeda sighed.

Zuryzel closed her eyes, thinking very hard. Finally she murmured, "If we could avoid being seen, then we'd even up."

Shartalla's head shot up. "Yer right! Just do what all yeh land creatures do with yer camouflages. They're definitely too tired t' make sense of any trickery like tha'!"

Dejuday suddenly nudged Zuryzel. "Princess?" he muttered, so low that no one else heard.

"What?" Zuryzel asked, her lips not moving.

Dejuday leaned forward slightly. "Where's Mokimshim?" he muttered in her ear.

The princess glanced around. "There. He's watching the open ground."

Dejuday persisted. "He's too far away to be helping in the planning. Why is that?"

Zuryzel frowned. Now that he mentioned it, it *was* unusual for Demeda to exclude the heir to the throne of Arashna from her planning. And upon further thought, it was even more unusual for her to hesitate before making a move like this on an army that had already suffered a serious defeat. It was as if she expected the foxes to be told that this attack was coming and unify in preparation for it. Was Demeda afraid that the spy Fawn told Biddah about was still at large? Zuryzel had almost forgotten about him.

Zuryzel stared hard at the map. "The trees are very thick," she insisted. "It wouldn't take much to out-maneuver them."

Demeda nodded. "True."

Zuryzel lowered her voice so only her mother and Shartalla could hear. "Lurena's dead, so she won't be telling Hemlock anything. It would be dangerous for Knife's spy just to show up to Hemlock and say we know where they are, and neither Claw nor Eclipse will believe the word of *Knife's* spy."

Demeda nodded again. "That is true," she agreed. She squared her shoulders. "Keep your eye on your older brother when I explain the plan to the army."

"The sneakin' plan?" Shartalla asked.

Zuryzel nodded, her eyes fixed on Mokimshim. He was gazing out across the open ground to the trees, his back to his watching sister, paying no attention to her.

Or are you, Mokimshim? Zuryzel thought. *Are you watching me? Were you shamming all those times at Mirquis? Why? What is going on in your mind?*

Shartalla saw the alert and contemplating look on Zuryzel's face. "Yeh okay?" she asked.

Zuryzel nodded, her eyes still fixed on Mokimshim.

Maybe her brother felt the intensity of his sister's gaze because he half-turned to see Zuryzel's face. Their eyes met; in Mokimshim's there was a trace of resentment, as well as a small amount of slyness. In Zuryzel's there was an open and calm challenge.

When the small army from Pasadagavra made it within a hundred or so yards of the glade, there were still the sounds of arguing from the Darkwoods foxes. To Zuryzel's surprise, Shartalla sniffed and then made a noise of disgust. "There's been some fightin'," she muttered. "I c'n smell blood."

"I'm grateful my sense of smell isn't as keen as yours," Zuryzel whispered to her friend.

Shartalla only smiled wryly.

Demeda gestured briefly to Shartalla and Zuryzel. Shartalla's crew eased through the forest to the other side of the clearing.

"Thank Cerecinthia we spent two weeks or more clustered round this place," Shartalla muttered. "Tha's the only advantage I c'n think of that we got over those kelpheads."

"Kelpheads?" Zuryzel chuckled. "Descriptive. And since when did pirates say 'thank Cerecinthia?'"

"I am not just a corsair," Shartalla murmured in response, her words now urbane and cultured. "I am also a princess."

She brushed forward through the trees. Zuryzel stared after her in astonishment. "You're a princess?"

"Sort of," Shartalla muttered, abandoning her fine speech. "My brother's a *nikora* on the eastern shores. That's like a king who's answerable to a High King."

"There were once rulers like that here," Zuryzel whispered. "I didn't know there were still High Kings."

"In the east. Only the east." She quietly unsheathed her sword. Zuryzel, looking forward, saw the foxes. She could hear Hemlock yelling furiously at Eclipse and Eclipse rounding on Claw for support.

"So your brother is like a king?" she whispered to the corsair.

"One of 'em is. The other, the younger, is a merchant. They're only my 'alf-brothers, y' see."

Zuryzel heard a familiar chickadee's cry. "Mother's getting ready to attack," she informed the corsair.

Shartalla made a few obscure gestures to her crew. They all drew their swords as silently as their captain.

Claw yelled something Zuryzel wished she hadn't heard over Hemlock's shrieking cries.

"'E's a jellyfish," Shartalla muttered, grinning.

"You mean a nutcase?" Zuryzel chortled.

"'Is brain's turned to jelly, whatever the word," Shartalla grinned back.

"Your word is more appropriate, then," Zuryzel breathed.

Another three chickadee's calls sounded across the woodland. "Count to five," Zuryzel whispered. "One … two …"

Claw unleashed a barrage of obscenity at Hemlock.

"Three … four …"

Hemlock shrieked in fury at Eclipse, who replied in a more controlled voice.

"*Five.*"

A whistle of arrows pelted across the glade and several foxes around Hemlock fell dead. Eclipse and Claw simultaneously cried, "*What?*"

Hemlock looked at them in confusion and demanded, "What's wrong?"

"'E's blind, deaf, mad, an' stupid," Shartalla whispered gleefully. "Now, crew!"

They quickly stormed into the clearing, and the corsairs, though undisciplined and rough, moved in perfect unison. Twenty seconds Demeda had said, and for twenty seconds, they slashed at the disoriented Darkwoods foxes, and then, as one, they jumped out of the melee into the forest. To say they disappeared or faded would be an exaggeration; they jumped behind trees and were quiet enough that no one heard them over the cries coming from the other side of the clearing as another war party attacked.

"Did you see Eclipse's face?" Shartalla smirked. Her eyes blazed with the joy certain creatures found in battle.

"What about Claw's?" Zuryzel chuckled.

"Don't take this the wrong way, but you'd make a good corsair," Shartalla replied. "Now where do we go?"

Zuryzel slipped through the trees, Shartalla and crew behind her, to a point a little bit east of their starting point. They still stayed well away from Eclipse's soldiers, just in case they really had come up with a way to fight corsairs.

Zuryzel watched carefully for another hail of arrows. Three seconds after that, they would charge into the clearing again, which at the moment was in a state of such confusion Zuryzel thought it funny. Then she noticed something odd. It was Claw—and it looked as if he'd had enough. He was waiting by a big rock, pressed against it watchfully. When an opening appeared between him and the woods, he shot out. Like an arrow, he vanished into the trees.

"Stay here," Zuryzel whispered to Shartalla. "Three seconds after the next arrow volley, charge in, fight for twenty seconds, and get out. Then go east around the clearing. I should be back by then."

Shartalla nodded to show that she understood, and the princess took off through the forest.

Claw left a trail that even Shartalla could follow. And if he was going to Knife and the others who had managed to get away from Darkwoods, then Zuryzel was on the right course. Scorch was probably with his fellow apprentice, Poison.

After running for a few seconds, Zuryzel caught sight of Claw's burnt orange pelt. He was running as fast as he could, but Zuryzel was fast, too. As he ran, Claw looked back over his shoulder at her, and he looked terrified.

I have you now! she thought. Her ears rang as she closed in on her quarry, and a burst of energy enveloped her. Claw was running for his life now, and he knew it.

Then he tripped.

He was back on his paws by the time the princess reached him, but he couldn't run. In desperation, he drew his weapon, but with a single blow, Zuryzel stunned his paw, and he dropped his sword.

"Where were you going?" she inquired, her own sword prodding Claw's chest.

"Anywhere."

Zuryzel smirked. "And you thought you could get away?"

Claw flinched at the danger gleaming in her eyes. "I am not the one who murdered your father. Scorch is."

"And where is he?" Zuryzel inquired acidly.

"Gone," Claw replied flatly. "Out of your reach—at least, for the time being."

Zuryzel did not lower her blade. That would have been arrogant. "I have a long reach, Claw. *Where is he?*"

"I don't know," Claw replied, and he obviously wasn't lying. "Whoever survived at Darkwoods separated. Most of the soldiers you saw in the clearing were brought there by Eclipse. The others were those that fled from Darkwoods and were found by her army. I don't know where Scorch is."

Zuryzel nodded. "I believe you." It didn't matter much. He was her prisoner now. "Come with me."

Claw shook his head. "Not a chance. I'd rather be dead than be a captive."

"I can arrange that."

"You owe me your life," Claw retorted before Zuryzel could move her sword. "I saw you and your friend made of fire in that tree."

He paused while Zuryzel digested the meaning of that statement.

"It would have been well within my rights to point you out," he continued. "But I didn't. You're alive because of me."

"My kingdom owes you nothing. I take you in the name of the Wraith Mice."

"What is left of my kingdom is dying because I let you live," Claw retorted. "You owe me my life."

Zuryzel didn't have time for a thoughtful, careful decision—she had to get back to Shartalla. She had to keep Claw here. For a moment more, she watched him, her sword pointed at him warningly, but he refused to move. In one quick motion, she slashed her sword across his torso and one of his paws.

He howled in pain and fell to the ground. "I'm sorry," Zuryzel said, her voice cold, "but I can't take you with me, and I can't have you running off."

Nor would he. The slash on his paw would make walking impossible, and the wound on his chest would make crawling impossible.

"Someone will be back here soon enough," Zuryzel went on. "In the meantime, don't move, or your wounds will get worse."

With that, she turned and pelted through the trees back in the direction of the battle. Her own words echoed in her ears. She knew she hadn't had time to take Claw captive. She should have killed him … but in cold blood … She wasn't sure her father would have liked her to do that. But were two deep wounds better? Well, it was too late to change that now. She hadn't had time to think it through.

I have a long reach, she had said. *I can arrange that.* In the past, it had always been "King Hokadra," not "I." But she had earned the use of the pronoun. She had come into her right as a Wraith Mouse princess.

Shartalla's pelt appeared through the trees, and Zuryzel saw that she was still fighting in the clearing. She berated herself inwardly for being gone so long, but Shartalla clearly knew what she was doing. When her crew bolted back into the trees, she pressed against an oak and grinned at Zuryzel.

"Do we wait fer another volley?" she panted.

"Not this time. Just a signal—three chickadee calls." Zuryzel was panting hard, but there was a grim smile of satisfaction on her face.

The wait took only half the time Zuryzel expected. Eclipse had managed to pull her warriors into a circle, so at least they were fighting decently. Hemlock was in the center, a shield protectively over his head. The foxes were occupied fighting a company of Wraith Mice on the north side of the clearing. The chickadee's cry echoed around the clearing, and Shartalla unpressed herself from the oak.

"Here we go!" she grinned. "Against these jelly-nut fish cases!"

Zuryzel laughed with delight at Shartalla's frankness.

She hadn't bothered to sheathe her sword, so she followed Shartalla right into the clearing.

Eclipse had learned a thing or two from her many, painful days at Arashna. She yelled an obscure word to her soldiers, who immediately understood. The circle broke apart, and the foxes dispersed throughout the clearing. The idea was to create confusion, so that at least some of the foxes could get away. In only ten seconds, Zuryzel saw a score of her allies fall. But the foxes were tired by now, and they simply didn't spread out quickly enough.

Demeda snatched a lance from a fallen soldier and ran through the chaos of the battle, indifferent to the battling pairs around her, until she was face-to-face with the vixen that had besieged her beloved Arashna for so long. It shocked her to see that Eclipse was barely older than Zuryzel, but she did not let that revelation shake her steely resolve.

"You have an opportunity to surrender," Demeda informed her, pointing the lance right at Eclipse's throat.

The dark fox had no hope in her eyes, a fact that didn't bother the Wraith Mouse Queen. She was positive Eclipse had looked at many from whom she herself had taken hope, and in her eyes had been the same glow that was now in Demeda's eyes.

Eclipse stared wordlessly at the Wraith Mouse Queen for a full ten seconds before lowering her sword, gripping it by the blade, and extending the hilt to the victor.

Zuryzel, fighting beside Shartalla, saw the gesture and ducked away from her opponent. "Eclipse has surrendered!" she cried above the battle noise. "Your leader has surrendered!"

The fighting stilled. The foxes from Arashna stared at their trusted leader, saw her swordless paws and her shameful eyes, and each one threw down his or her own weapon.

Shartalla grinned at Zuryzel. "It's over now," she said in a voice as calm as a summer noon.

Zuryzel glanced away from her friend and saw a familiar pair of black eyes watching her. Dejuday raised his sword and saluted her, grinning tiredly. Zuryzel smiled back.

Lady Raven's Friends

Four days later, the sun rose mistily over the tops of the pines, which had miraculously escaped the fate of the Ashlands. Creatures had begun to set off for their homes. Or rather, what was left of their homes.

Arasam left Pasadagavra first (to Zuryzel's and many others' relief) with his crew. Zuryzel had never trusted him, and indeed, he demanded the highest payment from Pasadagavra. Jaccah had given it all over willingly; she had no need for the silks, barrels, beads, and trinkets Arasam demanded. He left at dawn.

Sadly, Shartalla was the next to go. Zuryzel had come to like the devious, brave, loyal friend she had found in Shartalla.

Before her crew marched off toward the Okirraray River where several boats were kept, Shartalla pulled Zuryzel aside.

"Listen, Zuryzel," Shartalla hissed. "I had another dream from Time last night. 'E showed me the scene I guess 'e'd shown yeh; o' Current an' 'is oath of allegiance. Then he warned me o' great trouble that would touch me on'y if I chose t' touch it. Why 'e couldn't speak plainer … but, either way, I'm an adventurer, so I'll get inter it no matter what. But I 'ave this nasty feelin'… Zuryzel, I know yer mother is one o' the best rulers in the world, but all the same, keep on yer toes. Yeh'll be needed."

"Mokimshim will settle down; it will be all right," Zuryzel insisted. But when she had intended it to be forceful, it came out desperate.

Shartalla's next words left her stunned. "What if 'e became yer *enemy* … Y' wouldn't want 'im ter be a good leader then, would you? What if 'e *turned evil*?"

Zuryzel blinked. That thought had never occurred to her—why should it? But Shartalla's words opened up a whole range of frightening possibilities. Creatures had told her that she would lead someday, or why else would the Bear King have given all the abilities to lead to her and not to her brother? But what if he *hadn't*? What if Mokimshim did have the ability to lead and he had concealed it? And why would he conceal it?

Shartalla grinned and lowered her voice. "Let's not worry about tha', though, at least not yet. Yer mother has a good few seasons ahead o' 'er, an' a lot o' things could 'appen in a few seasons. Just stay prepared for anythin'." She drew from her sleeve a roll of parchment. "Anyone named on here," she murmured, "you can trust with yer life an' yer kingdom if trouble shows. I swear it on me own soul. But I do not believe trouble will show fer a long time. Well," she shook herself. "I've got a beauty o' a ship waitin' fer me t' sail again, an' adventure loomin' on the horizon. See you sometime at Arashna, Zuryzel."

"You'll always be welcome there, my friend," Zuryzel replied.

Shartalla grinned. She gave one holler, and her entire crew gathered behind her. As they set to march off, Grayik the ferret looked to Ailur.

The mercenary shook her head, wincing as she twisted her wounded neck. "Yer gonna get yerself killed one day, pal. Go on, but don' come crawlin' back ter me!"

Grayik bounded down and joined Shartalla's crew, waving back to all his former shipmates.

Zuryzel turned to Ailur. "You'll be going next?"

Ailur shook her head. "I made a promise, to Lady Raven, 'tis why I was in Diray. I'll foller yer back ter Arashna 'fore I 'oists me sails t' the coast. I'm seein' yeh back."

"You made …?"

"Yeah. The Lady knew somethin'd 'appen, an' now I'm in charge o' the ring she started. But first, I take yer back 'ome. Ye'll need the company, anyway."

Zuryzel was shocked to see tears coming to Ailur's eyes. "I take it I'm not supposed to know about this."

Ailur shrugged. "Don' make much difference, now. Besides, Lady Crow'll want ter question me, so let's set off soon as possible, please."

Amusement shook Zuryzel's heart for the first time in days. "Well, I'll question you for her. Out of curiosity, what was a slave doing, pretending to be a captain? And Jironi, your second mate? And Redseg …"

"My brother was always on the alert fer trouble," replied Ailur.

"Redseg, captain of the *Deathwind*, your brother?" Of course, she had heard that! But it hadn't set in.

Ailur nodded keenly. "Lady Raven an' yer mother arranged it all. They knew trouble was comin' and comin' fast. They'd both 'ad experiences outside o' the 'omeland; yer mother called on old friends. Lady Raven was just one, I was another, Redseg was a third, an' Fotirra was a fourth. See, she'd been with Lady Raven through most adventures; she could pass fer a captain, not many others could. If she did this, she was promised her freedom."

"And Shartalla and Arasam?"

"I decided on them," Ailur explained, swelling herself out proudly. "I can tell yeh, I was desperate. I didn't much trust Arasam, but he had a score t' settle wi' one o' the captains called by Knife, so he was useful. Shartalla I didn't trust either, but I knew her father. He was the most feared, respected creature on the coast, and 'is daughter thrived on the reputation, but I knew Shartalla was cunning and more a liar than even Knife." Ailur blinked. "She ain't what she used t' be, an' that's a good thing. Fer once."

The puzzle was beginning to fit together, but there was one question that had to be asked. "Ailur, how did you know Lady Raven?"

Ailur's eyes gleamed ruefully. "I was betrayed when I was younger and taken slave aboard the *Sea Monster* alongside Raven. I'd been living in a village on Pelleck Island, out to the west, where most corsairs grow up. I'd, er, gotten this *proposition*, an' I was betrayed. But it is a long story, an' now would be a bad time t' tell it."

Zuryzel sighed. "Well, that sums it up, more or less. Thank you, friend."

Ailur looked nervously toward the mighty gates of Pasadagavra.

"Yer family needs you, Zuryzel," she commented, catching Zuryzel off guard. "One day, the whole world'll need you, just wait 'n' see."

On that happy note, Ailur moved off and began arranging her crew for the journey seaward. Zuryzel felt a tapping on her shoulder. She turned to look at Johajar.

"Zuryzel," he hissed, "I need to talk to you. Come over here."

Without waiting for her response, he led her over to the wall and leaned against it. Zuryzel looked to make sure there was no one |else around. "What?"

"Mokimshim and I were in Dombre," Johajar explained, "during the battle. Mother told you about the plans, right?" Johajar paused, and looked around to make sure no one could hear. "Well, I was poking at him for his lack of strategy and he attacked me."

"Attacked you?" Zuryzel echoed blankly.

"We were in this dark alley," Johajar explained. "He said he could kill me then and no one would know any different, that he could make up some story."

Zuryzel blinked in disbelief. "He said *that*?"

Johajar nodded anxiously. "He didn't kill me obviously, but I had a job talking him out of it."

"You think he *would* have killed you?" Zuryzel gasped incredulously, at first blaming Mokimshim's reckless tongue. Then, Shartalla's words began to ring in her ears.

"He said he was proud of how hard he worked," Johajar murmured. "That I hurt his pride."

"Well," Zuryzel reasoned, "that could be true. He is proud."

"Not that proud," Johajar argued. "Not so proud that he'd kill for his pride. And if he was proud, he wouldn't admit it."

"What are you accusing him of?" Zuryzel asked, her voice thin.

Johajar looked intently at his sister. "I think he is Hemlock's spy."

Zuryzel lost her voice completely. Johajar, accusing their brother of this …

"Think about it!" hissed Johajar. "Hemlock said he had a spy that knew the secrets of Mirquis and Dombre. He's the only one who would know said secrets since our father passed them along to him in case something happened and Mokimshim never heard. The only other who knew was our father, who was definitely not the spy." He paused, before continuing hesitantly. "I know you thought Hemlock was just bluffing when he said that his spy knew the secrets of Mirquis and Dombre. I thought so, too—I mean, those secrets have never been leaked. But the more I think about it, the more I think it would have been a stupid bluff. He would have had to live up to that and tell the other Oracles the secrets about the fortresses and be right, or else they'd mutiny. He must actually have known them."

Great Cerecinthia, he was right. It made too much sense, even after what her mother had said. All along, she had suspected others—Orgorad and Dikiner and everyone else—when Hemlock had said the magic words. *He knows the secrets of Mirquis and Dombre*. Mokimshim was the only one who knew the secret tunnels going out of those cities. Zuryzel felt a chill of fear when she guessed that her father had arrived at the same conclusion when he had chosen to use a new tunnel.

"What can we do about it?" Johajar asked eagerly.

Zuryzel shook her head to clear it. "We have no real evidence. Let's just watch him for a few cycles."

Johajar nodded earnestly. "Fair enough."

"Have you told mother?"

"I didn't think she'd listen to me," Johajar confessed. "But I knew you would."

Zuryzel looked at him. "I still don't think he would have the heart. Besides," she added, feeling heartened, "Lady Raven saw someone who was a spy because he thought Mokimshim couldn't rule. And he was also pleading for Sibyna's life. I don't think Mokimshim has his eyes on Sibyna." She did not tell her brother that the spy could have been Orgorad or Crispisin playing Demeda's script.

Johajar was silent for a moment. "Zuryzel, do you remember that time we decided that Hemlock, Knife, *and* Ice had spies? Well, Ice obviously got her information from Lady Raven—"

"You were eavesdropping."

"I didn't mean to. Anyway, whoever was speaking to Hemlock was the spy."

Zuryzel remembered the day Johajar had brought her up short with his reasoning and suspicion. She suspected he was about to do it again.

"We don't know who Knife's spy was. Couldn't it have been Mokimshim? And Hemlock just overheard him telling Knife—or maybe Mokimshim spied for both?"

Yes, he had done it again. A chill feeling went right through her soul. She looked at Johajar with fear. "I pray you're wrong."

"I don't," shrugged Johajar. "I despise him anyway, but that's not why I'm 'accusing him,' as you put it."

"He's our *brother*!" Zuryzel protested.

"Oh, yes," Johajar muttered sarcastically. "He was such a brother when he attacked me in Dombre."

"Johajar, you were in the middle of a terrible battle!" Zuryzel insisted. "He may have been under stress and didn't want to admit it, so he made up this story about pride!"

"Zuryzel, stop being so blind!" Johajar hissed impatiently. "He never did anything like that before. He has a lot of vices, but *he isn't that proud.* He would have admitted it if he were under stress because he wouldn't have cared about his reputation and would merely have tried to stay out of trouble. He isn't proud enough to care one drop about his reputation. Not like you are," he added.

He'd said those last four words before, but in a more complimentary way. Zuryzel bristled. "I am not … arrogant!"

"No," Johajar said after a minute. "You're not. But Mokimshim isn't, either, not like that—not except in the lowest possible way."

"So Mokimshim could have been angry at your derision!" Zuryzel protested, half pleading.

"Anger at derision comes from pride." Johajar's tone was growing heated.

"Not always, surely!" Zuryzel pointed out.

"Zuryzel, he may not be a spy, but there's something wrong with him!" If this conversation kept up, Johajar would be shouting.

Zuryzel remembered Shartalla saying, "Just 'cos they're a foe t' our foe, don' make 'em friendly; they could be our enemy too." She had only been talking about the Moor Tribe squirrels—or had she? She had also said of Mokimshim, "What if 'e became yer *enemy* … What if 'e *turned evil*?" Shartalla was a corsair captain, so she would probably know about betrayals. This wasn't the sea, though. Could Shartalla just be overreacting?

No, not if Johajar, who had almost no experience in that matter, had seen the same thing.

Would Johajar's suspicions and Shartalla's foreboding prove true eventually?

When the army of Wraith Mice stopped to rest on the march back to Arashna, Zuryzel strode among the pitched tents and dripping trees. She had already helped set up the tent she shared with her mother. Now she was looking for her brothers.

Where was Johajar? Where was Mokimshim? They had set up their tent and disappeared, going opposite ways.

When she was scanning a row to her left, still walking, she ran headlong into Dejuday.

"Princess Zuryzel," Dejuday smiled, catching her shoulder to steady her.

Zuryzel's face grew hot. "Dejuday," she said curtly. "Have you seen either of my brothers?"

Dejuday nodded briskly. "Prince Johajar is speaking with the armorer, and Prince Mokimshim is on the other side of the camp."

"Doing what?" Zuryzel inquired.

Dejuday shrugged. "Keeping watch, I guess."

Zuryzel was on the verge of walking off after her brother when she hesitated for a moment, looking at her shoes.

"Will you show me?" she asked finally.

She glanced up, and saw a small smile on Dejuday's face.

"Follow me," he replied.

Very sharply, she jerked her head upright. What was the matter with her? She was a soldier and a princess, by the stars, and she had just been staring at her shoes and blushing like some air-headed fool! But when she followed Dejuday, her knees knocked, and her tongue felt as if it was wrapped in cotton. Shyness had *never* been a problem for her, so the sensations were completely unfamiliar.

As she and Dejuday crossed the camp, she kept her mind very firmly on Mokimshim. But when she saw her brother, she no longer needed to concentrate in order to focus on him.

He was speaking very quietly to himself. Zuryzel couldn't tell what he said, but his eyes swept the rows of tents as if looking for a watcher. When he saw his sister, he inclined his head briefly and smiled—but with no warmth or familiarity of any kind in either gesture.

Zuryzel expected to feel afraid, but instead her heart beat in anticipation.

She *knew* then that Johajar hadn't been seeing things. There was something Mokimshim was planning, and the coldness and malice in his eyes more than told her that. Fearlessly,she returned his cold smile with one of her own.

If you want a fight, she thought, *then so be it. I'm ready for you now.*

She turned around and started away, murmuring to Dejuday, "Come with me."

The princess and the soldier set a slow pace, as if they were doing nothing more than taking a stroll. When Zuryzel judged they were sufficiently out of Mokimshim's senses, she murmured to Dejuday, "I spoke with Queen Demeda about getting you a position as a palace guard at Arashna."

Dejuday gave her a smile. "Thank you, Princess."

She stopped dead and turned to face him. "That would put you in a position to learn quite a bit about anyone in the palace," she stated.

Dejuday didn't react; it was a fact they both knew well.

"When you do take up your duties—"

"You want me to see what I can learn about your brother," Dejuday finished. His eyes were expressionless, but Zuryzel could almost hear him say, *Your brother. Your own brother.*

Or maybe it was her own conscience saying that.

"If he's done nothing wrong, then there is nothing to find," she said, as much to herself as Dejuday.

Dejuday gave her a knowing look. "But you think he has."

Zuryzel nodded slowly. "Yes. And if he has, then something is going to happen in the near future. I do not want to be caught by surprise."

Dejuday nodded in response. "As you wish, Princess."

"I cannot order you-"

Dejuday waved his paw. "You need not."

Zuryzel smiled. "Thank you, Dejuday."

A cheeky smile quirked at one corner of his mouth. "Anything for you," he said lightly. Then his eyes darkened. "I don't want to be caught by surprise either," he murmured. "But there's not much the two of us can do if Mokimshim has some kind of scheme up his sleeve."

Zuryzel smiled. "We're not alone," she told Dejuday softly. From her sleeve, she drew out a roll of parchment.

"This is a list of pirates Shartalla swears on her soul are safe to contact," she explained in a low voice. "And all of them know how to find her in a moment. If trouble shows, this is where we go." She tucked the parchment back up her sleeve.

"We?" Dejuday murmured, expressionless.

"Don't push your luck," Zuryzel warned him in a normal voice. She gave him a warning look that was still friendly and walked past him.

Whatever was coming, she would be ready.

Dejuday watched her walk off. For a long time, his expression didn't change. Then a small, slow smile crept up his face.

30 Homeward Bound

Fawn, the former Oracle, had never in her life seen a place so bright as Miamur!

She held Rosemary in a sling wrapped around her shoulder and stared at the white towers gleaming in the sun so intensely as if made out of white light!

The Miamuran banner, two white wings on a blue field, drifted from every arch and spire. She had spent her whole life in Darkwoods, the forest, or Pasadagavra, and none of those was nearly as radiant as Miamur. It actually hurt the fox's eyes to look at the palace!

The little village around the palace was also made out of stone, and it was there that Fawn was destined for. Thank the Bear King it wasn't as bright! She held the child of her best friend close and murmured, "Almost home, Rosemary. Almost home."

She looked out toward the plains, and frowned. Odd. She'd heard one could see Danaray Mudriver's tribe's home from here, but the prairie was empty. She shrugged. Maybe Mudriver had decided her tribe needed to move to a different place for a while—they were, after all, semi-nomadic. As Fawn used to be.

Well, she was no more. She would make a home for herself and this little fox in the village of Miamur. A *permanent* home.

"Almost home, Rosemary," she whispered one more time.

Going home to Harboday, now that the foxes were there no longer, was a joy to Ol'ver and Ran'ta. With them, they carried the baby mouse Nathan'el, who had been cared for by Biddah, the squirrel.

Ol'ver had made a promise to himself; he would not let war touch his mate, or this child they had adopted, again. Perhaps, one day, he would fight again if called to, and he would take up arms to keep the fighting away from his family.

When they reached what was left of the small house he owned, they found it wasn't too badly destroyed. Ran'ta was even optimistic when she inspected the rooms.

"Only a few things were broken," she reported brightly.

"I guess there's an advantage to having nothing too valuable." Ol'ver smiled.

Ran'ta shook her head. "Ol'ver, this house is going to be the most valuable thing on earth: it's going to be a happy home."

Ol'ver laughed. He couldn't help it. "Ran'ta," he smiled, "I'm glad you're here."

"I would hope so," she laughed in return.

The forests in the south were quiet in spring. Birds trilled in the trees, and a few streams trickled along in muted harmony. The woods smelled green and pleasant, and a soft breeze played through the branches.

Danaray Mudriver looked around her at the trees. A stream grandiosely called the Othyrn River—the word *Othyrn* meant *rainbow-hued*—glided along behind her.

"Why didn't the sea otters come *here?*" she asked. "You could build a city as grand as Pasadagavra in this glade."

Kermunda, her healer, nodded his agreement. "I know what you mean. One also has to wonder why Shorefish or Moonpath or some of the other river otters didn't claim it."

"It's not their *ancestral land,*" Danaray replied. She was getting sick of hearing those words.

"It's better than their ancestral land," Kermunda countered. "For river otters, anyway. I doubt it would suit the sea otters. It's too far away from the ocean."

Danaray nodded. "There's probably some legend about ghosts and spirits and whatever else."

Kermunda sighed. "You're probably right."

A twig cracked behind them, and both of them whirled around, weapons raised.

Anamay stood there.

It was fully ten seconds before anyone said a word, and it was Anamay who broke the silence. "I didn't recognize you with the javelin, Dana," she said hoarsely.

Danaray lowered the weapon. She kept a blank face, but there were a thousand thoughts running through her head—*My little sister* and *What do I say* but mostly *I'm sorry.*

Kermunda mercifully spoke for her. "Anamay, you haven't been eating," he scolded. "Look at you. You're as thin as a new-hatched sparrow. And you're not getting enough iron, and—"

"Kermunda," Anamay reproofed, though she smiled.

"Sorry," Kermunda grinned back, completely unrepentant. "Force of habit."

Kermunda's bantering tone did not do anything to lighten the swamp of unshed tears in Danaray. But it did break the ice. Without a word, Danaray stepped forward and hugged her baby sister.

Both of them were blinking back tears. Both of them were struggling to say, "I'm sorry," Anamay for running away and Danaray for losing her temper. Danaray was vaguely aware of Kermunda in the background, but she couldn't bring to mind the fight that had tormented her conscience.

It was Anamay who drew back first. "What are you doing here?" she asked, trying to start a normal conversation.

"Let's take a guess at that, shall we?" Kermunda grinned.

Anamay smiled back. "Darkwoods is defeated then?"

"Well," Danaray replied, "scattered. It may take some time to hunt down every one of the Darkwoods foxes. However, all the Oracles have been captured or killed, and the original inhabitants have moved back into the castle. It's called Lunep again, and Burnish is king there again."

Anamay's smile brightened. Then it faltered, and she touched the silver filigree around her sister's brow. "And Father?"

"He died the day I got back to the tribe. Almost the exact moment."

Anamay closed her eyes and her shoulders hunched. "He must have been waiting for you to get back."

For us *to get back,* Danaray thought. But she didn't say that out loud. She'd laid enough guilt on Anamay already without mentioning that she'd failed to fulfill their father's last desire.

There was silence in the glade for a while, and then Anamay said, "Dana, I can't stay long. Suspicion and fear are running high among the sea otters right now."

"Really?" Kermunda replied. "That's pretty smart, considering how many river otters want them dead."

Anamay tilted her head sideways. "And me?"

Kermunda grinned wolfishly. "Your sister is chieftainess of the largest river otter tribe in the world. I wouldn't worry too much."

"They can wish you dead all they want," Danaray said lightly, "but to actually harm you is to cross me. No one will dare cross me."

Anamay frowned. "They didn't have a problem crossing Father."

"True," Danaray agreed, still in the throwaway tone. "But I've met with other chiefs once or twice, and I have established my reputation as … how do I put this …"

"Exponentially more volatile and far more dangerous," Kermunda suggested, grinning with pride in his chieftainess.

"That works," Danaray replied, smirking.

Anamay shrugged. "More hot-tempered than Father? *That's* not hard."

"True," Danaray agreed. "But I managed to shock Moonpath, Doomspear, and Shorefish, nonetheless."

"You should have seen their faces," Kermunda chortled.

Anamay laughed. "You like being chieftainess, don't you Dana?"

Danaray tossed her javelin in the air and caught it again. "Yes, I confess I do."

Anamay laughed once more; then her face grew sad. "I have to go," she said apologetically.

Danaray put a paw on her sister's shoulder. "You'll see me again," she promised. "Maybe sooner than you think."

Anamay nodded. She started backing away into the undergrowth until Kermunda's voice stopped her.

"Anamay?"

She turned to him. "Yes?"

Kermunda's face was about as stern as it ever got. "Keep yourself warm, drink lots of water, and whatever you do, no wine whatsoever."

Anamay smiled and put a paw over her increasing midriff. "Is it that obvious?"

"Only to healers, Anamay," Kermunda replied. "Only to healers."

Anamay laughed and slipped into the undergrowth with a promise of "I'll remember!"

Danaray watched her, worry creasing her brow. Kermunda stepped up beside her. "I expected it to be more emotional," he said jokingly.

"That would have been more painful and much harder," Danaray replied softly, a catch in her voice.

Kermunda smiled at her. "You are your father's daughter," he said proudly.

Danaray continued to gaze off into the woods where Anamay had disappeared. "She'll be all right," Kermunda promised, smiling.

"Will she?" Danaray whispered. "There are a lot of creatures who want her dead."

Kermunda laid a reassuring paw on his chieftainess's shoulder. "There are a lot more who want her alive," he replied, as the sweet fragrances of a woodland spring drifted around them.

In the middle of summer, one veteran warrior was finally going home.

"Can't you just *tell* me where it is?" his mate laughed. She had tied a blue kerchief around her head, and it made her brown eyes vivid.

"What fun would that be?" Feldspar teased.

Glor'a readjusted her pack again. "Come on, Feldspar," she pleaded, though they were only playing. "How much further? I've been waiting to see it for forever!"

"Not much," he replied casually. "I told you, we'd reach it today."

"'Today' is a long window," Glor'a replied.

Barely had she finished speaking when they broke out of the trees and Graystone stood before them.

Contrary to its name, Graystone was built out of wood. There was a plain wall around it with houses with thatched roofs inside. Some farming fields surrounded it, all of which were full of crops half-grown.

"It's not as nice as Pasadagavra," Feldspar chuckled. "But it sure is more of a home."

Glor'a squeezed his paw. "It's just the place to go home to," she murmured, gazing at it.

The fields were empty of workers; this made Feldspar smile. "Come on," he murmured. "We have to get up to the gate. Then we'll have the distinct pleasure of telling Chite's sweetheart that he's two days behind us. Let's get it over with."

They had just started onto the fields when what Feldspar had taken to be a rock stood up into the shape of a mouse. He grinned.

The lone mouse stood absolutely still for a minute; then she started running through the crops. They met on a pathway between fields, the third mouse staring at Feldspar incredulously.

"You're taller than I remember," Feldspar said lazily.

Opal's eyes were still amazed, not daring to hope, but her voice was sarcastic. "Adventure didn't work out for you, Feldspar?"

"Oh it did, Opal," Feldspar replied, putting his paw on his mate's shoulder. "I got all I wanted out of it."

Opal turned to look at Glor'a. "Indeed. And who is—?"

"This is Glor'a," Feldspar replied. "My mate. Glor'a, Opal—the leader of Graystone, as I understand it."

A smile flitted across Opal's scruffy features. "You understand rightly, my friend. Glor'a, welcome to Graystone, the finest town you will see anywhere."

"I can well believe it," Glor'a replied.

Opal, laughed in joy that her oldest friend had finally come home,. "Come on in," she invited, half-turning for the town, "and you just might make suppertime."

Epilogue: Clouds on the Horizon

Starfish, a little sea otter, had a baby brother not old enough to swim and a father, but her mother had passed away when her brother was born.

In early spring, her father called Starfish from her playmates.

She bounded over, curious. Mollusk was not the young, carefree otter he'd been when he was courting Anamay. He looked older, rarely spoke, and never smiled, though it had been over a cycle since Anamay had died.

Mollusk took his daughter inside. On a bundle of warm cloths, Starfish's younger brother, Conch, the babe her mother died to give birth to, gurgled softly. He'd always been quiet. Starfish watched as her father sat down next to Conch, watching his son with a kind of longing. Finally, he said, "Put on your best dress, daughter. We are going to meet someone. But you cannot tell anyone about this, remember!"

Confused, Starfish obeyed as her parents had taught her. She put on her favorite dress—a blue one with a white rose embroidered on the front, made for her by her father's sister—and turned back out to her father. "What is it?"

Mollusk held Conch gently. "Come on." He walked calmly out the backdoor. Starfish followed, overcome with curiosity. Where were they going? Who were they meeting?

Mollusk did not take the customary path to the river but slid through the woods. Starfish was even more curious. Then she remembered she could not tell anyone, so where they were going was a secret! But *where?*

For an hour, they trod along through the woods until they reached the sluggish Dellon River. Here, the river forked into two, the Kyaagha Brook and the Huakka Creek. Mollusk lay flat on his back in the water, holding Conch high and dry, calling, "Wait there, Starfish!"

Starfish stood in the creek's sand, watching as Mollusk set Conch down on the bank where the river split. Then he hastened back across the river, where he carried Starfish in the same manner toward the other bank.

"Be quiet," he warned.

Starfish sat on a stone, careful not to get her dress muddy. "What is going on?"

Mollusk shrugged. "Listen, Starfish, do not panic. You're in no danger. Do not make a noise, if you can help it. Look!" He nodded toward the strong-flowing Kyaagha.

A brown head was just above the river, still against the current. *River otter*! The otter dove and was lost to sight.

"She won't hurt you," promised Mollusk.

The river otter emerged, dripping wet, on the bank. Mollusk stood, and Starfish nervously stood too. The otter shook herself off and took a few strides up the bank.

"Danaray." Mollusk spoke with a curt greeting.

"Mollusk." Danaray's voice was emotionless. She really did not know what to feel; so much had happened because of Mollusk. But all the same, he was Anamay's mate, and his children were her kin.

Mollusk gently indicated each one of them. "This is Starfish, and this, Conch."

"Who are you?" Starfish asked boldly.

Danaray knelt down in the mud; it was easier to face them than Mollusk. "I am Danaray, your mother's sister."

Starfish's eyes widened in comical surprise. "Pleased to meet you," she smiled, putting into effect what her father's sister had taught her.

Danaray smiled. "Pleased to meet you, too." She knelt down and began to converse with the two young ones. Conch pretended to be shy, but Starfish could not feel shy in the presence of this … this strange female.

"Do you remember your mother, Starfish?" she asked.

Starfish nodded. "Yes, a little."

"Her name, *Anamay*, is in a language called Miamuran," Danaray explained. "As is mine. Her name comes from the word *Anam,* which means 'warbler.'" As she said the word, she brushed her paw across Starfish's brow. "You share the blood of river otters, little one. And a river otter will not know the name Starfish; a river otter will know the name *Anam*, Warbler."

Then she gently touched the younger child. "And Conch," she whispered. There was a strange sadness in her eyes, as if she were seeing a long and dark road ahead of Conch. "My name comes from the word *Danar*, which means 'wren.' Take that name now so that when another river otter happens upon you, he or she will know you are my nephew and the grandson of a chief."

She turned to both of them and, somehow, still faced Mollusk. "This is all I can give them. Anything else from a river otter chieftainess would put them in the way of ridicule and alienation."

Mollusk nodded. "I know."

Before too long, she stood back up. "Mollusk," she said urgently, "I cannot stay longer. But I must warn you that terrible danger for the sea otters is coming fast. The river otters have become even more restless; they are gathering more and more frequently, and their talks become increasingly violent. Those who have never set paw in this area are clamoring for sea otter blood."

"And what side will you take?" Mollusk inquired.

She looked him gravely in the eye. "If I were to stand before the otters who attacked those that lived here before, then I would fight them. Yet the creatures who fought in those wars, on both sides, have passed on, and the creatures who live now were born in the lands they are in now." Her eyes flashed with annoyance. "It has been so long that I doubt any river otter alive can claim anything was stolen from him or her by the sea otters."

She sighed and shook her head. "At the last gathering of chiefs, I spoke of this. I urged the others to not stew in their fathers' wars but to look ahead—as my sister did. A few, I think, listened to me—Wave and Rain, who rule at Kwang-ha`el, for instance, and Streamcourse, as well, and maybe some others. On the other paw, Doomspear and Shorefish were silent, and I am sure they are brooding on violent plans; Moonpath openly declared that she will stop at nothing to regain her father's land." She looked tired. "But after all this time, these lands are yours," she murmured. "And I will help you keep them."

"Thank you," Mollusk murmured. "I know the risk you have taken in telling us this."

Starfish clung to her father's paw. She didn't know what the adults were talking about.

"These two ..." Danaray trailed off, her gaze landing fondly on Starfish and Conch. "Mollusk, you must look after yourself. Shorefish has been vowing revenge on her father's killer, but since ... since Anamay is ... well, Shorefish can't let go of a blood-oath, but I do not know who she now targets in retribution for her father's death. It may be she will exact her vengeance on you."

Mollusk nodded. "I'll be careful. But what about these two?"

Danaray smiled down at Starfish's bewildered face and put a reassuring paw on her brow. "These two are safe. They are under the protection of a mighty river otter chieftainess. Neither Shorefish nor Moonpath nor Doomspear will dare tangle with me—they both know that if I am provoked I can eliminate their whole tribes. The whole world knows what will happen to the one who tries to harm these two."

She sighed. "I should go. I wouldn't want to cause you trouble."

"Thank you," Mollusk said expressionlessly.

"You'll see us again, though?" piped up Starfish. She had grown to like her aunt.

Danaray knelt in front of her. "I'll never be far away. Do you know where the Othyrn River is?"

Starfish nodded. "Father took us there once."

"My tribe has settled just across it," Danaray told her gently. "If you ever have need of me, I'll be there. If you ever wish to speak to me, I'll be there. Even when it seems that I'm not, I'll be there. Always. I swear it."

With that, Danaray Mudriver disappeared into the river, hardly able to bear the trusting look in her niece's eyes.

She popped up some way downstream and waved four times, a loving smile on her face.

A sneak peek into the next exciting book in the Darkwoods Series:

GRAYSTONE

By Marta Stahlfeld

Book 3 in the Darkwoods Series

Graystone

In the wilds between Arashna and the Keron River, a waterfall, sparkling in the moonlight, fell into a pool about thirty feet in diameter and at least forty feet in depth. In the center of the pool, a river otter stood upon a pinnacle of rock with a flat top. Around the pool were gathered more river otters. A large number of them carried elegant knives, leaned on javelins, and sported thin filigrees of silver or gold around their brows.

Those with the knives, javelins, and coronets were chiefs; those clustered around them were some of their tribe members.

Chieftainess Danaray Mudriver waited in the shadows outside the gathering, watching as the moonlight fell on the otter in the center. She had the smallest retinue of any chieftain there—only her healer, Kermunda Bluebrook, and her aide, Audayin Creeksand.

"You're going to have to join them soon," Kermunda murmured, anxiously twisting his tunic.

"How badly do you think they'll react to your ideas tonight?" Creeksand asked, just as anxious.

Danaray coolly counted the chiefs there. "Just as badly as they always do," she predicted. "Come on. Rain still isn't there, but we may as well make ourselves known."

She calmly strode out of the shadows, flanked by Kermunda and Creeksand, and found a spot between two chiefs, Lorwin and Orionyap. Lorwin gave her a chilly nod, but Orionyap said, "Good to see you!"

She detected a huge note of relief in his voice, barely hidden under the jollity. Danaray reminded herself that she couldn't rub her allies the wrong way. Though she made her opponents edgy, she couldn't do the same to her supporters.

She could see them all now: Orionyap, next to her; Arpaha, a few otters to her right; Streamcourse, around the pool to her left; and Shinar, almost directly across from her. Shinar's eyes were hardened and eager, but Arpaha looked about her warily. Streamcourse showed only lazy disinterest. There were a few other otter chieftains who shared her points of view, but she couldn't pick their faces out from the ring. Then there were otters, like Doomspear and Moonpath, who wished her dead.

She caught sight of Rain as he eased himself beside Streamcourse, his aunt, with his sister, Wave, behind him. On Streamcourse's other side, Danaray noticed Shorefish, and she swallowed. It had been too much to hope for, she thought, that Shorefish might be absent. Thank the Bear King she hadn't made any plans revolving around that hope.

After several more minutes, the otter in the middle of the pool stood up. "This gathering, this Conference of Chieftains, now begins. Who among the river otters is here? Shorefish?"

"I am here," Shorefish replied, gritting her teeth. The otter was listing tribes by size from least to greatest. This was the fourth Conference of Chieftains with Shorefish on the bottom.

"Lorwin!"

"I am here," the otter beside Danaray answered.

Danaray firmly quelled her impatience. There were over a hundred river otter chieftains here—this was needless. Most of them were only here to watch the debates!

"Lukkal!"

And on and on it went. Moonpath, Streamcourse, Doomspear, Shinar, Arpaha, among many others. Then finally it was Orionyap—the lists were nearly done.

"Rain!"

"I am here," Rain replied.

"Danaray Mudriver!"

"I am here!" Danaray called. Her gold bracelets and coronet glinted in the moonlight.

The otter in the middle sat down. "The tribe representatives are assembled. The conference shall commence!"

"Not before time," Kermunda muttered. Orionyap flashed him a grin.

The first to speak was Shorefish—she always was, and it was for that reason Danaray had hoped her absent. "My tribe has a plea," she said firmly. "For justice!"

The word would have rung dramatically around the pool and rocks, but Orionyap blew an exasperated sigh. "You want for us to unite and help you drive off the sea otters from your great-grandfather's land—*again*. How many times must we go through this?"

Next to Danaray, Lorwin snorted. Everyone knew that Orionyap was not neutral on the issue of the sea otters. He was all for letting them keep their land.

"Justice for what?" Danaray called across the water. "Not one of the living sea otters has harmed you in any way."

"They killed my father!" Shorefish cried out.

"As I recall, you and your father were the ones to attack their camp and try to steal their young," Arpaha reminded her.

"After they invaded our land," Shorefish retorted.

Lorwin, who had never lived anywhere near the sea otters, rolled his eyes heavenward. "Here we go again."

"The old invaders are dead," Shinar answered Shorefish. "And you cannot blame children for the crimes of their parents."

A cold hiss carried across the water. "The sea otters' crimes were not wholly committed in our grandfathers' times. Did they not take Zurez just before the reign of King Hokadra of Arashna?"

"What is that to you, Moonpath?" Orionyap demanded.

"What the sea otters have done has affected every river otter on earth!" Doomspear cried out, raising his spear. "They have desecrated the honor of our brethren!"

There was a general outcry of agreement, and Danaray thought she even heard some war cries. If something wasn't done fast, this conference would become a council of war.

"They never affected my tribe," Shinar exclaimed.

"The attacks on Zurez were unfortunate," Streamcourse shouted over the others. "But this matter is not the responsibility of those unconnected with the land or with the Wraith Mice. There are many tribes they have *not* harmed, and many tribes who have *no* right to that land. If the Wraith Mice do not wish to retake Zurez, then we have no reason to get excited over it either."

Her words somehow stilled the sudden outcry, but ripples of war frenzy still reached Danaray. She thanked the Bear King for Streamcourse, the skilled peacemaker.

"They also attacked me in my lifetime," Moonpath added.

"In your *infancy*," Rain muttered.

But Moonpath did have a point. One sea otter clan had taken over half her father's territory; ages later, they took over the other half, scarring Moonpath and killing her family. But those warriors had been killed in raids long ago; now it was the younger generation who suffered.

"Should this be allowed to go without revenge?" Moonpath challenged Rain, touching the veil that covered her hideous scars.

"Will revenge heal you?" Rain challenged back.

"It *has* been avenged," Streamcourse pointed out. "You have led many successful raids in the past, and you have certainly annihilated the warriors who wronged you."

"Except for Current," Doomspear pointed out.

Danaray and her allies had no answer to that; Current was still alive, and most of them wanted to tear his throat out. But Arpaha called, "Would you have many suffer the punishment of one? Moonpath, you lost your hold on that land long ago, and you haven't taken it back yet. Your rights to it are nonexistent. If you took it now, you would be the invader. Would you force the sea otters back to their cold, barren islands where their young will freeze in winter and the older will be destroyed by corsairs?"

"She is right," Streamcourse added. "That is why they left in the first place. I have no love for them, as they caused the death of my father and sister Sky. But we surely did not have it as badly as they would have if we had won."

"And of what value is their 'mercy?'" Moonpath hissed furiously.

Doomspear finally spoke. "You go too far, Moonpath," he said softly. Yet he would back her up when asked his opinion.

The other tribe chieftains watched the debate hungrily. They, too, thirsted for sea otter blood—and for the land the sea otters lived on, lands that had never belonged to their tribes in history.

"You speak of forcing them back to horrid conditions on their old lands," Shorefish snapped. "But what about my tribe? We are the ones who wander, homeless and freezing in the winter!"

"You've had plenty of time to find a new home, cousin," Rain pointed out.

She eyed him icily. "Moving from the land your ancestors inhabited for generation upon generation is not as easy as you might think!"

"I haven't had a problem with it," Danaray cut in. It was time she bore the brunt of the argument. "And my home is nothing like my old one."

"Which begs another question," Lorwin spoke up. His contempt and boredom were the least aggrandized emotions at the conference. "As

Streamcourse said, the sea otters are not the concern of most otters here. When will we discuss other questions?"

"What other question would you raise, Lorwin?" Danaray inquired.

"Many. For a start—why did you leave your father's land?"

Danaray grew rigid, curling her paws into fists. "I thought that was obvious. I moved so that I could look after my sister's children."

She had struck a chord, and its note seemed to reverberate across the water. Silence reigned for some time as it always did at the mention of Anamay among river otters.

Across the pool, an otter called Kway-han twirled his tribal knife in his paws. "Wren and Warbler," he murmured. "The children of a poor sea otter and a rebel princess."

"The children of a kind sea otter and a brave princess," Danaray snapped back.

Moonpath spoke, her tone suddenly honeyed. "Is this why you defend the sea otters? So Anamay's children will be safe?"

"I do not defend the sea otters. I urge you to keep out of a feud that has outlived itself."

"Perhaps we should test that," Shorefish muttered. "Kill Wren and Warbler and then see if you're still willing to speak up for the sea otters."

Danaray closed her paw around her tribal knife. "Try all you like, Shorefish. If you so much as look at Wren or Warbler, I'll make you know exactly how strong my tribe is!"

Have you read Book 1 of the Darkwoods Series?

DARKWOODS

By Marta Stahlfeld

The death of the foxes' ruling oracle, Scythe, bodes ill for the Wraith Mice around Darkwoods and their allies near and far. With the change in leadership, all sides know their uncertain relationship with the foxes will, too soon, erupt into a vicious war. Possessing the ability to melt into the darkness and renowned in warfare, the Wraith Mice rally the squirrel tribes, Ranger Mice, and others to defend their territory—and their very lives.

A young one among them, Princess Zuryzel understands the gravity of the situation and rises fearlessly to the challenges of the ruthless invaders. Possessing the traits of a natural leader and wise beyond her years, Zuryzel knows she must follow the difficult path before her. But can she overcome the challenges in time to defeat the hated foxes?

What Readers Are Saying about *Darkwoods*

Darkwoods was an interesting, fun read in the tradition of J.R.R. Tolkien's *Lord of the Rings* Trilogy and the *Chronicles of Narnia* series by C. S. Lewis. Within reading the first chapter, you will realize that the author has a creative and unique imagination. I was hooked into the book. I instantly forgot that the characters were animals. The main character, Zuryzel, is strong-willed, and every reader, young and old, can relate to her. I recommend the book to everyone.

Billy Burgess, Author

This book was a fabulous read. It was exciting from start to finish and hard to put down. Each character in the book had their own special skill, which made it exciting to relate to the characters. I'd recommend this book to any preteen/teen that likes action, adventure, and fantasy. I'm waiting for the next release [*Pasadagavra*].

Andrew, age 12

Darkwoods is an action-filled adventure. It really pulled me in when reading it, and I didn't want to put it down. It was so exciting! All the different characters and their abilities, the plot, everything was amazing! This is a great book for teenagers. I can't wait till the next book comes out!

Emily, age 15

"[*Darkwoods*]'s impressive because it's very elaborate and well written," says Allison Lee-Moore, owner of Burien Books who has hosted two book signings for Stahlfeld. "As an author, she has a great passion for her work and can keep her audience captivated by imagination without having to rely on shock value, sex, or violence," says Lee-Moore.

Lee-Moore complimentarily compares *Darkwoods* to Brian Jacques' popular Redwall series of which Stahlfeld is also a fan. Lee-Moore is personally and professionally happy to offer a book she can recommend to young readers and adults alike. "As an adult, you don't feel like you're reading a kid's book," she says.

The Highline Times, 08/24/2011

Darkwoods *is available at Barnes & Noble and other local bookstores, or it can be ordered from Amazon.com.* ***Darkwoods*** *is also available in eBook formats.*

Want to ask Marta a question or send her a comment? You can email her at ***DarkwoodsBooks@AOL.com***
Find her on Facebook at
Facebook.com/DarkwoodsBooks